MIDNIGHT LOVING

The wind caught Briana's hair, whipping it across her face. Her skirts billowed out around her.

"Come along," Devlin said. "It's time we were going inside." He took her arm and led her back inside the cabin. In the dim light, he stood towering over her, and with one swift movement of his hand he slid the ribbon from her hair. The heavy, red-gold waves came cascading down around her face and over her shoulders. His hands lingered, pushing her hair back from her face, tilting her head back. His eyes held hers and she saw the swift stirring of desire in their smoke-gray depths.

She stiffened and drew away. "I think I may already have taken a chill. Perhaps I should go to bed."

No sooner were the words out than she longed to call them back. A smile touched Devlin's lips. He bent his head and brushed his mouth lightly over hers.

"I spent last night out here on the sofa," he said. "You needed a good sound sleep then. But tonight . . ." His arms closed around her.

She put her hands against his shoulders and tried to push him away. But his lips claimed hers and her own hunger stirred and began to rise in a swirling tide. And now she was no longer trying to hold him off. She felt her body tingling, molding itself against his.

The kiss deepened, and with one swift, easy movement, Devlin lifted her, cradling her against his chest. Then he carried her through the doorway to his sleeping quarters and set her down on the bed. . . .

MY DEAREST LOVE

Diana Haviland

ZEBRA BOOKS
KENSINGTON PUBLISHING CORP.

ZEBRA BOOKS are published by

Kensington Publishing Corp.
850 Third Avenue
New York, NY 10022

First Printing: September, 1996
10 9 8 7 6 5 4 3 2 1

Printed in the United States of America

One

The driver cracked his whip and the small hired carriage moved forward into the brilliant sunlight of the Charleston afternoon. As the carriage pulled away, Briana turned her head for a last glimpse of the house on the Battery, with its wide piazzas, fretted ironwork and tiled roof.

Her mother had leased the fine house, with its high-walled garden, for a year; she had furnished it lavishly, determined to spare no expense in making a favorable impression on the best people in Charleston. But now Mama was gone, and Briana was leaving the city for good.

What other choice did she have? Even as the carriage rounded the corner, bound for the docks, she caught sight of a curtain raised, then swiftly lowered, on the second-story window of the mansion belonging to the Sherbourne sisters. And there would be plenty of others watching her departure. By late afternoon the ladies of Charleston would be gossiping with relish over her abrupt departure.

She could imagine what they would be saying about her.

To think of the poor creature—only eighteen—forced to make that long voyage all alone.

But my dear, what else is there for her to do?

No respectable family can ever receive that Cameron woman's daughter again.

Yes, that was how they would speak of her in Charleston from now on. As "that Cameron woman's daughter."

The doors of every respectable home would be closed to her.

And as for her mother's fond hope of finding Briana a suitable husband—that, too, was gone forever.

She raised her chin and fixed her amber eyes straight ahead. She was running away; no use denying it. But she refused to give the ladies of Charleston cause to pity her—her pride would not permit it.

Although she was leaving with unseemly haste, less than a week after Mama's funeral, she was determined to keep her grief private. That was why she had put on one of her most fashionable gowns from Paris. Not black, but lilac, suitable for half-mourning, a most becoming dress with a close-fitting bodice that accented the rounds of her firm breasts, the curve of her narrow waist. Her skirt, trimmed with four flounces and edged with purple ribbon, was so full that it billowed out over the whole width of the carriage seat.

Had it really been less than a year ago since she and Mama had stood in one of the dressing rooms at Worth's elegant shop in Paris? "All Charleston will be dazzled by your daughter, madam," the saleswoman had said to Mama. "She will have all the gentlemen vying for her favors."

Mama should not have spent her money so recklessly to provide a costly wardrobe. She remembered how, when Mr. Purdom, their family lawyer, had cautioned her mother about spending her money so freely, Mama had laughed and said, "Briana's face will be her dowry. It will be enough."

"For the young men, perhaps," the lawyer had agreed, "but their parents may expect something more substantial."

And yet the most eligible young men in the city had chased after her, and Hugh Mandeville had begun trying to talk his parents around. Maybe he and Briana would have been married by winter—had it not been for the shocking manner of Lynette Cameron's death.

Hugh had sent a brief, formal note of condolence a few days after word of the scandal had spread through Charleston—but he had not attended the funeral. Briana had read his words as if they were those of a stranger.

She had not loved him, she thought. She had been attracted by his elegant appearance, his gallant manners, his skill as a dancer. He would have been an excellent match. And he had wanted her for her beauty, her charm and wit perhaps. But as for love, he had not known the meaning of the word. Otherwise he would have stood by her, no matter what the circumstances of her mother's death.

Now, as the carriage turned into Dock Street, she heard in her mind the sound of the pistol shot. She flinched inwardly, remembering Mama, lying across her ornate canopied bed, the blood soaking the front of her silk robe. The shrill cry of her mother's maid.

Briana blinked back the tears that stung her eyelids and forced herself to hold her parasol steady, as if to shade her face from the glaring sunlight. Her fingers tightened around the beaded reticule that held the ticket for her passage to San Francisco, aboard the clipper ship *Osprey*.

And the letter from her uncle, Alexander. ". . . Since my late brother's daughter has no other relatives to take responsibility for her . . . my wife and I are prepared to do our duty. We trust the girl will be willing to make herself useful. . . ."

A strangely cold letter, thought Briana. And the last part still left her bewildered. Mr. Purdom had told her that Uncle Alexander owned a thriving shop in San Francisco. No doubt her uncle owned a fine house as well, with a staff of well-trained servants. How was she to make herself useful?

Perhaps, since her aunt was childless, she might be in need of companionship, Briana thought. If so, she would be pleased to read to the older woman, to play the piano and sing for her, to accompany her on social calls. Briana's ample wardrobe should be suitable for the social life in her new home. Two wagons laden with her trunks were already on their way to the waterfront.

Now, as her carriage turned onto the waterfront to merge with the stream of slow-moving vehicles, Briana felt a slight rise in spirits.

"There she is, ma'am," said the driver, pointing his whip in the direction of a tall, trim clipper ship. "That there's the *Osprey*."

He drew the carriage to a halt, got down and helped Briana out. The passengers, most of them men, dressed in coarse flannel shirts and heavy denim pants, were already hurrying up the gangplank. A slight frown creased her brow. They were certainly not the sort of traveling companions she and Mama had encountered aboard the great ship that had carried them to Charleston.

She tried to draw reassurance from the sight of a portly man in an army uniform, accompanied by his wife; the woman looked a bit dowdy but thoroughly respectable in her black bombazine. She smoothed the purple silk ribbons of her wide-brimmed bonnet and headed in the direction of the gangplank. But a moment later she stopped short, hearing someone speak her name.

"Ye said Miss Briana Cameron'll be travelin' on yer ship, Cap'n Rafferty."

"She's on the passenger list," a deep voice replied. "But she'll have to leave that mountain of baggage behind."

Briana peered through the milling crowd and caught sight of one of the two teamsters she had hired to carry her trunks. He stood in the glare of the fierce midday sunlight, his red face shining with sweat.

"An' what'll I do with this load, then?" he demanded. The driver of the second wagon sat on his high seat, listening to the exchange in silence.

"Take the trunks back where you got them." The captain spoke with the assurance of a man used to having his orders obeyed without question.

But this time he would not have his way, Briana told herself indignantly. She lifted her full skirts and hurried forward to confront Captain Rafferty.

He towered over her, his dark blue, gold braided coat emphasizing the width of his massive shoulders and broad chest.

"I am Miss Cameron."

"Captain Devlin Rafferty, at your service."

His words were polite enough, but his gray eyes were cool and appraising under his straight black brows. She wavered under his scrutiny. The man's powerful body, the hard masculinity in the deeply tanned face with its firm jawline and jutting chin sent a disturbing sensation coursing through her. For a moment she was thrown off balance by her unforseen response.

But she overcame the unexpected impact of his presence and forced herself to speak. "My lawyer, Mr. Purdom, booked my passage," she reminded him. "I have my ticket right here. Please have my trunks carried aboard at once."

"You're traveling alone, Miss Cameron?"

His implication was plain enough. A young, unmarried lady should not be making such a journey unless accompanied by a female relative, or a personal maid. But in her present straitened circumstance, Briana hadn't enough money to hire a maid.

The captain's eyes moved over her, from the swaying plumes atop her bonnet to the ruffled hem of her billowing silk skirt Did his glance linger on the rounded thrust of her breasts, pushed high by her tightly laced stays?

The low-cut neckline of her close-fitted bodice had been suitable in Paris, where the dashing Empress Eugenie had set the style for such daring fashions. But now, standing on the dock, she felt uneasy. Was it possible that Captain Rafferty had formed the wrong idea about her? Did he think she might be one of the loose women flocking to California, avid for a share of the miners' newfound fortunes?

"I am bound for San Francisco to live with my aunt and uncle." Her tone was firm. "And since I do not plan to return to Charleston I am not about to leave my trunks behind."

"The other female passengers are going to make do with a single trunk. You'll have to do the same."

He spoke with an accent she couldn't quite place. The *Osprey*'s home port was Boston, but she had met a few New England gentlemen in Charleston, and none of them had spoken like Captain Rafferty.

Perhaps he came from some remote northern fishing village. That might explain his accent, and his deplorable lack of manners.

"Since I've paid for my cabin you are obliged to take me, and my trunks, aboard."

"Your cabin won't hold more than one of those trunks. The voyage around Cape Horn's a rough one. We'll be at sea two, even three months, depending on winds and tides." He gave her a brief, sardonic smile. "You'll soon have more to think about than your fancy fripperies."

"I have sailed before, Captain."

"Around the Horn?"

"No, but—"

"Then do as I say. Send all but one of the trunks back to your home without delay. We sail within the hour."

There was no mistaking the barely controlled impatience in his voice.

"If only one trunk will fit into my cabin, you may store the rest in the cargo hold," she persisted. "That large, brass-bound trunk up there on the first wagon contains valuable china and crystal. You must make sure the contents arrive undamaged."

"The hold's already filled to the load line." His massive chest swelled as he drew in a deep breath. "The *Osprey*'s no coffin ship, Miss Cameron."

Coffin ship. The words sent a chill coursing through her. For a moment she nearly gave way before the driving force of Rafferty's will.

The brilliant glare of the sun was starting to make her a trifle giddy. Her legs felt unsteady.

"I beg your pardon, ma'am." She turned to see a gentleman, slender but well built, who wore a dark brown frock coat, fashionably tight fawn-colored trousers and an embroidered satin vest. He raised his tall hat and bowed. "Since I, too, am sailing aboard the *Osprey*, I may be able to be of service." He bowed. "I am Cole Forrester of Oleander."

She had lived in Charleston less than a year, but the Forrester name was familiar to her, and she had heard of Oleander plantation: four hundred highly productive acres on the Ashley River. Her tension began to dissolve.

Captain Rafferty scanned his passenger list. "Cole Forrester." He spoke curtly. "You'd best be going aboard."

But Forrester made no move toward the gangplank. "My cabin's larger than some of the others."

"The largest on my ship."

"Then I shall exchange quarters with Miss Cameron. No doubt she'll find space for her luggage—all of it—in my cabin."

The captain studied the contents of the two heavily laden drays. Then he nodded.

She knew it wasn't strictly correct to accept such a favor from a stranger, but she could see no other choice. "I should be most grateful."

"The pleasure is mine," said Forrester. Before he could say anything more he was surrounded by a group of well-dressed gentlemen who had come to see him off. He raised his hat to Briana, bowed, then moved off with his friends.

Briana found herself confronted by a tight-lipped Captain Rafferty, his eyes like chips of gray ice. "Seems you've lost no time in finding yourself a protector."

She flinched and felt the heat rise from the neckline of her bodice to the roots of her hair. A protector: She knew well enough that the word had more than one meaning. The ladies of the demimonde in Paris—Mama among them—had been kept in high style by the gentlemen they called their protectors.

Briana glared at the captain. "Please have my luggage unloaded and carried to—"

"To the gallant Mr. Forrester's cabin," Devlin Rafferty interrupted. It was impossible for her to ignore the sardonic tone. He shrugged and motioned to a couple of longshoremen.

"Start getting those trunks down," he ordered. "Take them aboard the *Osprey*."

Briana, still shaken, turned and joined the stream of passengers heading for the gangplank. But though she no longer had to endure Rafferty's hard stare, she could not forget his words.

You've found yourself a protector.

By sunset the *Osprey* was under sail, heading down the coast. The last rays of light gilded the white sails and slanted through the porthole to touch Briana's hair with sparks of red-gold fire.

She lingered at the porthole a moment longer, then turned to look with satisfaction at the trunks piled against the bulkheads. The smallest of the trunks had been placed at the foot of her bunk.

The chiming of a gong and the tramp of hurrying footsteps from the deck told her it must be time for dinner. She'd had only a cup of coffee and a few buttered biscuits early that morning. She was hungry and couldn't wait to eat. She started for the cabin door, then stopped short.

The deck was crowded with men, and although there was no time for a complete change of clothes, she must do what she could to make herself less conspicuous. She opened the small trunk, found a black lace shawl, and draped it over her hair; then she wrapped the ends about her shoulders to conceal the creamy swell of her breasts above the deeply rounded neckline of her bodice.

Once out on deck, she kept her eyes fixed on the scrubbed planks and moved along quickly. Then she had to stop short. A man in a blue and yellow plaid suit stood blocking her way. When he raised his hat she caught the heavy smell of the Macassar oil on his hair.

"Nice evenin', miss," he said. "A bit breezy, but that's a welcome change from the infernal heat back in Charleston, isn't it?"

"Yes, indeed," she agreed, and tried to get past him. But he moved, too, so that she could not get by. The unfamiliar motion of the deck made her stumble slightly. He caught her arm. She tried to free herself, but his grip tightened.

"Easy, there. You don't want to go into the dining saloon alone and have to fight for a place at one of the tables, do you? What you need's a fella to see you're not annoyed by this riffraff."

"What she needs is a real man to look out for her—ain't that right, missy?" A short, apelike man in dirty canvas pants and a frayed shirt moved in. "On your way," he told the man who was holding her arm. "The lady's goin' to eat with Jacko Muldoon tonight."

Muldoon grabbed the other man's shoulders and yanked him away, then threw him against the rail. The man slipped and landed on the deck. Other passengers stopped to watch what promised to be a lively brawl.

"Now, missy," Muldoon began, "just you come with me." But the man in the plaid suit was back on his feet. He lunged at Muldoon, landing a blow on his jaw. The apelike man swayed but remained standing. The rest of the men closed in, forming a circle.

"Cut his guts out, Jacko!" someone shouted. "Show him how us Kentucky fellas fight."

Muldoon pulled a long, wicked-looking knife from his boot. Briana's shocked cry was lost in the men's raucous shouting.

"No knives—bare fists!"

"The hell with rules—no holds barred!"

"Slice 'is ears off, Jacko!"

"Toss'm overboard an' let 'm swim t' San Francisco!"

The circle was tightening now, hemming her in. Rising panic held her immobile. She could feel the lust for battle moving over the crowd like a hot wind. She gagged at the rank smell of dirty clothes and unwashed male bodies.

She had to get away, back to her cabin. Then she realized that some of the men were no longer watching the combatants. She turned and saw Devlin Rafferty striding down the length of the deck. An officer, a towering bearded giant, moved close behind him.

The captain stopped a few feet away, drew a Navy Colt from his belt, and fired a shot straight up. The men began to move uneasily, like a herd of cattle before a storm.

Rafferty handed his weapon to the bearded officer and pushed his way to the center of the circle. He took hold of Briana, his arm around her waist, his fingers hard against her ribs. With a single movement he thrust her behind him.

"You there. Hand over the knife."

Muldoon hesitated, clutching the knife handle. The captain kept coming, his gray eyes alert, stopping just out of range of the blade. Muldoon's thick features creased in a jagged-toothed grin as his friends began to urge him to stand his ground.

Devlin Rafferty moved in swiftly, feinted with one arm, leaped to the opposite side, and seized the thick, hairy wrist that held the knife. He raised his knee and brought Muldoon's wrist down in one quick movement.

Briana flinched when she heard a crack of bone. The knife clattered on the wooden planks. Muldoon dropped to his knees, clutching at his arm, his features contorted with pain. He tried to rise, but Rafferty stepped closer and locked his fingers together. Then with one swift, powerful movement, he struck his hands against the back of Muldoon's neck. The apelike man dropped facedown on the deck, jerked convulsively, then lay still.

"He's dead," Briana whispered, scarcely able to recognize her own voice.

The captain turned Muldoon onto his back with one booted foot and looked him over briefly.

"Still breathing," he said. He turned his cold gray stare on the man in the plaid suit, who was trying to hide himself in the crowd.

"It wasn't my fault, Captain. I only wanted to help the young lady."

Rafferty kept his eyes fixed on the man, saying nothing.

"Seeing as how she is all by herself, I offered to take her down to dinner," the man went on shakily. "Only trying to help."

"And did the lady accept your invitation?"

"Well, now—you know how the ladies are, sir. Takes a bit of persuasion sometimes—"

The man's voice trailed off.

Rafferty looked over the crowd. His deep voice rang out. "Hear this, all of you! Any man aboard who forces his attentions on an unwilling female or gets into a brawl with weapons or bare knuckles will be put in irons by Mr. Quinn, my first officer." He jerked his head in the direction of the big, bearded man. "And thrown ashore in the nearest port of call."

There were a few muttered protests and then, as Rafferty's icy gray gaze swept the crowd, the men fell silent. Now Briana heard only the shuffling of boots on the deck, the crack of the wind, filling the canvas sails overhead, the clatter of crockery from the dining saloon.

Devlin Rafferty stood still for a moment, his eyes moving from one face to another, as if seeking the slightest sign of rebellion. Then he gave a brief nod of satisfaction.

He turned to Briana, lifted her against his chest, and moved down the deck with a long, easy stride. The men dropped back to make way for him.

Because she wasn't sure she would be able to stand alone, she made no protest. She felt the roughness of his coat against her cheek, the hard pressure of his gold buttons.

"Makes a tidy armful, she does." Briana caught the words from somewhere in the crowd.

"Travelin' alone, ain't she?"

"Maybe not fer long. Maybe the captain needs company—long way to San Francisco—"

If Devlin Rafferty heard the talk, he ignored it. He paused before her cabin door, kicked it open, and carried her inside.

"You may put me down now," Briana said coldly.

But he didn't loosen his grip and Briana felt a swift lash of fear. She went rigid for an instant, then arched and twisted her body, struggling to get free.

"Let go of me!" she demanded. "Now!"

He dropped her down on her bunk with an unceremonious movement. She fell backward and her shawl slipped off, baring her soft white throat and the tops of her breasts. He stood looking down at her, his gray eyes narrowing slightly under his straight, dark brows.

Fear caught at her throat as she remembered his display of naked force up on deck only moments before.

And realized that she was completely powerless against him.

For the remainder of the voyage this ruthless, cold-eyed man controlled the destinies of every man and woman aboard the ship.

Including hers.

Two

Briana raised herself quickly, her wide skirt and lace-trimmed petticoats billowing up around her knees. It wasn't easy for her to rearrange her garments with Devlin's eyes fixed on her, but somehow she managed. She smoothed the folds of her skirt down around her ankles, then drew her shawl over the soft swell of her breasts, half-revealed by the deep neckline of her bodice.

A gentleman would have turned away. But Devlin Rafferty was no gentleman. He didn't even avert his eyes. She flinched inwardly, remembering the strength of his powerful arms around her, the roughness of his coat against her cheek, the masculine scent of him.

Had he heard the crude remarks of the passengers as he had carried her to her cabin? It scarcely mattered; he had already made it plain that he had no high opinion of her morals.

He kept his steady gray gaze fixed on her. The silence drew out until she found it unbearable and she seized on the first remark that came to mind. "I'm grateful to you for rescuing me from those dreadful men, Captain Rafferty."

"Spare me your thanks. I only did what was necessary. It's my job to get my passengers safely to San Francisco." His eyes raked over her. "Having a female like you aboard doesn't make it any easier."

Damn the man! From the moment they had met at the docks he had treated her like a trollop. Now his eyes, no longer cool and remote, swept over her again. She felt as if he were stripping her naked.

"I expected that Forrester would take you down to dinner,"

he went on. "Haven't you had time to make your arrangements with him yet?"

She bridled at the irony beneath his words. "Cole Forrester's not the sort of man who would expect to be repaid for an act of courtesy. Such behavior comes naturally to him, but you wouldn't understand that."

"Suppose you enlighten me, Miss Cameron." She saw the corner of his mouth twitch with barely concealed amusement.

"The Forresters are a fine old family. Their plantation, Oleander, was given to them through a land grant from King Charles the Second. Mr. Forrester is a gentleman."

"Even a gentleman expects some return on his investment," Devlin cut in.

"Investment?" She stared up at him in confusion.

"His ticket cost three times as much as yours. The cabin you were to have occupied is about the size of a broom closet."

"But my lawyer said he'd booked me a first-class cabin."

"First class only means it's up here on deck," Devlin said patiently, as if instructing a not overly bright child. "Second-class cabins open directly into the dining saloon."

"And what about the rest?"

"Third-class passengers sleep in the saloon. They have to wait until the tables are cleared; then they pull down their bunks. And they have to get up before the tables are set for breakfast again."

"But that's downright uncivilized, Captain Rafferty. Why would they tolerate such conditions?"

"Gold fever," he told her. "But you can spare those men your sympathy; there are plenty of others who'll be sleeping out on deck."

"What if there should be a storm?"

"There will be more than one." He spoke with calm certainty. "The worst storms will strike as we round the Horn. Gales that'll bring the waves sweeping waist-high across the decks. Snow squalls, and icebergs three hundred feet high, some of them. But the deck passengers know the risks."

Her amber eyes went dark with indignation. "You said you weren't running a coffin ship."

"A coffin ship is a floating hulk, no longer seaworthy. She's dangerously overloaded with passengers and cargo. But if she goes down, the owners are well satisfied to collect their insurance money."

Her voice shook slightly. "I didn't know."

"There's a lot you don't know about sea travel," he told her. "You still don't seem to realize how foolhardy you were, to embark on a voyage like this one, and without a traveling companion."

"I've always traveled with my mother."

"Why isn't she with you this time?"

Her throat tightened. "My mother died—a few weeks ago."

She thought she saw a flicker of genuine compassion in his eyes. "You might have hired a maid."

"I couldn't have paid her wages."

His eyes took in her elaborate gown, then shifted to her trunks, stacked against the walls. "And you wouldn't have considered selling your precious wardrobe." His mouth tightened. "Still, you must have gotten a good price for your family's slaves."

"All the servants in our Charleston home were free men and women of color." Her indignation made her speak with uncharacteristic bluntness. "After I'd settled our debts I had barely enough left to pay my passage to San Francisco."

He leaned closer, searching her face. "A moving tale, Miss Cameron." She caught his brief, ironic smile. "How much of it is true?"

Her voice was tight with resentment. "I was foolish to try to explain my circumstances to you. I should have known better than to expect a common Yankee seaman to understand."

"I'm not a Yankee," he interrupted.

"But I thought—where do you come from?"

"Australia."

She searched her memory, trying to dredge up what little she knew of that far-off continent, but she could find only a vague memory of her governess, back in Paris, pointing to a pink blob on a globe.

"You have heard of Australia?"

"Certainly I have." She sprang up from the bunk and confronted him. "The British government uses Australia as a dumping ground for thieves and cutthroats, doesn't it? Habitual criminals of the worst kind. Lawless, vicious men who are beyond reformation . . ."

His look of icy rage silenced her abruptly. His cheekbones jutted under his tanned, tightly drawn skin. Two hard lines, like twin scars, bracketed his lips. The muscles stood out against his jaw. He took a step toward her and she shrank away.

What had she said to bring on such a swift, terrifying reaction? Was he responding with such anger merely because of an insult to his native land? Or was it possible that Devlin Rafferty had once been a convict, transported to Australia for having committed some unspeakable crime? And if he had been, had he served his sentence—or had he escaped?

Visions of rape, of murder, surged up in her imagination. She fought back her panic, sensing that it would be a mistake to betray the slightest sign of fear to such a man.

Somehow she forced herself to keep her eyes fixed on his. "I want you to leave my cabin. At once."

He didn't move, but stood looking down at her, his muscles tense. Then he drew a deep, steadying breath. "No doubt you've forgotten that the *Osprey* is my ship. I am master here."

His words, and his implacable stare, made it difficult for her to go on. But she must not back down, not now. "I haven't forgotten. But this is my cabin. That gives me the right to ask you to leave."

"Cole Forrester paid for your cabin," he reminded her.

"As soon as we get to San Francisco, my uncle will repay him."

"Your uncle is another wealthy gentleman, an aristocrat like Mr. Forrester?"

"Alexander Cameron is a respected citizen who owns a fine mercantile establishment," she retorted.

She wished she could offer more proof of her uncle's social standing, but she knew so little about him. "My family's affairs are no concern of yours," she said.

He shrugged slightly. "True enough," he conceded. "My only concern is this ship, and I've already taken away enough time from my duties." He started to turn away.

She ignored his rudeness. "Just a moment, Captain. Since I've had no dinner, please see that a tray is brought to my cabin."

He paused, torn between annoyance and unwilling admiration. She had ordered him around as if he were a servant, back there on the dock in Charleston. And although she had been genuinely afraid of him a few moments before, she hadn't given way before his rage.

She had stood her ground and faced him down; had held her head high and kept those extraordinary amber eyes locked with his. Perhaps she wasn't the experienced adventuress he had first thought her to be, but an arrogant, pampered young lady, coddled by her mother and deferred to by the servants. No doubt her looks had made it easy for her to get her own way with any man she met.

She was a beauty, make no mistake. He tried to ignore the tightening in his loins, the heat that went coursing through him at the memory of her body, cradled in his arms. The need aroused in him when a strand of her red-gold hair, tossed by the breeze, had brushed across his cheek. He remembered the sight of her, lying back on the bunk. The enticing swell of her breasts, before she had covered herself with her shawl.

Plenty of other men must have been moved by her lush, feminine allure. All sorts of men. Cole Forrester, with his high-toned ways. The brawling Jacko Muldoon. And many others, no doubt. Perhaps she had been the belle of Charleston society.

But this wasn't Charleston. And the voyage would be rough enough without his being distracted by Miss Briana Cameron.

Please see that my dinner is brought to my cabin.

Where the devil did she think she was, in some luxurious hotel? Although she had just told him she was nearly penniless, she still did not seem to understand fully what the reversal of her fortunes would mean.

She was young to be on her own—seventeen, maybe eighteen. He'd been a lot younger when he'd found himself far from home, surrounded by indifferent strangers. But she was a woman; it was different for her. He tried to ignore a brief, unexpected stirring of pity.

"You'll be having all your meals here in your cabin," he told her. "And you are not to go up on deck alone again, for any reason."

She stared at him, her eyes wide with disbelief. "You can't mean to keep me a prisoner here for the rest of the voyage!"

"I'll escort you for a walk on deck whenever the weather's suitable and I can find the time."

"That's most considerate of you." She spoke with unmistakable irony.

"Even the masters of convict ships bound for Australia allow their human cargo some fresh air. You're entitled to equal consideration, I suppose."

It took all her willpower to hold back the angry words she longed to say. How dare he compare her with a "cargo" of common criminals?

Her hands closed into tight fists, but she forced herself to remain silent as he left the cabin. She started as she heard a key grate in the lock.

Devlin Rafferty had imprisoned her here. She would remain his captive until he chose to set her free.

She stood beside her narrow bunk and stared at the heavy door, fighting down her impulse to run to it, to pound her fists against it and scream for someone to come and let her out. But she mustn't give way to panic.

She had to regain her composure, to keep a tight rein on her emotions and not let herself think about the miles that stretched between the Carolina coast and San Francisco Bay.

She forced herself to consider her situation as calmly as possible. Even if she did call for help, if one of the crew had the courage to defy the captain's orders and release her, she would still have to face the mob of unruly men on deck.

Some might be respectable farmers, bank clerks, teamsters, and shopkeepers who had left home, seized by "gold fever." But probably there were more like Muldoon, who would assume that any female traveling alone was fair game.

She turned from the door and caught sight of her reflection in the wavy mirror over the chest of drawers across the cabin. Her cheeks were drained of color; her eyes had gone a dark, glittering amber. For a moment she felt as if the walls of the cabin were closing in on her . . . as if they might crush her. . . .

She shut her eyes and tried to seek out some untapped source of strength inside herself. If only she had known her father, she might have found some legacy of courage in her remembrances of him.

James Cameron had been a fine man, so Mama had told her; hard-working and respected; a prosperous cotton factor whose business dealings often took him from his native South Carolina to England and France. He and Mama had been staying in Paris when he had died of a heart attack.

"That was a few months before you were born," Mama had said.

"But why didn't you go home to Charleston afterward?"

Mama had shrugged and smiled wistfully. "I no longer had any relations there. Besides, I'd always adored Paris. So, with your dear Papa gone, I chose to remain."

Her mother had done well for herself in the frivolous, profligate society of Second Empire Paris. She had hired an elegant phaeton, complete with liveried coachman and footman, and had gone out driving on the Bois de Boulogne every afternoon.

It hadn't been long before the young widow, whose fashionable black gowns set off her blond hair, creamy skin, and graceful, well-rounded figure, caught the eye of a dashing French nobleman.

"Unfortunately, the duke was already married," Mama had said with a sigh. "One of those dreary arranged marriages, you understand. But he was in love with me from the moment he saw me. And he has been most generous with me."

Indeed, Mama's wealthy protector had provided a fine house in the rue de Rivoli, a collection of expensive jewelry, and a dazzling wardrobe; a fine carriage, a staff of well-trained servants, and a succession of nursemaids to take little Briana out to the Luxembourg Gardens for her daily walks.

Briana's earliest memories were of Mama's lavish parties, attended by fashionable gentlemen and ladies who were part of her mother's world—the gilded society of the demimonde. Beautiful, sweet-scented ladies decked out in low-cut gowns with billowing skirts from the House of Worth, and jewels from the shop of Froment-Meurice.

Mama had never explained to Briana why she and the duke had parted. After he had left there had been a succession of equally generous titled gentlemen to take his place.

But when the male visitors who gathered in her mother's salon had started casting admiring glances at Briana, now on the threshold of dazzling womanhood, Mama had realized it was time to leave Paris.

"We will return to Charleston." Mama had made her decision in her swift, impulsive way. "There you will make a respectable marriage."

Now, remembering the tragic aftermath of Mama's decision, Briana set her lips in a firm line. As soon as she arrived in San Francisco, settled with her aunt and uncle, she would make Mama's plan for her future a reality.

Aunt Gertrude and Uncle Alexander would take care of the necessary preliminaries. They would present her to the cream of San Francisco society, give balls and receptions and teas in her honor, and see to it that she was invited to the right sort of homes. Introduced to the right sort of young gentlemen.

She bent and opened the small trunk at the foot of her bunk and found her silver-mounted comb and brush set, the tissue-

wrapped cakes of fragrant almond soap, the lotion of glycerin
and rose water to keep her hands smooth and white, the flask
of lilac cologne and the tiny box of lip salve.

She placed them carefully on top of the chest, then started
putting away her nightgowns, pantelettes, and ruffled petticoats.
If this was the best cabin on the ship, Captain Rafferty might
have provided more storage space.

She had already noticed a second bunk, above her own. This
cabin was meant to accommodate two passengers, but Cole Forrester had booked it for his exclusive use. A gentleman like him
would not have deigned to share his quarters with a stranger.

She went on putting away her undergarments, trying to ignore
the uproar outside. The passengers had finished dinner and
come back on deck. Some were talking loudly about their plans
for the future, of the fortunes they would make in the California
goldfields; others were singing raucous ballads.

She heard the hoarse male voices bellowing out a song about
a pair of ill-fated lovers. Although she didn't understand all of
it, she caught the meaning well enough to feel a hot blush rise
to her cheeks.

> *Frankie she worked in a cribhouse*
> *Cribhouse had only two doors,*
> *Gave all her money to Johnny*
> *To spend on those parlor whores. . . .*

She flinched, then once more turned her attention to putting
away her clothes. She was arranging tiny beribboned sachet
bags in the top drawer when she heard a rap at the cabin door.
Had Devlin Rafferty come back? Her heart speeded up and she
stiffened with apprehension.

Then she gave a sigh of relief at the sight of a boy with
cropped, sun-bleached hair who wore a striped shirt and wide-
bottomed denim pants. He carried a heavily laden tray.

"Evenin', miss," he said. "Tommy's my name. I'm the captain's cabin boy. Cook's fixed ye a nice fresh pot o' coffee. But

if ye'd rather have tea, just say the word." When she did not reply at once he went on, "Hope ye ain't feelin' seasick, this bein' yer first night out, miss."

"I didn't have even a touch of seasickness when I crossed the Atlantic," she told him.

He set the tray on a small wooden table fastened to the wall, then drew out a chair for her. "You're lucky." He gave her an approving grin. "First time I went to sea I was sick as a dog. Puked up my guts every day for near a week, I did." He flushed. "Beg pardon, miss. Guess that ain't no way to talk in front of a lady."

"How long have you been at sea, Tommy?"

"Since I was ten. Leastways, I think I was. Never did know my right age for certain."

"But surely your mother must have told you."

"Never had no mother—no father, either." He spoke without a trace of self-pity as he set down the covered dishes and poured the coffee.

Then he glanced over at the chest of drawers. "If you mean to keep all them female fripperies there, you'll be needin' a rack to hold them steady. We'll be havin' some rough weather."

She remembered Rafferty's talk of the dangers of rounding Cape Horn, but she tried to hide her uneasiness.

"A strip of wood to keep your things in place, so they won't get smashed to pieces. I could make you one."

She gave him a warm smile. "I'd be most grateful," she began. She hesitated. "Maybe I shouldn't take you away from your regular duties. I wouldn't want you to be punished by the captain on my account. I'm sure he must be a hard master."

"Captain Rafferty's more than a match for any man. You seen how he handled that Muldoon fella. But he couldn't be a clipper ship's master 'less he could deal with scum like that."

"I suppose not," she conceded.

"He looks out for his passengers, though," Tommy assured her. "Especially the ladies. He said I was to make myself useful an' see you were as comfortable as possible."

"He did?" Her amber eyes widened in surprise.

Tommy nodded. "Like I said, he takes good care of the passengers. An' gets them where they're goin'. We'll make it safe to San Francisco with the captain in command, miss—you'll see."

"You think well of him, don't you?"

"He's the best man I ever knew, miss. Why if it weren't for him, I'd've ended up in jail, or maybe dead in some alley—" Tommy's eyes glowed with conviction.

Before she could question the boy further he said, "Now don't let me keep ye from yer dinner." He started for the door. "I'll be back in an hour to clear away."

Briana, her naturally healthy appetite restored by her talk with the friendly cabin boy, began her meal. The chicken, baked to a golden brown, was tender and succulent, the biscuits hot and fluffy, the coffee delicious.

She remembered the cook back in the house on the Battery, saying, "Coffee supposed to be as pure as an angel, strong as love, black as the devil, an' hot as hell."

She tried to ignore a stirring of homesickness for the sun-drenched city she had left that afternoon; for the scents of mimosa, wisteria, and tea olive bushes in the walled garden. For the long, lazy afternoons, followed by evenings of dancing in the ballrooms of Charleston's finest houses.

It was harder to dismiss the memory of her mother. Her mouth tightened with resentment. She could imagine the spiteful gossip that had flown from one home to the next after the night of her mother's death.

Had Mama been a bad woman? No, never that. Foolish, perhaps. Impulsive, indiscreet. Mama needed a man to take care of her, to provide her with luxuries, to shower her with flattery.

But she was not like her mother. She would take care of herself until a suitable gentleman came along with a proposal of marriage.

But what about love? Her delicately arched brows drew together. Her husband would be young, handsome, and deeply in love with her. Surely she would learn to love him. For a lady love came after marriage.

She had finished her dinner and was standing at the porthole, looking out at the moon-silvered sea, when Tommy returned. He surveyed the dishes with a grin.

"That's the way, miss," he said. "With a long voyage ahead, you got to keep up your strength."

As he piled the dishes on the tray, he continued, "Now that missionary lady who's travelin' with her brother, she's in her cabin sippin' tea and moanin'. An' her brother ain't much better off, neither."

"I didn't know we had missionaries aboard," she said. "Are they bound for China? Or India, perhaps?"

Tommy laughed. "Not them two. They're goin' to do their soul-savin' in San Francisco."

"But I thought missionaries were sent out to save the heathens."

"There's more heathens on Pacific Street than in Peking; that's what the captain says. Miss Griscomb an' her brother'll have their work cut out for them, tryin' to save the Chinese slave girls from the men wot brought them over to work in the cribhouses—"

The boy went beet red and looked away. "Sorry, miss. I never meant no offense."

She tried to shift the conversation to spare the boy further embarrassment. "I—didn't know Chinese were used as slaves in California."

"Only the girls. Sold by their own fathers, they are, when they're no more'n nine or ten. An' the way they're treated, they don't last long—" Once again he lapsed into awkward silence.

He did not meet her eyes as he picked up the tray, mumbled a quick good night, and went off, locking the door behind him. She thought about his startling revelations and shivered slightly. Then she told herself that every large city probably had its dark side; that her aunt and uncle would make sure she never saw any sights unsuitable for a young lady.

Quickly, she went about preparing for bed. Dressed in her

nightgown and robe, she took the pins from her hair and began brushing the red-gold waves. A hundred strokes each night, Mama had said. Briana's arms began to grow weary. Once in San Francisco, no doubt she would be provided with a personal maid to do such services.

Back in Charleston, Odette, Mama's pretty quadroon maid, had also seen to Briana's needs. She had brushed her hair, and arranged it in the most becoming styles, had attended to her wardrobe and helped her dress.

It had been Odette who had been first to rush into Mama's bedroom at the sound of the pistol shot that terrible night; Odette who had cried out and then had tried to keep Briana from entering the room. But Briana had freed herself from the maid's restraining grasp and run to her mother.

Once again her memory was seared by the vision of Mama, blood staining her nightdress, the man who had been with her looking down at her body. Then he had pushed past Briana and fled downstairs.

In the days that followed Briana had only pieced together the barest outline of the tragedy. The man, the Marquis de Valmont, had come to Charleston as a visitor. He had known Mama in Paris, where they had had a brief liaison.

From what little Odette had told her, she understood that the nobleman had wanted to resume the affair in Charleston. But her mother, bent on keeping up a respectable reputation so that Briana might marry well, had refused. And when the marquis had said he would make public the facts about Mama's life in Paris, she had threatened him with the small pistol.

"Yo' mama never meant to hurt that man," Odette had insisted. "She only wanted t' scare him—make him leave her be. But he must've tried to take the gun away from her—an' it went off—an' yo' mama—poor lady who never would've harmed a soul—"

Briana's fingers shook as she set down her brush and braided her hair. She mustn't think about the way Mama had died. She must remember only those carefree years in Paris. The parties in the salon of the house on the rue de Rivoli. The silk-hung walls, the white-and-gold furniture and glittering chandeliers.

She blew out the candle and climbed into her bunk, pulling the blankets over her. But, tired as Briana was, sleep eluded her.

Even after she managed to dismiss the memory of that terrible night in Charleston, other, more immediate thoughts kept her awake.

She couldn't forget the unfamiliar, disturbing sensations that had coursed through her when Rafferty had lifted her in his arms and carried her back to her cabin. The fear that had seized her when he had tossed her down on the bunk and stood looking at her with those smoke-gray eyes.

She thought of the miles of ocean that stretched ahead, and remembered that as long as she was aboard the *Osprey*, her fate lay in Devlin Rafferty's hands.

I am master here.

In spite of her exhaustion it was long after midnight before Briana finally found escape in sleep.

Three

The early morning sunlight spread a glowing path across the sea and turned the sails to gold as Devlin Rafferty led Briana out on deck. She had arranged her hair in a simple chignon, but had scarcely had time to finish doing up the row of small buttons on the bodice of her dove-gray linen gown before she had heard his brisk knock at her cabin door.

She hoped he would have no reason to find fault with her gown; its lace collar fastened at the neck and the sleeves concealed her arms. But her bonnet, like all the others she had brought along, was a frivolous creation, designed to catch the masculine eye. Its wide gray brim was lined with shirred, rose-colored satin to cast a warm, flattering glow over her face, and the crown was decorated with a cascade of pink silk blossoms.

"Fine morning, Miss Cameron." Devlin took her arm. "We've a good following breeze to speed us along."

She breathed in the fresh salt air appreciatively, then caught the rich smell of sizzling ham and steaming coffee from the galley. "I've not had breakfast yet."

"You certainly have an excellent appetite." He gave her an amused smile. "I wouldn't have expected that." His silver-gray eyes raked her trim body.

Before she could decide whether to reproach him or pretend not to have noticed his appraising glance, he went on. "Breakfast's waiting in my cabin."

She hesitated for a moment at the foot of the short flight of stairs leading to his private domain on the quarterdeck. Passengers and crew were moving about the main deck. She suspected that, in spite of her subdued costume, she already had caught their attention. She remembered the bawdy remarks she had overheard the night before, as Devlin had carried her to her cabin.

Should she refuse his invitation now? It was unquestionably improper for an unchaperoned lady to dine with a gentleman in his private quarters.

"Come along," he urged.

He stood aside, his look challenging her. She started up the steps and he followed; together they entered his quarters. Tommy was setting out breakfast on a round table covered with a spotless white cloth.

"Mornin', miss." He gave her a wide, amiable grin. The mouthwatering smell of breakfast—fried ham, eggs, and potatoes, along with biscuits and coffee, stirred her appetite. "Hope you slept well."

"I did, thank you."

"If we need anything more, I'll call you." She had hoped the boy would remain, but Devlin dismissed him with a gesture. He drew out a seat for her, then took the chair opposite.

"If the wind holds steady, we'll drop anchor in Havana harbor tomorrow," he remarked.

"You are stopping to take on more passengers?" He'd said the *Osprey* was already booked to capacity.

"We need a good supply of oranges and lemons. Limes, too. I can get them at a reasonable price in Havana." Then, seeing her questioning glance, he added, "Citrus fruits ward off scurvy."

"Your concern for your passengers does you credit, Captain."

He shrugged. "Sick passengers can be a nuisance. But I'm more concerned for my crew. I want every seaman in prime condition, able to handle his share of the work."

He passed her the hot biscuits, then filled her coffee cup. She was surprised to see that the porcelain dishes were of fine quality. The blue and white plates, cups, and platters were decorated with a pattern of curving bridges, pagodas, flying cranes, and gracefully drooping willows. She glanced around the cabin. Above the polished mahogany sideboard there were shelves of leather-bound books. A wide leather sofa stood against the opposite wall.

Through a half-open door at the rear of the cabin, Briana caught sight of a bunk, already made up with a patchwork quilt, the pillow covered with a neat white case. She quickly turned her eyes away. This glimpse of his sleeping quarters reminded her of the impropriety of the situation.

Then she realized that, while she had been inspecting his cabin, he had kept his eyes fixed on her.

She started on her generous portion of ham, eggs, and potatoes. He began eating, too, but his gaze did not waver from her. "I hope my choice of costume pleases you, Captain."

His mouth curved upward at the corners. "I'm no judge of ladies' fashions. But I suppose that dress is less likely to cause a riot than the one you wore last night," he said.

"I'm glad you approve, Captain Rafferty."

"Only from a practical point of view," he said.

She gave him a puzzled frown.

"Personally, I preferred the way you looked last night, down in your cabin. Flat on your back with your skirts up around your knees and that lace shawl slipping down."

She drew in her breath, shocked by his words and the picture they evoked. She pushed back her chair and stood.

"Where do you think you're going?"

"Back to my cabin. And there's no need for you to escort me."

"You've scarcely started breakfast."

"Have Tommy bring my breakfast down to my cabin. I refuse to remain here and be insulted."

"Sit down, Briana."

She remained on her feet, glaring at him across the table.

"I was paying you a compliment." His voice was low and deep. "Hair like yours shouldn't be hidden under a bonnet. Or a fancy lace shawl. And as for those trim ankles and your—"

She cut him short; her voice shook with anger. "You wouldn't have seen my—ankles—if you hadn't flung me down on my bunk, as if I were a sack of potatoes."

"No man could possibly mistake you for that." He was amused by her tirade. But now another emotion stirred inside him. Her eyes narrowed like those of an angry cat. He'd never seen eyes quite like hers: warm amber with glittering flecks of green and gold, and shaded by her thick, dark lashes. Even the slant of her brows, now drawn together in a deep frown, only made her more enticing.

And that dress. Worn by another female, it might have looked completely respectable, even prim. But on Briana it was damn near as exciting as last night's outfit.

The lace collar, buttoned at the throat, was proper enough for a deacon's daughter. But the perfectly fitted bodice drew attention to her firm, pointed breasts. His palms began to tingle at the thought of the way those breasts would feel cupped in his hands. He tried to ignore the growing heat in his loins.

"Sit down and finish your breakfast." He tried to keep his voice crisp and impersonal, as if he was giving an order to one of his crew. But she ignored his command and started for the door.

Before she could reach her destination he was on his feet. He overtook her with a few long strides, grasping her firmly by the arm.

"Have you forgotten the fracas you caused when you went out on deck alone last night?"

"Hardly. And I haven't forgotten how evil-minded people can be, either." She tried, unsuccessfully, to free herself from his grip. "I was wrong coming to your cabin as I did. But maybe if I leave right now, those men will have no cause to—to think the worst."

"The worst?"

"Don't pretend not to understand. They'll think I'm your—" She broke off, warm color flaring in her cheeks.

"Go on," he urged.

"I won't be the object of contempt—or pity—as I was in Charleston. No scandal will ever touch me again."

"Scandal?" The pain in her voice awoke his curiosity. Yesterday, seeing her on the dock, he had assumed she was an ordinary adventuress, bound for the choice pickings to be found in San Francisco. Now . . . he was no longer sure.

Her words came rushing forth in a torrent. "Those trunks I brought aboard . . . the clothes inside would have been my trousseau."

"You were betrothed to someone back in Charleston?"

"There hadn't been a formal announcement. Not yet. But Hugh said he didn't care about the meager dowry. He'd nearly talked his parents around. He and I would have been married by winter."

He saw her lips quiver and heard the ache in her voice.

"And then?" His arm went around her shoulders.

"Then a visitor came to Charleston, a nobleman from France. He and Mama—they had been—"

"I think I understand."

"But Mama wanted so much to make a fresh start. For my sake. So I could make a respectable marriage."

The bitter grief in her voice was unmistakably real.

"Go on."

"The kind of life Mama had led in Paris—" She looked away. "She couldn't let it be known that she had been—indiscreet. She was careful to make sure no one in Charleston had cause to suspect. Not until that dreadful man arrived. As soon as he saw Mama again, he wanted her."

She broke off abruptly. He led her to the sofa and drew her down beside him. "Tell me the rest."

She searched his face, then shook her head slightly. "I doubt you'd understand. What could you know about Charleston society?"

"Enough. The rules of polite society are pretty much the same, on the Battery or Beacon Hill, in Boston. I do know this much: No matter what kind of scandal followed your mother to Charleston, that suitor of yours was a pompous, spineless jackass to let you go."

"Hugh was a gentleman. The Mandevilles were a highly respected family. They would never have accepted me, not after what happened."

His arm tightened around her shoulders, "Were you in love with him?"

"I thought I was. But now—I don't think I could have been."

"Then forget him. You'll find a husband fast enough, once you get to San Francisco. There's still a shortage of females. A girl like you will have a dozen proposals before you've been there a month."

"I don't want a dozen proposals. I'll take my time and choose carefully."

"You sound as if you think choosing a husband is like laying out a ship's course."

"Perhaps it is, for me. I certainly won't marry the first man who asks me. I need a man who can give me the respectable life Mama wanted for me."

"I doubt you know what you need. Not yet."

The swift change in his voice, the warmth in his eyes, should have put her on her guard. But she was still too shaken by her memories of those last weeks in Charleston.

Before she realized what was happening he had turned her around to face him. Then she was in his arms, her breasts crushed against the hardness of his chest.

She cried out, but he ignored her protest. He bent his head and his mouth brushed hers. The touch, light though it was, sent flickers of excitement darting through her.

All at once she was caught up in a headlong tide of emotion. It surged inside her, sweeping aside her innate caution.

She felt his fingers touch her throat as he unfastened the ribbons of her bonnet. He tossed it aside then tilted her face upward. His mouth claimed hers again with growing urgency. Her lips parted, inviting his tongue to explore the moist warmth inside. Somehow she was clinging to him, her fingers pressing into the powerful muscles of his shoulders.

Her tongue sought his and the contact sent shock waves pulsating through every nerve of her body.

His lips moved to the curve of her throat. And lower still. The heat of his mouth burned through the layers of fabric that covered her breasts. Beneath the layers of linen and lace, her skin began to tingle. Her body was coming alive, lifting, pressing, melding with his.

Slowly, purposefully, he opened the first few buttons at the top of her bodice. His hand moved inside, and she caught her breath as his fingers cupped one of her breasts. He moved the ball of his thumb across her nipple. The friction sent a tide of scalding waves down the length of her body. She was startled and bewildered by the swift heat that stirred deep within the moist, untouched core of her womanhood.

From somewhere far off she heard an intrusive sound. It jolted her back to reality. Someone was knocking at the cabin door.

Devlin let her go, got to his feet, and strode across the cabin. She raised herself from her half-reclining position. With unsteady fingers, she buttoned her bodice, then tucked a few stray wisps of hair back in place.

As the door swung open, she caught a glimpse of the huge bearded officer who had accompanied Devlin when he had come to break up the fight on deck. She searched her memory. Mr. Quinn; that was the man's name. The *Osprey*'s first mate. Today Quinn had an enormous marmalade-colored cat perched on his shoulder.

"You'd best come an' take over," the man blurted out. "That pestiferous missionary female an' her brother are raisin' hell." He broke off at the sight of Briana. "Sorry, Cap'n. I didn't know you had company."

"Go on," Devlin rapped out impatiently. "What are the Griscombs up to?"

"That slab-sided harpy an' her brother mean to hold a prayer meetin' in the dining saloon this evenin'. But some of the other passengers want to play cards down there after dinner."

"I shouldn't have taken those two aboard," Devlin said. "I hoped they might keep to their cabin for a few more weeks at least, seasick as they were."

"Even a bout of seasickness ain't enough to stop a couple of psalm-singin' do-gooders like them for long. The female's the worst of the pair, screechin' about how cards are the tools of Satan. When I tried to quiet 'er down she swung that damn parasol like a belayin' pin."

"Did she land a blow?" His gray eyes glinted with a touch of mockery.

"It ain't funny," Quinn grumbled. "I can deal with her brother or any man on board, an' you know it. But a fractious female's a different matter entirely."

Devlin turned to Briana. "I won't be long," he said.

He and Quinn left the cabin. The marmalade cat rode easily on the first officer's massive shoulder. The beast's tail twitched slightly, as if in anticipation of the conflict that lay ahead.

Briana forced herself to wait until she could no longer hear the men's footsteps on the companionway. Then she got to her feet. She smoothed the folds of her skirt and retrieved her bonnet. She mustn't be here when Devlin returned.

Last night she had been afraid only of him; now she had cause to fear her own treacherous emotions even more. She went hot all over, remembering the hard pressure of his body, the heat of his fingers stroking her breast through the fragile barrier of her chemise.

She hadn't fled from Charleston only to give herself to an arrogant stranger. What did she know about him? He might once have been a common convict, shipped off to the penal colony in Australia for heaven knew what unspeakable crimes.

How was it possible that his embrace had stirred such a powerful response in her? Was she more like her mother than she had ever suspected?

Swiftly, she wheeled around and fled the cabin, as if pursued by demons. Her legs were shaky and her heart hammered against her ribs. She paused long enough to steady herself. The freshening breeze caught at her hair, whipping it across her cheek.

She put her bonnet back on and was tying the ribbons when she heard a voice from the deck below. "Good morning, Miss Cameron."

Cole Forrester stood at the foot of the steps, a dignified figure in his plum-colored frock coat and starched white cravat. He raised his tall hat and smiled up at her. Had he seen her coming out of the captain's cabin? Or had he caught sight of her only after she was already standing out on the quarterdeck? She hurried down to join him.

"I hope your first night at sea was a restful one," he said.

"Yes, indeed. Your cabin is most comfortable. I dropped off to sleep the moment my head touched the pillow." She hoped her words would at least convince him that she had not spent the night with Devlin Rafferty.

But she was still shaken by the wayward emotions Devlin had aroused in her. She needed time to steady her whirling thoughts. If she could keep Cole at her side, and get him to escort her around the deck, that would help.

But what of the command Devlin had issued only last night, that no male passenger was to force his attentions on any lady? She mustn't repay Cole's kindness by getting him into a confrontation with the master of the *Osprey*. She hadn't forgotten Devlin's capacity for violence.

She caught the puzzled look in Cole's eyes and searched her mind for a solution. Devlin had warned the men not to force themselves on unwilling females. She would make it plain that she welcomed Cole's company.

She tilted back her head and gave him a warm smile. "I was hoping to see you again soon," she said. "There's a small matter I wish to discuss with you."

"And what might that be?"

"Perhaps we might talk it over while we stroll about the deck," she suggested. "This sea breeze is most refreshing." She lowered her lids and looked at him from under her dark, curving lashes.

He offered her his arm and they started off together.

"Captain Rafferty has told me I am in your debt," she began. "He explained the difference in the price of our passage money. I've never traveled alone before and know nothing of such details. But I do want to assure you that as soon as we arrive in San Francisco, my uncle will reimburse you."

He gave her an indulgent smile. "A small matter, indeed," he said. "I should be most honored to call upon you, Miss Cameron. With your uncle's permission, of course. As for the exchange of our cabins, think no more about it."

She felt a sense of reassurance. Cole was behaving exactly as she had hoped he might. She should have known that a gentleman like Cole Forrester would dismiss a favor to a lady as a matter not worthy of discussion.

"Will this be your first visit to San Francisco, Miss Cameron?" he asked.

"It's more than a visit," she told him. "San Francisco is to be my home."

"And mine," he said. "A most fortunate coincidence."

He guided her around a group of men who were gathered on deck, arguing over how and where to make a gold strike most quickly. "I came back east only to take care of some family business at Oleander," he went on.

"You prefer San Francisco to Charleston?"

"It's not easy to make comparisons. Charleston has a dignity, a mellow charm that only comes with time. But San Francisco's a young city, vital and exciting. Perhaps you will allow me to show you about, once you're settled."

"I should like that." She broke off; she had caught sight of Devlin.

He was speaking to a man and a woman, both of them tall and thin and clad in black. The woman wore a no-nonsense bonnet with a brim like a coal scuttle, and gripped the handle of a large, serviceable parasol. Although she seemed to be the more forceful of the pair, perhaps even she had been subdued by her encounter with Devlin.

He had turned away from the missionaries and was making his way along the deck when he caught sight of Briana and Cole. Now he headed in their direction. She moved closer to Cole, looking up at him and giving him her most dazzling smile. She had to make it plain that she was his willing companion.

"Good day, Captain," Cole said. He glanced up at the billowing canvas sails. "I should imagine we're making good speed, with this strong following breeze."

"We'll get to Havana by tomorrow if the weather holds," Devlin said. He turned to her. "Our breakfast will be cold by now. Tommy'll bring us a fresh serving." He grinned at Cole. "It's most gratifying to discover a young lady with such—hearty appetites, don't you agree, Mr. Forrester?"

Cole was plainly taken aback. He released her arm and drew away. "I did not realize I had interrupted your breakfast with the captain." The warmth had disappeared from his eyes.

Before she could think of a suitable reply, Devlin said, "I was called away from my quarters to settle a small dispute between the Griscombs and some of the other passengers. No doubt Briana grew restless and came out for a breath of air."

How dare he make it sound as if they were already on such friendly terms? And to call her by her given name on so short an acquaintance! She glared at him. "I believe I made it plain that I wished to eat in my cabin," she said.

"Come along, then." He took her arm, his grip strong and possessive. She couldn't hope to break free without making a scene. Surely no one on board had forgotten that two men had been fighting over her only last night. Some of the passengers already had paused, no doubt hoping to witness another brawl.

Miss Griscomb stared at Briana, then turned to her brother. "Disgraceful . . . no better than she should be. . . ." The words, although spoken in an undertone, carried to the closest passengers, who grinned at one another.

Anxious to escape from what was becoming an impossible situation, Briana said, "Good day, Mr. Forrester," and allowed Devlin to escort her back to her cabin.

"You did that on purpose," she accused him. "You deliberately led Cole Forrester to believe that my visit to your quarters was—that you and I were—"

"Close friends?"

"More than that." Damn the man! He was deliberately pretending not to understand.

"I didn't realize you were so anxious to win Forrester's approval."

"And if I am?"

"It's a little late for that, isn't it? You gave me the idea that the scandal you spoke of had set tongues wagging all over Charleston. Surely he would have heard about it."

Her tone was icy. "Cole—Mr. Forrester—only returned to his plantation on family business. Oleander's some distance from the city. I doubt he had the opportunity to hear the local gossip And now he plans to settle in San Francisco, to make his home there."

"You managed to learn a good deal about him during your little promenade. But I suppose when a determined young lady's interested in a man she starts by finding out all she can about his prospects."

"I've no idea what you are hinting at."

"Don't you? A lady on her own, with no money and no female relatives to guide her, must arrange her own future."

"Mr. Forrester is a chance acquaintance, nothing more."

Devlin laughed softly. "But surely you can change that. He'd be a good catch for any girl. No doubt he receives a good income from that plantation of his."

"Cole Forrester's income isn't of the slightest concern to me."

He gave her a quizzical stare. "You told me you planned to choose your future husband carefully. Wouldn't any young lady prefer a gentleman who is not only respectable but wealthy?"

Under his relentless mockery, her temper flared and she lashed out at him. "What would you know about a lady? No doubt you've only consorted with waterfront trollops—"

Swiftly, his eyes turned the cold gray of the sea. Under her fingers, she felt the muscles of his arm harden. He escorted her the rest of the way to her cabin in silence. So much the better, she thought. She wanted no further conversation with him.

But when they stopped outside the door and he took out a ring of keys she couldn't restrain a wordless sound of protest. Although she hated having to beg a favor from him, she couldn't stop herself.

"Don't lock me in again. Please."

He paused, searching her face. "It's for your protection," he reminded her.

"I won't go walking on the deck alone. I won't cause any trouble for you. But being locked up—it makes me feel as if the walls are closing in—as if I am trapped in a cell—"

She braced herself for a sardonic reply or a cold refusal. Instead, she saw a curious shadow move in the depths of his eyes. In a moment it was gone, but he spoke quietly, without a touch of mockery. "I'll leave the door unlocked from the outside."

She managed a shaky smile of gratitude.

"But there's an inside bolt, and I advise you to keep that one locked, especially at night."

"I will, Captain. I give you my word." She turned and went

inside. Quickly, she found the heavy bolt and pushed it into place. Only then did she hear the sound of his retreating footsteps.

She stared at the locked door in bewilderment. Would she ever understand the contradictions in this man? He had mocked her mercilessly, grown furious when she had turned on him. Why, then, had her plea moved him so?

Bewilderment gave way to gratitude, but even that gradually ebbed away. Devlin could well afford to give in to a small request when he was still in control of her as long as she was aboard his ship. There was no one else she could turn to for protection; not now, after he had alienated Cole with his suggestive remarks.

"A young lady of hearty appetites"; that was what he'd called her, knowing that those simple words could be taken in more ways than one.

How dare he give Cole Forrester the wrong idea about her?

She sat down on the edge of her bunk. She longed to deny Rafferty's words, but how could she? Her face grew hot as she remembered her overpowering response to his touch.

He had caught her off guard. She had allowed him to hold her only because she had thought he was being kind. How could she have realized that his gentle caresses would change so quickly? Or that he could arouse her as no other man ever had?

She would be on guard against her own bewildering responses from now on. But how could she fend him off, if he decided he wanted her? She tried to still her whirling thoughts, to make plans for the immediate future.

Tomorrow, if the breeze held, they would drop anchor in Havana harbor. Rafferty had told her he planned to go ashore to buy supplies. She would be safe from his advances for one day, maybe two.

But what would happen after that? She cupped her burning cheeks in her hands and tried not to think of the long weeks that lay ahead before the *Osprey* arrived in San Francisco.

Four

The dawn sky over Havana was a blaze of crimson and gold. The *Osprey* had dropped anchor an hour earlier, and now she rose and fell with the tide. The grim stone fortress of El Morro loomed to the left. Beyond the ships from a dozen nations lay the red rooftops and narrow streets of the sprawling tropical city.

A light breeze blowing in from the sea ruffled the wide skirt of Briana's blue silk gown, making it billow over her wide crinoline petticoats. It tugged at a ringlet of her red-gold hair, whipping it out from beneath her bonnet and across her forehead.

She stood at the rail directly outside the door of her cabin, trying to ignore a small twinge of guilt. She had promised the captain she would not go walking on deck unescorted, but now she told herself that she wasn't promenading about, only standing here a moment, so that she might catch a glimpse of the city and draw in a breath of fresh air. It was a bewitching medley of scents she inhaled: the salt tang of the sea, the pungency of tar, hemp, spices, sugarcane, and the fragrance of dew-soaked tropical foliage.

She lingered at the rail, assuring herself that if any of the male passengers came near her, a few short steps would take her back inside her cabin, where she could bolt the door behind her. Meanwhile, she reveled in the delicious sensation of freedom.

Hearing footsteps behind her, she turned away from the rail to find herself face to face with Cole Forrester. She felt a stir of uneasiness, remembering the humiliating circumstances of their parting the day before.

After Devlin had hinted at his intimacy with her Briana wouldn't have been altogether surprised if Cole had pretended not to see her, or even turned away and walked in the other direction.

Instead he paused, raised his hat, and greeted her with a smile and a polite "Good morning."

Relieved at this show of friendliness, she relaxed slightly. There was a brief, awkward silence, while she searched her mind for something—anything—that would help to erase the false impression Devlin had created.

Tommy appeared, hurrying about his duties. "Mornin', miss," he said with a cheerful grin. "If yer lookin' for the captain, he's already gone ashore."

"The captain's whereabouts are a matter of complete indifference to me."

She hadn't meant to speak so coldly to the amiable young cabin boy, but the words were the first that came to her mind and she could only hope that they would help to undo the harm Devlin had caused by his insinuations.

"Yes, miss." Tommy's grin faded. He touched his cap and hurried off, looking startled and a little crestfallen. Again she was left alone with Cole. Together they looked out over the turquoise water at the city, with its houses of pastel green, blue, and yellow.

"Is this your first visit to Havana, Miss Cameron?"

"I'm afraid I won't get any closer to the city than I am now," she told him.

"And why not?"

"The captain has given me strict orders to remain in my cabin. I suppose he would be furious if he knew I was out here on deck, even for a moment."

Cole stared at her in disbelief. "But that is intolerable."

She wasn't being entirely fair to Devlin and she knew it. After all, he had been moved by her plea and had agreed that she need not be locked inside her cabin, at least during the day. And although he had gone ashore on ship's business this morning, she did not doubt that he would keep his word and take her for a walk on deck whenever he had the time.

"How dare he keep you a prisoner in your own cabin?" Cole's face was tight with indignation. "Such behavior toward a lady is quite unforgivable."

"I suppose he feels it's for my own good," she interrupted. "The men aboard the ship are a rough lot."

"I don't dispute that," he said, "but there's no reason for you to remain aboard the ship all day when Havana is so close. It has been called the 'Paris of the Caribbean.' "

Briana gave a wistful sigh. "I doubt it could live up to its namesake."

"You've visited Paris?"

"I was born and raised there," she told him. "But I will try to learn to think of San Francisco as my new home."

"I hope so. But there's no need for you to miss the charms of our 'Paris of the Caribbean.' I've already hired a boat to take me ashore. Please say you'll join me."

She stiffened at his words. "Forgive me for speaking so bluntly, Mr. Forrester, but whatever unfortunate impression the captain may have given you, I assure you I couldn't possibly accept your offer."

"My dear Miss Cameron, I am not accustomed to forming an opinion of any lady on the word of another."

"Still, I'd like to explain about—what happened yesterday. Captain Rafferty agreed that I could not spend the whole voyage in my cabin. He offered to accompany me on an occasional stroll about the deck, and I agreed."

"But he's not here today. We're lying at anchor, and by mid-day there won't be a breath of air in your cabin. You must allow me to take you ashore, at least for a few hours."

"I couldn't possibly go ashore without a chaperone."

He gave her a reassuring smile. "I understand your scruples, and I respect you for them. But you're coming with me. I promise to take you for a drive about the city, show you the sights, and have you back aboard long before the captain returns."

She wavered in her resolve, and he was quick to pursue his advantage. "We'll be under sail again before sundown, and this is our last port of call until we reach the west coast of South America."

Still she hesitated. "The Paris of the Caribbean," he reminded her. "I'll hire a *volante* and show you some of the local sights. It won't be like the Bois de Boulogne or the Tuileries gardens, but I think you will enjoy your excursion."

When she remained silent he added, "The shops are filled with elegant trifles to please a lady. Perhaps you will wish to do a little shopping."

She laughed softly. "Surely you haven't forgotten the captain's fit of temper when I wished to have my luggage carried aboard in Charleston."

"He had no right to speak to you that way. And he'll not do it again, I promise you. You are a passenger aboard this vessel, not a member of the crew. If Rafferty speaks disrespectfully to you again, I will deal with him."

Briana felt reassured at his words. During her brief months in Charleston she had gotten to know many gentlemen like Cole Forrester; soft-spoken Southerners with outwardly easygoing charm who were capable of swift violence if provoked. They reminded her of the dashing French noblemen she and Mama had known in Paris. Charleston, too, had its share of expert duelists, ready to fight on the slightest provocation.

Now that she had corrected Cole's false impression of her, she would be able to rely on the code of the southern gentleman. Yet, as Cole helped her down the gangplank, she still felt a little uneasy.

Although she might have convinced Cole that she was a proper young lady, it wasn't so easy for her to deal with the hard core of honesty inside herself. She couldn't deny that she had not only gone willingly to Devlin's quarters but had allowed him to take the most shocking liberties.

Face it, she told herself, *Captain Rafferty never forced himself on you. You wanted him to hold you, kiss you, to touch your breasts, to . . .*

She remembered vividly the rising hunger between them. The

way her breasts had grown turgid and heavy under his hands and her nipples had peaked and hardened, stroked by his fingers. Suppose Mr. Quinn had not interrupted them when he had?

She looked away, as if fearful that Cole could read her thoughts in her eyes. But he was speaking of more mundane matters.

"The captain's being sensible, taking on a cargo of fruit here in Havana," he was saying.

"I doubt many of the other passengers would agree with you. They seem eager to reach San Francisco as quickly as possible. I'm sure they resent even a day's delay."

"That's because they've never been around the Horn before."

They had reached the foot of the gangplank. Cole signaled to an olive-skinned man in cotton pants and a straw hat who held the reins of the horse harnessed to a curious-looking carriage. Cole spoke to him in rapid Spanish and handed him a few coins; then he helped her into the carriage and took the reins in his gloved hand. He cracked the whip and the *volante* moved forward. The vehicle merged with the procession of others moving slowly along the cobbled street.

"I saw the effects of scurvy during my first voyage to California," Cole went on. "Whatever his other shortcomings, Rafferty's concern for the welfare of his passengers does him credit."

"No doubt. But let's forget the captain for today; you promised to show me the sights of Havana."

"And so I shall. I don't think you'll be disappointed."

It was good to be off the ship, if only for a few hours. Briana leaned forward and looked with pleasure at the profusion of fine shops dealing in jewelry, silver, millinery, perfume, ladies' shoes, and imported laces.

The single-story houses were painted blue or green, with enormous, iron-barred windows. "Are there no gardens?" she asked.

"There are, indeed," Cole assured her. "And they're most charming, with orange trees, mignonettes, pomegranates. But you can't see them from the street because each of these houses is built around its own courtyard, secluded from public view."

The *volante* was forced to move slowly because of the ever-growing crowd. "This is a most unusual sort of carriage," she remarked.

"It was designed especially for traveling about the island," Cole said. "See how large and high the wheels are—nearly six feet in diameter—and the body of the vehicle, slung low between the shafts. The Cubans never got around to paving the roads outside the city."

Even in early morning the narrow streets were growing crowded and noisy. Other *volantes* carried groups of dark-eyed ladies who fluttered their fans and chattered like so many tropical birds as they went about their shopping.

Briana stared, wide-eyed, at the window of a jewelry shop, where the emeralds, diamonds, and rubies in the window caught the sunlight; at a fashionable dressmaking establishment with gowns of organdy and tulle, suitable for the tropical climate.

She noticed that many of the ladies wore dresses that looked as if they might have been imported from the famous salons of Paris—perhaps from the House of Worth itself.

When she remarked on this Cole nodded. "These ladies are the wives and daughters of the sugar planters." Briana noticed that as the ladies made their way out of the shops they were followed by small black boys in satin livery, who carried their purchases.

She was glad she had worn her fashionable blue silk over its wide crinoline. This time, however, she was taking no chances; she had covered her low-cut bodice with a shawl of Lyons silk.

"Havana does remind me of Paris—a little. Except that there, the ladies never started their shopping until afternoon."

Cole smiled. "By noon Havana is far too hot for anything but a siesta," he told her.

He drew rein in front of a large café and motioned to a dark-skinned street urchin, who hurried forward to hold the reins.

"This is the Dominica," he told her. "They serve a delicious assortment of ices and sherbets. You must sample their refreshments."

"I'm not sure I should," she began.

"It's perfectly correct for a lady to come here, so long as she is accompanied by a gentleman. Or her duenna."

Before she could offer further objections he had alighted from the *volante* and was holding out his hand to her.

As she entered the café on Cole's arm, Briana still felt a certain trepidation. She didn't want Cole to get the wrong idea about her; not again. But why was it so important to her to make a good impression on Cole Forrester? To convince him that she was every inch a well-bred young lady?

The answer came with startling clarity.

Because of Mama. Mama, who had defied convention and then put an ocean between herself and Paris, only to be caught up in the shadows of her past. Mama, who had fought so hard to protect her from the slightest breath of scandal. Mama had given her life, trying to protect Briana.

It had been Mama's last wish that Briana should make a respectable marriage and take her place in polite society. Very well, then, she vowed; Mama would have her wish. Once the *Osprey* reached San Francisco, she would set about finding a suitable husband. In the meantime she would do nothing to compromise her virtue.

A few minutes later she and Cole were seated at one of the small round tables in the marble-floored dining room of the Dominica. She spooned a mound of lime and pomegranate sherbet as she watched the rainbow patterns cast on the ceiling by a glittering fountain.

"I suppose I do miss Paris more than I thought I would," she said softly. "I haven't dined in a café like this since Mama and I left there."

"Your mother chose to remain behind in Charleston?"

"Mama passed away some time ago." The familiar ache of loss caught at Briana's throat.

Cole didn't reply at once, and her grief gave way to a brief flare of panic. She had to know whether whispers of the scandal had reached him at Oleander. "It was malaria," she said.

Now he murmured his condolences. "Most unfortunate. Our South Carolina climate; those great swamps near the city. Too near. They are the breeding ground of malaria and yellow fever."

She stifled a sigh of relief. Cole hadn't heard the scandal that had rocked Charleston. And why should he? Immured on his plantation upriver, eager to conclude his family business and return to San Francisco, he knew nothing of salacious gossip surrounding "that Cameron woman."

Even now Briana felt a stab of deep resentment toward those who had been so quick to judge her mother, especially against Hugh, who had professed to love her and then turned away from her. Was any man to be trusted? she wondered.

"You have no family at all in Charleston?" Cole was saying.

She shook her head. "And I've never even met Uncle Alexander or his wife, Gertrude. Still, it was most generous of them to offer me a home after—" She caught herself in time. "After my bereavement."

The café was growing crowded now. Ladies seated themselves at nearby tables. It wasn't easy for them to find room for the wide crinolines that billowed around them. Once more Briana noticed their fashionable gowns. "These Cuban planters must be quite wealthy."

"They are, indeed," Cole said. "Most of them travel to Europe every year. And they've also built the finest opera houses and theaters right here in the city. When they are on the island they prefer to spend their time in their homes in Havana."

"But how do they manage to run their plantations from such a distance?"

Cole shrugged. "They have overseers to take care of all such mundane details," he said. "Not like so many of our South Carolina planters, like my father and mother. And Keith, my younger brother. They seldom leave Oleander."

Briana didn't like the careless, half-contemptuous way he spoke of his family's devotion to their plantation. "I should think that when a planter and his family live on their land the mistress of the household is more likely to concern herself with the welfare of her slaves."

"My mother would agree with you. She takes on the burden of responsibility for our people. She nurses them when they fall ill. She even provides them with the services of a traveling preacher for the good of their souls."

It was plain from Cole's tone and the faint flicker of amusement in his blue eyes, that he regarded his mother's concern for the family slaves not as a duty, but as a harmless feminine foible.

"And when you return to Oleander someday, what then?"

"I've no intention of returning," he told her.

"Are you, too, possessed by this gold fever?"

"Good Lord, no! For every man who makes a profitable gold strike a hundred go home empty-handed. If they survive to get home at all."

She looked at him, puzzled. Why would any man twice undertake a long and dangerous voyage to San Francisco, if not to hunt for gold?

"I am a lawyer by profession," he said. "I've already formed a partnership with Martin Padgett, a Virginia gentleman who also sees the possibilities for the future in California."

"But what about Oleander?" she persisted.

"It will go on running smoothly, producing a fortune in cotton. My father's a born planter, tied to the land. With Keith to help him, the plantation will flourish, as it has these past three generations."

Briana was relieved by his words. Even back in Charleston, she had felt a certain distaste for the institution of slavery, although she had done her best to conceal her opinions.

But San Francisco was a free state and, without the climate for growing cotton or sugarcane, it was likely to remain so.

Perhaps Cole, for all his seeming indifference, shared her views. Maybe that was part of the reason he was leaving the south. She found herself hoping it was.

Even if she had married Hugh Mandeville, she doubted she could have adjusted easily to being the mistress of a plantation.

Briana reprimanded herself sharply. What possible difference could it make to her what Cole Forrester's opinions on slavery might be?

She set down her spoon abruptly. What was she thinking of? She scarcely knew Cole Forrester. Any thoughts about a possible future for them were totally ridiculous.

Captain Rafferty's words came back unbidden. *A lady on her own, with no money, must arrange her own future. . . . He'd be a good catch for any girl. No doubt he receives a good income from that plantation of his. . . .*

As if fearing that Cole could somehow read her thoughts, she felt the heat surge into her cheeks. Devlin Rafferty was a crude, impossible man who had said what he had only to rouse her temper.

"Is something wrong?" Cole's voice jerked her back to the present, to the Dominica and the chatter of Spanish voices.

"No, indeed. But it is growing warm and close in here."

"Not much warmer than our own Charleston," he said. "But I'm forgetting; you are more accustomed to the climate of France."

He signaled to the waiter. In a few moments they were back in the *volante.* "Perhaps a ride along the beach would refresh you," he suggested. "Havana is quite impossible in the middle of the day."

As they left the center of the city, the houses and shops grew farther apart. The sea breeze cooled her face, and she inhaled the scent of the orange trees, the pomegranates and mignonettes. Butterflies fluttered their iridescent turquoise wings among the blossoms.

They turned off the road and onto a stretch of palm-fringed beach overlooking the harbor. She caught her breath in sheer pleasure. "Such a beautiful view."

"Beautiful," he agreed. But he wasn't looking at the dazzling white sands or the glittering water. His eyes were fixed on her face, and it was impossible for her to mistake his meaning.

All at once she was aware of her vulnerable position. She

shouldn't have come here to this deserted spot with a man she scarcely knew.

Seeking to divert him, she said, "I should think that Oleander is lovely in its own way. You've said you won't miss it, but perhaps in time you will grow homesick and wish to return."

"I won't have time to be homesick," he told her, "even if I were given to such vaporing sentiments. I'll be fully occupied in building my law practice."

"The law must be a fascinating profession," she said politely.

"No doubt. But I don't intend to practice for more than a year or two. After that I'll go into politics."

His blue eyes took on a metallic glitter. "California's a new state with infinite potential for a man who can reach out and take what he wants. All the gold doesn't lie in the mines. There's a fortune waiting for anyone with the will to grasp it. Fortune," he repeated. "And power."

Although she knew little about politics, she was disturbed by the avid hunger in his voice when he spoke of power. Then she told herself that surely it was natural for a man like Cole, raised and educated in an atmosphere of privilege, to seek to rise to the top, wherever he might be.

"I've made all my plans carefully," he was saying. Why did she find his look, his tone, so distasteful?

Remembering the events of the past few months, she said, "We are sometimes forced to change our plans, Mr. Forrester. Unforeseen circumstances . . ." She bit down on her lower lip, fearing that she might still betray herself.

But Cole went on with growing self-assurance. "If circumstances change, a clever man can always find a way to turn such changes to his own advantage."

She felt the force of his ambition reaching out to envelop her, to overwhelm her. Outwardly easygoing, there were unknown forces in this man. His blue eyes looked beyond her, to the curve of the palm-fringed beach and the blue-green waves with their creamy foam.

She heard herself saying, "I wish I could be as sure of my own future."

He smiled down at her complacently. "Ah, but a lady is different. Her future is shaped by her husband's."

Such a view was widely held, of course; and yet something inside her longed to deny it. Why should a woman of strength and intelligence allow her husband to mold her to his will?

He was still speaking, his eyes fixed on hers. "A suitable wife," he was saying. "A lady of beauty and breeding, who will be an ornament to his home. But even those qualities are not enough."

The complacency of the man roused a rebellious streak, and it was hard for her to keep a fixed smile on her lips. She was beginning to wish she hadn't come ashore with him after all. His words droned on, blending with the surge of the waves. ". . . capable of running his household, raising his children properly . . ."

"Children?" she heard herself repeating.

"A man does not marry for practical reasons alone," he said. His voice was deep and husky. He drew her against him and cupped her face, tilting it up to his, pressing his mouth against hers.

His kiss deepened. He was trying to force her lips apart, yet she felt not the slightest response.

She was remembering the fierce urgency Devlin Rafferty's kiss had aroused in her. She went rigid for a moment, turned her face away, set her hands against Cole's chest, and pushed hard.

She knew she was no match for his wiry strength. And, against all her misgivings, she had come ashore with him; had allowed him to drive her out here to this deserted beach. "Let me go! At once!"

To her surprise, he complied instantly. When he spoke again it was without the slightest trace of resentment or even wounded masculine vanity.

"I'm sorry, Miss Cameron—Briana— I forgot myself. But only because you are so very lovely."

She drew away, keeping her eyes fixed on the beach.

"You must forgive me for taking such liberties. It won't happen again, I promise you." He smiled faintly. "But perhaps it would be as well to return to the ship now. Otherwise I might be tempted to forget myself again."

While she smoothed the folds of her blue silk skirt and resettled her bonnet, he picked up the reins and turned the *volante* in the direction of the city.

During their drive back to the ship he confined himself to impersonal comments on the various sights of interest in the city. She nodded from time to time, making suitable replies.

Cole Forrester hadn't the slightest understanding of her, or of her reason for rejecting him. She could be grateful for that much at least.

She had pushed him away not because he had overstepped the bounds of propriety but because his caresses had left her unmoved. Yet Cole was exactly the sort of gentleman Mama would have wanted for her. And, what was equally important, he knew nothing of the scandal in Charleston. If she played her cards right, she might be able to hold his interest while keeping him at arm's length, until she was under the protection of her uncle. After that Alexander Cameron and his wife would provide her with the proper background of respectability.

As they ascended the gangplank, he asked: "You have forgiven me, haven't you, Briana?"

She lowered her eyes. "I'm not sure."

"If I promise to behave, will you allow me to call on you in San Francisco?"

Remembering Mama's lectures, the proper reply came to her automatically. "Perhaps, Mr. Forrester. If my uncle is willing."

Devlin was already on board, standing at the rail some distance away. He gave her a long, cold stare, then turned his attention back to the sweating stevedores who were loading cases of fruit into the hold. When the task was nearly complete he turned to Quinn. "Make ready to sail," he ordered.

She watched the sailors snap to action at Quinn's bellowed

commands. Some swarmed up the rigging, while others ran to remove the gangplank. Already fearing Devlin's response to her flouting of his orders, she tried to formulate an explanation.

"Look alive there, ye lazy buggers!" Quinn's roar startled her out of her self-absorption. There was a flurry of motion at the top of the gangplank and a curse from one of the sailors, followed by a shrill cry of protest. She caught a glimpse of a parrot green skirt and a dark mane of hair.

"Take your hands off me! Let me talk to the captain!"

A girl, scarcely older than herself, struggled and broke free from a sailor's restraining grip. Her high heels clattered across the deck.

"You, there!" Quinn shouted to the girl. "Get yer arse off this deck or I'll have ye tossed into the harbor!"

Ignoring the first mate, the dark-haired girl made straight for Devlin. She clutched at his arm. "Captain—"

He spoke calmly enough. "There's no business for you here, girl. We're getting ready to sail."

"I'm not what you think!"

He looked her up and down, taking in the loose, heavy mane of black hair, the painted mouth, the sheer white cotton blouse.

"I want to sail with you. As a passenger." The sweat was streaming down her face and her blouse clung damply to the lush curves of her breasts.

"I'm taking no more passengers. Get off my ship. Now!"

His voice was harsh, but the girl did not move. Instead she kept her grasp on his sleeve. He knew desperation when he saw it, and he felt a brief stirring of pity. Her dark eyes were imploring.

The passengers began to gather around, impatient to set sail yet briefly diverted by this unexpected bit of drama. "I can't go back—I won't go!"

"Then I'll have you put ashore," he told her.

She glanced about at the gathering crowd. "Let me speak with you alone, Captain. Only a moment."

He pulled her aside, into the shadow of the quarterdeck. A

glare at the crowd, and they retreated. She looked up at him, speaking urgently, her eyes never leaving his face.

"Allow me to escort you to your cabin," Cole was saying, but Briana shook her head. Something about this girl, the desperation in her face, held her where she was.

The girl was speaking softly, so that Briana couldn't catch a word. Poor creature; no matter her reasons for begging passage, she'd have little chance of moving Devlin Rafferty.

Briana was startled when, after a few more moments of talk, Devlin took the girl by the arm and led her not to the gangplank but straight to Briana.

"Miss Briana Cameron, this is Poppy Nolan. Or so she calls herself."

"It's my name. And I am an American citizen. I swear it."

He brushed aside her words. "Miss Nolan says she's a member of some kind of theatrical troupe. Stranded in Havana and without passage money."

"I scarcely see how this unfortunate young woman's predicament can possibly concern Miss Cameron," Cole protested, but the captain ignored him.

"As you've heard, she wants to sail with us," Devlin went on, his gray eyes fixed on Briana's face. "It's up to you whether I take her along."

"Up to me?" His words made no sense, but he was obviously quite serious.

"You're the only female traveling alone and there's a second bunk in your cabin. If you'll share your quarters, she comes with us. Otherwise she goes ashore."

Briana stared from Devlin to the terrified girl, then back to Devlin again. She heard Cole's protesting voice. "You insult Miss Cameron by suggesting she share her quarters with this—this—"

If Briana agreed to share her quarters with an actress—or whatever the girl might be—she would forfeit Cole's respect. She had her own future to think about. Then her amber eyes met Poppy Nolan's brown ones. She tried to look away but couldn't.

The girl had some urgent reason for needing to leave Havana at once. Devlin must think so, too, or he never would have considered taking her along, not for one moment. Whatever his virtues, if any, charity wasn't one of them. And yet . . .

Devlin spoke directly to Briana. "What's it to be? Will you share your cabin? Or do I have Miss Nolan put ashore?"

Five

Tommy tossed a thin mattress, a blanket, and a pile of linens onto the upper berth, then climbed down and stared doubtfully at Poppy Nolan. Briana suspected that he, like Cole Forrester, disapproved of her decision to share her cabin with the dark-haired dancer.

Maybe if Devlin hadn't forced her to make an immediate decision, she would have refused to spend the rest of the long voyage in such close quarters with a girl she scarcely knew. Perhaps he had even hoped she would say no, taking the whole matter out of his hands. Remembering his look of surprise when she had agreed to the arrangement, her lips curved in a faint smile.

Tommy had already started for the door when Poppy called to him. "How about bringing me a few buckets of water to wash myself?" She looked down at her soiled dress with a frown of distaste. "And my clothes could use a good scrubbing, too."

The cabin boy paused, but he didn't answer her. Instead, he gave Briana an inquiring look. So far as he was concerned, this was still her cabin; he would take his orders from her.

"Please bring as much water as you can spare," Briana said. "And a tub, if you can find one."

"If that's what you want, miss," he conceded.

The crimson and gold sunset had already given way to twilight, and the *Osprey* was moving out of Havana harbor when Tommy and another seaman came in, carrying a small bathtub made of tin, with a wooden bottom and a handle at each end. They set it down, went out, and returned again, this time with several buckets of water, which they emptied into the tub.

As soon as they were gone, Poppy started taking off her soiled dress. Briana stared at her in surprise. Under Poppy's parrot-green dress the girl wore another, this one of vivid yellow-and-blue-flowered muslin.

"And I've got on three petticoats, two camisoles, and two pairs of drawers." Poppy grinned with satisfaction as she went on removing layer after layer of sweat-dampened clothing.

"Our company's manager—dirty little bugger—went off with every cent he owed us," she said. "And the landlord of that flea-ridden boardinghouse swore he'd have the law on us for not paying our rent. He said he'd see all of us in jail for debt. So I had to get out of there fast. I put on as many clothes as I could and went sashaying down the front steps and out through the lobby, like I was goin' for a promenade. Then I took off and ran for the docks."

"I left my trunk behind," she went on. "Otherwise the landlord would've known right off that I wasn't coming back. But even so, it wouldn't have taken him long to figure out he'd been rooked, and then he've had them Havana police on my tail."

"But it wasn't your fault that your manager left without paying what he owed you," Briana protested.

"That don't matter. They would've tossed me in jail and thrown away the key." Poppy shuddered.

Briana saw the fear in the other girl's dark eyes. Seeking to distract her, she said, "You must have been dreadfully uncomfortable in all those clothes."

"I would've been a hell of a lot more uncomfortable if the police had caught up with me. I heard about them Havana jails—real hellholes, they are." She tried to speak casually, but she couldn't conceal her revulsion.

She stripped off her remaining garments, then stretched her

arms over her head and gave a deep sigh of relief. Her full-breasted, long-legged body gleamed tawny gold in the light of the swinging overhead lamp, but she showed not the slightest trace of self-consciousness.

Briana took a cake of lilac-scented soap and a fresh washcloth from the top drawer of the chest and handed them to her.

"Say, this is real nice of you, honey." Poppy hesitated for a moment. "I never did get around to thanking you proper for letting me share your cabin. To tell the truth, I took you for one of them la-de-da, stuck-up ladies who pulls aside her skirts so as not to brush up against a girl like me."

She stepped into the tub, sat down, drew up her knees, and began to lather her face and shoulders. "When I've finished bathing I'll give my clothes a good scrubbing. Wish I'd have been able to take my trunk, but that would've given me away for sure. No matter—once I'm in San Francisco I'll have them miners fighting to buy me all the fancy duds I want." Her even white teeth flashed in a grin of anticipation. "From what I've heard, them fellas out there are real generous. I mean to get my share of all that gold."

"Are you going to find work as a dancer?"

"It's what I do best," she said. "That manager of ours, he had a lot of fancy ideas about putting on 'uplifting classical drama,' back there in Havana."

"Don't Cubans care for drama?" Briana asked.

"Maybe—if it's in their own language. None of us could speak more'n a few words of Spanish. But dancing—that's different. A girl who's got a good pair of tits and a nice round arse and knows how to move 'em—she can make any man hotter than a pistol without sayin' a word."

Briana caught her breath, her face scarlet with embarrassment at the other girl's words. Mama had always been careful to shield her from such bawdy talk. Indeed, the women of the Parisian demimonde, though they lived beyond the pale of polite society, assumed the manners of the most elegantly bred ladies—at least in public.

"What happened to the other members of your troupe?" Briana asked.

"Guess some of them got away. Maybe a few of the men were able to get work as seamen." She laughed. "They'll sure be gettin' their nice soft hands blistered, pullin' ropes and scrubbin' decks."

"And the other ladies in your company?"

"There're plenty of bawdy houses in Havana, same as in any other seaport. But that ain't for me. If I don't fancy a man, I won't have him in my bed. Know what I mean?"

Although Poppy's frank speech shocked Briana, she did understand. She remembered that Cole's kiss had left her completely unmoved. The thought of giving herself to him, even in the sanctity of marriage, was faintly distasteful.

But Devlin . . . His lightest touch had sent flickers of desire through her whole body. Her nipples had hardened and peaked under the stroking of his fingers. . . .

"And what about you, honey?" Poppy's voice jerked her back to the present. "Why're you heading for San Francisco?"

"I'm going to live with my aunt and uncle."

"You're lucky to have your own folks waiting for you." Poppy sounded a little wistful as she raised one leg and ran the washcloth down its shapely length. "And that high-toned gent who was with you on deck—is he a relation, too?"

Briana shook her head. "I met Cole Forrester just as I was boarding the *Osprey* back in Charleston. He offered to exchange cabins with me, so I'd have more room for my trunks."

"The way he was making such a fuss about your sharin' a cabin with me, I figured he might be your brother or your cousin."

"He had no right to say what he did, even if he was only trying to—" She broke off in embarrassment.

"To protect you from getting mixed up with a girl like me. I guess I can understand that. A well-bred lady isn't supposed to have anything to do with my kind." She looked at Briana over the rim of the tin tub, her dark eyes troubled. "Hope I ain't spoiled your chances with this—Mr. Forrester."

"My chances?"

"Honey, with your looks an' your high-toned ways you can have him hooked and landed by the time we get to California."

"I'm not at all sure Cole Forrester's the sort of man I'd want to—hook and land."

"Then maybe you got the hots for the captain, is that it? Now there's a handsome devil."

"He is good-looking in his way, I suppose."

"You suppose! You know damn well he is! Wide in the shoulders, narrow in the flanks, and moves like a prize stallion. I'll bet he knows how to pleasure a girl between the sheets and have her begging for more."

"Poppy!" Her voice wavered; how could she deny the other girl's words when, even now, she was remembering her overwhelming response to Devlin's kisses? Her body began to tingle as if, this very moment, she could feel his warm hands stroking her shoulders, curving around her breasts, teasing the nipples until they hardened like twin pebbles under his touch. The skin of her thighs began to heat, and a sweet-hot need, a nameless wanting, stirred deep in her loins.

"You mustn't say such things! They aren't—decent."

Poppy sighed and shook her head slightly. "Guess a girl like you don't look at a man the same way I do."

She wriggled deeper in the water, ducked her head under, and then came up with her heavy black mane soaking wet. She scrubbed her hair until the dark strands were covered with billows of lilac-scented suds.

"I guess maybe you don't let yourself think about a man unless you figure he'd make you a proper husband. I can't say I know much about marriage myself, but I bet that if things ain't right with a man and woman between the sheets, they can't be any good in the parlor, neither."

She smiled ruefully. "Sorry, Briana. There I go, forgetting

myself again. You've been real decent to me. I sure don't want to make you sorry you gave me a chance to get out of Havana."

"I could never be sorry for that."

"But you wish I'd watch what I say, right?"

When Briana didn't answer the girl went on. "Don't you worry; I'll speak as nice and careful as a preacher's daughter—when I'm around you."

In the days that followed, as the *Osprey* sped southward under full-spread canvas, Briana was grateful for Poppy's company. Although the dancer, in spite of her promise, didn't always remember to choose her words carefully, her good qualities more than made up for her occasional lapses in decorum. Poppy was used to taking circumstances as they came and making the best of them. She didn't fuss over the minor inconveniences of shipboard life, as a more gently reared young lady might have done. And she was quick to appreciate every small comfort that came her way.

"Say, the ship's food's a lot better than that swill they gave us in the boardinghouses, when I was traveling with the troupe. The bunks are cleaner, too." She laughed a bit ruefully. "I would like to go up on deck without that Quinn fella trailing after me, though," she admitted.

Devlin had appointed Quinn to take Poppy for her daily walks. Briana sometimes smiled at the picture they made: Poppy, with her graceful walk, and Quinn plodding along beside her, his huge orange tomcat perched on his massive shoulder.

"I guess the captain knows best, though," Poppy conceded. "Two good-looking females like us would keep the other men hot and achin' from here to San Francisco. I don't relish the thought of getting jumped by a fella with a bulge in his breeches, looking for a quick—" She stopped short. "Sorry, Briana. I keep forgetting."

As for Briana, she went on taking her walks about the deck with Devlin whenever he could spare the time from his duties.

During these encounters he kept his conversation carefully impersonal.

When the ship's course took them close to shore he would identify some points of scenic interest.

"Over there, that's Brazil. The harbor at Rio de Janiero is excellent," he said. "Ordinarily I might put into port there, but my passengers are eager to reach their destination. And we have all the provisions we'll need until we reach the west coast of South America."

He pointed out a school of silvery flying fish or the fin of a shark, slicing through the water. He even explained the way he used the ship's navigational instruments to plot their course at noon each day.

When Cole happened to be passing by he raised his tall hat and gave Briana a polite smile and a formal bow, but it was plain that he disapproved of her willingness to allow Poppy to share her cabin.

Remembering Cole's embrace on the beach in Havana, Briana wondered whether she could have gotten him "hooked and landed" had she refused to have Poppy as a cabin mate. But perhaps it wasn't too late to win Cole's respect again, even now.

Respect—no, it had been more than that. Much more. His kiss had told her that. Once more, her common sense was at war with her turbulent emotions.

Cole had all the qualities she had been taught to look for in a suitor: social position, wealth, and ambition. As for her complete lack of physical response to his kiss, perhaps that would change in time.

Uncontrolled emotion could be dangerous. Briana would keep her own feelings under control. She would never allow herself to yield to the treacherous lure of her desires, no matter how strong the temptation.

A week after the *Osprey* crossed the equator, a heavy copper-colored cloud bank appeared on the horizon, blotting out the pale blue sky. The wind sprang up and tall waves battered at the clipper, which rocked and shuddered beneath the driving force of the angry sea.

Devlin took the wheel and Quinn began shouting orders to the crew. Men scurried up the mast, swaying perilously on their perches high overhead.

Confined to their cabin, Briana and Poppy huddled together in the lower berth. All night long the wind keened like a soul in torment; it drove torrents of rain against the locked porthole and clawed at the sails. Briana flinched at the cries of the men, who were battered by knifelike shards of flying wood.

The storm began to die away toward dawn, and the two girls sank into an uneasy sleep. When Tommy brought breakfast a few hours later they saw that his striped shirt and canvas pants were soaked through and his sandy hair was plastered to his forehead in lank strands.

"Breakfast ain't much, but you'll have to make do," he said with a grin.

He set a tray on the table. "It's a proper shambles out there. Lots of rigging fell on deck during the night. We got to cut it away. An' we got sails to mend, an'—" Even as he spoke, they heard the roar of Quinn's voice; the sailors' bare feet slapping against the deck; the pounding of the carpenter's mallet. "We'll have plenty to do before we get the ship seaworthy again. But don't you worry; the worst's over. For now."

"For now?" Briana's voice was unsteady, her nerves still taut. "You mean there'll be other storms like this one?"

"This weren't nothin' special," he said. "Wait 'til we get to the Horn, miss. Goin' around old Cape Stiff—that's what us sailors call 'er. We'll be running into the worst of it then."

Briana and Poppy stared at each other in disbelief. Then they both started to laugh. The sound was shrill, with an edge of rising hysteria. Tears ran down their cheeks and they clung to each other, still rocking with laughter.

Tommy stared at them, baffled by this unexpected outburst.

Females were a strange lot and no mistake, he thought. He sighed, shook his head, and left the cabin.

Early one afternoon, nearly three weeks later, Briana stood on deck, her head tilted back as she studied the slate-colored sky. She was disobeying Devlin's orders again, but she didn't care. It had been three days since her last walk, and she could no longer bear the confinement of the cabin. She had chosen a spot at the foot of the stairs leading up to the captain's quarters. After these weeks at sea the passengers had come to know that Devlin Rafferty's orders were not to be taken lightly. Even the roughest of the lot wouldn't be likely to give her any trouble.

But the weather was another matter. She gasped as a raw, chilling gust of wind tore at her skirts. The ship heeled, and billows of white foam went scudding over the deck. Briana clutched the rail as she struggled to keep her footing.

"Looks as if it'll be starting soon." Even as she heard Devlin's voice behind her, she felt his arm about her waist, steadying her.

"Another storm?" She tried to sound unconcerned.

"Not just another storm," he told her.

His arm tightened and she felt an inner stirring at the hard pressure. She tried to stiffen her body so that she wouldn't be forced to lean against him.

Although it was early afternoon, the sky was already darkening overhead. "You see those birds?"

He pointed out to sea, while he kept his other arm firmly around her. "They're called storm petrels."

"And that larger bird, the one that's wheeling overhead— what's it called?" she asked.

"That's an albatross."

A vague fear from the past stirred in the depths of her memory. "An albatross is supposed to bring bad luck, isn't it? My governess read me a poem once . . . about a ship that carried a curse. . . ."

"But, if you remember, the ship in the poem met with disaster because one of the crew had shot the bird. With a crossbow." He gave her a reassuring smile. "We carry no crossbows aboard this vessel."

She hadn't imagined that a man like Devlin was given to reading poetry, but she remembered the shelf of books she had seen in his cabin on her first morning aboard the ship.

She had tried, over and over again, to blot out the memory of that morning, but now it came back to her with shocking clarity, awakened by the scent of him: salt and soap and brandy. By the pressure of his tall, wide-shouldered body, pressed against hers to shield her from the force of the rising gale.

"Let's hope this albatross is a good omen," she said. "See how it wheels and rides on the wind."

"There's beauty in the sea and its creatures," he said softly. "But these birds give warning of danger, too. We're nearing Cape Horn now, Briana. We'll be facing the roughest part of the voyage until we've rounded her."

"That's what Tommy said."

"You'll have to keep to your cabin from now until we've come around and entered Pacific waters."

"How long will that be?"

"Impossible to say. Cape Horn's treacherous. We'll be going through the Strait of Le Maire, between Cape San Diego and Staaten Island. That's where we'll be most likely to run into a blizzard."

"A blizzard? In June?"

"We're below the equator now," he reminded her. "Down here the seasons are reversed. The icebergs are the worst of the hazards we'll be facing. They can crush a ship to splinters."

"You're trying to frighten me."

"I'm trying to prepare you for what's ahead; that's all. And to make sure you don't take a notion to go strolling on deck."

"You won't lock me in again?"

"I promised I wouldn't. But once you're back inside your cabin today you are to bolt the door on the inside. Don't even think of coming out again, no matter what."

She moved closer to him, too frightened by his words to care about the proprieties. She could feel the heat of his breath against her cheek. His eyes, gray and unfathomable as the rising sea, held hers. She couldn't look away. With one swift movement he pushed back her cloak. His hands rested on her shoulders, and she felt the warm strength of his fingers through the silk of her gown.

"Listen to me, Briana, and remember what I say. I will get the *Osprey* through the storm."

"But how can you be sure? After all you said about the blizzard, the icebergs—"

"I've never lost a vessel yet. And the success of this voyage is particularly important to me."

Her heart soared at his words. Was this his way of saying that he would use all his strength, all his skill, to get the ship through because her safety meant everything to him?

His next words shattered her brief illusion.

"I finally managed to get together enough money to buy the *Osprey* from the fat-bellied directors of the shipping line back in Boston. The ship belongs to me now." His fierce intensity stirred her to the depths of her being. "I never let go of what is mine."

She might have known that a man like Devlin Rafferty would put his feeling for a ship before his passion for any woman. Yet she was moved by the emotion in his voice. She drew reassurance from his words, and the pride that lit his eyes There was a hard, unshakable determination in this man, an inner strength a woman could rely on.

If only he felt for her what he felt for his ship With a man like Devlin at her side, watching over her, she would fear nothing.

But what was she thinking of? He had nothing to offer her. She reminded herself of what Mama had wanted for her: a home, social position, respectability. Devlin was a wanderer over the face of the earth. Once this voyage was over she would never see him again. She looked away. He mustn't guess what she had been thinking, feeling, only a moment ago

She forced a smile as she looked up at him from under long, curving lashes. "I'll put my trust in your seamanship, Captain," she said. "Since you will no doubt make a good profit from this voyage I'm sure you'll do everything in your power to get the ship—and its passengers—safely to San Francisco."

He cupped her face in his hands and his eyes held hers. It was impossible for her to hide her feelings when he looked at her this way.

His voice was deep and husky. "You're safe with me, Briana."

She was thrown completely off guard by the swift glow of warmth in his gray eyes; the intimacy in his look. Her breathing grew unsteady and her pulses quickened. She wanted to turn away from him, but it was too late.

He pulled her to him. Her breasts were crushed against the hardness of his chest. Even through her skirt, her petticoats, she could feel the steely pressure of his thighs. Heat stirred in her loins, then spread to every part of her body. She breathed his clean male scent as she gave herself up to his embrace. His mouth found hers, urging, demanding, his tongue invading the moist warmth within. Her arms tightened around him.

When he took his lips away she made a soft, wordless sound of protest.

For the first time in his life he longed to share his feelings with a woman. He wanted to tell her how she had moved him. "Briana, I want you to know—I want—" His voice was shaking with the need to make her understand. How easy it had always been for him to arouse a woman, to take his pleasure with her. But now there was only the harsh, ragged sound of his breathing mingled with the crash of the waves against the hull, the crack of the wind in the sails overhead.

He drew away, thrusting her from him. "Go to your cabin." He saw her look of bewilderment but forced himself to ignore it.

"Devlin . . ." She looked up at him in bewilderment.

"Do as I say. It's not safe for you to be out here, not now." His voice was brisk and impersonal once more. "At least you won't be alone. Tommy tells me that you and Poppy Nolan are getting to be good friends."

"Does that surprise you?"

"I didn't think friendship would be possible between a well-bred lady like you and a female who has displayed herself on the stage. You never cease to surprise me, Briana."

"As you surprised me when you took her aboard. You said you would take on no more passengers. And she didn't even have any money to pay her passage."

"I had my reasons." He took her arm and turned her in the direction of her cabin. "Now get off the deck. Leave me free to go about my duties."

"Not until you've explained why you allowed Poppy to sail with us."

"Maybe I didn't want to think about her locked in a rat-infested cell, with no way to protect herself from the scum who guard such places." His grip tightened on Briana's arm, and she allowed him to lead the way back to her cabin. "Bad enough for a man in prison. For a girl like Poppy it can be pure hell."

"I didn't know you felt that way. I think I can understand why you let her stay aboard."

"You understand? You, sheltered, guarded from the least glimpse of ugliness or violence."

The intensity of her feelings swept away her caution. "I haven't always been sheltered."

"You were left short of money after your mother died," he said evenly. "That must have been hard for someone like you. But once you're settled with your uncle, decked out in your Paris finery, you'll forget all that." He gave her a brief, hard smile. "If you should happen to meet Poppy on the street, you can pretend you don't know her."

She flinched under the irony of his words. "If you believe I could do that, you know nothing about me."

They had reached her cabin door. "Get inside," he ordered. "Or must I carry you in?"

"I prefer to walk." She started to turn away. Then, over the sound of the rising wind, she heard his voice.

"Please yourself. And remember what I said: I'll get you to San Francisco, safe and sound. You—and those precious trunks of yours."

Six

During the hours that followed Briana kept repeating Devlin's words to herself. Now, as the clouds thickened, blotting out the sky, she stood looking through the porthole and saw the driving rain change first to sleet and then to heavy snow. White flakes clung to the glass and froze there, blurring her view of the deck and the sea beyond. She caught her breath as she watched the waves, rising ever higher, like steep gray-green cliffs.

Over the pounding of the sea and the howling of the wind, she heard Devlin shouting orders to the crew. The sound of his voice, powerful and commanding, helped to control the surge of panic that threatened to engulf her.

The ship reared up, as if lifted by a giant hand, then came slamming down into a trough; rose again and heeled over so that the cabin floor slanted sharply. She clutched at the narrow frame of the porthole, lost her grip, and stumbled backward. Her shoulder struck the wall with bruising force.

Poppy staggered over and caught her around the waist.

"Come away from there. We'll both be safer in the bunk," she said.

Clinging together for support, they stumbled to the bunk and climbed into the lower berth. Poppy took hold of one of the posts, and Briana quickly followed her example. "We're in for it now an' no mistake." Poppy gave a short, rueful laugh. "And

I thought those blizzards back in Lowell were the worst ever. But at least there I had the solid ground under my feet."

"You're from Massachusetts?" Briana guessed that her companion was making conversation to distract them both, and she was more than willing to do her part.

Poppy nodded. "I was born and grew up there. I was working in that stinking cotton mill in Lowell when I was twelve. All of us girls stood for fourteen hours a day at one of the looms, with the windows shut tight. The air was so filled with lint, we could hardly draw a breath."

It was the first time Poppy had spoken about her early life, and gradually Briana found herself listening with mingled interest and sympathy. How different from her own pampered childhood in Paris!

"Ma died in one of the company boardinghouses after a day at her loom. She coughed her life away with lung fever. I took her place in the mill because I needed to earn a living and I didn't know any other way. But I didn't stay for long. After nearly a year I ran off and never went back."

"But how could you possibly manage on your own?"

Poppy gave a crooked little smile. "It wasn't easy, but I got along. I was dancin' for pennies outside the saloons in New York 'til I joined up with a third-rate touring company. After that—I sure saw a lot of different towns, all the way from Pittsburgh to St. Louis. I remember one time, we were playing in a tent along the Mississippi—"

She broke off. "What was that?" They stared at one another in dismay, terrified by the crash of falling timber. The sound had come from just outside their cabin. The heavy oak door shuddered in its frame. "Oh Lord—look down there!" Poppy gasped.

Briana went rigid with fear when she saw a stream of water sloshing in under the door. Her heart lurched and her hand went to her lips to stifle a scream. Then, as the ship rolled over in the opposite direction, the water went streaming out again. But with the pitching and tossing of the ship it would be only a matter of time before the cabin was flooded.

Surely the door was too solid to give way. But already she seemed to feel the icy sea reaching for her, engulfing her.

She set her jaw hard and fought back her panic. Her eyes moved quickly about the cabin. "We've got to push something against the door. We can use my trunk."

Poppy looked down doubtfully at the small trunk at the foot of the bunk. "That's not nearly heavy enough."

"Then we've got to get one of the larger ones!" Briana grabbed a post of the bunk and pulled herself to her feet. The ship heeled over, and she and Poppy made their way across the slanting cabin floor.

"Get hold of one of the handles," Briana said.

"It's no use—the trunks are all tied down."

"We'll have to undo the knots."

It was far more difficult than either of them could have imagined, and the water was soon ankle deep. Their nails were broken and their fingers scraped and bleeding, but still the knots held.

"We'll have to find something sharp—to cut the ropes—" Briana said.

"You got a knife—a pair of sewing shears?"

Briana shook her head. Then her eyes lighted on the silver-mounted mirror atop her chest: a present from Mama.

On her hands and knees, Briana dragged herself over to the chest. She felt a moment's hesitation. Then picked up the mirror and struck it hard against the chest.

"Careful—don't cut your hand," Poppy warned. She tore a length of cloth from her petticoat and wrapped it around her fingers; then she gave another strip to Briana, who did the same.

They sloshed their way back and, after what seemed an agonizing eternity, they managed to loosen the knots enough so that the rope gave way. "Take hold of a handle," Briana said.

Together they pulled and tugged, the perspiration running down their faces. Somehow, they managed to drag the trunk halfway to the door, stopped to steady themselves, and were bending to go on with their task when a powerful fist began pounding against the door.

"Slide the bolt open!" Briana recognized Quinn's hoarse bellow and clawed her way to the door. He pulled it open and she gazed out at the deck.

A seaman's broken body lay stretched close to the threshold. His neck was twisted at an impossible angle and his eyes stared sightlessly at the sky. Even as Briana took in the terrible sight, a mountainous gray wave reared up. It seemed to tower, motionless, over the ship, before it came crashing down. The seaman's body was swept over the side, along with a tangle of shattered timber and broken rigging.

"Cut away those lines!"

Through the dazzling white curtain of snow, she caught a glimpse of Devlin, moving quickly, purposefully, about the deck. His cap was gone and his dark hair was plastered to his forehead, but he was a commanding presence, nevertheless. Briana took heart at the sight of him, shouting orders above the fury of the storm.

"Secure the boats! Topmen to the rigging!"

Then Quinn slammed the door shut behind him and drew a heavy knife. "Couldn't get here no sooner," he said as he cut one length of rope and then another from the coil he carried over his arm. "Get into the bunk, both of you." He glanced briefly at the trunk. "What's that doin' there?"

"We were going to use it to brace the door—" Briana began, but he interrupted with a bark of mirthless laughter.

"Good try, but it wouldn't stay in place five minutes. Once I get the two of you trussed up good and tight the carpenter'll be coming to nail the door shut."

Briana gave him a startled look and he added, "Captain's orders."

As soon as they had climbed into the lower bunk, he took a length of rope, tied it around Briana's waist, and fastened it to one of the posts. Then he did the same for Poppy. He tugged at the knots. "They'll hold," he said.

"My trunk—it has to be tied down."

He stared at her as if he thought she had lost her wits. "What for?"

"My mother's glassware, her china, are inside."

"Holy saints, girl! Are you daft, worryin' over them knick-knacks at a time like this?"

"We'll make it through. Devlin said we would. Please, Mr. Quinn—see to the trunk."

"You're one stubborn female," he said, but there was a faint gleam of admiration in his eyes. He shoved the trunk back against the wall and made it fast once more with another length of rope.

Then he was wading through the water and out the door, leaving Briana and Poppy tied securely to the bunk, facing one another.

"You think Captain Rafferty'll get us through?" Poppy asked.

Briana nodded. "I know he will." She was remembering how he had held her close as he assured her that they would arrive safely at their destination.

If only she could be with him now, to draw strength from his presence. For a moment she was seized by the need to run out on deck to find him, to throw herself into his arms and bury her face against his chest. But even if she could get to him, he would send her back to the cabin. And he would be right. He needed all his strength and skill for the ship. Not only her life, but the lives of everyone on board, rested in his hands.

"You sure think a lot of Rafferty, don't you?" Poppy was saying.

"As an experienced seaman, nothing more."

"You sure about that?" Poppy forced a smile. "Let's hope you're right about his gettin' us through. I haven't come this far to miss out on my chance at a share of all that gold."

Later they heard the sound of hammering as the carpenter boarded up the door. The storm roared down on the ship with ever-increasing fury. Briana's lips moved, whispering Devlin's name, like an incantation against the menace of the sea, as the *Osprey* pitched through the night.

* * *

It was midmorning before the worst of the storm abated. They heard the boards being wrenched away from the cabin door, and a few hours later Tommy appeared with a tray.

"Captain Rafferty—is he safe?" Briana asked.

" 'Course he is, miss." His mouth tightened and his voice shook slightly. "We lost a few of the men, though. Two of 'em were washed overboard, an' another was crushed by a fallin' block."

Then he set down the tray and cut the ropes that held Briana and Poppy to the bunk.

"Only cold biscuits and rum; we had to douse the cook stove."

Briana looked doubtfully at the mug of rum he thrust into her hand.

"It'll warm you better'n coffee," he told her. "Once we get the deck cleared and the stove's workin' again I'll bring you both a proper meal."

Briana hadn't realized that she was hungry until she bit into one of the biscuits. "Wash it down with the rum, like he said," Poppy advised. "Then maybe we can get some sleep."

Although Briana had never tasted rum before, she swallowed, coughed, and felt grateful for the warmth that spread through her. Every muscle in her body ached from the tension of the night before. Now, as she began to relax, her eyelids drooped.

Poppy climbed up into her own bunk, leaving Briana to stretch out and pull the blanket over her. Exhausted, she sank into the swirling darkness. . . .

And now she was with Devlin. They were drifting on the gray-green waves of the sea, naked bodies entwined. . . .

Strangely, she felt no shame, only a rising need to be one with him. The waves cradled them, rocked them with a rhythm as old as time itself. . . .

She woke with a start, still lost in the spell of her dream. She swung her legs over the side of the bed, made her way to the porthole, and saw that the snow had changed back to driving rain.

"Cut loose those spars!" Devlin was shouting. She caught a glimpse of his tall figure, moving about the deck. And she knew that the worst was over.

The *Osprey*, her deck cleared of the debris left by the storm, and with all sails set, was moving swiftly through the Strait of Le Maire. Briana, in a hooded blue wool cloak, was walking with Devlin, relishing the clean, salty air after her confinement to the cabin.

He raised his arm and pointed out Cape Horn before its snow-shrouded headland disappeared from view. "We're entering Pacific waters now. The rest of the voyage should go smoothly, with any luck," he said.

"That's welcome news, indeed." Cole came to the rail to join them. He bowed to Briana, then turned to Devlin. "You are to be commended, Captain," he began.

"I am well paid for what I do." Devlin nodded curtly, then led Briana past the startled Cole and on along the deck.

The night before the *Osprey* was to enter San Francisco Bay Poppy went to bed early. "I've got to look my best tomorrow," she said. "Soon as I've found myself a place to stay, I'll start making the rounds of the theaters and concert saloons."

Briana was about to suggest that Poppy stay at her uncle's home, but she hesitated. A respectable businessman like her uncle might not approve of her friendship with a girl who had performed on the stage.

Briana was taking the pins from her hair and brushing the one hundred strokes, as Mama had taught her, when she heard the knocking at the cabin door.

"Open up." In spite of herself, she felt a surge of anticipation at the sound of Devlin's voice. He stood outside in the fog-shrouded night.

"We'll be dropping anchor tomorrow morning," he said. "I need to talk to you now."

"Poppy's sleeping," she cautioned him. "We mustn't disturb her."

"Then come outside." He glanced at her dark-blue dress. "You'll need more than that to keep you warm," he said.

She picked up the cloak that lay neatly folded on the chair, then followed him onto the main deck. "Not here," he said. The passengers, their excitement at fever pitch now that they were so close to their goal, were milling about, gesturing, talking loudly, staring into the fog, eager for their first glimpse of the city.

He took her arm and led her up to the quarterdeck. The wind whipped back her cloak and she shivered slightly as the damp night air enveloped her.

"Come inside the cabin."

But she shook her head. The memory of her dream returned, and she was grateful for the darkness and the fog that shielded her face. She dared not risk being alone with him again.

"We'll be dropping anchor tomorrow morning," he told her. "We'd better decide how to get you ashore."

"I will disembark with the rest of the passengers, of course."

"That may not be so easy," he interrupted. "Your uncle knows you're arriving on the *Osprey*?"

"Mama's lawyer must have written to him about my travel arrangements. As soon as he gets word that the ship's docked, he'll come down to meet me."

"And if he doesn't?" Devlin interrupted.

"Then I will hire a carriage."

"This isn't Charleston," he said. "Once we drop anchor here, all hell will break loose." Before she could speak he went on quickly. "You don't know what you'll be getting into when you leave the ship. Before '49, I'd have followed the usual routine. I'd have sent the crew aloft to furl the sails, then steered for anchorage."

"And now?"

"Now I'll have to bring her in under full sail, drop anchor, and let go the braces and sheets. After that it'll be every man for himself." He jerked his head at the frenzied crowd, milling about the main deck. "Those fools'll be trying to get hold of the small boats, as if this were a plague ship and they were escaping for their lives. Some damn idiots will jump overboard and try to swim for shore."

"You can't mean that."

"Wait and see. I want you to stay in your cabin, while I take care of business, filling out the ship's papers, handing over my manifests to the authorities. As soon as I've finished, I'll take you ashore myself."

If he had smiled at her, if she had seen the slightest warmth in his gray eyes, she might have agreed, but he was making it plain that he regarded his offer as another one of his duties. "In case your uncle's not there to meet you I'll see you get to his home. Where does he live?"

"I—don't know." His dark brows shot up in surprise, and she went on quickly, "I have the address of his store. It's on Pacific Street."

She heard Devlin draw in his breath harshly. "Pacific Street! You're sure?"

"It's called Cameron's Emporium. On Pacific Street. I've read his letter over until I know it by heart."

"Then that settles it: I'll have to go with you and try to find this store. Or whatever kind of dive he's running down there."

She glared at him. "I don't know what you're implying. My uncle came out to San Francisco in 1850. He's built up a successful business in the short time he's been here. Mama's lawyer told me so."

"I'm not questioning your uncle's prosperity," Devlin said with a sardonic smile. "Pacific Street taverns are doing a roaring business. So are the gambling hells. And the parlor houses."

Her voice shook with outrage. "Are you saying that my uncle—that any member of my family—"

"Sorry if I've offended you, but you'll be hearing a lot worse language if you're planning to live on the Barbary Coast."

"The Barbary Coast?" The very name had a sinister ring to it, and she felt a stirring of doubt.

"That's what they call a certain part of the waterfront district. It was named after a hellhole on the North African coast that used to be the lair for pirates, slave traders."

"But surely you're mistaken about Pacific Street—"

"It's one of the most notorious in all San Francisco." He spoke with a certainty that chilled her to the bone.

"My father's brother would never have opened a tavern or a—house of ill repute."

"All right then. Maybe he does own some kind of a store. He may even have gotten rich profiteering—buying barrels of flour back East at five dollars each and selling them here for fifty. Last time I was in San Francisco eggs sold for a dollar a piece."

"My uncle's an honest businessman!" But even as she spoke, she could not shake off her rising fear. What did she really know about San Francisco? Or the Barbary Coast?

What did she know about her uncle?

Devlin was wrong; he had to be. Or he was lying for some devious purpose of his own. "You're saying these awful things to frighten me!"

"And why should I want to do that?"

"Maybe you're trying to keep me from meeting my uncle because you have other plans for me."

"Go on."

"What's to keep you from taking me to one of those—houses—on the Barbary Coast."

"You don't believe that."

"How do I know what you're capable of?"

He took a step forward and looked down at her, his eyes hard. She stood shivering in the thick, damp fog that blanketed the quarterdeck.

"Don't deceive yourself, Briana. If I'd wanted to take you by force, I could have done so during the voyage."

She started to turn away, but his hand closed around her wrist. "I've never forced myself on any woman."

"Let me go." She tried to free herself, but his grip tightened.

"As for you, I doubt I'd have needed to use force." His voice was soft, but she flinched at his words. "Surely you haven't forgotten that morning in my cabin. Have you?" His hands moved to her shoulders. "If Quinn hadn't interrupted us, how long would it have taken for you to forget your virginal fear and give yourself to me?" His powerful arms encircled her waist, and his voice came to her, low and intimate. "You're not afraid now, are you?"

He bent her backward and the hood dropped back, so that her red-gold hair fell about her face and over her shoulders. Then he buried his face in the soft waves and breathed their perfumed fragrance.

She wanted to resist, to thrust him away, but she was caught up in the urgency of her own rising need. Her hands moved to his back, drawing him closer. She arched her hips, her body demanding to be one with his.

Her lips parted willingly. His tongue plundered the moist softness of her mouth, exploring, tasting, savoring.

When he opened her bodice she could make no move to stop him; she longed to feel his touch, with no barrier between her tingling flesh and his questing fingers.

She moaned as he teased her nipples to firm rosy peaks. Then she drew his face down against the soft swell of her breasts. His tongue flicked at the hardening peaks and still she wanted more.

It was as if a magic, born of the night, the sea, the swirling silver fog, had changed her dream into reality . . . as if they were drifting together on the surface of an enchanted sea, their bodies entwined. . . .

But a moment later he shattered the spell as he released her and stepped back, holding her at arm's length. His eyes mocked her. "You see, my sweet? Force wouldn't have been necessary . . . not with you. . . ."

She stared up at him, humiliated to the depths of her being. He had chosen this way to prove to her that she didn't know herself at all. That she would have been his for the taking.

She was standing here on the quarterdeck with her breasts bared, her hair tangled and falling over her shoulders, like any dockside trollop. Humiliation surged up within her, blotting out every other emotion. She struggled to button her bodice with fingers that had turned stiff and clumsy.

"Let me help you."

Her amber eyes narrowed with outrage. "I don't need your help, Devlin Rafferty! Not now, or ever. I never want to see your face again."

She turned away and hurried toward the steps leading down to the main deck.

"Briana—wait!"

There was an urgency in his voice that made her pause in spite of herself.

He moved to her side and looked down at her. "Why do you try to deny your own feelings—to pretend you're made of ice when we both know better?" When she remained silent he went on quickly. "Stay in your cabin tomorrow and let me take you ashore. If your uncle's waiting on the dock, you can go with him, and after that you'll never have to see me again."

She hesitated. What if her uncle wasn't there to meet her? How could she manage to fight her way ashore through the mob of frenzied passengers and make her way to her uncle's store?

"If my uncle's not there to meet me, I will ask Cole Forrester to take me to his store."

"You're sure you want to take that risk?"

"No gentleman would refuse to offer his help to a lady in such a situation."

"You're probably right about that. You know more about the breed than I do. But do you want the elegant Mr. Forrester to see your uncle's place on Pacific Street?"

She hadn't thought of that. If Pacific Street was really as Devlin had described it, how could she possibly allow Cole to know she was living there? But Devlin had been mistaken—or else he was lying, for reasons of his own. He had to be.

"You've no need to concern yourself with me, Captain," she

told him. She eyed him coldly. Then, lifting her skirts, she ran down the short flight of steps to the main deck and shoved her way through the crowd.

Somehow she got to her cabin, shut the door, and pushed the bolt into place.

From long-established habit she braided her heavy copper hair into a single thick plait. She could hear Poppy's even breathing from the bunk above.

But even as she changed into her lace-trimmed cambric nightdress, climbed into her bunk, and buried her face in her pillow, she feared she would have little rest tonight. Had she fled from the gossiping tongues in Charleston and come all this way only to find herself in real danger, here in this unknown city?

Seven

The morning fog that swirled in over the bay and drifted across the waterfront and the hills of San Francisco slowly began to lift, as Briana, dressed in a gray silk gown and a long-sleeved jacket trimmed with black braid, started down the *Osprey*'s gangplank. The breeze, damp and salty, tugged at her red-gold curls and ruffled the ostrich plumes atop her small pearl-gray velvet bonnet.

She paused for a moment to take in the panorama spread before her. San Francisco. Her new home. She felt a little overwhelmed by the sheer noise of the waterfront and the crowd milling about on the wharf below.

In the years following the discovery of gold in John Sutter's millrace in Coloma, the small settlement of Yerba Buena had changed into the city of San Francisco, lusty and brawling with its 30,000 men and women from all parts of the world, drawn here by the lure of the fabulous riches to be had for the taking.

The iron wheels of drays and carts rattled over the wet wooden planks; stevedores shouted and swore as they unloaded cargoes from distant ports. From the doorways of saloons came the music of pianos, concertinas, and guitars. Adding to the cacophony were the rattle of dice and the shouts of the players who crowded around open gambling booths.

Although Briana would have remained where she was a moment longer, she found herself pushed along by the sheer pressure of the frenzied passengers behind her and she clutched tightly at the handle of her carpetbag, to keep it from being pulled out of her grasp.

Not until she had reached the foot of the gangplank was she able to extricate herself from the others and to stand aside while the men went stomping past her, bound for the straggling row of crude, unpainted wooden shacks that lined the muddy thoroughfare beyond. Prostitutes in gaudy finery approached the newcomers boldly, and the woman-starved passengers were only too eager to follow them into saloons, alleys, or cellars.

Briana looked about, anxious to catch sight of her uncle's carriage, but she saw only heavily laden wagons and carts splashing through the mud. She took a step forward, and the next moment a sailor jostled against her. She turned her face away as she caught the powerful fumes of whiskey on his breath. He swayed slightly. "Don't be shy, little lady," he said, with a gap-toothed grin.

He caught her by the arm, then reached into his pocket, pulling out a handful of coins. "Look here, I just got in from a whalin' voyage. Here's my pay, and I'm all set to spend it on a good-lookin' piece like you." He reached down and fumbled with her hair, knocking her bonnet askew. "Always was partial to a redhead—pay you double, I will—"

"Let go of me!" Briana cried, fear and disgust surging up inside her. But the sailor only laughed and ignored her protest.

A prostitute, her heavy breasts half-bared by her unbuttoned bodice, her round face white with rice powder, her lips and cheeks rouged, shoved her way out of the stream of humanity that moved along the dock and took in the situation with a practiced eye. Pushing Briana aside, she seized the sailor's arm. "Don't bother with that skinny little bitch," she said. "You come with me, sailor, an' I'll show you a good time."

Trembling with relief, Briana watched as the woman led him off, across the muddy thoroughfare and into the nearest alley. She was safe, for the moment, but she dared not remain here much longer.

With mounting anxiety, her eyes moved over the crowd. Surely her uncle would have gotten word that her ship had arrived by now. Where was he? Her hand tightened around the handle of her carpetbag.

It still wasn't too late to go back on board the *Osprey* and wait for Devlin to take her to her uncle. But how could she face him again, after what had happened between them last night? She went hot with shame as she remembered the pressure of his body against hers, the tumultuous feelings that had coursed through her.

Poppy had urged her to wait for Devlin, but she had refused. "What about all those trunks?" Poppy had protested. "You're not going to leave them behind."

"My uncle will take care of them," she had assured her friend. "He'll have them delivered to his home."

"Why not wait here in the cabin until he comes to get you?" Poppy had persisted.

"And what about you? Aren't you going ashore alone?"

"That's different," Poppy had said with a faint, rueful smile. "I'm experienced. I know how to take care of myself."

But when Briana had insisted on going ashore at once, and alone, Poppy had given up, embraced her, and wished her luck. The weeks they had spent together, the dangers they had shared, had formed a bond between them.

But now Briana was beginning to feel more lost, more unsure

of herself with every passing moment. Had it been reckless, even dangerous, for her to have left the ship alone?

"Briana."

She wheeled about quickly and gave a sigh of relief at the sight of Cole, who was as smartly dressed as ever in a perfectly fitted frock coat, an embroidered satin vest, a spotless cravat, and dark blue trousers.

"You shouldn't be standing about here alone," he told her. His tone was stern, his look disapproving. But that didn't matter. At least there would be no repetition of the incident with the sailor, not while Cole was at her side.

"I was expecting my uncle to be waiting for me."

"I'll stay here with you until he arrives. Or shall I hire a carriage and escort you to his home?"

Only last night she had assured Devlin that Cole would be more than willing to take her to her uncle. But she hadn't approached him earlier this morning, and even now she hesitated to accept his offer; she was remembering Devlin's warning.

Suppose Pacific Street was the notorious place Devlin had said it was? How could she possibly allow Cole to discover that her uncle kept a store on the Barbary Coast?

And why on earth hadn't her uncle included the address of his home in his letter? Such a cold, matter-of-fact letter, she thought. No word of condolence over her mother's recent death; no word of welcome for her. True, she and her uncle had never met, but she was his brother's child.

"You must not allow your opinion of San Francisco to be shaped by your first sight of the waterfront," Cole was saying.

If he had misinterpreted the reason for her anxious silence, perhaps it was better that way, she thought.

"It is rather—overwhelming," she managed to say.

Her eyes widened as she caught sight of a couple of bearded men, wrapped in furs and carrying snowshoes strapped to their backs. Welcoming the distraction, she asked, "Whatever possessed them to dress that way?"

"No doubt they were misled by some pamphlet they bought

back East, written by a man who never set eyes on San Francisco. Men come here from all over the world, without the slightest notions of what to expect when they arrive," Cole said with a faintly derisive smile. "Last time I was here I actually saw some foolish fellow from England, wearing a white linen suit and a pith helmet. Seems he'd been told that the climate here is similar to that of Egypt."

An answering smile tugged at the corners of her lips.

"Frenchmen, Chinese, Italians, Germans—they all come rushing here, leaving their families, their businesses, their homes. And when they don't strike it rich overnight they come straggling back to San Francisco, some of them without even the passage money to take them home."

"But what becomes of them?"

"What does it matter?" He looked down at her, his eyes cool and devoid of pity. "A pack of credulous fools, most of them. And there are always those who find other, better ways to make a fortune here. Without even leaving the city."

"They run the saloons and gambling houses, I suppose," she said with distaste.

"Some do. But not all. A dry goods dealer from Bavaria, Levi Strauss, arrived here a few years ago with needles, thread, scissors, and heavy canvas. They say he intended to make tents for the miners. Instead, he has done remarkably well, making canvas trousers.

"A Chinese called Wah Lee opened a laundry at Washington and Grant streets. And there was a Mexican who landed a few years ago with a cargo of cats. He asked eight to twelve dollars for each and got his price for every one of the beasts."

"Now you are teasing me," she said, her spirits rising slightly.

"I give you my word. This city was plagued by an army of rats. They invaded the warehouses, the granaries, and devoured the food. The Mexican sold his cats and went home a prosperous man. So you see, there is no limit to what a man may accomplish in a city like this, if he's clever and enterprising. No need to tramp out to the diggings at all."

"Mistuh Forrester." A large, dark-skinned man in coachman's livery stepped out of the crowd. "Welcome back, suh."

"Good to be back, Roscoe," said Cole. "I hadn't expected Mr. Padgett to come down to meet me."

"Mistuh Padgett, he couldn't come. But Miz Padgett, she had me hitch up the team soon as she got word your ship come in, suh. She's waitin' right over there."

The coachman pointed to an elegant barouche; the passenger, a young lady smartly dressed in bottle green velvet, with a matching feathered hat set atop her brown curls, half-rose from the leather seat and waved to Cole.

"Miss Padgett is the daughter of my law partner," Cole told Briana.

Even from this distance Briana could see the eagerness in the girl's face. "You mustn't keep her waiting," she said. "If you'll find me a carriage for hire, I'll go straight to my uncle's store."

"There's no need for that," he assured her. "Miss Padgett will be pleased to drive you directly to your uncle's home."

Before she had time to explain that her uncle hadn't sent her his home address, Cole had handed her carpetbag, and his own, to the coachman; then he lifted her into his arms. "You mustn't soil your dress in the mud," he said as he carried her to the waiting coach. He set her down next to Miss Padgett, took the seat opposite, and then performed the introductions.

Eleanor Padgett turned a melting smile on him and said that she would, indeed, be delighted to drive Miss Cameron to her destination, but Briana caught the frosty look in the other girl's eyes.

"What is the name of your uncle's store?" Eleanor asked.

"It's called Cameron's Emporium." Briana braced herself, anticipating the inevitable question. She raised her chin and met Eleanor's eyes squarely. "It's located at the intersection of Pacific and Kearny streets."

If she had set off a stick of dynamite inside the carriage, she couldn't have caused a more stunned reaction from her two companions. "Oh, my dear! You must be mistaken, surely! Pacific Street—why that's . . ."

The expression on Eleanor's face, the horrified tone in which she spoke, made it plain to Briana that Devlin had told her the truth last night. She could deceive herself no longer. She had fled from Charleston only to find herself facing an even worse future in San Francisco.

Although Cole, too, had been taken aback by her revelation, he smoothed over the situation as best he could. "There's no need for you to go to your uncle's store. Surely he will expect you to go to his home."

Briana clasped her hands together in her lap to keep them from shaking. "He didn't put his home address in the letter."

Cole, his face impassive, leaned forward and spoke to the coachman. "Pacific Street at Kearny," he said.

Roscoe turned his head and Briana saw that he, too, looked shocked. "Yessuh," he said, then brought down his whip with such force that the team sprang forward, spattering mud over the passersby.

Eleanor sat rigidly in her seat; then, ignoring Briana, she directed her gaze on Cole. "You will be having dinner with Papa and me, of course. And you must stay at our home until you find suitable lodgings."

Before he could reply, she added quickly, "I trust your voyage wasn't too dreadful, Cole. I shall never forget what it was like, coming out here with Papa." She gave a high, tinkling laugh. "I do believe he decided to settle in San Francisco permanently rather than suffer through another trip around the Horn."

"It's a difficult voyage under the best of circumstances," Cole conceded.

"If Papa and I ever go back to Virginia, I'll insist that we travel across Panama." Eleanor leaned forward and put a small, lace-gloved hand lightly on his arm.

"Certainly it's easier to cross Panama now that they've built the railroad line," he said.

"And you, Miss Cameron: If you should decide to return home—"

"I'll never go back to Charleston! Never!" Eleanor gave her a startled look and Briana realized too late that the vehemence in her tone had aroused the other girl's curiosity.

"But surely you must have family and friends there who will miss you."

"My aunt and uncle are my only relations," Briana said with a finality that discouraged further questions.

How quickly her Charleston friends had turned away after the scandal surrounding Mama's death. She fixed her eyes on the maze of unpaved streets and lapsed into silence.

Devlin, having completed the paperwork that was a necessary part of docking in any port, left his cabin and went down to the main deck. Quinn, his cat seated on his broad shoulder, was overseeing the unloading of the cargo when he caught sight of the captain, heading for Briana's cabin.

"If you're thinkin' of takin' the young lady ashore, you're too late," he said. "I saw her just awhile ago, drivin' off in a carriage with Forrester. There was a lady with them."

"Her aunt, I suppose." Briana had said her uncle had established a prosperous business here in the city. His store might be on Pacific Street, but he had probably used the profits to buy one of the fine new houses being built on Rincon Hill.

Quinn shook his head. "The lady wasn't her aunt," he said. "From what I could see, she wasn't no older than Miss Cameron."

A cousin, perhaps, thought Devlin. And why the devil should he waste any more time brooding about Briana, her relations, or her future here in San Francisco? She had made it perfectly plain last night that she never wanted to see him again.

"What about those trunks of hers?" he demanded. "Did her uncle send word where he wanted them delivered?"

Quinn shook his head. "I never saw hide nor hair of any uncle," he said.

Devlin's lips tightened. He might have expected as much. Briana Cameron had been nothing but trouble since the moment he took her aboard in Charleston. He had only to order her luggage dumped on the wharf, or sent to the nearest warehouse, to be held until her uncle came to dispose of it. Then he could put her out of his mind and spend a well-earned liberty ashore. He had no doubt he would be besieged by passengers, eager to make the return trip east.

"I want this ship cleared by noon," he told Quinn.

He was in a bad temper and no mistake, but the first mate persisted. "And Miss Cameron's trunks?"

"Have them thrown into the bay."

"Is that an order?"

Devlin drew a deep breath. He couldn't forget the red-haired, amber-eyed girl who had stood her ground and insisted that her luggage be carried on board and carefully stowed away. Shaken by the loss of her mother, facing an uncertain future, she had nevertheless found the strength to face him down and get her way.

"The trunks, Devlin." Quinn's impassive voice brought him back to the necessity of dealing with the immediate problem.

"Hire a wagon or two and have the damn trunks delivered to Cameron's Emporium at Pacific and Kearny." He turned and headed for the gangplank. "When I've finished my business at the custom house I'll meet you at Belle Cora's place."

He turned and strode down the gangplank, shouldering his way through the crowd and heading for Battery Street. But his thoughts weren't on his business with the customs officials.

Why the devil had he spoken to Briana so harshly last night, frightening the wits out of her with his description of the Barbary Coast? He hadn't been exaggerating the dangers that might lie in wait for a girl on her own down there. He had been trying to persuade her to let him go with her, that was all; to let him see for himself what sort of place her uncle was running; but all the same, he might have chosen his words with greater care.

As it was, he had shocked and frightened her, so that she had turned to Cole Forrester instead. Better that way, he told himself. A girl like Briana Cameron wasn't for him.

She would use her beauty and breeding to make a good marriage. She would find a man who would give her the secure, sheltered life she craved.

And as for him, he would find the only kind of female companionship he needed at Belle Cora's place. A few weeks ashore and then he would be back aboard the *Osprey*, bound for the next port of call.

Briana, her slender body tense beneath the gray silk, sat stiffly on the seat beside Eleanor Padgett. As the carriage drove through the streets of the Barbary Coast, she saw that the saloons and gambling tents were doing a brisk business, even at this time of the morning. And there were other buildings, their shades drawn, a red glass globe beside each door. Were these the bawdy houses Devlin had spoken of last night?

At the entrance to an alley two painted trollops fought over a burly sailor, each tugging at him like a pair of alley cats fighting over a scrap of meat. Their voices rose shrilly. "I saw'm first, you ugly cow!"

"Cow, is it? Why, you pox-ridden slut, I'll snatch you bald-headed." The sailor laughed as he separated the two and held them apart.

"None o' that, now. I been at sea these three years on a whalin' voyage. I'll take the both of ye, an' keep ye busy 'til tomorrow mornin'."

The carriage rolled on, then jerked to a halt at last before a long, one-story building with a sloping wooden awning. A signboard with the name CAMERON'S EMPORIUM in large black letters, creaked in the breeze.

Miners, sailors, farmers, and clerks elbowed each other, try-

ing to get through the narrow doorway. A few of them paused
briefly to stare at the handsome carriage and pair and the liveried coachman. No doubt such a sight was rare down here on
Pacific Street, thought Briana.

All these weeks at sea, when she had woven her brightly
colored daydreams about her future, she had imagined that she
would find an elegant shop like those she and Mama had patronized in Paris; a fine stone building with glittering show
windows displaying the finest merchandise.

She flinched from the stark reality before her: a crude wooden
structure with a single dingy window, half-hidden from sight
by a hodgepodge of crates and barrels. Only the realization that
Eleanor and Cole were watching, waiting to see her reaction,
forced her to pull herself together, to keep her face carefully
expressionless.

Before the coachman could get off the high seat, Cole had
descended and was holding out his hand to her. Somehow she
managed a tight, set smile. He set down her carpetbag beside
her. At least there was a wooden walk in front of the store, so
she didn't sink ankle-deep in mud.

She was smoothing the skirt of her silk dress when she caught
sight of the tall, big-boned woman in black bombazine who
stopped in the doorway, then came forward with a brisk step to
meet her.

"Aunt Gertrude?" Briana asked.

The woman pushed a straggling lock of iron-gray hair away
from her face. "I'm Gertrude Cameron." She looked Briana up
and down and grimaced with distaste. "I guess you're Alexander's niece from Charleston."

Briana nodded. If she had hoped that her aunt would embrace
her, or even shake her hand, she quickly realized that no such
warm greeting awaited her. "I looked for Uncle Alexander at
the dock," she began. "I do hope we didn't miss each other."

"You did not," her aunt snapped. "He couldn't waste the time
waiting around for you. He heard of a bargain in hardware, down
at Ferguson's warehouse, and went there first thing to bid on it."

Her uncle *had* heard of the arrival of the clipper, then. But he hadn't been willing to take the time to go to meet her.

Gertrude turned her head and stared at the carriage. "Whatever were you thinkin' of, girl—hirin' yourself such a fancy rig?"

Briana went scarlet with embarrassment, but before she could answer Cole intervened. "This is not a hired vehicle. It is Miss Padgett's carriage, ma'am. Her father is my business partner, and she was kind enough to offer your niece a ride."

Few women could have been immune to his smile, his polished manners, but Gertrude only gave him a cold glance, then cut him short. "You can be on your way now, young man. I got no time to stand out here jawin' while the store's full of customers and only that lazy Enoch to wait on them." It was less a suggestion than an order, but Cole wasn't so easily fazed.

"Miss Cameron's had a long and difficult voyage," he said. "No doubt she is fatigued. We would be happy to drive her on to your home, ma'am, where she can rest and recover from the ordeal of her travels."

Gertrude gave a short, mirthless laugh. "Our home's right across the alley, back of the store. Guess Briana can walk that far."

It took all Briana's willpower to conceal her revulsion and remain silent. But even as she bit back her protest she told herself that she couldn't live here. She couldn't.

Yet where else could she go? Somehow she managed to thank Cole and Eleanor, bend down and pick up her carpetbag. She caught the smug little smile on Eleanor's lips and understood its meaning all too well.

From the way Eleanor had been looking at Cole, she was obviously taken with him. He was her father's business partner and he would be staying at the Padgett home. Although Eleanor had appeared somewhat shaken by her first sight of Briana, there was no doubt she was reassured now. How could this red-haired stranger, in spite of her fashionable clothes, her polished speech, and her good breeding, be a rival for Cole?

Now that Cole had met her aunt, and seen the sordid surroundings in which she was to live, he would probably do his best to forget whatever shipboard friendship had sprung up between them.

As the carriage pulled away, Briana followed Gertrude into the store, where the customers, all male, crowded around the counter. "Don't keep the customers waitin', Enoch," she called to a heavy-set, moon-faced young man in a soiled apron. Then, as if it was a matter of little importance, the woman jerked her head in Briana's direction and added, "This here's Mr. Cameron's niece. She came off the *Osprey* this morning."

The clerk stared in openmouthed admiration, and he wasn't the only one. The customers, too, looked her over and exchanged appreciative glances.

"Ain't seen nothin' like her since I left St. Louis."

"A real fine, high-steppin' little filly, ain't she?"

"Come along, girl!" Gertrude ordered. She led the way through the store, and Briana, hurrying after her aunt, scarcely had time to gather more than a brief impression of her new surroundings. What she saw did little to raise her spirits.

Crates and barrels of all sizes were piled against the unpainted walls. Rolls of cheap calico and muslin lay on one counter, and stacks of tin pans and enamel coffeepots stood on another. Briana wrinkled her nose at the smells of linseed oil, cheap tobacco, pickles, onions, and salt pork, mingled with the stench of unwashed male bodies and sweat-soaked clothes.

She was thankful when, after stumbling through a badly lit, cluttered stockroom behind the store, she and her aunt came out into the alley. Here at least she had a chance to fill her lungs with the clean, fresh breeze blowing in from the bay.

"Come along," her aunt urged. "Got no time to stand here." Raising her skirt with one hand, to try to keep it out of the mud, and holding tightly to her carpetbag with the other, Briana obeyed. "Once we get you out of that fancy rig you're wearin' you'll go back to the store and help Enoch. He's the laziest clerk your uncle ever had." She looked over her shoulder at Briana and shook her head. "Lord knows, you don't look like you'll be much use either. But your uncle figured it was his duty to take you in, and once he gets his mind set there's nothing can change it."

"This here's your bedroom." Gertrude led Briana into a low-ceilinged cubicle on the second floor of the small, shabby wooden house. The room was scarcely larger than the cabin she had shared with Poppy, and far less inviting.

Her aunt pointed to a sagging calico curtain stretched on a string at one side. "You can use that for your closet. Take off your dress and hang it away. You won't have any use for it around here."

"Aunt Gertrude—"

"No need to waste time thankin' me," her aunt interrupted. "You'll earn your keep." She gave Briana a scornful look. "You sure don't look like you can add up a column of figures, or make the right change. But I suppose you can unpack the goods when they come in, and sweep out the store."

Briana felt a surge of rebellion, but this wasn't the time for a confrontation.

"Take off that fool bonnet."

Startled by the unexpected command, Briana did as she was told.

"Red hair." Her aunt's mouth pursed with displeasure. "Most red-haired females are no better than they should be." Then she shrugged. "I'll find you a dustcap to cover it."

Before Briana could speak she heard a pounding at the downstairs door.

"What's that racket?" Her aunt hurried to the window overlooking the alley and pulled aside the limp muslin curtain. Briana stood beside her, staring down at the two large wagons piled high with her trunks.

* * *

Nearly an hour later, Briana and her aunt faced each other in the upper hallway, now blocked by her luggage. "You mean to say you came here with enough dresses to fill all these trunks? Where'd you get all them clothes?"

"Mama had my wardrobe made at the House of Worth, in Paris."

It was plain from her aunt's blank stare that the name of the most famous salon in all Europe meant nothing to her.

"You can have a couple of my old dresses to wear in the shop. You'll have to make a few alterations, but that shouldn't take you long." Her eyes moved over Briana's body. "Don't make them fit you too tight, though. If you show off your shape, all the men'll be after you like a pack of tomcats."

"I don't know how to sew," Briana told her aunt.

The older woman looked at her with undisguised contempt.

"My governess taught me to do embroidery and crewelwork, but I've never altered a dress."

"And I suppose you've never done your own laundry or washed a dish, either. You have a lot to learn, and you'd best be quick about it, or out you go."

Briana took a deep breath and pressed her lips together. It was all she could do to keep from telling her aunt that she would be only too pleased to leave at once. But suppose her aunt turned her out? Where on earth would she go from here?

She stood in numb silence, trying to collect her thoughts, to form some plan of escape from the dismal future that confronted her. A chill breeze enveloped her as the downstairs door swung open. "There's your uncle now."

Briana peered down and caught sight of a tall, thin man with sandy-colored muttonchop whiskers framing a long, narrow face.

"Enoch told me the girl was here."

He climbed the stairs and then, after a prefunctory glance at Briana, stared at the trunks, his pale eyes widening under his bushy brows. "What's all this?"

"It's your niece's luggage. From Paris, no less."

"Must've cost your mother a fortune. No wonder she died a pauper and left you on my hands." He shook his head in disgust. "Your father was a good, sound businessman, but he never did have a lick of sense when it came to women. Else he wouldn't have married a flighty piece like your mother. I told him she'd bring him nothing but trouble, and so she did."

Although, under other circumstances, she would have been crushed by her uncle's cold reception, she had no room for any feeling except resentment at his insult to her mother. But before she could speak out, Gertrude said, "Unless I miss my guess, this one's no better than her mother. You ask her what she was up to during the voyage, Alexander. Just you ask her."

"What's she talking about, girl?"

Gertrude gave her no chance to reply. "The teamsters told me that the captain of the *Osprey* paid the freight charges on all her baggage, that's what."

Briana stared at her aunt in shocked disbelief. "Devlin—Captain Rafferty paid to have my trunks delivered here?"

"Don't look so surprised, miss. The man must've had his reasons for laying out good money that way."

"Look here, girl," her uncle said, his voice tight with disapproval, "I don't know what sort of life you led in Paris, or what you were up to on the voyage here. But long as you're under my roof, you'll behave yourself like a decent, God-fearing female. Otherwise, out you go."

Somehow Briana managed to rein in the fierce resentment that threatened to overwhelm her.

"I will give you no cause for complaint so long as I'm under your roof." She kept her eyes fixed on the floor and spoke quietly, but inwardly she was seething with rebellion.

"See that you do." He turned and started down the hall. "Come along, woman," he called to Gertrude. "We've got no time to waste on any more chatter." And to Briana, he said, "You get yourself settled, girl. And soon as Enoch Slocum's got some free time he'll move those trunks of yours into the storeroom across the hall."

After the two of them had left her alone in the house Briana walked slowly, reluctantly, down the hall to her room, went inside, and closed the door. She sank down on the narrow bed with its chipped enamel headboard and looked about at the rest of the meager furnishings: a scarred wooden chest of drawers, a table with a tin basin and a pitcher, and a single straight-backed chair.

She turned away and stared out the open window into the alley below, where teamsters were unloading their wagons. A slatternly woman came out of the house next door and emptied a bucket of slops. A drunk went stumbling along, singing a bawdy tune in a loud, off-key voice.

She slammed the window shut and drew the curtains.

Her mother's lawyer had said her uncle was a prosperous businessman; and the store, for all its unprepossessing appearance, seemed to be a thriving business. Was Alexander Cameron a miser, that he should choose to live in such surroundings?

Now she began to understand the meaning of the lines in his letter. . . . *We trust the girl will be prepared to make herself useful.* . . . She had come all this way to work in his store, to live with him and her aunt in this shabby house.

She felt a powerful impulse to pick up her carpetbag and leave without a backward glance. But where could she go? Cole would be staying with the Padgetts, and even if she were to find him, what right had she to ask him for help?

As for Poppy, she had no idea where her friend might have gone. And she knew no one else here in San Francisco.

No one except Devlin Rafferty.

Suppose she were to leave her uncle's house, go back to the *Osprey*, and ask him to take her aboard for the return voyage. But how could she face him after last night, when she had boasted of her independence and insisted she needed no help from him?

And there were other, far more urgent reasons why she hesitated to go back to Devlin. It was her own passionate nature she couldn't trust.

At the thought of him she felt the hot need surge up within her and take possession of her body. Memories came flooding back, sweeping away all reason. It was as if, even now, she could feel the touch of his questing hands. His tongue, pillaging her mouth, sending shivers of ecstasy coursing through her, until her own tongue came up to meet his, joining in a ritual dance older than time.

She clenched her fists so tightly that her nails bit into her palms. Forget Devlin; the dark-haired, gray-eyed captain could be no part of her future.

She forced herself to stand up, then slowly started to unbutton the bodice of her silk dress. Her lips tightened with distaste, but she knew Aunt Gertrude was right. Such a costume would certainly be unsuitable for working in Cameron's Emporium.

And that was what she must do, at least for now. She must take orders from her aunt and uncle, and do what was expected of her, without complaint.

She raised her head, her amber eyes narrowed with determination. She would accept the hand fate had dealt her.

But she would never surrender her dreams—Mama's dreams—for her future.

Eight

Alexander helped his wife into the buggy, climbed up on the seat beside her, and flicked his whip over the bony back of the horse. As the shabby vehicle moved away from the store and merged with the traffic on Pacific Street, Gertrude looked back over her shoulder with a troubled frown.

"You sure we should leave that girl to tend the store by herself?"

"Enoch's there to help out," Alexander reminded her. "And if it comes to that, Briana's a whole lot better at the job than he is. She's a hard worker, she's quick at figures, and the customers like the kind of service she gives them."

"They like her looks, you mean—and the little minx knows it. I've seen the way she goes sashaying around the counters, flaunting her shape at the men."

"She takes after her mother. Lynette was a conceited female. Good-looking in a flashy way, I'll grant that much. But forever primping and putting on airs. And decking herself out in a wardrobe fit for a duchess, though she was only the daughter of a French artist who died in debt."

Although Gertrude nodded dutifully, she was paying little attention to the recital of Lynette's many faults; she had heard the account of her brother-in-law's unfortunate marriage many times. James Cameron had been in Paris on business when petite, blond Lynette Desmoulines had caught his eye. She had recently found a position as a governess and had been escorting her young pupils for a walk in the park when he had seen her for the first time.

"If I'd been over there in France with him, I'd have talked some sense into him," Alexander went on. "But by the time he brought her back to Charleston they were already married. She was fifteen years younger than him, a flighty piece if there ever was one. And she drove him to an early grave with her extravagant ways."

"I don't doubt it. But it's Briana who worries me," Gertrude persisted. "That girl's got too many fanciful notions for her own good." Her pale eyes narrowed. "I don't trust her out of my sight."

"Then maybe you'd like to get out of the buggy right now and walk back to the store to keep an eye on her, instead of going to that Ladies' Civic Improvement meeting over at Mrs. Yancey's."

"I should say not! That new missionary, Mr. Griscomb, and his sister are going to be speaking about their crusade against vice, and I want to hear all they've got to say." She sighed and shook her head. "I only hope we don't come back and find

Briana's moved everything in the store around, like she keeps wanting to."

"You needn't worry," he assured her. "I set the girl straight about those foolish notions." His thin lips twitched in a brief, self-satisfied smile. "I had my doubts about letting her come out here to live with us, but I made the right choice and no mistake. Why, she gets twice as much work done as Enoch. We don't have to pay her a salary. And she won't be grabbing a shovel and running off to the gold fields, neither."

"She'll make mischief all the same. You just mark my words, Alexander. She's headed for trouble."

"What kind of trouble?" he demanded impatiently.

"Man trouble, that's what! How can any man help but notice a girl who looks like she does? I've seen the customers mooning around her like a pack of hound dogs. And why not? That red hair is downright indecent—makes her look like a loose woman."

"She didn't choose the color," he reminded her. "And who's going to see her hair under that God-awful dustcap you make her wear?"

Alexander pressed his thin lips together and lapsed into silence, as he concentrated on driving the buggy through the heavy traffic of Pacific Street. Gertrude was a sensible, thrifty woman—hard-working, too—but she did try his patience when she went on nagging him about Briana.

Clerks were still hard to find in San Francisco, and even harder to hold on to. Let them hear a rumor of a gold strike and off they went, without giving even a day's notice. Briana would stay put.

Too bad Gertrude had taken such a dislike to the girl. Probably his wife was jealous of Briana's trim shape and pretty face. She had certainly done all she could to make the girl look a fright, but even that baggy black dress and shabby dustcap couldn't hide Briana's vivid coloring, her red lips and glowing cheeks, and the graceful movements of her slender young body.

* * *

Briana stood at the door of the shop looking after the buggy as it disappeared into the stream of wagons, drays, and handcarts that rumbled along Pacific Street day and night. She had been on her feet since six o'clock that morning, waiting on a crowd of impatient customers; now she welcomed the brief midafternoon lull. With her aunt at the ladies' meeting for a few hours, she would be spared the older woman's constant carping.

Although her eyes still were fixed on the street outside, Briana let her thoughts drift away, back to those long, lazy afternoons in Charleston . . . she and her mother together in their high-walled garden . . . one of the housemaids serving them and their guests with lemonade and cakes. If she tried, she could almost recapture the well-remembered fragrance of wisteria, mimosa, and new-cut grass.

But she mustn't allow herself to look back; to be caught up in poignant memories of the past. Such daydreams only made it more difficult for her to return to the dreary reality of her present surroundings. She sighed and reached up to set the hateful-looking dustcap more firmly on her head. During the past weeks the gesture had become automatic. If even a single stray curl escaped, her aunt was quick to reprimand her.

There was no doubt that Gertrude had taken an instant dislike to her, seeming to be set on making her look as unattractive as possible. She stared with loathing at her shapeless, hand-me-down black dress. Had her aunt deliberately altered it to make it hang like a sack?

Although Briana had tried to stifle every outward sign of rebellion, and had treated her aunt with proper respect, she had never once managed to win a friendly word or a smile from Gertrude.

At least Uncle Alexander, although he showed her no affection, had offered her an occasional word of grudging approval. Only yesterday, when she had caught several errors in Enoch's accounts, he had remarked, "You're quick at figures, miss; I'll say that for you. From now on you can handle the day's receipts and enter them in the ledger. Your father was a good businessman.

Let's hope you take after him, and not your flibberty-gibbet mother after all."

Coming from her uncle that was a lavish compliment. She had taken it as such, and had forced herself not to protest openly against his slighting remark about Mama. Instead, encouraged by his praise, she had ventured to offer a few suggestions for rearranging the stock so that the store might look more orderly and inviting to their customers.

"We could keep one part of the store for the miners' tools and another for the clothes—workshirts and boots. And those shelves behind the back counter for canned goods and patent medicines. And why couldn't we set aside one corner for a ladies' department? I think—"

"You leave the thinking to me, miss," he snapped. "We have those sunbonnets over there. And there's plenty of bolts of calico and black bombazine. Those ought to be enough to satisfy any decent woman. Not that we get many female customers coming in here."

"But we might get more if we gave them a reason to come."

The dour look on his long, narrow face had warned her that it would be useless to pursue the matter. She stifled a wistful sigh as she remembered the smart shops of Paris, where Mama and her women friends had gone to browse and spend their money lavishly on whatever elegant trifles caught their fancy: a lace and jet pelerine to be worn over a summer gown; a Longchamps bonnet trimmed with ostrich plumes and satin roses; dancing slippers with pearl and sapphire buckles.

Was it possible that one day there might be such stores here in San Francisco? She smiled in self-mockery at the unlikely notion.

But this afternoon, at least, she would have Cameron's Emporium to herself for a few hours, and she was determined to make certain minor changes Surely her uncle couldn't object if she were to arrange the stock in a more orderly way.

She turned from the door and walked back quickly to the shelves behind the long counter at the rear of the store. Stacks of canvas pants, red flannel miners' shirts, waterproof slickers, woolen socks, and high boots vied for space with a jumble of patent medicines, potted meats, and bottles of vinegar. Boxes of biscuits were mixed in among tins of tobacco and snuff and jars of ginger and horehound drops.

She dragged over a ladder and started to climb up, intent on starting her self-imposed task.

"Your uncle won't like for you to go changin' stuff around the minute he turns his back," said Enoch Slocum, who had just emerged from the stockroom.

He gave her an ingratiating smile that revealed his uneven yellowish teeth. "What do you want to wear yourself out for? You'll get no thanks for it."

She didn't answer him, but he wasn't easily discouraged. "As long as we got the place to ourselves for a bit, why don't we take us a little rest? That there horsehair sofa in the storeroom's right comfortable." His grin widened. "And it's plenty big enough for two."

She gave the fat-faced clerk a frigid stare. He had been after her since the day she had started working here and she knew it. He had made it a point to brush against her when he had to pass her behind the counter; he never missed a chance to press his thick thigh against her as they knelt side by side to unpack crates.

"You go and rest if you're tired," she snapped. "Or better yet, you might start unpacking those blacksmiths' tools that were delivered yesterday."

But he only shrugged a meaty shoulder and remained where he was, his small eyes fixed on her with a salacious gleam. She began to rearrange the lowest shelf, but though she tried to keep her mind on her work, she was uncomfortably aware of his presence. The back of her neck began to prickle and she repressed a shiver of distaste. She searched for an excuse to get him away from her, if only for a few moments.

"If you don't want to help rearrange the stock, at least you can get me a few rags so I can dust these medicine bottles." She held one out for his inspection. "I can't even read the labels."

But her abrupt movement caused the ladder to sway. She clutched at the wooden sides, and then she felt his heavy arm encircling her waist. "Careful, dearie," he said. His hand crept upward to squeeze her breast. She pushed him away with such violence that she nearly lost her balance.

"Easy, now. That ladder's none too steady."

"Keep your hands off me, Enoch Slocum!"

"No need to be so uppity. I was only tryin' to save you from takin' a nasty spill."

She got down off the ladder and confronted him. "I know exactly what you were trying to do." She kept her voice steady with an effort. "If you put your hands on me that way again, I'll tell my uncle."

"Tell him what? I ain't done nothin' wrong." He gave a harsh, derisive laugh. "You better get over your touch-me-not ways, Miss Briana, and try acting a little more friendly. Otherwise I might just take it into my head to leave the store and go off to the diggings again. Then you'll have twice the work to do."

His threat was a hollow one and she knew it. Her uncle had told her that Enoch had already spent a few months in one of the mining camps along the Yuba River. He had found the brutally hard work of panning for gold while standing waist deep in icy water not at all to his liking. He had come limping back to the city with holes in his breeches, his boots worn through, his hands blistered, and not an ounce of gold dust to show for his efforts. "He was only too glad to come to work here at the store, and sleep in that lean-to alongside the stockroom," her uncle had said.

She was about to remind him of this, when she heard the *ring* of the bell over the front door. She gave a sigh of relief. With customers about, he would make no further advances. She looked toward the door, expecting to see an unshaven miner or a sailor just off his ship. Then she gave a cry of pleasure. A moment later she was running across the length of the store, her eyes aglow, her lips parted in a smile.

"Poppy! How did you find me down here?"

Heedless of Enoch's curious stare, the two girls threw their arms about one another.

"It wasn't hard. I just asked around, and somebody told me there was a Cameron's Emporium at Pacific and Kearny. I figured it might be your uncle's place."

Poppy stood back and looked Briana up and down with dismay. "What've you done to yourself?" she demanded. "You sure didn't get that awful dress in Paris. And that cap!"

Before Briana could explain Enoch came bustling forward, wiping his hands on his soiled apron. He took in Poppy's enticing figure and gave her a smile. "Can I help you, miss?"

"Miss Nolan's not a customer. She's come here to visit me."

Briana wondered if she should take the chance of inviting Poppy across the alley to the house. As long as her aunt and uncle were out, why not? "Come with me," she said. But her friend paused to look around the store.

"Wait a bit. As long as I'm here, I could use a new dress." The yellow and blue muslin, one of the two she had worn for the whole voyage, was looking threadbare.

"Uncle Alexander doesn't stock ready-made dresses," Briana told her regretfully. "Only those bolts of calico and bombazine."

Poppy glanced over the drab display with distaste. "That stuff wouldn't do for me. What I need is a costume—one that'll make them sit up and take notice when I'm doing my dance."

"Then you've found work?"

"I got me a job right off, performing at the Black Pearl."

"You're dancing in a real theater?"

Enoch snickered. "The Black Pearl ain't a theater—it's a concert saloon."

Poppy ignored him. "I got hired there a couple of weeks ago," she said. "Jack O'Keefe—he's the boss—wants me to get a good-looking new outfit. Something real fancy that'll knock the customers out of their seats."

"I'm afraid you won't find anything like that here," Briana said with a sigh. She linked arms with Poppy. "We'll go across the alley to my uncle's house, and you can tell me all about what's been happening to you since we arrived in San Francisco."

"Your uncle lives down here on the Barbary Coast?" She looked at Briana with sympathy. "This sure isn't much like what you were expecting, is it?"

"What is a concert saloon?" Briana asked. She had taken Poppy upstairs to her room and had given her the only chair, while she perched on the edge of the bed.

"It's a—sort of like a theater, with a stage up front, and a piano player. Only there's tables, too, where they serve drinks during the performance. Jack O'Keefe hired me right off after I danced for him and sang a few songs."

"Do you like the work?"

"It suits me all right. I don't have to wait on the tables. Or go into the private booths with the men. I settled that with O'Keefe before he took me on." Briana caught her meaning and looked away. "The audiences like me. But if I'm going to stand out from the rest of the dancers, I've got to have a real special costume. I tried a couple of fancy shops, but the dressmakers told me right out they don't cater to my kind. I guess they're afraid I'd drive their high-toned customers away." She spoke without a touch of self-pity, as if she was used to such treatment. There was an unbreachable wall between respectable ladies and girls like Poppy, who displayed themselves on the stage.

Maybe San Francisco wasn't all that different from Charleston after all, Briana thought. She was silent for a moment as she tried to figure out some way to help Poppy with her problem. Of course! Her lips curved in a smile, and she sprang up from the bed. "I think I may have what you need, after all," she said.

She seized Poppy's hand and hurried her across the hall to the dusty little room where Enoch had stored her trunks. Her eyes moved quickly among them until she caught sight of the one she wanted: a large black Hussar, complete with a covered tray for a bonnet box and parasol case. She opened the monitor lock and raised the lid. Poppy leaned forward, then drew in her breath as she examined the contents.

"Oh, Briana! These gowns are—they're the most beautiful— why, any one of them would be perfect!" But a moment later the pleasure faded from her dark eyes, to be replaced by a troubled look. "Oh, but I couldn't pay you for any such gown." She paused, then added hopefully, "How would it be if I gave you a few dollars on account and the rest a little each week?"

"As if I'd let you pay me!" Briana interrupted. "We're friends, aren't we? Just pick out the dress you want and it's yours."

Her throat tightened and she felt the sting of tears as she looked at the trunk and its contents. "These belonged to my mother," she said. "They're far more sophisticated than the ones she chose for me."

"Are you sure you want me to wear one of your mother's dresses—in a concert saloon?"

Briana's lips curved in a poignant smile. Of course, Poppy knew nothing about Mama; otherwise she would not have asked such a question. One day, perhaps, she would tell her friend the truth about the life her mother had led in the demimonde society of Paris. Of the scandal that had rocked Charleston and forced Briana to leave the city forever. But this wasn't the time for such revelations.

"I do believe there's one particular gown that would suit you perfectly," Briana said as she went through the gowns, carefully folded away in their sheer muslin wrappings. "Here—this is it."

Poppy's lips parted, her dark eyes aglow with admiration, as she reached out and stroked one of the black sequined flounces.

"Let's go back to my room so you can try it on," Briana urged.

Soon after her arrival at her uncle's store she had come across a cheval glass in the storeroom; because it had been badly cracked and was therefore unsalable, she had persuaded her uncle to allow her to keep it for herself. Even so, her aunt had found cause for complaint. "What do you want with a full-length mirror? You'll only be wasting valuable time preening yourself in front of it."

Briana helped Poppy take off the worn muslin and put on the shimmering black gown. Poppy smoothed the bodice, so that it revealed the enticing curves of her firm breasts, and shook out the flaring skirt around her; then she gave a cry of delight and whirled about, so that she could see her reflection from every angle.

The skirt was trimmed with three deep flounces, while the black point lace overskirt added to the seductive elegance of the garment. The bodice, cut daringly low, with a cluster of crimson silk flowers on one shoulder, accented the smooth white skin of her bare shoulders.

"I believe there's a black lace fan to go with it. And slippers, too, with jet buckles. Let's go look for them."

But Poppy couldn't tear her eyes away from her reflection in the cheval glass. "Those other girls will be pea green with envy when they see me decked out like this." She paused. "You're really sure you want me to have this? You may want to wear it yourself sometime."

Briana repressed a sigh. "That's not likely."

"If Cole Forrester should come calling, you sure wouldn't want him to see the way you look right now. That dress—it's like a coal sack. And that awful cap makes you look like one of the mill girls back in Lowell." With a swift, impulsive gesture, Poppy pulled it from Briana's head and tossed it aside. "Now, that's a little better."

"It makes no difference how I look," Briana said, her voice taut with long-repressed anger. "Cole Forrester's not going to come calling on me, not now that he's seen where I live."

"This sure isn't the kind of house I expected to find you living in," Poppy admitted as she glanced around the shabby bedroom. "Lord knows, with prices as high as they are here your uncle must've made plenty of money. He could have one of them big places on Rincon Hill."

"He could," Briana agreed. "I've been working at the store

long enough to know how much he's taking in. But he's a miser, and my aunt's no better."

"Don't you worry. With looks like yours, it shouldn't matter where you're living right now."

"It might not matter to some men," she conceded, "but Cole has high ambitions. He told me all about his plans for the future when he took me driving in Havana. He means to go into politics, and when he does he'll want a wife who'll be a credit to him. A girl like Eleanor Padgett would be suitable. And I'm sure she'd jump at the chance to marry him."

"Who's Eleanor Padgett?"

"She's the daughter of Cole's law partner. She drove us down here in her carriage, the day the *Osprey* arrived. Cole never did see this house, but my aunt let him know that it was right across the alley from the store. He looked positively relieved to get away."

"And you haven't heard from him since then?"

Briana shook her head. "He's probably forgotten all about me."

"Not likely. Men don't forget a girl like you." Poppy gave Briana a mischievous smile. "Devlin Rafferty sure hasn't."

"Devlin's probably halfway back to Boston by now."

"No, he's not! He came to the Black Pearl a couple of nights ago, and he asked me if I'd seen you. He tried to make it sound like he didn't much care, but I know enough about men to be sure he does."

Devlin was still here in San Francisco.

Briana caught her breath and her heart leaped with uncontrollable excitement. A swift warmth went flooding through her. She turned away for a moment, unwilling to let Poppy see her reaction to this wholly unexpected news.

When she spoke again Briana hoped she sounded more indifferent than she felt.

"I should have thought he would set sail as soon as he had a cargo and passengers."

"He planned to," said Poppy, "but after word got around about that big gold strike at Seven-Up Ravine, his crew took off."

"All his crew are gone?"

Poppy shook her head. "Tommy stuck by him. And Quinn, too. But it takes a lot more men than that to handle a clipper like the *Osprey*. Right now she's moored in Yerba Buena Cove. Devlin's living aboard her, and trying to round up a new crew."

Briana's heart still was thudding erratically, and although she tried to conceal her feelings, she didn't succeed.

"Maybe if you were to come to the Black Pearl tonight, he'd be there."

"Why should I want to see him? He means nothing to me."

"If you say so." Poppy obviously wasn't convinced. "But why not come anyway? I'm going to wear this new outfit tonight when I dance."

"My uncle would never allow me to visit a concert saloon—" she began, then broke off abruptly.

"I guess he's kind of strict with you, even though he lives down here on the Coast. I don't blame him. But I wish you could come, just once."

"I don't see how I could manage without my uncle finding out," she said.

And even if she was somehow able to sneak out after dark and get to the concert saloon, it wouldn't be wise—not if there was a chance she would meet Devlin again.

During the weeks she'd been living on Pacific Street, Briana had managed to keep her spirits up in spite of her dismal surroundings. She had told herself that this was only an unavoidable delay. Sooner or later she would get away from the store. She would leave the Barbary Coast and never come back.

She hadn't forgotten Mama's plans for her future, or the sacrifice her mother had made. Briana's amber eyes hardened with determination. Somehow she would make a good marriage. She would have wealth, security, an unassailable position in society. She had suffered defeat in Charleston, but here, in this new city, throbbing with vitality and promise, she had a chance to start fresh. And she would make the most of it. Somehow . . .

Poppy was speaking, and Briana forced herself to listen. "Tell you what," her friend said. "Even if you can't come to the Black Pearl, I'm going to give you a special private performance, here and now. There's a song I learned right after I got to the city. It's a real favorite with the men."

Briana seated herself in the chair, an audience of one. "It would help if I had a piano player. But here goes." Poppy lifted her silk skirt above her ankles, whirled around, and tossed her mane of black hair so that it fanned out around her face.

Although her singing voice wasn't exceptional, it was strong and bubbling with bawdy good-humor.

> *The miners came in forty-nine*
> *The whores in fifty-one*
> *And when they got together*
> *They produced the native son. . . .*

"What's going on here?"

Briana sprang up and saw her aunt standing in the doorway. Gertrude's face was mottled with ugly red splotches, and her eyes burned with indignation.

"Who is this—this shameless female?" she demanded, pointing at Poppy.

Although Briana was too stunned to speak, her friend gave Gertrude a hard, unflinching stare. "My name's Poppy Nolan. Briana let me share her cabin aboard the *Osprey*."

"I might have known!" Her aunt cast a poisonous look in Briana's direction. "You, miss, with your airs and graces! I leave you alone for a few hours and come back to find you with a foul-tongued slut."

Briana had borne her aunt's insults all this time, but she wasn't about to stand by while Gertrude reviled her friend. "Don't you dare—"

"Your uncle will deal with you when he gets back!" Then

her aunt turned on Poppy. "As for you, get yourself out of my house, and don't let me ever see you around here again!"

"Now maybe you'll listen to me, Alexander!"

Briana, seated at the dinner table, kept her eyes fixed on her untouched plate of mutton, cabbage, and boiled potatoes. Her aunt had given her highly embellished account of Poppy's visit, but now she launched into a repetition.

"No decent girl would have anything to do with a female who flaunts herself in a concert saloon. You should have seen the creature, kicking her legs in the air and—"

"Poppy's my friend," Briana began. "She—"

"Hold your tongue, girl." Her uncle fixed his pale eyes on Briana. "We gave you a home when you had nowhere else to turn. And this is how you repay our charity."

"Charity? I've worked hard since the day I arrived here."

"In exchange for your room and board. We're all the family you have left," he reminded her. "If I turned you out in the street tonight, what would become of you?"

"I'm good at figures; you said so yourself," she reminded him. "I believe I could find another position. One where I was paid for my services."

"Of all the ungrateful creatures!" Gertrude began, but her husband silenced her with a gesture. Briana wondered if her threat might have hit home. It wouldn't be easy for her uncle to find another clerk. Most men who came to San Francisco could scarcely wait to go off to the gold fields to make their fortune. Hadn't Devlin's crew jumped ship, possessed by "gold fever"?

But Alexander quickly recovered himself, and his thin lips curved in a contemptuous smile. "You are a fool, girl. Have you any notion what would happen to you if I turned you out tonight? Yes, you'd find another job—working in a bawdy house."

"You'd be no better off than those Chinese slave girls," Gertrude chimed in. "Locked up, forced to submit to any man who wanted you. Then, when you lost your looks, you'd be cast out into the gutter." Gertrude, like the other ladies at the Civic Improvement Society, had been shocked and titillated that afternoon by the Griscombs' lurid description of conditions in the Chinese brothels.

Although Briana wanted to believe that her aunt was only trying to intimidate her, she suspected Gertrude's dire predictions might be true enough. From the day she had boarded the *Osprey*, on her own for the first time in her life, she had begun to realize just how vulnerable she was. During the time when she'd shared her cabin with Poppy and listened to the other girl's talk, she'd learned about a side of life that had been hidden from her before.

She saw that her uncle was watching her now with a look of smug satisfaction. Maybe he believed he had broken her rebellious spirit. But he was wrong.

"I don't think you would put me out on the street, Uncle Alexander. That lazy lout, Enoch, might take it into his head to go off to the gold fields again."

"He might," her uncle conceded. "But you can't. A female, even one as bold as you, doesn't have a man's freedom. You'd do well to remember that. Otherwise I'll be forced to give you a lesson you won't forget."

Surely he couldn't be threatening her with physical punishment. Her insides tightened at the very thought. She pushed back her chair and started to get up.

"Stay where you are," her uncle ordered. "You'd better hear me out, miss." Her knees turned weak and she sank back into her seat.

"I suppose you're not entirely to blame for your reckless ways, considering your upbringing. That mother of yours—"

"I won't listen to another word against my mother."

"She used her looks to turn my brother's head. She made a fool of him. His house in Charleston wasn't good enough for her. She had to have a mansion on the Battery. Trips to Paris. Her extravagant ways drove him to bankruptcy and an early grave."

He paused, his eyes holding hers. "But I'll see to it that you don't follow in her footsteps. It's my duty to discipline you as I see fit."

The threat was unmistakable.

"You have no right!"

But he did, and she knew it. As her only male relative, her uncle had every right to exert whatever discipline he chose.

She lapsed into silence, and his thin lips curved in a tight, self-satisfied smile. "I think you're beginning to take my meaning," he said. "Am I right?"

For a moment she sat in silence, her jaw set, fighting back the scalding tide of anger that surged up inside her. Then she took a deep, steadying breath and made herself answer respectfully. "Yes, Uncle Alexander."

She could scarcely get the words out, but she realized that she had little choice. For now she would give her aunt and uncle no cause to reprimand her. She would act meek and submissive; work hard in the store and help Gertrude with the household chores. She wouldn't even think about slipping out to see Poppy at the Black Pearl; she could well imagine the consequences if she were caught in such a forbidden escapade.

"May I be excused, Uncle Alexander?" she asked. He nodded brusquely. She rose and hurried from the room. Her legs felt unsteady and she stopped for a moment, before climbing the stairs.

No doubt he was convinced that he had cowed her completely; now he and Gertrude were deep in a conversation that had nothing to do with her.

From what she could hear they were making plans to take the ferry across to Oakland next weekend. "There's plenty of land for sale there, and it's still cheap," he was saying. "If we buy a dozen acres and hold on to them for a few years, prices are bound to go up."

"We could make us a handsome profit," Gertrude agreed.

After she had gone upstairs to her room Briana didn't even consider going to bed. Instead, she began to pace the floor, too deeply absorbed in her own thoughts to notice the now-familiar din from the alley outside.

It would take time, but somehow she would devise a plan for getting away from her aunt and uncle; from Pacific Street and all it stood for. And when she did she wouldn't forget her mother's hopes for her future. She would make those hopes, those dreams, a reality.

She stopped her pacing and thought about Poppy's unexpected revelation. Devlin was still here in San Francisco. All at once she felt an overpowering need to see him again, to appeal to him for help. Although he had lost most of his crew, she was confident that a captain as experienced as he would find a way to round up more seamen and take the *Osprey* back east again. If she appealed to him, he might be persuaded to let her come along.

But she pushed the treacherous thought aside; she had no doubt of the price she would have to pay in return for her passage. And although he might desire her, he would not marry her; he wasn't the marrying kind, of that she was sure.

Her only hope was to remain here, under her uncle's roof, until she could find another way to escape from the Barbary Coast; to make a respectable marriage and achieve the sort of life her mother would have wished for her.

Nine

Devlin Rafferty sat at one of the front tables near the small stage of the Black Pearl Concert Saloon, his lips curved in a crooked smile as he watched Poppy's performance. She certainly looked a whole lot different from the bedraggled girl who had come running up the gangplank of his ship in Havana harbor. The row of gas footlights played over her clinging black sequin bodice and the flounced silk skirt that flared out around her as she danced. Her song was bawdy, just the sort to please the raucous Saturday-night crowd here at the concert saloon.

With her rhinestone garters, and her black silk tights
She landed in Frisco, one Saturday night. . . .

Although Poppy didn't have any outstanding vocal talent, her skill as a dancer made up for the deficiency; her shapely body moved with a combination of grace and sensuality that stirred the men who watched her.

Maybe under other circumstances, Devlin thought, he would have been aroused like the rest of them. He, too, would have hungered to possess the dark-haired girl up there on the stage.

But now, although he could appreciate her skill and admire her looks, he felt no particular desire for her. Or for any other woman in the room. He didn't want to admit the reason, but he knew it well enough.

After all this time he couldn't get Briana out of his mind. Ever since she had left the ship and gone riding off with Cole Forrester he had found himself thinking about her. He told himself that it was unlikely that their paths would cross again; that even if he was to meet her by chance, she probably would rebuff him again, as she had that last night on the quarterdeck of the *Osprey*.

Lost in his own thoughts, he was only half aware of the men in the audience—miners, sailors, gamblers, clerks—who were now pounding their glasses on the tables and shouting their approval of Poppy's performance. Saturday nights were even more uproarious than all the others in the concert saloons, the gambling houses, and the brothels of San Francisco.

"Kick up yer heels, girl!"

"Let's see them fancy garters!"

"Show us yer tights, Poppy!"

She threw her audience a brilliant smile, pulled her skirts above her knees, and kicked one long, well-shaped leg high in the air. The men shouted their approval. A gold nugget hit the stage and landed at her feet; it was followed by a dozen more. Miners tossed the heavy pokes of gold dust they had toiled for during months of back-breaking labor in the camps along the American, the Yuba, and the Feather rivers. Gamblers threw the winnings from their all-night games of faro, monte, and poker.

Twirling around on one satin-slippered foot, Poppy spread her arms wide, as if to embrace all of her admirers at once. Then, bending with a fluid movement, she gathered up her loot and dropped it into the deep pocket in her skirt.

She paused, tossed back her dark hair, winked, and tucked one of the nuggets into her bodice, between the lush curves of her half-bared breasts. The men were on their feet now, applauding and shouting for more. She pulled up her skirts again, slid off one of her rhinestone garters, and tossed it to a gray-bearded miner at a front table. She put her fingers to her lips, blew kisses to the audience, and then whirled off the stage, her skirts flying.

Devlin had already half-emptied the bottle before him, but the whiskey had no more effect on him than plain spring water. He stared moodily at the scarred table. And thought about Briana.

Earlier that evening, before she had gone onstage, Poppy had come to his table and told him about her visit to Cameron's Emporium. "From what Briana says her uncle's done well for himself."

"I don't doubt it, with prices sky-high here in the city." He paused, his dark brows drawing together in a frown. "And yet you say she's living with him and his wife down on Pacific Street, across the alley from the store."

"Briana says her uncle's a miser. She works in the store and helps her aunt with the chores, but he doesn't pay her a cent, only gives her room and board. And that house she's living in! It's nothing like she's used to."

In spite of himself, he felt a twinge of pity. Briana, who had made the long, dangerous journey all the way from Charleston, now found herself living amid the vice and squalor of the Barbary Coast. He had tried to prepare her, the night before they had dropped anchor, but she had refused to believe him.

"I hardly recognized her at first," Poppy said. "She was wearing a black bombazine—a hand-me-down from her aunt—and she had her hair pushed up under a dustcap." Poppy shook her head, her eyes filled with sympathy for her friend. "That aunt of hers is a regular harpy. She was furious when she found me in her house. I'd have told her off, but I didn't want to make any more trouble for Briana."

Now Devlin poured himself another drink and tried to close his mind to Briana's predicament. After all, he told himself, she was young and healthy. A little hard work would do her no harm. It might even be the best thing for her. Sooner or later she would have to learn to cope with reality, difficult though it might be. At least her uncle was what he claimed to be: a respectable shopkeeper. She might have done a lot worse. She might have ended up in a parlor house or a waterfront crib. . . .

But try as he might, he couldn't put her out of his thoughts. Briana, well-bred, pampered, was working on Pacific Street, waiting on sailors and miners.

He could see her now, as she had looked that afternoon on the dock in Charleston: a bewitching picture in her lilac gown, with her red-gold hair glowing like molten copper under her plumed bonnet.

He shifted in his chair, remembering the pliant warmth of her body, as he had carried her to her cabin; her body, slender yet curved in all the right places; had been cradled against his chest, and her hair had brushed his cheek.

She had been afraid of him, but even when he had tossed her down on the bunk so abruptly that her petticoats had billowed up around her knees, had tried to humiliate her, she had refused to cringe. Instead she had glared at him with fiery defiance in her amber eyes. Somehow she had found the courage to challenge his unquestionable authority over her. She had gotten to her feet, had confronted him, had ordered him from her cabin.

He tried to distract himself, glancing around the crowded room, with its haze of blue smoke, its long, polished bar, its much-advertised "pretty waiter girls." One of these, a plump young blonde in a low-cut blouse and a crimson skirt, was making her way through the crowd to join him. He knew she would try to get him to buy another bottle, then lead him to one of the velvet-curtained booths on the balcony overhead. Once inside, he would be free to use her as he pleased, so long as he kept buying the drinks. Whiskey or brandy for him; cold tea for her.

The Black Pearl was no different from a hundred other such dives, from the Mersey waterfront in Liverpool to New York's South Street; from Panama City to Rio and Marseilles.

There had been a few saloons back in Sydney, but he'd been too young to sample their pleasures when he had been a lonely, desperate twelve-year-old boy, hanging around the docks and waiting for his chance to stow away on a ship—any ship that was leaving Australia.

He had known he would never return. He was leaving the country of his birth; escaping from the tyranny of his grandfather, Colonel Trevor Pendleton, commandant of one of the convict settlements in New South Wales.

His grandfather should have been a handsome man, with his dark hair, touched with gray at the temples; his tall, ramrodstraight body, and deeply tanned face; but his eyes were as cold as pale granite chips, the set of his mouth hard and pitiless. The colonel's own troopers had feared him almost as much as the luckless prisoners over whom he exercised absolute power.

Perhaps Devlin, his only grandson, had feared him most of all. He still remembered the terrified child he had been all those years ago. How often had he approached the door of his grandfather's study with slow, reluctant steps, having committed some act of defiance and fearing whatever new punishment awaited him.

Even now he felt his insides tighten. His fingers clamped around his empty glass and he stared down into it, unseeing. The uproar here in the concert saloon, loud and raucous though it was, could not drown out the echo of his grandfather's harsh voice. The old man had rarely called him by his name. Instead, it had been "convict's bastard," and "rebel's spawn."

The blond girl was beside him, resting a hand on his shoulder. He caught the mingled scent of strong violet perfume and perspiration. "You shouldn't be looking so glum, a handsome gent like you." She slid her fingers into the open collar of his shirt and her rouged lips curved in an enticing smile. "What you need's another bottle," she said. "And a little company. Just you come with me, Captain. There's an empty booth up there. We'll close the curtains and have ourselves a good time."

But he shook his head. "Not tonight," he said. He'd had enough to drink, and as for "company," he felt no desire for the girl's skilled but meaningless caresses. She shrugged and sauntered off, in search of a more willing customer.

Never before had he sought anything more than a casual night's pleasure ashore. But since he had known Briana all that had changed. The realization hit him with the force of a blow.

It was his enforced idleness that was causing him to brood about the girl this way. Once he was back at sea, where he belonged, he would forget her.

But that was the problem: So far he had not been able to find workmen to make the necessary repairs on his ship. And he hadn't been able to get together a new crew.

Meanwhile, with the *Osprey* stranded in Yerba Buena Cove, he would have to find some other way to keep himself occupied. During the past few days he had begun to consider a scheme that could bring him a handsome profit. Tommy would be in on it, and Quinn: the only two members of his crew who had stood by him, in spite of the lure of the goldfields.

Quinn had urged him to gather enough men to make up another crew, by whatever means might be necessary. "I'll hire a few crimps and we'll go down to Mother Pigott's place. A little whiskey laced with laudanum, a rap on the head, and toss 'em into the hold. By the time they come around we'll be out to sea."

But he had refused. "I'll take no men by force. They'll sign on of their own free will or not at all."

"And meanwhile the *Osprey* will rot out there in the cove."

Devlin knew that Quinn couldn't understand his refusal to

get together a crew by whatever means were necessary. Most clipper captains had no qualms about shanghaiing a crew. But Devlin had his own reasons for his decision; reasons too private to share, even with Quinn.

He pushed his chair back from the table and got to his feet. He'd walk back to Yerba Buena Cove, where the *Osprey* lay beached. For now the clipper still belonged to him, even if he could find no way to take her back to sea.

Early the following evening, Enoch Slocum made his way through the jostling crowd on Pacific Street. He grinned with anticipation as he considered the possibilities before him. Alexander and his wife had taken the ferry across the bay to Oakland at dawn; it would be at least a few more hours before they got back. And since the store was closed on Sunday, Briana would be in the house alone.

He had gone from one saloon to the next, and had fortified himself with several shots of whiskey, so that by now his footsteps were a little unsteady. As he approached the juncture of Pacific and Kearny, he felt the hunger growing stronger inside him.

Ever since Briana had come to work in the store he had wanted her. She was special, with that fancy way of talking and that touch-me-not manner of hers. Only last week, she had made a big fuss when he had put his hands on her.

But she wouldn't keep him at arm's length, not tonight. Because he knew her now for what she really was. No respectable young lady would be friendly with a girl who worked in a concert saloon.

Tonight she would drop into his hands like a ripe peach. He felt a stirring in his groin as he imagined how she would look, stretched out before him, stripped of her clothes. He ran his tongue over his lips. Would he be the first man to have her? It wasn't likely. But if it should turn out that she was still a virgin, he'd teach her a thing or two about pleasuring a man.

* * *

Briana had finished the last of the many household chores her aunt had ordered her to do. Now she climbed the stairs to her room for a brief rest.

A few hours before, she had breathed a sigh of relief as she had seen Enoch coming out of the lean-to that served as his living quarters. He had discarded his well-worn working garments and had changed into a checked suit and a plug hat with a curved brim. No doubt he would be taking advantage of her uncle's absence to enjoy a night on the town.

She reached her room, where she removed her dustcap and her black dress and slipped into one of her own embroidered cambric wrappers. Then she slid the pins from her hair and let it fall around her shoulders. She brushed the heavy, red-gold waves until they glowed in the light of the kerosene lamp overhead. She went to the bed and stretched out with a sigh of pure pleasure.

She made herself ignore the discomfort of the thin, lumpy mattress. Her eyelids closed, and now she could almost imagine that she lay on her wide, canopied bed in the house in Charleston. She felt a stirring of nostalgia as she conjured up the memory of her high-ceilinged room overlooking the garden . . . the French windows opening onto the balcony to catch the sweet-scented breeze. . . .

She started abruptly, jerked back to the present when she heard the sound of heavy footsteps downstairs. Surely her uncle and aunt hadn't returned already. She sat up and listened more closely: a man's footsteps coming from the parlor. She got up quickly and fastened the belt of her wrapper around her waist. "Uncle Alexander, is that you?" But there was no answer. Moving cautiously, she left her room and went down the short hallway to the head of the stairs.

"Uncle Alexander?" She felt a growing uneasiness. The parlor door was locked; she was sure of that. But what about the back door? Had she remembered to lock it, too, after she emptied the scrub bucket into the yard?

She leaned over the banister. Enoch stood at the foot of the stairs. She caught her breath and felt a sinking sensation deep inside. He had lit one of the kerosene lamps and now he held it high, his eyes fixed on her. She mustn't let him even guess that she was afraid.

"What are you doing in here?" she demanded. She hoped she sounded more confident than she felt.

His gaze moved over her, and she flinched as she realized that the sheer wrapper revealed every curve of her body.

"I figured you might be feelin' lonesome all by yourself." His speech was slurred. "How about comin' down and fixin' us some supper?"

Her first impulse was to retreat back to her room, but already he was climbing the stairs, the lamp clutched in his hand. His shadow, huge and wavering, moved along the wall.

"I am not at all lonesome," she said evenly. "Please leave. At once." Her words had no effect. He stood before her and reached out; his free hand closed on her wrist. "Come on," he urged. "You don't want to make me feel unwelcome, do you? How about a nice friendly meal, for just the two of us."

As he leaned closer, she caught the smell of raw whiskey on his breath, and she knew it would be unwise to refuse him outright.

She forced her mouth to curve in the semblance of a smile. "All right, then. Just let me go upstairs and change, and I'll prepare supper for you." There was a bottle of whiskey in the kitchen. Maybe if she could get him to take a few more drinks he would pass out.

But he tugged at her arm so that she nearly lost her balance. "You needn't bother putting on a dress. You look a whole lot better in what you're wearin'." He stared fixedly at her breasts. "A whole lot better . . ."

She drew a long breath, then let him lead her downstairs into the parlor. She had to hold him off as long as possible. "You wait here." She edged him toward the plush settee. "Make yourself comfortable and I'll get you a drink, while I prepare supper."

But he set down the lamp on the table beside the settee. "Supper can wait," he said, his voice husky. Beads of sweat gleamed on his forehead and ran down his flabby cheeks. His hands moved to her breasts, and his thick fingers began to knead her flesh.

"No—you mustn't!" Briana cried. "Stop it!"

"You can't fool me—not any more. You're no better'n that saloon girl friend of yours—" He tugged at the belt of her wrapper until it opened. She tried to pull the wrapper around her, but he forced her hands away. He pushed her down on the settee and flung himself on top of her, holding her immobile with the weight of his thick body.

She fought with all her strength, writhing and twisting under him, until she sensed that her frenzied movements only aroused him more. "Can't wait, can you? Bet you want it as much as I do—" He was fumbling with his breeches. She drew in her breath and screamed. "None of that now!" But she screamed again.

"Stop your damn caterwauling!" She clawed at his face. He caught her arm and forced it behind her. Then he slapped her hard across the cheek, so that glittering spots of light danced before her eyes. Although she went on struggling, she felt the last of her strength ebbing away.

Through the darkness that was beginning to swirl up around her, she caught the creak of hinges. A damp breeze came blowing in from the alley.

"Let go of her!"

At the sound of her uncle's harsh voice, she went weak with relief. In the wavering light of the lamp she caught sight of Alexander's face, frozen with outrage. He seized Enoch by the back of his collar and twisted it until the other man's eyes bulged.

Now Gertrude, too, was in the parlor. Seeing her husband struggling with Enoch, she seized a cane from the stand beside the door and raised it menacingly. "What's he doing here?" she demanded. "You, girl! Speak up! What've you and him been up to?"

Enoch scrambled clumsily to his feet, trying to button his breeches. The clerk's face was purple and he was panting as he fought for breath. "—wasn't my fault, Miz Cameron—Briana— she asked me in—she flaunted herself at me—"

Briana stared at Enoch in disbelief. How dare he tell such a blatant lie? She must convince her aunt and uncle of the truth, at once.

She grasped the carved side of the settee and pulled herself up. "It's not true, any of it. He came in—he forced himself on me!"

"I'm not so sure of that." Gertrude's eyes raked over Briana's body, taking in the open wrapper, the thin chemise and petticoat. "Look at her, Alexander. Half-naked, with her hair down, like some trollop out of a sporting house!"

Her uncle glanced at her with distaste. "Cover yourself, girl." As Enoch seized on the distraction and started for the door, her uncle glared at him. "You stay right where you are, until we straighten this out."

Then he turned to Briana. "Go to your room, girl!"

"I'm not leaving until you get Enoch to admit the truth," she protested.

Her uncle turned on her. "You'll do as you're told."

She shook her head. "I won't have that—that toad lying about me when I'm not here to defend myself," she insisted.

Her uncle's thin lips twisted as he took hold of her shoulder. She gave a cry of pain at the cruel grip of his bony fingers. "Upstairs, girl. Or must I take a strap to you?"

The threat sent a cold shiver racing the length of her body. She headed for the stairs; then, clutching the banister, she began to ascend.

"We'll settle this with Enoch, here and now," she heard him saying. "We'll deal with the girl afterwards."

Briana sat on the edge of her bed and tried to still the shudders that still shook her body. Her arm throbbed from her uncle's ruthless grip and she rubbed it, trying to ease the pain. Surely neither he nor her aunt could believe Enoch's lies. If she had lured the clerk into the house, if she had thrown herself at him, why would she have been screaming for help when her aunt and uncle had returned? They must have heard her cries halfway down the alley.

Uncle Alexander would get the truth out of Enoch and turn him over to the authorities. Or, if he wished to avoid a scandal, he would at least dismiss the clerk and send him packing at once.

She got to her feet and poured water from the pitcher into the basin to bathe her flushed face. Then she smoothed her hair back. She could hear the rise and fall of voices from the parlor below, but she couldn't make out what was being said.

Then she heard the front door close. She drew aside the curtain and made out Enoch's heavy figure, stumbling in the direction of the lean-to beside the store. He had confessed, she thought, with a sigh of relief. Now he would pack his few belongings and be on his way.

She turned from the window as she heard her aunt and uncle coming upstairs. They stopped outside her door. "Time enough to tell her tomorrow," Gertrude was saying.

"Why wait?" her uncle asked. "The sooner she gets used to the idea, the better."

The door swung open. Briana pulled her wrapper around her. She was puzzled and faintly troubled by what she had overheard.

Probably her uncle would tell her that, until they could find another clerk, she would have to do all the work in the store. She'd manage somehow. At least she wouldn't have to see Enoch's face again That would make it easier to put the memory of this awful night behind her

The bedroom door opened, and her aunt and uncle came in. "It didn't take you long to start more trouble, did it?" Her uncle's words caught her completely by surprise.

"Surely you don't believe I was to blame for what happened tonight?"

"Seems to me there's enough blame to go around," her uncle

said. "Enoch had been drinking; he admitted as much. But you should've known better than to invite him in."

"I didn't! You must believe me."

"It's his word against yours," Gertrude said. "I never did trust you, not from the first day I laid eyes on you. I told your uncle you were no better than you should be. Getting around the captain of the ship that brought you here, so he paid to have your luggage delivered. Sharing a cabin with a saloon girl. Asking her into my house, the minute my back was turned."

"That'll do," her uncle interrupted. "Enoch's sorry for what he did. But he's willing to make it up to you."

Briana stared at her uncle in bewilderment. "Make it up . . ."

"He's willing to marry you, girl."

"Best thing for both of you," her aunt said smugly.

This was a nightmare. It had to be. How could her uncle and aunt believe that she would even consider such an arrangement?

"I won't do it."

"You'll do exactly as you're told," her uncle said. "First thing tomorrow I'll have a preacher down in the parlor. He'll make it legal. Then you and Enoch can live in the lean-to next to the store."

"I won't—you can't force me to marry that—creature."

Her uncle's face hardened. "I figured you might be sensible about this, but I see I was mistaken." As she watched, her eyes wide with disbelief, he unbuckled his leather belt and took it off. It was in his hand as he advanced on her. Numb with revulsion and terror, she stared at him, then took a quick step back. Her legs went weak and she sank down on the edge of the bed. "You'll give me your word right now that you'll marry Enoch. Otherwise, you'll regret it."

He brought the belt down on the table beside the bed with a resounding crack. Her breath caught in her throat. "What's it to be?" he demanded. "Will you do as you're told?"

She shook her head. "I won't—I can't—" She could scarcely get the words out.

"Then you'll have to be made to change your mind, the hard way."

Briana drew up her legs and crouched on the bed, her eyes fixed on the belt. "When I get finished you'll be pleading to marry Enoch." He raised the belt, but her aunt seized her uncle's arm.

"Not yet, Alexander!"

"And why not?" he demanded.

"We don't want her marked up," Gertrude warned him. "Else she's liable to show the preacher her bruises, and say she's being forced into marriage against her will."

Her uncle hesitated, weighing his wife's words. "A forced marriage might not be legal," he said slowly. "But the girl needs taming, or she'll bring shame on us."

"I'm not saying she doesn't deserve a beating," her aunt agreed.

She turned on Briana with a baleful stare. "Once you're married to Enoch it'll be up to him to teach you to behave like a dutiful wife."

Although her first impulse was to tell them both that no threats would force her into marriage with Enoch, she hesitated. Her uncle still confronted her, his hand firmly wrapped around the belt. She dared not risk arousing his temper to the point where even her aunt wouldn't be able to control him.

"If I could be alone—to get used to the idea." She kept her voice low and respectful. "Marriage is a serious step. I need time to think. . . ."

Her uncle shrugged. "Think about it all you please tonight," he said. "But tomorrow you'll marry Enoch."

He turned and stalked out, followed by her aunt.

She sat staring at the closed door. If she didn't give in, her uncle was capable of carrying out his threat; she was sure of it. She had to wait until her aunt and uncle were asleep and then get away. She had to be out of the house before morning.

She slid off her wrapper, glancing down with distaste at the black dress and dustcap she had discarded earlier. Then she tossed them into a corner. She would never wear those hated garments again.

She pulled aside the curtain from the space that served as her makeshift closet and took out the gray silk dress and jacket she had worn when she had arrived here. Quickly, she put them on, her fingers shaking so that she found it difficult to manage the buttons.

Carefully, she turned the doorknob and breathed a sigh of relief. Her uncle hadn't taken the trouble to lock her in. Did he really believe that, in spite of her reluctance to marry Enoch, she would go through with the wedding? Or that she wouldn't dare to leave because she had no place to run?

She paused, confused, uncertain as to her next move. Even if she could slip out of the house, where was she to turn for help?

If she went to Poppy, her uncle might come looking for her at the Black Pearl. She mustn't make trouble for her friend. Poppy was a saloon girl; Alexander Cameron was a respectable shopkeeper and Briana's only male relative. Should he decide to call in the authorities, it was likely she would be returned to his home.

She needed to seek refuge with someone strong enough, determined enough, to protect her.

Devlin Rafferty.

He had offered his protection once before; had said he would see her safely off the ship. Maybe he would protect her now.

Men don't forget a girl like you. Devlin Rafferty sure hasn't. Devlin had come to the Black Pearl and had asked about her. *He tried to make it sound like he didn't much care, but I know enough about men to be sure he does.*

The *Osprey* was beached in Yerba Buena Cove, so Poppy had said. If only he would agree to keep her aboard his ship until he found another crew, she would talk him into taking her back East.

But what would he ask of her in return? She knew well enough, and she felt a swift current of heat coursing through every nerve of her body. How could she forget the hunger in his bold gray eyes whenever they moved over her; the hard, driving passion with which he had held her; the burning touch of his tongue, invading, possessing her mouth; his hands caressing her breasts. . . .

He had never said he loved her.

But he had wanted her—he still did. She was sure of it. If she took refuge aboard his ship, how could she hope to keep him at arm's length during the long return voyage?

She dared not let herself think about that. It would take every ounce of courage and determination she possessed to leave this house and risk the dangers that lay in wait for her outside, on the twisting, fog-shrouded streets of the Barbary Coast.

Ten

Holding her shoes in one hand and her carpetbag in the other, Briana left her bedroom in her stocking feet, moving as noiselessly as possible. She went down the hallway with no more than a glance at the door of the room where her trunks were stored.

Even now she remembered her first meeting with Devlin, on the Charleston dock; how she had quarreled with him, insisting that she wouldn't sail unless all her trunks were carried aboard. Yet now she was leaving those treasured possessions behind without a qualm. All that mattered was that she get out of this house as quickly as possible.

Keeping close against the wall, she went down the stairs and through the parlor. She averted her eyes from the plush sofa where, only a few hours before, Enoch had tried to force himself on her. Into the kitchen and now, at last, out the back door into the alley.

Her legs were unsteady and she was feeling a little lightheaded, but she fought back her weakness. She couldn't give

way. If she could find her way to Yerba Buena Cove and get
aboard Devlin's ship, she would be safe.

The thick, damp fog was rolling in from the sea, so that she
could scarcely see more than a few feet ahead of her. But she
could hear the uproarious sounds of revelry that seemed to echo
from every street and alley along the waterfront. Never before
had she been out alone in this notorious district after dark. She
shivered, remembering all she'd been told of the Barbary Coast.

Even now, long past midnight, the saloons, the gambling
houses, the cellar dives, were crowded and noisy. The alley was
filled with the discordant blending of pianos, fiddles, banjos,
and melodeons; the shrill off-key singing of a saloon girl, the
shouts and curses of drunken brawlers.

She hurried on, hoping to avoid the roving eye of a woman-
hungry sailor or miner, who would consider any girl out here
alone fair game. Or worse yet, she might fall prey to a bully
from one of the brothels, who wouldn't hesitate to drag her off.
She remembered her aunt's description of such places, and her
insides churned with fear and revulsion.

She had nearly reached the livery stable at the end of the alley
when she heard a man calling to her. "You there!" A horse-drawn
wagon came looming out of the fog, bearing down on her.

She tried to dodge to one side and hide herself in the shadows,
but she missed her footing and slipped. She lost her grip on her
carpetbag, heard her silk skirt tearing, and cried out as her knees
struck the ground with bruising force.

The man jumped from the wagon seat, and a moment later
she felt his strong hand grasping her shoulder. Terror shot
through her as she struggled to get free.

"Are you hurt, miss?" She thought she heard genuine concern
in his tone. "This fog," he was saying, in a thick, foreign accent.
"I did not see you until—almost under my horse's hooves, you
were."

He helped her to her feet. Her skirt, her petticoat, were torn
and soaked with mud from the alley. Her knees were scraped
and aching. In the faint glow of the lantern that hung beside

the wagon seat, the man peered at her more closely. "It is not right, a young girl like you should be wandering around this part of the city. And at such an hour."

Although he looked respectable enough in his dark, shabby suit and derby hat, she wasn't entirely reassured.

"I wasn't just wandering around." She tried to sound self-possessed as she smoothed her torn dress. "I'm looking for Yerba Buena Cove. Can you tell me how to get there?"

"Which wharf?" he asked. She recognized his accent now. He spoke like the German tourists who used to visit Paris when she and Mama had lived there.

"Is there more than one?"

He nodded. "And hundreds of ships beached in the cove."

"The ship I want is a clipper called the *Osprey*."

He shook his head. "You can't go walking around these alleys in the fog, asking strangers for directions."

He turned to climb back on the wagon and her heart sank.

"I must get to the *Osprey*," she insisted.

He climbed onto the narrow seat and looked down at her. Then he said, "Give me your hand. Who knows, maybe we can find a sailor who'll know where this ship, this *Osprey* might be."

Although she knew she was taking a risk, she had to follow her instincts. She retrieved her soiled carpetbag and passed it up to him, then gave him her hand. He helped her up onto the seat beside him.

He cracked his whip and the horse started forward, with the small, heavily laden wagon bumping and jouncing along. She clutched at the seat as the wagon hit a rut. "It's kind of you to help me," she said.

He shrugged. "I'm a peddler," he said. "I go past the cove on my route. First to the fort, to sell my goods to the officers' wives, then on to the mining camps. Grass Valley, Calaveras, Hangtown. Those miners are my best customers. They buy cooking pots, pickaxes, shovels. And cards—always they want cards. You would think it is enough of a gamble for them, looking for gold. But as soon as they get together a few nuggets, they start up a card game."

He broke off as a seaman came striding by. "We're looking for a ship—the *Osprey*," he called out. "You maybe know where she's beached?"

The seaman scarcely paused. "Never heard the name," he said. "There's nearly six hundred vessels out there. It's a sorry sight they are. But why should a man slave for sailor's wages when he can fill his pockets with gold out there in the diggings?" He turned away and went through the swinging doors of the nearest saloon.

Briana was beginning to realize how foolhardy she had been to think that once she was out of her uncle's house she would be able to find her way straight to Devlin's ship.

"We'll keep asking," the peddler assured her. "Don't you worry. Meantime, you're safe in my wagon." He gave her a rueful smile. "As safe as anybody can be, here on the Coast."

He pulled back the side of his worn coat and she saw the butt of a pistol protruding from his belt. He shook his head. "It doesn't seem possible. Me—Jacob Perlman. Back in Hamburg I kept a shop with my brothers. I never even handled a pistol. But here, I got to have one."

Her body tensed as she remembered Devlin's talk of the dangers that lay in wait for the unwary along the Barbary Coast. "A man isn't safe here. It's those criminals," Jacob Perlman went on. "The Sidney Ducks they call themselves. They're the worst of the lot."

Under other circumstances Briana would have smiled at the peculiar name, but now she caught the look of fear in the peddler's eyes. "They're mostly escaped convicts," he explained. "From Australia, they come."

Devlin had come from that distant continent, too. He had told her so, the first night of the voyage. And she had caught the hard edge of resentment in his voice when he had spoken of the Australian penal colonies. Did he know of them from his own experience? She felt a shiver of apprehension as the peddler went on.

"They serve their sentences, or maybe they escape, and then they get across the ocean and head straight for San Francisco. Thieves, they are, and murderers. The scum of the earth."

She stiffened, remembering her earlier misgivings about Devlin. Even now she knew little about his past. Was she making the mistake of a lifetime, seeking refuge with him? But there was no turning back for her. She couldn't return to her uncle's home, not ever.

The peddler had caught sight of a man in the gold-braided uniform of a ship's officer. "You, sir," he called out. "You know where we can find a ship called the *Osprey*?"

It was near dawn when Devlin returned to the wharf. He headed for the *Osprey*, which was beached at the far end of the cove, surrounded by so many other ships. Their sails were furled; their masts rose dark against the sky.

He climbed aboard his ship and stepped onto the deck, where he found Tommy waiting for him. The boy looked up at him uneasily.

"Trouble?" Although there was little enough to steal from the ship, he had taken the precaution of leaving Tommy to guard her each night.

"It's Miss Briana, sir."

Briana. The sound of her name sent a wholly unexpected tide of pleasurable anticipation sweeping through him. He had resolved to put her out of his mind, but he hadn't been able to.

"She came aboard about an hour ago," Tommy went on. "I helped that peddler fella get her aboard. She looked kind of pale and shaky, like she might be gettin' ready to keel over. Her dress was torn and muddy, and I think she might've been knocked around some. I put her in your cabin, 'cause I figured you'd want me to."

But Devlin didn't wait to hear any more. He was already heading for his quarters. He took the steps two at a time, flung open the door, and went through the outer cabin to the smaller one beyond.

By the light of the kerosene lamp that hung from the ceiling beam, he caught sight of a torn, mud-spattered silk gown and petticoat tossed across a chair. A carpetbag and a pair of small, kidskin slippers lay on the floor. And Briana, asleep in his bed, her coppery-red hair tangled about her face.

He bent over the bed and stared down at her. He drew in his breath. One side of her face was swollen. His mouth hardened as he drew back the blanket and saw the livid bruises on the smooth white skin of her shoulder. "Who the hell did this?" He hadn't meant to speak aloud, but the words came unbidden, fueled by his anger.

She woke with a start and her eyes flew open. They were wide with fear for a moment. "It's all right," he said softly. "I'm here now."

He sat down on the edge of the bed. She reached out to him, and then she was in his arms, clinging to him. Her voice was muffled against his shoulder. "I had to get away before morning—and I didn't know where else to go—"

He held her close and stroked her hair. Her breasts, firm and round, were pressing against his chest, and he was inhaling the delicate, familiar scent of her skin. But for the first time he felt an unfamiliar sensation stirring inside him, not the fierce hunger to possess her. Right now he wanted only to comfort her, to protect her from further harm.

He held her a moment longer, then unclasped her clinging arms. He turned to the bedside table, poured cool water from the pitcher into the basin, and soaked a cloth. He pressed it against her swollen cheek, her bruised shoulder. "This should make you feel better," he said softly.

She took comfort from his reassuring words, his gentle touch. In the time she had known him, she had seen the violent side of his nature often enough. But how could she have guessed at his capacity for kindness, for caring?

He pushed the blanket down, and now his hands moved over

her body, exploring her collarbone, the arc of her ribs. "Nothing seems to be broken," he said. "Are there any more bruises?"

"I scraped my knees when I stumbled back there in the alley."

"Take off your pantalettes."

She shook her head and drew away. He made an impatient gesture. "Pull them up over your knees, then.

"I'll try not to hurt you," he said, as he washed the abrasions carefully. His eyes lingered on the graceful curves of her lower legs, the delicate shape of her ankles and small, high-arched feet. For a moment he felt a hot stirring in his groin, but he forced himself to ignore his need. Briana had been cruelly mistreated. She needed time to rest, to recover. He drew the blanket back over her. "Get some sleep now. Tomorrow you'll be feeling better."

She reached out and her fingers closed around his hand. He was moved by the look of complete trust in her amber eyes. No woman had ever looked at him that way before.

"I was so afraid I wouldn't be able to find your ship," she murmured. Her voice was growing drowsy, and her eyelids were closing. "If it hadn't been for the peddler . . ."

He eased her back against the pillows. "You can tell me about it tomorrow," he said. "Sleep now. No one will hurt you again. You're safe here with me."

Exhausted by her ordeal, she slept through the following morning and late into the afternoon. When she awoke Tommy brought her a light but satisfying meal on a tray.

Her dress and petticoat were dry now, although still stained with mud. Then she dressed, brushed her hair and fastened it back from her face with a length of ribbon.

It wasn't until sunset, when she joined Devlin outside on the quarterdeck, that she told him what had happened to drive her out of her uncle's home.

"I won't go back to live with him and Aunt Gertrude, not ever," she finished.

"Damn right you won't." He put his arm around her waist, and she felt reassured by his gesture.

They stood close together in silence, and she looked out at the last rays of the sun glittering on the wind-ruffled surface of the bay, the steep rise of the distant hills.

"What do you figure on doing now?" Devlin's matter-of-fact question reminded her that, although she was safe from her uncle and the prospect of a forced marriage to Enoch, her future was still unsettled.

She remembered the vague plans she had made before she had run away, but she couldn't yet bring herself to ask him to take her along with him when he sailed. Instead, she kept her eyes fixed on the bay. "So many ships out there," she said. "Have they all been abandoned by their crews?"

"Most of them have. They'll never put out to sea again. Some will lie beached until they rot and go to the bottom."

"But you won't let that happen to the *Osprey*!"

"Not if I can help it. There are other, more profitable uses for abandoned ships. Plenty of businessmen are buying them up and converting them into hotels, stores, gambling houses. The city's growing fast, and there's a shortage of buildings."

"You wouldn't sell your own ship—you can't!"

"I'd rather sell her than let her lay beached here until the wind and rain turn her into a rotten hulk."

"But you told me how much the *Osprey* means to you. It was that day just before the storm struck, rounding the Horn; remember?"

His eyes darkened and his mouth clamped into a thin, hard line.

"Surely you don't want to sell her, do you?"

"I may not have a choice. I can't put out to sea with only Tommy and Quinn to help sail the ship."

"You can at least try to find another crew."

"Why should it matter to you whether I do or not? Why do you care what happens to my ship?"

She couldn't delay any longer. She looked up at him and

drew a steadying breath. Now she would have to offer her proposition; and if he agreed, it would be on his own terms.

"I hoped that when you set sail again you would take me with you." Before she could lose her nerve she went on quickly. "If you're going back to Boston, I may be able to find some sort of respectable position there."

"You want to work for a living," he said, with a touch of irony. "That's quite a change, isn't it?"

"I've had experience in my uncle's shop. Even he had to admit that I was useful. Or I can try to find a family who'd hire me as a governess."

"But why in Boston? Do you have friends there?"

She shook her head. "No, but—that's the *Osprey*'s home port, isn't it?"

"Don't you understand that I have no way to get back there without a crew?"

"You can't give up so easily," she protested. "Now you're master of your own ship, you'd never be content to stay ashore."

Her words caught him off-guard. He had told her little enough about himself during the voyage. How had she managed to penetrate his deepest, most closely guarded feelings? He looked down at her uneasily. It was as if those amber eyes of hers could see into his very soul.

"The sea is a part of you—it's your only real home."

He drew a harsh breath. She understood more about him than he would have thought possible, and he didn't like it. "That's enough! If you knew anything about ships, you'd see that this one's in no fit condition to put out to sea again, not without my spending a fortune for repairs. And I don't have a fortune right now."

"But surely not every other ship that was battered by a storm coming around the Horn will stay out here."

"Wealthy owners of shipping lines, men like Aspinwall and Howland, can afford to pay exhorbitant prices for repairs. I can't."

He slammed a closed fist against the quarterdeck rail, his

face dark with frustration. "Dammit, Briana! You think I want to lose my ship? To see her turned into a gambling house or a hotel? I have no other choice. Even if I could get her repaired, I'd still need a crew."

He stared out across the bay. The rosy light of the setting sun was fading now; the chill wind grew stronger, and the thick gray fog came billowing in.

She put her hand on his arm. "You won't let the *Osprey* go," she said softly. "Feeling as you do about her, you'll find a way to keep her."

"Feelings are a luxury I can't afford." His eyes were cold and remote now. "Quinn wanted me to let him hire a few crimps and shanghai a crew."

"You couldn't—" she began.

"I've shanghaied crews in my time," he interrupted. "But that was when I was commanding other men's ships. And I always swore that when I was master of my own vessel my crews would sign on willingly or not at all."

She searched his face, surprised by the intensity in his voice. "Why should it trouble you to force men to sail your ship against their will? That first night out of Charleston, you broke that man's arm before you knocked him unconscious."

"It was my duty to keep order aboard my ship. But shanghaiing a crew, that's different. No man should be imprisoned without cause."

"Imprisoned?"

"What else would you call it? A man who's drugged or knocked unconscious and taken to sea against his will is a prisoner."

No better off than a convict who was sentenced unjustly and shipped out to that damned penal colony in New South Wales. As my father was . . . He forced the hated memory from his mind and turned away.

But not before Briana had seen the cold rage in his gray eyes, the tensing of his jaw. She sensed that he had said more than he'd meant to. He had come close to revealing a side of himself that he'd kept hidden from her until now.

The wind caught at her hair, whipping it across her face. Her skirts billowed out around her.

"Come along," he said. "It's time we were going inside. That dress is too thin to protect you from the night air."

He took her arm and led her back inside the cabin. In the dim light he stood towering above her. With one swift movement of his hand he slid the ribbon from her hair. The heavy, red-gold waves came cascading down around her face and over her shoulders. His hands lingered, pushing her hair back from her face, tilting back her head. His eyes held hers, and she saw the swift stirring of desire in their depths.

She stiffened and drew away. "I think I may already have taken a chill," she said. "Perhaps I should go to bed."

No sooner were the words out than she longed to call them back. A smile touched his lips. He bent his head and brushed his mouth lightly over hers.

"I'll see you get to bed soon enough," he said. "But first we'll have a drink." He poured a glass of brandy for her, and one for himself. "To help ward off that chill." She hesitated, then swallowed and felt the heat moving through her. He emptied his glass and set it down, then drew her to him.

"I spent last night out here on the sofa," he said. "You needed a good sound sleep then. But tonight . . ." His arms closed around her.

She put up her hands against his shoulders and tried to push him away. But his lips claimed hers, his tongue seeking entrance to the moist softness within. Her own hunger stirred, rising in a swirling tide. And now she was no longer trying to hold him off. She felt her body tingling, molding itself against his.

The kiss deepened. With one swift, easy movement he lifted her, cradling her against his chest. He carried her through the doorway to his sleeping quarters and set her down on the bed.

Her body ached with longing for him, but she tried to hold back. She couldn't give herself to him, not like this. He had never said he loved her, never once spoken of a future for them, together. How often had she told herself that she would never allow her emotions to rule her, to destroy her? Yet now none of her careful plans seemed important.

There was still time to hold back the tide of passion before it engulfed them both. There was no mistaking the hunger in him. And yet he had told her that he would never force her to yield to him. If she gave herself now, it would be of her own free will.

Fool. You mustn't let him . . .

Then the warning voice was gone, drowned out by the fierce desire that swept all else before it.

He stripped off his shirt and tossed it aside. Her breath caught in her throat. The hanging lamp above the bed cast a pattern of light and shadows over the muscles of his chest, his wide, powerful shoulders.

He pulled off his boots, then unbuckled the belt around his lean waist. She began to turn away, but his words stopped her. "Don't look away, love. There's nothing for you to fear." She told herself that he was right, but it took an effort for her to obey. Her breath caught in her throat; her heart speeded up. And her eyes widened with wonder at the first sight of his naked body. She had never known that any man could move her so. He stood before her, tall, magnificent—beautiful in his proud masculinity. Her gaze moved from the tapering line of his torso to the muscled ridges of his abdomen, and lower still. She did not, could not, avert her gaze from the hard shaft of his manhood. He was ready to take her now. Her senses whirled with mingled desire and apprehension.

He came closer, then lowered himself to the bed beside her. A tremor ran through the length of her body and she longed to draw away. "Briana . . ." His voice, deep and husky, made the sound of her name a caress.

All thought of the future slipped away. There was only tonight . . . this wondrous moment. . . .

He raised himself up on one arm, reached out, and began to

unbutton her bodice. He drew off her camisole, baring her breasts to his gaze.

Without any trace of lingering modesty, she pressed herself against him, moving her breasts against his chest. The crisp dark hair there sent a delicious, exciting sensation racing through her, teasing her nipples into hard, tingling peaks. A hot current of tantalizing need began to move downward from her breasts. . . . Ripples of desire spread through every part of her. Possessed with her aching need, Briana held out her arms and drew him to her.

He longed to take her at once, but he mastered his own hunger. He lay his cheek against the satin swell of her breasts. His lips closed around one rosy nipple, drawing its sweet hardness inside his mouth, caressing, teasing, then suckling avidly. He couldn't get enough of her.

His fingers stroked her throat, the curve of her shoulder, the swell of her breasts. He looked down at her face and saw her eyes in the lantern light. He saw the desire reflected there, but he also caught a flicker of lingering doubt in their amber depths. The glowing waves of her red-gold hair spread in burnished glory about the white oval of her face.

Slowly, hesitantly, her hands reached out and began to caress the muscles of his back. But when the hardness of his manhood brushed her thigh he heard her draw in her breath sharply.

"Devlin, please . . ." Was she pleading for release—or for more time to ready herself to receive him?

He would hold back as long as he could, arousing her, gentling her, readying her for the moment of their joining. He parted her legs and caressed the coppery curls at the apex of her thighs. Now he moved deeper and found the tight, hard bud, the source of her womanhood. He fondled her, tantalized her until he felt slick, moist heat beneath his fingertips.

He drew his hand away and nudged her legs apart with his knee, positioning himself between her thighs.

She caught her breath at the first hard thrust and tried to pull away. But it was too late; he was inside her, the pain was ebbing, and she clung to him as he drove deeper, filling her with his powerful manhood.

She reached up to draw him closer yet. Her hips lifted, drawing him into the center of her being. He was moving inside her silken sheath, slowly at first, in long, lingering strokes.

The rise and fall of her hips quickened, and he answered her need, his thrusts harder, faster, more urgent. They were caught up in a fierce storm of sensation. She felt a pulsing within her loins and gave a wordless cry. Together they were lifted on the crest of the soaring wave. Together they rose up and up to touch the height of ecstasy.

Then, slowly, the storm subsided. She lay in his arms, savoring the sweet afterglow of their loving. With her head pillowed on his chest and his arm across her breasts, she felt cherished, loved. She moved closer to him, feeling the hardness of his body, still moist and warm against her. Sighing with complete fulfillment, she drifted off to sleep.

When Briana awoke the light was streaming through the porthole, sending long shafts of gold across the tumbled bed. She reached out for Devlin, but he was no longer beside her. She sat up, the blanket falling away from her body.

She got out of bed, put on her chemise, and went to the door of the outer cabin. He was not there either. After washing and dressing she brushed her hair and hurried outside.

The sun was high over the bay, and a fresh sea breeze caught at her skirts as she descended the steps to the main deck.

"Mornin', Miss Briana," Tommy hailed her. "Cap'n said not t' wake ye."

"Where's he gone?"

"He went ashore at dawn," the boy replied. "If ye want yer breakfast now, I'll fix ye some."

She shook her head. "Did he say when he'd be back?"

"He don't usually get back until late at night."

But surely, after last night, he wouldn't leave her here alone for so long!

"Maybe he's made up his mind to sell the ship," Tommy went on. "He's had a couple of offers already, but he's been holdin' off. It won't be easy for him to let the *Osprey* go, I guess."

Only yesterday evening she had used all her powers of persuasion to convince him to reconsider; to hold on to the ship until he could sail back to Boston.

Now it no longer mattered to her, so long as she and Devlin were together. A smile touched her lips and her amber eyes glowed as she tried to imagine their future.

"Has the captain told you what he means to do, if he does sell the ship?"

The boy shook his head. "You needn't worry about that. Whatever he does he'll get along fine."

"Perhaps he'll decide to settle down here in San Francisco after all."

Tommy shook his head. "Not Cap'n Rafferty. He ain't about to settle down nowhere." He gave her a searching look. "He won't be leavin' right away, though." She thought she saw a touch of concern in the boy's face. Was it possible that the boy, young as he was, guessed what had happened between her and Devlin last night?

But Tommy need feel no concern for her. Wherever Devlin might go, she would go with him. He wouldn't leave her, not after the passionate intimacy they had shared.

Yet he had talked of selling his ship. He wouldn't find it easy to part with the clipper, but he would do it if he had to.

Feelings are a luxury I can't afford.

She caught her breath and felt a sudden chill as she remembered his words. Was it possible that he might part from her, as he would from his ship, putting aside his regrets and moving on?

She wouldn't let herself think of the future. She would demand no promises from him. Tonight she would be waiting here, ready to give him all the passion, all the tenderness within her.

Slowly she turned and mounted the steps to the quarterdeck, where she paused to look out over the city. Yesterday evening, when she and Devlin had stood here, wrapped in the chill fog from the bay, she had sensed the dark forces that were a part of this man. Would he ever come to trust her enough to share his innermost feelings with her?

Eleven

It was late afternoon, and Briana, clad in her chemise and petticoat, had finished washing her hair in the basin beside the bed. She sat brushing the thick, red-gold waves over her shoulders, so that she would look her best when Devlin returned. She would wait up for him, no matter how late it might be before he came back to the ship.

At the sound of footsteps mounting the stairs to the quarterdeck she paused, then set down the brush. She rose, slipped into the wrapper she had brought with her in her carpetbag, and started for the door of Devlin's sleeping quarters, her heart quickening with anticipation.

Tommy had said he seldom came back to the ship until late at night, but now, contrary to his usual habits, he was returning early. Surely he, too, couldn't wait for them to be together again. Warmth flowed through her as she thought of the hours of shared passion and tenderness that lay ahead.

Her lips curved softly as she heard the outer door swing open, but her smile froze when she saw not Devlin, but Quinn, the first mate, standing there with his orange cat perched on his shoulder.

Quinn glanced at Briana in surprise, then cleared his throat.

"Didn't mean to come bargin' in on you like this, Miss Briana. I was lookin' for the captain." Obviously he hadn't expected to find her here in Devlin's quarters, clad only in her undergarments, covered by a sheer, lace-trimmed wrapper, with her hair tumbling about her shoulders.

Her face flushed, but she managed to meet his gaze. "Devlin went ashore early this morning, while I was still asleep," she said.

"Sorry, Miss Briana." The burly mate started for the door. "I'll come back later." Before he could leave the big orange tomcat jumped down from his shoulder and went padding across the floor to rub up against Briana's ankles.

She bent and stroked the cat's thick, soft fur. "There's no need to leave, Mr. Quinn," she said. "If you'll wait here, I'll join you in a few minutes. Do help yourself to the brandy while you're waiting, if you wish." She gestured toward the decanter on the sideboard.

Then she went into the sleeping compartment, followed by the cat, who stretched out on Devlin's bed and watched her as she changed from her wrapper to her gray silk gown and jacket, then quickly fastened her hair into a simple chignon.

Although she had been taken aback by Quinn's unexpected arrival, and disappointed at not seeing Devlin there instead, she wasn't ashamed of what had happened last night and she had no intention of trying to conceal their relationship. In any case, there would have been little use in trying now.

She fastened a few pins in her hair to keep the chignon in place and went to rejoin the first mate. When she entered the outer cabin, the cat stalking at her heels, Quinn was standing at the sideboard, holding a half-empty snifter of brandy in his huge hand. She seated herself on the sofa, and the cat sprang into her lap without the slightest hesitation.

"Here, Jigger!" Quinn said. "Mind your manners, you good-for-nothing rascal."

But the cat ignored him, curling up in Briana's lap. Quinn finished his brandy, an awkward silence growing between them.

Wanting to put the mate at ease, she forced herself to speak first. "I left my uncle's home last night. I couldn't stay there any longer." She didn't offer a reason for her sudden departure, but went on quickly, "I came aboard because I hoped that Devlin might give me passage back East. But he said he hadn't enough money to make the necessary repairs on the ship, and no means of hiring another crew. He told me he might have to sell the *Osprey*." She gave the mate a searching look. "You don't think he really would, do you?"

Quinn nodded. "I'm afraid I do. He don't want to let the ship go, that's for sure. Not after workin' aboard other men's vessels all these years. But like he told you, he's got no crew, an' knowin' him as well as I do, I doubt he'll leave her beached with her keel rotting in the mud 'til she turns into a useless hulk."

Briana hesitated, then spoke with a touch of uneasiness. "He said you wanted to hire some—crimps—and shanghai another crew."

Quinn shrugged. "I did. But Devlin wouldn't hear of it. An' I guess that didn't really surprise me. He has his own way of lookin' at such things, an' once he's made up his mind nothin' can budge him."

Since her first meeting with Devlin she had been plagued by many unanswered questions about his past. Here was her chance to find out something about the man who had come to mean everything to her. "You've known him a long time, haven't you, Mr. Quinn?"

The big man nodded. "That I have. We've made many a voyage together. Bristol to the West Indies, Salem to Hong Kong, the hellholes along the Ivory Coast—we've seen 'em all."

Although she felt guilty at prying, she couldn't stop herself. "Were you in Australia with him?"

"Not there—no."

Dread mingled with curiosity as she forced herself to continue. "But he spent some years in Australia, didn't he?"

"Devlin was born in New South Wales."

Her eyes widened in surprise, and she felt a deep sense of

relief surging through her. "Then he wasn't transported there from England—he isn't an ex-convict."

Quinn threw back his head and laughed. "Lord, no! Is that what you were thinkin', Miss Briana?"

"I had my suspicions," she admitted. "He's spoken of the conditions aboard the convict ships, more than once. And there was such bitterness in his voice."

"You thought he might have been transported to one of them penal colonies in Australia. And yet you trusted him enough to turn to him for help after you left your uncle's house." Quinn shook his head, obviously baffled, as always, by the strange ways of women. "You can put your mind at ease on that score, Miss Briana. Devlin never was a convict. But Liam Rafferty, his father, was an Irish rebel. Got himself transported for treason against the British government. Leastways the British called it treason. Me, I'm Irish, too, and as far as I'm concerned Devlin's father was a brave man, a patriot, fightin' for his country's freedom." He cleared his throat, aware that he had said more than he'd meant to. "I guess Devlin'll tell you all about himself when he's got a mind to."

"I'm not sure about that," she said, choosing her words with care. "Whenever I've asked him about his past he's put me off. He gets that closed look. It's as if he wanted to shut me out. And I have to know about him—the sort of man he really is."

Quinn drained his glass, set it down, and gave her a searching look. She thought she saw the same expression of sympathy in his eyes that she had seen in Tommy's, when she'd met the boy on deck that morning.

She forced herself to meet Quinn's eyes. "I'm not just prying out of idle curiosity. I have a right to know—now."

She was sure he understood her meaning well enough. "Guess maybe you do, at that. But Devlin—he don't like to think about how it was for him, when he was growin' up. Can't say I blame him."

"And why is that, Mr. Quinn?"

"He only talked about Australia to me that one time. Back

in Bristol, it was. We'd been without a ship for a few months, an' we were runnin' out of money. Livin' in a lice-ridden boardin'house on the waterfront, trampin' the docks, lookin' for a ship. Then he was offered a berth on a frigate bound for Australia, carryin' convicts. An' he said there was another berth aboard her for me. I couldn't hardly believe it when he came to the tavern where I was waitin' for him an' told me about the offer, an' then said he'd turned it down. I called him a damn fool—excuse me, Miss Briana.

"He said I could take a berth aboard the convict ship if I had a mind to. But he never would, not if he starved first. We emptied a couple of bottles, and then he started tellin' me about his father fightin' the British an' being tried for treason."

She leaned forward, determined to learn as much as she could while she had the chance. "And what about his mother? Was she a convict, too?"

"Lord, no! Not her. Miss Jessica Pendleton was a well-bred young lady. She was the daughter of the British colonel who commanded the convict settlement out there in New South Wales."

Briana leaned forward, wide-eyed, as Quinn went on to relate the brief, tragic story of Devlin's parents. In spite of all the barriers between them, they had been drawn to one another. They had fallen in love and risked everything to run away together, taking refuge in the barren wilderness beyond the settlement.

"They only had a few months together," Quinn said. "Then the colonel's troopers hunted them down and brought them back. Devlin's father was hanged. Later, his mother died giving birth to him. I guess his grandfather, Colonel Pendleton, never forgave Devlin for that."

Briana drew in her breath, growing hot with resentment at the injustice of it all. "Devlin's grandfather must have been a monster to blame an innocent child for what his parents did."

"He was a hard man, that's for sure. The sort they choose to run the penal colonies out there. An' he made Devlin's childhood a real hell, I know that much. Treated the boy as if he'd been one of the convicts. Punished him somethin' fierce. Devlin stood it until he was old enough to run away. Then he got himself a place as a cabin boy on a ship out of Sydney."

Briana sat listening in silence, her heart aching with pity for Devlin.

"Devlin's been on the move ever since he left Australia," Quinn was saying. "He'll never settle down anywhere, Miss Briana."

"How can you be so sure of that?" she protested. "Perhaps, one day, he'll have had enough of roaming the seas. He'll want a home, a place where he can feel he belongs."

Quinn shook his head. "He's got no ties with any country on the face of the earth. There was a girl once, in Boston. She was an innkeeper's daughter, young and pretty. Real fond of her, he was. I started thinkin' maybe he'd give up the sea for her. But he was offered command of a ship and he left her, like he's left all the others."

Briana couldn't conceal her dismay at this revelation. Handsome and virile as he was, Devlin must have had other women, many of them. But somehow she hadn't allowed herself to think of that—until now.

"Sorry, Miss Briana. But it's best you know."

"You're trying to warn me, aren't you?"

"Guess you might say that."

"He won't leave me." She spoke with conviction.

Not after the deep, all-consuming passion they had shared the night before. The tenderness and intimacy of their joining. "And he won't sell the ship, either. He'll find a way to get hold of another crew without going against his own standards; you'll see. And when he sails he'll take me with him."

"Maybe so," Quinn said slowly. "But don't you be countin' on it."

Although she tried to ignore his warning, she felt a rising uneasiness. The first mate had known Devlin far longer than she had. And Devlin had shared his past with Quinn, as he never had with her.

"Don't look so downcast, Miss Briana. There's some men in San Francisco who've struck it rich. An' a pretty young girl like you, ladylike an' all, won't have no trouble findin' herself a rich husband. A man who can build you a great big house up on Rincon Hill, maybe, with servants to wait on you hand and foot—like you're used to. You'll have fine ladies come callin' in their carriages to take tea with you."

She sprang to her feet so quickly that the cat scarcely had time to leap down from her lap. He fixed his round yellow eyes on her with a reproachful stare.

"I don't want a rich husband, a fine house. None of that matters. I only want—" She stopped short, startled by what she was feeling.

She wanted only one man: Devlin Rafferty. She stood in silence, stunned by the growing realization of the complete change in her. Her carefully laid plans for a respectable marriage and a place in good society; Mama's cherished hopes for her—she cast them aside without a trace of regret.

And all because of what had happened last night. In that brief, passionate interlude she had discovered that she and Devlin belonged together. Nothing, no one, could ever separate them.

She turned quickly as the cabin door swung open. As if summoned to her side by the depth of her emotions, Devlin was there, poised on the threshold. She responded to the sight of him with all her being. Her pulses speeded up and she felt a hot tingling racing through her as he strode to her side. He smiled down at her, then brushed a kiss across her lips. But there was something disturbingly casual in the gesture.

Before she could reach out to him he had already turned away to speak to Quinn. "Glad you're here," he said. He glanced at the empty glass on the sideboard. "I see you've started your drinking early. And why not? We'll have a drink all around." Although he was smiling, his teeth startlingly white against the deep tan of his face, Briana was sure she heard a forced heartiness in his tone.

"Suits me. What're we drinkin' to?" Quinn asked.

She saw the skin across Devlin's angular cheekbones tighten for an instant, and she sensed a lingering trace of regret in his gray eyes. Then he filled three glasses, took one for himself, and handed the other two to her and Quinn.

"A toast," said Devlin, raising his glass. "To the Rafferty Shipping Line."

"The Rafferty Shipping Line, is it? And what might that be?" Quinn's broad, weathered face furrowed with bewilderment.

"We'll have only one skiff to start with," Devlin said. "But as soon as we've made enough of a profit, taking our goods upriver and selling them to the miners, we'll be able to buy another."

"Slow down a bit. How do you figure on payin' for the first skiff?"

"That won't be a problem," Devlin assured him. "I got a good price for the *Osprey*."

Briana stared at him in disbelief. "You've sold your ship. But how—when—"

"As I told you last night, I've already had several offers for her. I decided there was no point in delaying any longer."

Her hand tightened around her glass. "When did you come to this decision?"

"This morning."

The morning after he had made love with her, while she still lay asleep, he was already making plans to get rid of the ship, to move on.

He took a sip of brandy. "I went to see the man who'd given the highest bid. He wants to open a fancy gambling house."

"Here aboard the *Osprey*?"

"It's not unheard of. The city council's making plans to fill in part of the cove." Whatever he might be feeling, his tone was matter-of-fact. "They're getting a steam excavator to level the dunes in Happy Valley, and a freight car to carry the earth where it's needed. Then they'll put down planks between the ships, to make the streets. But I'm not concerned with any of that. Now I have my money, I can go out looking for a skiff."

"The man who's buying the *Osprey* has already paid for the

ship?" Her voice was unsteady; she felt as if the cabin floor was shifting beneath her feet. Devlin had disposed of the *Osprey*, without a word to her.

Before she could gather her whirling thoughts Quinn was already asking, "You, me and Tommy, we're going to serve as the whole crew for this skiff you're talkin' about?"

"The three of us can handle her easily."

Briana set down her untouched glass and put a hand on his arm. The tightness in her throat was like a steel band. "You'll take me along?"

"I can't, Briana. You don't know what those mining camps are like," he said. He put his arm around her. "They're no place for a girl like you."

"You ain't just goin' to leave her here in San Francisco on her own!" Quinn said.

Devlin gave the mate a long, level look. "I've already made my inquiries," he said. "There'll be one of the Aspinwall ships going back East."

He turned to Briana and put a hand over hers. "I'll book passage to Charleston for you."

"Never!" she cried, her amber eyes locking with his. "I've told you why I can't go back there. I thought you understood."

Quinn bent, scooped up Jigger, and set the cat on his shoulder. "I'd best wait for you on deck," he said. Devlin nodded brusquely.

After the door had shut behind the first mate Devlin led her to the sofa, drew her down beside him, and put his arm around her waist. "By the time you return to Charleston I've no doubt the local busybodies will have found themselves a new scandal to cluck over."

"If you believe that, you don't know Charleston society. I'll always be thought of as the daughter of 'that Cameron woman.' And even if everyone else had forgotten, I never shall." She felt a coldness rise within her at the memory of Mama's limp body, the front of her lavender nightdress stained with blood.

"I won't go back there! I won't!"

His arm tightened around her. "Briana, try to understand

what I'm telling you. There's no way I can take a beautiful young girl to those camps upriver, full of woman-starved miners. You'd be nothing but trouble."

"Surely you're not afraid you wouldn't be able to protect me? You handled Jacko Muldoon easily enough, that first night of the voyage.

"That was different." She caught the impatience in his tone. "Now that I'm starting a shipping line of my own I'll have no time to spare for brawling with every swaggering river rat between here and Sacramento. Every mining camp bully who's hot for a quick tumble with a good-looking young female." Although he didn't raise his voice, he spoke with unshakable determination. "Accept what I'm telling you. You're going back to Charleston."

Her self-control gave way, and she spoke the first words that came to her lips. "Would you go back to Australia, even after all these years?"

She felt the muscles of his arm go iron hard and saw his gray eyes darken with barely leashed fury. "What the hell do you know about that?"

She longed to tell him all she had discovered about his past, but even now, as badly shaken as she was, she stopped herself. She didn't want him to turn his anger against Quinn.

"I won't go back to Charleston," she repeated, and now there was some measure of control in her tone. She set her jaw hard to keep it from trembling. He couldn't leave her. Somehow she had to convince him to take her along.

"Then how about Boston? I still have a few connections in Boston."

"The owner of a waterfront tavern, no doubt?" She hadn't forgotten what Quinn had said about Devlin's attraction to the innkeeper's daughter.

"I'm speaking of prosperous, respectable ship owners. You said last night that you might try to get a position as a governess."

She had said a great many things last night, but that was before he had taken her to his bed, before he had made love with her. They belonged together now. Nothing could separate them. Not even Devlin himself, with his insatiable wanderlust, his refusal to give all of himself to any woman.

"I'll provide you with suitable letters of reference," he went on. She recognized the iron determination in his voice and felt her heart sink. Was he so anxious to rid himself of her?

She wrenched herself away from his encircling arm and sprang to her feet. Her amber eyes narrowed and her body went taut with outraged pride. "I'm not one of your cargoes, to be shipped off to any port of call at your orders, Captain Rafferty! And you needn't concern yourself with my future. I'm quite capable of taking care of myself."

He rose and took her in his arms, holding her close. She felt his hand stroking her hair. "Briana, how can I make you understand?"

"I understand well enough," she said, struggling to keep back her tears. "You had all you wanted from me last night. Now you're ready to move on—just as you always have. How could I ever have expected anything more?"

He let her go and took a step back, then stood looking down at her. She saw the closed look on his face; the look she'd come to know so well. Once again he was withdrawing, shutting her out. "I made you no promises," he reminded her.

"And I asked for none." Although turmoil raged within her, she kept herself outwardly controlled. "Your conscience needn't trouble you. You've sold your ship; now buy yourself a skiff and take to the river. But as for me, I have no intention of leaving San Francisco."

"And how will you get along here?" he demanded. "Surely you don't want to go back to your uncle's house."

"I can't stay aboard the ship," she reminded him. "No doubt the new owner is eager to take possession."

She turned away, then walked swiftly into the sleeping cabin, where she gathered up her few belongings and pushed them into her carpetbag. Her hands were cold and trembled slightly, but somehow she managed the task.

Then she returned to the outer cabin.

He looked down at the carpetbag in her hand. "Just where do you think you're going?"

Without pausing to answer, she swept past him, her head high, her back straight. She flung open the door leading to the quarterdeck. Quinn was out there, leaning against the rail, his cat perched on his shoulder.

She started for the stairs, but Devlin moved to block her way. She tried to push past him, but he remained there, unmoving. "You're not leaving this ship until you tell me where you're going."

And indeed, she told herself, she couldn't go running off without any destination. She searched for some plausible solution to her immediate problem—finding a place to stay for the night. The light was already beginning to fade, and she could feel a chill dampness carried on the wind from the bay. She couldn't spend the night roaming the streets of the waterfront, but neither could she remain aboard the *Osprey*.

Cole Forrester. Could she possibly go to him, explain her predicament, and ask him to help her?

But no sooner had the thought crossed her mind than she dismissed it. The last time she had seen Cole he had been going to stay with Martin Padgett and his daughter Eleanor. That had been weeks ago, and she hadn't heard from him since. She had no way of knowing whether he was still a guest of the Padgetts, and she certainly didn't think Eleanor would welcome her with open arms. She hadn't forgotten Eleanor's possessive attitude toward Cole.

Devlin stood towering over her, and it was plain that he had no intention of letting her go until he was satisfied as to her destination. "I'll go to see Poppy at the Black Pearl," she told him.

He stared at her as if he thought she had taken leave of her senses. "You can't go there. Don't you know what a concert saloon is?"

"Poppy told me all about it. She dances on the stage and she sings, too."

"But you, my dear, are no performer. Or maybe you'll ask for work as a waitress. One of those 'pretty waitress girls'; that's what they're called on the sign outside the saloon."

"I suppose I can carry a tray and serve drinks if I have to." The idea was far from appealing, but she realized that, for the present, she might have little choice.

"Those waitress girls have to do a lot more than serve drinks," he told her. "There are curtained booths along the sides of the room, where a girl can take any man who wants her. Once she's inside, and the curtains are closed, the customer can do whatever he likes with her." His words and the look that accompanied them sent a wave of revulsion swirling through her. She remembered her terrifying encounter with Enoch in her uncle's parlor. She would be forced to endure far worse if she was to work as a waitress at the Black Pearl.

"I didn't know—"

"Now you do. So maybe you'll calm down and listen to reason. The *Osprey*'s new owner isn't going to take over for a few weeks. By then I'll see that you're on a ship headed for Boston."

"Damn you, Devlin Rafferty! I told you that you're not running my life, and I meant it. I'm staying here in San Francisco. Tonight I'll go and talk to Poppy. Surely she can help me find lodgings for a few nights. Meanwhile I'll look for a position as a clerk in a store."

"And if you can't find work in a store, what then?" His eyes were storm-gray, and for a moment she thought he might seize hold of her and carry her back to his cabin.

"I'll manage on my own." Even as she spoke she took renewed hope from his concern. He did care what became of her; otherwise why would he keep her here and question her so closely? Perhaps she could persuade him to change his mind; to take her upriver with him aboard his trading skiff when he was ready to sail.

"Maybe you can take care of yourself," he said. "You're certainly stubborn enough to try." Her burgeoning hope quickly faded. He reached into his pocket and offered her a couple of folded bills.

Her cheeks flamed with humiliation as she tried to push his hand away. "If you think I'll take your money in return for—"

"This is for your cab fare, and a room for the night. If you can find one," he said.

He forced the bills into her hand and closed her fingers around them. "It's getting late," he went on. "You can't go walking all the way across the city. This time you might not find an obliging peddler to give you a ride."

She wanted to fling his money back at him, but even now, shaken as she was, her common sense told her that he was right. No matter what her destination, she would be safer in a hired buggy. "There's a livery stable down there." He pointed toward a rickety wooden building not far off.

She thrust the bills into the pocket of her jacket. "I'll go with you an' hire you a buggy, Miss Briana," Quinn offered.

"That won't be necessary. I'm perfectly capable of taking care of myself." Although she spoke to Quinn, her words were intended for Devlin. He stepped aside. She lifted her full skirts and went swiftly down the steps to the main deck. She dared not pause, not for an instant, or she feared she might forget her pride. She might go running back to Devlin and plead with him to take her along when he went upriver.

Even when she was seated on the worn leather seat of the shabby hired buggy she had to fight against her need to return to the ship and to the man who stood on the quarterdeck. Was he watching her departure, or were he and Quinn already deep in conversation about their new venture?

The driver turned his head. "Where to, miss?"

Briefly she considered the possibility of returning to her uncle's house. No—that would be impossible. Even if Uncle Alexander didn't beat her for having run away, he would surely do so if she refused to marry Enoch. His reason for insisting on the marriage was plain enough; miser that he was, he relished the idea of having two clerks for the price of one.

The driver repeated his question, with a touch of impatience. "Where to?"

"Take me to—" she paused, her determination wavering for a moment, as she remembered Devlin's warning. She certainly had no intention of asking for work as a waitress, but no doubt Poppy would at least offer some suggestion as to where Briana might find a night's lodging. "To the Black Pearl—I'm not sure where it is, but I know it's a concert saloon."

She caught the driver's stare of surprise and disapproval. "I know what it is and how to get there," he said. "You sure that's where you want to go?"

"I'm sure." Although she hadn't seen Poppy since Aunt Gertrude had ordered the girl from the house, Briana was confident that her friend would try to help her.

The cab moved forward. In spite of her firm resolve she couldn't keep from turning once more, to catch a glimpse of the *Osprey*. The tall masts and sleek hull were blurred by the rising mist; pearls of moisture clung to the rigging. She was free now to give way to tears, but she could only sit in silence, numb with grief, as she watched the ship disappear from view.

Twelve

Briana, her carpetbag at her feet, braced herself and clutched the buggy's seat as the vehicle went jouncing along the rutted streets of the Barbary Coast. It came to a stop before a long, low building; by the light of a flaring gas lamp over the swinging doors she made out the name painted on the gilt sign. THE BLACK PEARL.

She handed the driver his fare and tried to ignore his curious stare. She hadn't wanted to come down here, and certainly not after dark, but she had to see Poppy.

She descended from the buggy, carpetbag in hand, then lifted her gray silk skirt to keep the hem from the mud-spattered wooden planks. There was no turning back now. She set her jaw and made her way through the swinging doors of the concert saloon.

No sooner had she stepped inside than her spirits plummeted; it was impossible for her to put Devlin's warning out of her mind. Her gaze moved over the room. It was even more disreputable than she had feared.

On the small stage, a row of dancers in low-cut black bodices and short red skirts kicked their legs high in the air. They whirled about, turned their backs on the audience, and lifted their skirts over their ample rumps to display their ruffled drawers to the men, who cheered lustily. The off-key thump of the piano, the shrill squealing of the fiddle, competed with the raucous shouts of the all-male audience. The miners pounded on the table with their beer mugs and whiskey glasses. Briana's cheeks burned as she overheard a few of their lewd remarks.

She turned her face away, then caught sight of the staircase leading to the balcony above. Sure enough, there were the booths Devlin had told her about; they were curtained in red velvet heavily fringed with gilt trimmings. Although it was early in the evening, the "waiter girls" already were doing a lively business; they led their customers up the stairs, giggling and pressing their scantily clad bodies against the men, who were already pawing at them, as if unable to wait until they reached the seclusion of the booths.

Tense with mounting anxiety, Briana drew her eyes away and looked about the room. Already a few of the customers were staring at her with undisguised interest. She had to find Poppy, and quickly. Since her friend wasn't on the stage, she might be in a dressing room, preparing for her entrance.

But when the dancers finished their performance and scrambled about, shoving and jostling one another, to gather up the nuggets the audience tossed onto the stage, after they hurried down to mingle with the customers, Poppy was still nowhere to be seen. A tall, skinny man in a green and purple striped suit came swaggering onto the stage and started singing an obscene ballad about a drunken sailor and the captain's daughter.

Briana cast a desperate look back at the swinging doors; she wanted to turn and run from the room, with its thick blue haze of cigar smoke, its overpowering stench of spilled beer and whiskey, unwashed clothes and perspiring male bodies. It surely would have been better had she waited until the following afternoon to come here seeking her friend. But she would have had to spend another night aboard the *Osprey*. Another night with Devlin.

But she wouldn't let herself think about him. She had to concentrate on finding Poppy. Surely Poppy would agree to share her living quarters for a few nights. What sort of lodging house was Poppy living in? She suspected it would be difficult for a girl on her own to find a respectable home in the city. No matter—it shouldn't take longer than a few days for her to find work in a store like her uncle's.

"You, there." One of the dancing girls, a round-faced blonde, pushed her way through the crowd, heading straight for Briana. The girl's large breasts, white with rice powder, spilled over the top of her sleazy satin bodice. She looked Briana up and down with an air of hostility.

"What're you doin' in here?" Without giving Briana time to answer she went on, "Jack O'Keefe don't want no outsiders comin' in here, takin' his customers from his own girls. If you know what's good for you, you'll be on your way. And make it fast."

The blonde's meaning was plain enough, but although Briana went hot with resentment at the implication, she didn't back off; she hadn't come this far only to be turned away before she got a chance to talk to Poppy.

"I'm not looking for—customers," she said.

The blonde's eyes moved over Briana with a dubious expression. "If you're after work as a waiter girl, you're wastin' your time. You ain't got enough meat on your bones, and besides—"

"I'm not looking for work here. I've come to see Poppy Nolan," she interrupted.

The other girl shook her head. "You won't find her here—not tonight."

"But she told me she works here."

"Not anymore she don't. She quit a few days ago. Went off with a gent who's openin' a real theater in Sacramento. Jack O'Keefe wanted her to stay. He even offered her more money, but she turned him down flat."

Briana's fingers tightened around the handle of her carpetbag. A wave of despair washed over her, leaving her weak and shaken. She hadn't even considered the possibility that Poppy might no longer be here. What was she to do now? She couldn't spend the night roaming the dangerous streets of the Barbary Coast.

"You a friend of Poppy's?" The blonde's air of hostility had disappeared; now she eyed Briana curiously, taking in her gray silk dress. Although it was clumsily mended and stained with mud at the hem, it was perfectly fitted and obviously expensive.

"Poppy and I came to San Francisco together," Briana explained. "We shared a cabin aboard—a clipper ship." She couldn't bring herself to speak the name of the *Osprey*; she didn't want to think about the ship, which Devlin had sold, so that it might be turned into a gambling house. Or about Devlin, who was already completely involved in his plans to leave San Francisco.

"Oh, sure—you must be Briana. My name's Hortense." Hortense's brightly rouged lips curved in a wide smile. "So you're the one Poppy told us about. You gave her that gorgeous costume, didn't you?"

She regarded Briana with growing interest, then took her by

the hand and led her to a nearby table. Her legs were shaky, and she sank down gratefully in the seat opposite the plump blonde.

"That outfit was really something special, let me tell you. It did a lot for her. Not that Poppy ain't a good dancer, no matter what she's wearin'. And she's got a good shape, I got to admit it. But if it hadn't been for that dress with all them shiny sequins and flowers, she mightn't have caught that gent's eye the other night. He was real high-toned. Called himself a theatrical im—imper—"

"Impresario?" Briana suggested.

"That's right! Anyhow, I think it was the dress that done it for Poppy. From now on she'll be dancin' in a real theater—not a dive like this."

Hortense leaned across the table, and Briana caught the musky scent of her patchouli perfume. "You know somethin'," she said. "If I could get me a costume like hers, one that'd make the men sit up and take notice, I'll bet I could talk Jack O'Keefe into givin' me the top spot on the bill. An' maybe someday I could get to dance in a high-toned theater myself."

She ran her plump hand over her sleazy black bodice, a look of disdain in her pale blue eyes. "A girl can't make the most of herself in a getup like this one. It wasn't nothin' special, even when it was new. And wearin' it every night, like I do, it'll look like an old rag soon."

She gave Briana an ingratiating smile. "Poppy told us a lot about you. She said you sailed from Charleston to San Francisco with a load of trunks, all of them filled with fancy dresses from Paris. Look, if you'd sell me one of those outfits, I could pay you real good."

"You tryin' to get yourself a fancy dress like Poppy's?" Briana turned and saw another dancer, who had paused beside the table to eavesdrop on their conversation.

"What's it to you, Millie?" Hortense demanded.

"I'd like to buy one for myself, that's what. I got a fistful of nuggets—guess they're as good as yours."

And before Briana knew quite how it had happened, the small

table was surrounded by the other dancers, all of them clamoring for her attention.

"There's been another big strike, up Hangtown way."

"The miners who've struck it rich have been real free-handed with their gold."

"I'd like to have a green satin, if you got one. With lots of lace."

One of the girls reached into her bodice and, from between her ample breasts, drew out a bulging deerskin poke. "I got plenty of gold dust in here," she said. "How much you askin' for one of them fancy dresses, miss?"

Briana stared from one dancer to another; taken completely by surprise by this unforeseen turn of events. Before she had left the *Osprey*, she had assured Devlin that she could take care of herself, and she had meant it. But her expectations had been modest; she had hoped only to find work as a clerk in a store like her uncle's. She had been resigned to long hours of hard, monotonous toil, at a salary that would barely cover her living expenses.

Now, as the girls kept up their clamor, she felt a swiftly rising hope. If she could sell even a few of the dresses she had brought with her, she would have enough to pay her expenses for the immediate future.

"How about it, Briana?" Hortense urged.

She started to speak, then hesitated, seized by the sudden realization that it might not be easy to get her trunks back. "I don't have the dresses, not with me," she said cautiously. "I left them stored away at my uncle's house on Pacific Street."

Even as she spoke she remembered the anger in her uncle's long, bony face as he had stood over her, his leather belt gripped in his hand. He and Gertrude would be even more furious with her now, after she had defied them, run away, and spoiled their plans for her marriage to Enoch. She could just imagine the uproar that must have shaken the walls of the house when they had awakened to find her gone.

The grim prospect of confronting the irate pair, of demanding the return of her trunks, sent icy darts of panic racing through her. But if she was to get her possessions back, what other choice did she have? She certainly couldn't slip into the house unseen, remove those heavy trunks, and carry them off by herself.

"What's it goin' to be?" one of the girls demanded. "Can you get us them dresses or not?"

For a moment she remained silent, torn with indecision. Then she stood up quickly. If she was to take advantage of this wholly unexpected opportunity, she would have to overcome her misgivings and take action, before she lost her nerve.

"I'll get you the dresses."

"Tonight?" Hortense asked, her eyes shining with anticipation. "Can you get them tonight?"

"Yes, I can. I'll bring them back here before midnight." She hoped she sounded more confident than she felt.

Swiftly she left the table and moved through the noisy, crowded room. She was scarcely aware that she had caught the attention of the men drinking at the tables, until she heard them calling out to her.

"Wait a minute, can't ye, honey?"

"What's yer hurry? Sit yerself down here with me. I'll show you a good time."

"Don't listen to him. I'll buy you a bottle of champagne. Best in the house. We'll go upstairs an' make a night of it."

A large, heavy hand touched her thigh, but she brushed it away. She was running now, her skirt swaying around her, her carpetbag clutched in her hand, as she headed straight for the doors. She pushed her way out and onto the wooden walk in front of the saloon, giving a deep sigh of relief, then paused to get her bearings. The swirling fog had grown thicker now, so that the gas lamps were blurred circles of light, dancing and shimmering before her eyes.

She dared not try to make her way to her uncle's house on foot. Last night she had been lucky enough to meet the good-natured peddler, Jacob Perlman, but she knew it was most unlikely that she would have another such stroke of fortune. If only she had told the driver of the hired buggy to wait for her.

She took a step forward on the slippery, uneven planks, lost her footing, and collided with a dark figure who came looming up out of the fog.

"Pardon me, miss." It was a man's voice, soft and cultured, and it sounded oddly familiar. He put out his hand to steady her and started to move on; then she heard the sharp intake of his breath. He stood still for a moment, peering down at her. "Good Lord! It's Briana!"

She tilted her head and found herself looking up into the face of Cole Forrester. He studied her closely by the light of the lamp beside the gilt sign that swung overhead. Then he swept off his tall hat and bowed. "I scarcely expected to meet you down here—and after dark."

She might have said the same to him. What business would bring a gentleman like Cole Forrester to the Barbary Coast at this hour of the night?

When he spoke again he had regained his customary self-possession. If he had seen her running out of the Black Pearl, he didn't make any mention of it. "May I be of assistance?" he asked.

Although he didn't question her, as to her presence in this notorious district, she felt she had to offer some explanation. "I'm—on my way to my uncle's house. I hadn't realized how late it was. . . ."

"Let me find you a cab."

Perhaps she should refuse his help; she couldn't forget that he had made no effort to see her during the many weeks she had lived with her aunt and uncle. Even now she felt a pang of wounded pride at the memory of his neglect. But her sense of self-preservation was stronger than her outraged sensibilities. "That would be most kind," she said.

He stepped off the plank walkway and into the fog. After a brief wait he caught sight of a cab that had stopped before a gambling house to discharge its passengers. He raised his malacca walking stick and called out to the driver.

Then he led Briana to the waiting cab.

"Where to, mister?"

Cole didn't reply at once. Try as he might, he couldn't take his eyes from Briana. She was even more beautiful, more desirable than he remembered.

Although he hadn't come calling on her since he had taken leave of her at Cameron's Emporium, he had thought of her often. But he had told himself that, no matter how strongly attracted to her he had been during the voyage, it wouldn't be in his best interest to call on a girl who lived on the Barbary Coast.

And then, too, there was Eleanor. She had never made any secret of her warm feelings toward him. After a few nights spent as a guest of the Padgetts, he had moved to a suite at the Tehama House, at the corner of California and Sansome streets. One of the city's few fashionable hotels, its verandas and colonnades gave it a somewhat Southern appearance.

But Eleanor, in the most ladylike way possible, had continued to show her interest. She had deluged him with invitations to dinner, and to the musicales, parties, and afternoon teas that now were becoming popular with the upper-class society in San Francisco. He had enjoyed her company, for she was pretty and well-bred, and a definite asset to him in his unswerving desire for advancement. Although he was a partner in the respected law firm of Padgett and Forrester, he hadn't wavered in his determination to enter the political arena when a suitable opportunity presented itself.

But now, as he stood in the silvery fog with Briana, Cole was stirred by the same powerful attraction he had felt for her during their visit to Havana. The wavering light from the carriage lamp flickered over the soft waves of her burnished red hair and accented the delicate features of her oval face. When she looked up at him, her amber eyes shaded by dark, curving lashes, he felt a hot stir of physical need.

Eleanor, pretty and charming though she was, had never once awakened such raw, primitive emotions within him.

He should help Briana into the cab and then allow her to go out of his life. He shouldn't make any attempt to take up their shipboard friendship again. That would be the sensible course, and he had always prided himself on his realistic outlook. But instead he heard himself saying, "May I accompany you to your uncle's home, Briana?"

Before she could refuse his gloved hand was firmly cupped beneath her elbow. He helped her onto the seat, then, without further hesitation, climbed in beside her and gave the driver the address.

Although he didn't question her as to the reason for her errand to the concert saloon, she felt that she had to contrive some sort of explanation. Knowing what she now did about the Black Pearl, she couldn't permit him to think she worked in such a place. But neither could she tell him everything that had happened to her since he had left her to drive off with Eleanor Padgett.

She couldn't speak to him—to anyone—about the hours she had shared with Devlin aboard the *Osprey* last night.

In spite of her determination to put Devlin out of her mind, his image rose up before her in the dimly lit carriage. His silver-gray eyes, his hard, angular features. And his tall, powerful body. She trembled inwardly, for even now she could feel the urgency of his arms tightening around her, the pressure of his hard-muscled thighs against her body. His fingers, stroking her bare flesh. An overpowering longing, hot and honeysweet, stirred deep inside her, went spreading through her. Devlin . . .

She might have spent another night, even another few weeks, aboard his ship. She might have given herself to him again, and gloried in the wonder of his loving. But that would have changed nothing; he would have left her as soon as the time came for him to take to the river.

She pressed her lips together and stared, unseeing, at the maze of streets and alleys beyond the carriage window.

"Briana." She heard Cole speak her name. "Are you all

right?" Was it possible that her emotions had been reflected in her eyes?

"Certainly. That is—"

"Do your aunt and uncle know where you were tonight?"

She shook her head, then folded her hands in her lap. "I left my uncle's home without telling him I was going," she began. "There were reasons why I couldn't stay there any longer."

"But why did you go to the Black Pearl?"

"I had hoped that Poppy Nolan might agree to share her lodgings with me until I could find work. But Poppy's gone off to Sacramento."

Her explanation seemed to satisfy Cole—at least for the moment.

"I should suppose your uncle's home wasn't at all what you had expected when you set out from Charleston."

"It was most—disagreeable." She chose her words cautiously, determined to tell him no more than was absolutely necessary. She wanted him on her side; it occurred to her now that he might be of help when she had to confront her aunt and uncle. "To live in such a dreadful part of the city was bad enough. But if my aunt and uncle had shown me the least family feeling or kindness, it might have been bearable."

"But they offered you a home; surely they must have felt some concern for your welfare."

Her face hardened. "So I thought. But I found out soon enough the reason why they sent for me."

"And that was?"

"My uncle is a miser," she said. That much, at least, was the plain truth. "He needed extra help in the store. I worked for my room and board."

Should she tell him about the revolting incident with Enoch? She thought for a moment, then decided against it. But she had to offer some reason for her running away. "Uncle Alexander is a cold, harsh taskmaster. And my aunt is a shrew."

"And yet you're going back to them now."

"Not to stay," she assured him quickly. "Only to fetch my

trunks. I left quickly, you see, with no more than I could carry in this carpetbag."

She held her breath, waiting. Mercifully, he didn't ask where she had spent the previous night.

"Some time ago I gave Poppy one of my gowns," she went on. "Tonight, Hortense—a dancer at the Black Pearl—offered to buy one of the others. And some of the other girls want new gowns, too."

Cole leaned closer and took her hand. "Briana—surely you're not being forced to sell your clothing in order to survive."

"It's a perfectly honest way of earning a little money."

"But since your uncle sent for you I'd say he's obliged to provide for you."

"I wouldn't take his money, even if he offered it. I can take care of myself. Since there is such a great demand for the dresses I brought with me, I should be able to make enough to keep me until I can find respectable work.

"You mean to go into the business of selling dresses?"

"I hadn't thought of it as a business, exactly," she admitted. "Only as a means of raising a little money for the time being. Besides, I'm not at all sure Uncle Alexander will turn over my trunks."

"Why not?"

"I left without his permission." She tensed at the thought of the coming encounter. "He'll be furious with me."

"Maybe so, but he can't keep you from taking back your possessions."

"You don't know my uncle."

"I know the law," he reminded her. "It's my profession, remember?" His fingers pressed her hand tighter, and he gave her a reassuring smile. "Don't worry. We'll get those trunks for you."

"So this is what you've been up to, you shameless trollop!" Gertrude, wrapped in a flannel bathrobe, stood in the parlor, at the foot of the stairs, confronting Cole and Briana. "You've been carrying on with your fine friend here." She gave a snort of contempt, her shrill voice echoing through the thin walls of the house.

"Marrying Enoch wasn't good enough for you, was it? But you were willing enough to sell yourself to a gentleman with fancy airs and graces." Her eyes swept over Cole, taking in every detail of his elegant attire. "I'll bet he paid you well for your services." She advanced on Briana, her eyes hard with dislike. "Your uncle always said that mother of yours was no better than she should be. And I can see you're no different."

Cole stepped in front of Briana "You've said quite enough, Mrs. Cameron. As it happens, I met your niece by chance less than an hour ago."

"So you say." Her voice rose, harsh and accusing. "But knowing the girl as I do—"

"What's going on down here?" Uncle Alexander came stalking down the stairs. He hadn't yet dressed for bed. Probably he had been going over the ledgers, as he did every night before retiring.

"So you've come crawling back here, miss. And I suppose you expect me to take you in, after you went junketing off at night." His eyes moved to Cole. "And who might you be, mister?"

"He's the girl's gentleman friend. He's the one who brought her here in a carriage, the day her ship docked."

"Your niece and I made the voyage from Charleston aboard the same ship." He ignored Gertrude and fixed a cool look on Alexander. "She has no intention of coming back to live with the two of you. She's returned only to collect her trunks." He gave Alexander a hard stare. "You will have them brought down at once."

"Don't you go giving me orders in my own home," her uncle began, but Cole cut him short.

"You will return your niece's property or I will take legal measures to see that you do so."

"Legal measures, is it?" Her uncle's long, thin face turned brick red.

"Mr. Forrester is a lawyer," Briana told her uncle.

Now her uncle gave Cole a wary look.

"Surely you don't wish to become involved in a drawn-out legal dispute, Mr. Cameron." Cole's tone was smooth, even amiable, but he kept his gaze locked with Alexander's. "A dispute that could prove expensive for you, as I'm sure you realize."

Alexander reared back, as if confronted by a rattlesnake. In spite of the unpleasant circumstances in which she found herself, Briana had all she could do to suppress a smile. Cole had sized up her uncle quickly enough and had hit on the most effective means of persuasion.

But Alexander wasn't prepared to give in easily. "I gave the girl a home. A *respectable* home. We treated her like our own daughter."

"You put her to work in your store and paid her nothing for her services," Cole cut in. "She owes you nothing. Now you're trying to withhold her property. That could be construed as theft, Mr. Cameron."

Alexander's face darkened, as if he might be about to have a fit of apoplexy.

"I'd advise you to settle the matter, here and now," Cole said. "If you agree, I am prepared to pay for a couple of wagons to carry the trunks away. Otherwise you'll be responsible for the freight charges."

"Freight charges—a couple of wagons—" Alexander sputtered. He clamped his lips together and tried to outstare his opponent, but Briana saw that he was giving way.

"Gertrude, you run across the alley and wake up Enoch. He'll carry down the trunks while I go get the wagons from the livery stable." He turned on Briana. "As for you, miss, you can take yourself out of here, right now."

Briana raised her head and gave Alexander a long, cool look. "Gladly," she said. She returned to the waiting buggy.

Her aunt's shrill voice echoed after her. "That girl's headed for perdition—you mark my words—"

The two wagons, laden with Briana's trunks, came to a halt in front of the Black Pearl. Cole helped her down from the buggy, but even as he was paying the driver, Hortense and the other girls, who had been watching for her return, came hurrying out of the concert saloon. Before the teamsters could even start to unload the wagons, the girls were clambering up to look over the contents of the trunks.

"Open them! Let's see what you've got."

"I want one with sequins like Poppy's."

"Do you have a pink one, with lots of lace?"

"What the devil's going on here?" A deep male voice silenced the girls, but only for a moment.

"We're goin' to buy ourselves some fancy new outfits like Poppy's, that's what," said Hortense.

"This here's the lady who gave Poppy that costume. She's got lots more."

"It'll be good for business, Jack—you'll see."

"I'll handle this," Cole said. He stepped forward to confront a stocky, muscular man wearing a heavy mustache.

"Mr. O'Keefe." Cole nodded to the other man. "Sorry for the disturbance."

"Evenin', Mr. Forrester," O'Keefe said. "Would you mind telling me what this is all about?"

"Your young ladies wish to purchase a few gowns from Miss Cameron," he said. "She was obliging enough to bring the trunks down here."

"Obliging my—" O'Keefe shot a glance at Briana. "My foot," he amended quickly. "This is no outdoor marketplace. I'm running a business, and your Miss Cameron's blocking traffic. And keeping the girls from their work."

Cole's eyes hardened. "That wasn't Miss Cameron's intention. She was trying to do your employees a favor."

A crowd of idlers had begun to gather, completely obstructing the entrance to the concert saloon. Streetwalkers, gamblers, and pickpockets slowed down to see what was going on.

"Sorry, Mr. Forrester," O'Keefe said, "but the young lady will have to do her selling someplace else." He grinned at Briana. "Maybe you can rent a store. Looks like you'd do a good business."

Briana stood still, taking in his words. A store of her own. She felt a surge of excitement coursing through her.

O'Keefe's suggestion had caught her off-balance. But why not? Her thoughts moved swiftly as she considered the possibilities. She had gained experience in keeping a store during the time she had worked for her uncle. She had wanted to take a corner of her uncle's store for a ladies' department, but he had dismissed her ideas as unworthy of consideration.

A store of her own. Not a general store, like Cameron's Emporium, but a tastefully decorated shop that would sell only ladies' apparel.

Hadn't Poppy told her there were few stores in the city that sold fashionable gowns? And the owners of those few that did weren't anxious to cater to women of dubious reputation. They were afraid that girls like Poppy and Hortense would drive away their respectable customers.

But Briana wasn't troubled by such concerns. So long as the girls from the Black Pearl and the other concert saloons could pay for the merchandise, she was prepared to serve them.

This wasn't at all what she had planned when she left Charleston and came to San Francisco. It was a far cry from Mama's dreams of luxury and social status for her daughter. But she was here on her own, and here she would stay.

Thirteen

The sails of the trim skiff *Monterey* caught the early morning breeze, and she moved swiftly along the mist-shrouded Sacramento River, between the steep banks lined with oaks, sycamores, and fragrant pines; the hills beyond were thick with chaparral and manzanita. Devlin, standing at the wheel, surveyed his new vessel with satisfaction. She had already brought him luck, for he had made an excellent profit at the two camps along the way; the miners had exchanged their nuggets for the onions, potatoes, coffee, beans, bacon, sugar, cheese, whiskey, heavy iron skillets and kettles, shovels, blankets, boots, canvas pants, and flannel shirts.

Although the river still ran high from the snowmelt of last winter, it wasn't difficult for him to handle the small craft with the help of Quinn and Tommy. He had needed a crew of twenty-five to man the *Osprey*.

His lips set tightly, he tried not to think about the clipper, but it was no use. She lay beached in Yerba Buena Cove, but now her decks were swarming with the workmen hired to make the elaborate and costly renovations that would change her from a seagoing vessel to a land-locked gambling house.

He had promised himself that he wouldn't set foot on the *Osprey* again, ever. He didn't want to see her bound to the shore, stripped of her sails, her tall masts cut down, her bulkheads moved to make room for the gambling saloon. The new owner had spoken of his plans for decorating the huge room with thick Turkish carpets, crystal chandeliers, gilt-framed paintings, and a long, polished mahogany bar. "You'll be welcome aboard anytime, Captain," the new owner had said. "Roulette, faro, poker, blackjack—you can take your pick."

Devlin fixed his eyes on the bend in the river, peering into the mist for the first glimpse of Gila Flats. It wouldn't be long before he reached the camp and started unloading his cargo.

"Here's your coffee, Cap'n." He turned, nodded at Tommy, and took the steaming mug from the boy's hand.

"You want me to start bringin' the goods up here on deck?"

"There'll be time enough for that, after we've dropped anchor."

The boy looked up eagerly, still relishing this new venture.

"What do you think the camp'll be like?" he asked.

Devlin shrugged. "Same as all the rest. Tents, a canvas gambling shed, and maybe a cribhouse with a couple of Peruvian girls."

"Then I guess it's as well Miss Briana didn't come along. These mining camps ain't no fit places for a lady like her."

Devlin kept his eyes on the winding course of the river. The mist was starting to lift now, and the ripples sparkled in the first rays of the rising sun.

"I hope Miss Briana's doin' all right back in San Francisco. You figure she found work by now, Captain?"

"Briana can take care of herself." Devlin was trying to convince himself, as well as Tommy. "I offered to get her passage to Boston. She went off on her own because that's the way she wanted it."

The boy hesitated, startled by the captain's harsh rejoinder. He scuffed his bare foot on the scrubbed deck, then blurted out. "But what she really wanted was to come with us. She asked you to take her along, just before she left the *Osprey*, an' you said no. You said—"

"At least she's not workin' at the Black Pearl." Devlin turned to see Quinn, who had come up from the hold with Jigger balanced on his shoulder. Although he didn't want to go on talking about Briana, he couldn't help himself; he needed to know that she was all right.

"How do you know?" he asked Quinn.

"I went down to the saloon just before we sailed, and one of them dancin' girls told me so."

"You talked to Poppy Nolan?"

Quinn shook his head. "Poppy's gone off to Sacramento."

Devlin's shoulders tensed, and he gripped the wheel tighter. Although Poppy wasn't exactly the kind of girl he would have chosen to look out for Briana, the two of them had become close friends during the time they'd shared the cabin aboard the *Osprey*. He had assumed that Poppy would take care of her until she could find respectable work; in a shop, maybe.

He didn't want to admit his concern, but he had to know more. "Briana's not working in that damn concert saloon, is she?"

"You should know her better than that." He cleared his throat and stared out at the riverbank. "I figure she'll do all right, now she's got Cole Forrester lookin' out for her."

His remark caught Devlin off guard. "Forrester! What makes you think she's with him?"

"Because that dancin' girl, Hortense, told me so. A big, good-lookin' blonde, she is. An' built like a brick—"

"What about Briana?"

"That's what I'm tryin' to tell you," the first mate went on patiently. "I would've said somethin' sooner, but every time I mentioned Miss Briana you said you didn't want to talk about her."

"I do now."

"Right after Miss Briana left the *Osprey* she went straight to the Black Pearl, an' when she found out Poppy'd left I guess she was shook up real bad. Anyhow, she left the saloon, that's what Hortense said. Then, awhile later, back she came, ridin' in a buggy with Forrester. They had a couple of wagons followin', with all her trunks. Them saloon girls were for buying some of them fancy clothes from her then an' there. But out come Jack O'Keefe—he's the fella that owns the place—an' he said—"

"Never mind O'Keefe." Devlin was startled by the hot jealousy that ripped through him on hearing that it had been For-

rester who had come along to help her. "I want to know why
you think Forrester's—looking after Briana."

"Because he took her to the Tehama House, the hotel where
he's been stayin', that's why." His broad, weathered face impassive, Quinn went on to tell him what else he had learned from
Hortense during his visit to the Black Pearl. "O'Keefe wouldn't
let Miss Briana sell her clothes in front of his place because
her wagons were blockin' the street, keepin' his customers from
gettin' inside. He said somethin' about, why didn't she open a
dress shop. And that's what she's gone and done. She rented a
place over on Sansome Street."

Briana had a shop of her own. But how was that possible?
He'd given her a little money; enough to take care of her immediate needs, but not what she would have needed to rent a shop.

How had she managed to raise that much cash? The answer
was plain enough: Cole Forrester must have set her up in business. And, in return, she had moved into his hotel. Into his bed.

Devlin felt his insides twist into a hard knot.

No, it wasn't true. It couldn't have happened that way. Another woman might have made such an exchange, but not Briana. Never Briana.

He tried to keep his full attention fixed on the curving river
ahead, but it was no use; even as he steered the skiff between
the sloping banks, he was seeing Briana, her amber eyes, deep
and unfathomable, watching him by the light of the lantern
above his bed. And now he was feeling the silken heat of her
pliant body in his arms, her nipples hardening against his chest.

He was remembering how her first reluctance had given way
to her awakening need. Her long legs had wrapped around his
hips, drawing him closer. And when, at last, he had lost all re-
straint, had thrust deep inside her, the warm moisture of her
woman's sheath had enclosed him. She had been ready, more
than ready, had held nothing back. Had given herself completely,
with a shattering intensity that had matched his own. Heat went
flooding through him at the memory of their night together.

Then it ebbed away, to be replaced by harsh self-reproach.

The next day he had let her go out of his life; had made it plain that there could be no future for them. She hadn't pleaded with him to change his mind; her pride wouldn't have allowed her to do that. But he had seen the unhappiness in her eyes. And he had chosen to ignore it.

What right had he to expect her to go into seclusion; to wait for him? He had made her no promises; had given her no reason to believe that he would come looking for her when he returned. He had pressed a couple of bills into her hand and allowed her to go walking down the gangplank and into the thickening fog of the waterfront.

How badly shaken she must have felt, when she had gone looking for Poppy, only to find that her friend was gone. Why the hell shouldn't she have turned to Cole Forrester for help?

Forrester had been attracted to her from their first meeting on the dock in Charleston; he had given her the use of his spacious cabin, the gallant gesture of a well-bred Southern gentleman. And even though Forrester had shown his disapproval when she had agreed to share the cabin with Poppy, he had, nevertheless, cared enough to drive her to her uncle's home the day they had disembarked.

Tommy's voice pulled him back to the deck of the *Monterey*.

"I don't believe Miss Briana went off with Mr. Forrester. I'll bet that saloon girl got it all wrong."

"Get below, boy." There was a hard edge to Devlin's voice. "Start carrying up those crates of ironware."

"But you said that could wait until we got to Gila Flat and dropped anchor before we——" Devlin silenced him with a cold stare. Tommy turned and scurried off, his bare feet slapping against the scrubbed deck.

"No need to take your bad temper out on the boy," Quinn remarked. "For all you know he might be right. Maybe that Hortense was lyin' about Forrester an' Briana."

"That's enough about Briana." Although Devlin didn't raise his voice, it shook with barely restrained anger. Jigger laid back

his ears and switched the end of his orange-colored tail, then
leaped from Quinn's shoulder and went padding away.

Quinn's broad face remained impassive; over the years he
had become accustomed to Devlin's shifting moods. "The ironware's a heavy load," he said. "Guess I'll be goin' below to help
Tommy with them crates."

Briana surveyed the small, tastefully decorated shop with its
walls painted a delicate shade of coral pink; its polished black
walnut counter. She, herself, had scrubbed the small front window until the glass sparkled in the sunlight. She had given careful thought to arranging her first window display: A
sapphire-blue bonnet trimmed with white and azure ostrich
plumes was set at a coquettish angle on its brass stand; on one
side she had placed an ivory-handled fan painted with bluebells,
on the other, a scarf of turquoise foulard, intricately embroidered with dark green silk.

Although the girls from the Black Pearl had been her first
customers, the gossip about the new dress shop on Sansome
Street had spread quickly. Miss Cameron, the customers agreed,
was "a real high-toned lady," but she welcomed the patronage
of the dance-hall girls, parlor-house madams, and women of
dubious virtue who were kept in expensive hotel suites by their
wealthy gentlemen friends.

Gentlemen like Cole.

That night, when they had driven away from the Black Pearl,
he had taken her to the Tehama House. She had felt slightly
uneasy until she heard him order the desk clerk to give her a
suite of her own, the most luxurious one available. Thoroughly
exhausted, she had slept through the following morning; it had
been late afternoon before she accompanied him to Sansome
Street for her first glimpse of the shop.

That was when he told her that he had already begun making
arrangements to purchase the property. "It's not charity, Bri-

ana," he had assured her. "With this district growing so fast, I'm making a sound investment."

But when he had wanted her to have the shop rent free she had refused. She had insisted that, although she couldn't give him the first month's rent in advance, she would repay him, and continue paying so long as she ran the shop. She wouldn't be indebted to him, or to any man.

That same night she had moved into the three small rooms over the shop. "There's no need for you to do this," he had protested. "Surely you would be far more comfortable at the hotel for now."

"The former owner left a table and chairs and a bed upstairs. I'll give the rooms a thorough cleaning, have the walls painted, and buy a few more pieces of furniture when I can afford to," she said. The unswerving determination in her amber eyes warned him that further discussion would be useless.

Now, as she looked about her shop, her lips curved in a smile of approval. Her business was growing; every day more customers came flocking to the shop. In the two small, chintz-curtained dressing rooms at the rear, a steady procession of customers tried on dresses, hats, capes and shawls, studying their reflections in the full-length mirrors.

She soon realized that many of her customers were taller and more buxom than she; they would need to have their purchases altered to fit properly. This was the one task to which she wasn't equal. But Abbie Dawson, a miner's widow, had proved herself equal to the challenge, and grateful for the chance to earn her living in such agreeable surroundings.

A small, energetic woman in her thirties, Abbie had been left penniless and adrift in San Francisco when her husband had been killed in a barroom brawl. She had no desire to return to Cincinnati and live with her elder sister, who had warned her not to make the perilous journey to California.

Abbie, hard-working and skillful, quickly proved invaluable to Briana. Taking in the seams of a dress was no great problem; it was far more difficult to add width to a bodice stretched to bursting by the billowing breasts of a full-figured customer or to let out a pair of sleeves that threatened to split every time the wearer moved her arms.

Abbie made clever use of lengths of satin ribbon or insets of lace. Briana, whose sewing skills were limited to a little fine embroidery, couldn't have managed that part of the business without her.

But, as even her dour Uncle Alexander had been forced to admit, Briana was quick at figures; and her manner, friendly yet dignified, made a favorable impression on her customers.

Now the shop bell tinkled, and she smiled as she hurried to greet Belle Cora, the madam of one of the city's most ornate and expensive parlor houses. Belle was the mistress of Charles Cora, a prosperous gambler. Although they weren't legally married, she chose to use her lover's name; and from what Briana had heard she was as faithful and devoted as any loving wife.

The tall, voluptuous woman, with her dark-brown hair and green eyes, had come to San Francisco a few years earlier. Ambitious and determined, she had set out to make her establishment the finest in town.

She lost no time in telling Briana the purpose of her errand that afternoon. "I need new walking costumes for my girls. The best you've got."

"Walking costumes?" In the brief time she had been running the shop, Briana had learned that the parlor-house girls rarely left their place of business; the madams usually came here to buy showy lingerie: satin and lace nightgowns lavishly trimmed with ribbons and sheer silk wrappers.

Seeing Briana's surprise, Belle smiled. "They're not going to do any walking," she said. "I've bought a great big open carriage. I had it shipped all the way from New York City. I'm going to have my girls dressed up in some of those elegant Paris outfits of yours, and hats with plumes—like that one you have in the window. Then I'm going to take them out driving every Sunday afternoon."

Belle's green eyes sparkled with enthusiasm. "It'll be good

for business. And it'll make a nice change for the girls, too. They can use a breath of fresh air—they hardly ever leave the house during the week."

Briana smiled politely. Since women like Belle were her customers it wouldn't do to show disapproval of their way of life. Besides, it would be hypocritical. She hadn't forgotten that, back in Paris, the ladies of the demimonde had displayed themselves in much the same way, driving their glittering phaetons and landaus through the boulevards and along the paths of the Bois de Boulogne.

As Belle explained her plans, she moved about the shop, looking over the merchandise. "That bowl there is a real handsome piece." She leaned over the display case to get a better look. The bowl, one of Mama's favorite's, was made of translucent pink glass trimmed with gold, and was set on a gold-plated stand supported by the figures of three cupids.

"When you're running a real high-class house like mine comfort isn't enough," Belle said. "The gents want plenty of luxury—and they pay well for it."

As soon as Briana had offered her mother's crystal and china for sale, the madams had been eager to buy. She had been making an excellent profit on these items; nevertheless, she couldn't quite stifle her misgivings.

Mama had left Paris for only one reason: to make a new beginning; to introduce Briana into respectable society. Yet here she was, running a shop whose customers were a part of San Francisco's rapidly growing demimonde. These weren't the pathetic group of whores from Peru, who had been first to sail north to serve the needs of the miners, back in Forty-nine; or the Chinese girls, some of them no more than eleven or twelve, sold into slavery by their own fathers and shipped across the Pacific to work in the waterfront cribs.

Her first customers had been the dancers from the Black Pearl, and then those from the other concert saloons, but now she was also catering to successful madams like Belle Cora; to the mistresses of wealthy businessmen and well-heeled politicians; and

to a few touring actresses who were appearing in the new theaters: the Adelphi, the American, and Maguire's Opera House.

Yet, even as her profits grew, Briana sometimes felt a twinge
of guilt—this wasn't the sort of life her mother had wanted for
her.

Belle, who was running her fingers over the pink glass bowl,
remarked, "Lucky for you that this made it through the voyage
in one piece. Lots of fragile pieces get smashed to smithereens
along the way. What with the rough weather, and those storms
the ships run into, going around the Horn . . ."

Briana nodded, but even as she and Belle discussed the price
of the bowl and a few other decorative items, she was thinking
of her own passage around the Horn; the shrieking winds, the
sleet-swept deck of the *Osprey*. Of the glimpse of Devlin at the
wheel. The sight of him, tall and commanding, had given her
courage. She had crouched in her bunk, telling herself that
Devlin would get her safely to San Francisco.

"I'll pay well for these pieces," Belle was saying. "My
place'll be the talk of San Francisco."

Quickly, Briana completed the transaction and promised to
have the pieces packed and delivered the following day. "And
as for the walking costumes, if you'll bring your young ladies
in, Mrs. Dawson will take their measurements."

After Belle had left Briana started for the rear of the shop to
look over her selection of walking costumes. Her brows drew
together in a slight frown. With her business flourishing, she
already was starting to run low on merchandise. Where on earth
was she to find dresses of the same fine quality as those Mama
had bought in Paris when the time came for her to replenish her
stock?

Before she had time to think about it the shop bell tinged
and she turned to see Cole. She smiled at him, but there was
no answering warmth in his face.

"Wasn't that Belle Cora I saw, coming out of here?" he demanded.

"It was. She's ordered my finest walking costumes for all her young ladies."

"Young ladies." He made no effort to hide his contempt. "They're parlor-house girls. I'd have thought that by now you would have tried to encourage a better class of customers."

She made an effort to control her rising irritation. "If I don't think of a way to replenish my stock, I won't be able to cater to any sort of customers." She forced a smile. "When I brought all those trunks from Charleston I thought I wouldn't need another gown or bonnet for ever so long. But it never occurred to me then that I'd be running a shop."

"Maybe you won't be, not much longer."

She was puzzled by the intensity in his blue eyes. "Surely you're not planning to raise my rent." She tried to break the growing tension between them with a teasing smile, but he didn't respond.

"Briana, this isn't a suitable occupation for a lady, and you must know it. I won't have you catering to saloon girls and women like Belle."

She pressed her teeth into her lower lip to hold back a sharp retort. Cole owned the shop, but as long as she paid for the use of it, what right had he to dictate to her how she ran her business? "I've been selling my gowns to the actresses who are appearing at the Adelphi and the—"

"An actress is not received in the best society," he interrupted.

"The social standing of my customers has nothing to do with you."

"You're wrong about that, Briana." His hand closed over hers, and she caught the sudden tension in his face. She couldn't mistake the look of desire that flared in his eyes.

He had done so much for her already: He'd helped her to get back her possessions from her uncle; he'd given her a start in the shop. Was he now about to demand payment—to ask her to become his mistress? And even if he were, what possible difference could it make to him that she dealt with saloon girls, or women like Belle Cora?

"Briana, surely you must know how deeply I care for you." His gaze locked with hers, and she couldn't look away. "From that first day we met, back in Charleston, I haven't been able to get you out of my thoughts."

She gave him a wry smile. "You managed well enough, all that time I was living with my uncle on Pacific Street."

"I didn't forget you, even then," he persisted.

"But you didn't want to get involved with a girl from the Coast."

"All that's changed now. If you were to give up the shop at once—"

"And go back to live with Uncle Alexander and Aunt Gertrude?"

"That would be out of the question." He drew her against him, and she felt the heat of his breath on her cheek. "I don't want you to have anything more to do with those two."

"But if I leave the shop—" His look silenced her.

"Briana, I'm asking you to become my wife."

He meant it. He wanted to marry her. Her thoughts began to whirl in a dizzying spiral, and it took all her will to think calmly.

This was what Mama would have wanted for her; what she had hoped for when she had brought Briana from Paris.

She told herself she should accept Cole's proposal right now. She should marry him and take her place among the wealthy, respectable ladies in San Francisco society. She owed Mama that much.

He would insist that she give up the shop: Cole Forrester's wife mustn't work for a living. She could agree to that, although, even in so short a time, her business had become a source of pride to her—an indisputable proof that she could succeed on her own. But Cole was right. If she went on catering to women like Belle Cora, like Hortense and the others from the concert saloons, she would soon forfeit all claim to respectability.

She mustn't give herself time to think it over; she would say "yes" right now. She would allow him to take her in his arms and raise her lips for his kiss.

But she couldn't. Not now—not ever. Because of Devlin.

"Briana?" Cole was waiting for her answer.

She had been taught the correct way to refuse a proposal of marriage, the carefully chosen words that would turn away a hopeful gentleman while soothing his disappointment. But now she forgot all that.

"I can't marry you, Cole."

He took a step back, but he didn't release her hand. If her manner of refusal had caught him by surprise, he didn't show it. And she could guess the reason. Mama had said that it was acceptable for a young lady to refuse a proposal once, even twice, as proof of her girlish hesitancy, and then to accept, as she had intended to do all along.

"It's unconventional to propose without first asking the permission of your relatives," he was saying. "But under the circumstances, I doubt that I would get a friendly reception from your uncle."

"My uncle has nothing to do with it. I can't marry you because—" There was one way to be sure he would accept her refusal; that he would never ask to marry her again.

But even as she considered the possibility, she knew she couldn't tell him about Devlin; she couldn't speak about the night of loving they had shared. She couldn't say that, although Devlin had made love with her, he had let her leave. He hadn't even tried to see her again before he sailed.

"I am fond of you, Cole. And grateful for all you've done for me. But even if I were to give up the shop, I wouldn't be the right wife for you. That day back in Havana, you spoke of going into politics. I wouldn't be a suitable wife for a rising politician."

He was silent for a moment as he considered her words. "Perhaps it would be best if I were to give you time to think over my proposal." He raised her hand to his lips. "But you'll still dine with me tomorrow night at the Tehama House restaurant, as we planned?"

She hesitated for a moment, then agreed. Cole was a gentleman; he would keep his word and give her more time to consider his offer of marriage. He wouldn't pressure her.

As he drove his buggy away from the shop, Cole thought over his encounter with Briana. From their first meeting she had intrigued him, with her often contradictory behavior. She had been cool and unyielding when he had kissed her that afternoon in Havana, the model of a well-bred Southern lady. Yet a few hours later she had readily agreed to share her cabin with Poppy Nolan, a common slut.

She had left her uncle's house and fled into the streets of the Barbary Coast, but he could scarcely blame her for that. Yet she had gone straight to the Black Pearl, a disreputable saloon, to seek out Poppy again; surely that proved she considered the girl her friend.

Although he had made no attempt to force himself on her the night she had stayed at the Tehama House, she had insisted on moving out the following day. She had never once invited him upstairs to her living quarters over the shop.

He was obsessed with her beauty; her burnished red-gold hair, her seductive amber eyes, her soft, enticing lips. A young lady of breeding, graceful in her movements, impeccable in her speech.

But who was the real Briana? How much did he know about her?

She had told him she had been born and raised in France, the daughter of a respected Charleston businessman, a cotton factor. That her mother, Lynette, had chosen to remain with her in Paris until Briana had turned seventeen.

Had James Cameron left his wife and daughter so well provided for that they had been able to live in luxury all those years? And what had caused Lynette to decide to return to Charleston with her daughter?

He had accepted the reason Briana had given him for leaving Charleston so abruptly. Her mother had died of malaria; she'd been left alone, without even a distant female relative to act as her chaperone.

Yet why would a girl like Briana, strong-willed and independent, have come all the way to San Francisco to seek shelter with relatives she had never met?

Before he offered to marry her again he would find out all he could about her past. As he guided his horse through the crowded streets, he set about shaping his plan with the same logic that had served him so well in his profession.

Charleston: That was the sensible place to start. His family lived at Oleander, but they came into the city occasionally. And he had many friends there, too; surely one of them might be able to tell him what he wanted to know about the beautiful but elusive Briana Cameron.

Fourteen

A brisk sea breeze tugged at the satin ribbons on Briana's bonnet as she drove her new dark green phaeton toward the Embarcadero. The phaeton was a handsome vehicle, another tangible proof of her growing business success; its lacquered sides and polished brass trim sparkled in the September sunlight, and the horse, a sleek, brown filly, moved along at a brisk trot.

Her spirits rose at the prospect of a few hours away from the shop, and she smiled as she breathed in the heady scent of the salt air, but she hadn't driven out on a pleasure jaunt. Her stock of dresses had dwindled to the point where she was finding it difficult to meet the demands of her customers: she didn't need Abbie to remind her that she would have to replenish the merchandise as soon as she could.

She had already taken the first step. She had ordered paper

patterns for the latest styles in dresses, mantillas, and cloaks, along with a copy of *Madame Demorest's Mirror of Fashions.* But although they had arrived from Philadelphia only last week, they would be of no use to her unless she could also find a wide selection of suitable fabrics. If she had to send all the way to Paris for silks, satins, and laces, it would take far too long before they arrived and Abbie could begin working on the new collection.

But luck was with her, for only this morning Belle Cora had visited the shop and told her about the arrival of the China clipper *Star of Canton.* "The ship dropped anchor a few hours ago. My girls'll be plenty busy for the next few nights. We won't be getting any of the common sailors—only ships' officers, with plenty of pay to spend on my best-looking girls and my finest champagne."

"What cargo does the vessel carry?"

"Tea, silks—the usual trade goods from the Far East. No Chinese slave girls, though. Captain Obadiah Tyler doesn't carry that kind of merchandise."

Even as she wrapped Belle's packages, Briana's thoughts raced ahead. She must not miss out on this opportunity. No sooner had she shown Belle to the door than she hurried upstairs and changed from the black silk she wore in the shop to a honey-colored taffeta street dress she had set aside for herself. Then she put on a matching bonnet trimmed with russet plumes and set out for the Embarcadero.

Thank goodness Belle had chosen to visit the shop that morning—and with such useful information. But then, Belle always knew everything worth knowing about what went on in the city. Her patrons included San Francisco's newspaper editors, from James Casey, who supported the interests of the South, to James King, whose *Daily Evening Bulletin* advocated the preservation of the Union. Lately, the growing friction between North and South had reached as far as California. But Belle welcomed sympathizers on both sides, along with the city's most prominent judges and aldermen. Mayor Van Ness himself was a frequent visitor to her luxurious parlor house.

Now, as Briana maneuvered her horse and phaeton through the crowded streets, her elation ebbed slightly; her brows drew together in a faint frown. What a pity that Cole still criticized her for selling her gowns to Belle and the other ladies of easy virtue. Although he did not conceal his disapproval, she couldn't let him influence her business decisions.

It had been over a month since Cole had proposed to her and she wondered if, perhaps, he had accepted her refusal as final. He hadn't asked her to marry him again. But he had gone on squiring her about the city, taking her to dinner and the theater. Only last week they had attended the city's new opera house, the Metropolitan, with its resplendent foyer, deep plush seats, and gilded pillars.

Seated beside him in his private box, she had smiled warmly and said, "This is a treat. I haven't been to an opera since Mama and I left Paris."

"You and your mother lived in Paris for many years?"

"I was born there, a few months after Papa died. Mama preferred to remain." She hoped he would drop the subject, but he persisted.

"I should think your mother would have wanted to return to Charleston after your father passed away."

He leaned toward her, his blue eyes alert as he waited for her to reply. During the time since he had proposed, she had often caught him looking at her that way, and it always made her uneasy.

"Mama enjoyed the gaiety of Paris. And she had a—wide circle of friends there." Then, fearing he would go on with his cross-examination until she made a slip and revealed too much about Mama's background, she deftly changed the direction of the conversation.

"Madame Anna Bishop sings so beautifully," she remarked as the conductor raised his baton, and the curtain began to rise on the second act of *Der Freischutz*. A gaslight moon shone above as Agatha, the lonely maiden, stood at the window waiting for her lover, praying for his safe return.

Briana had been startled and dismayed to feel the sudden sting of tears. She blinked them back and tried not to think of Devlin, far away on the river. She felt a sudden, overpowering need to see him again. Then she turned her head and saw that Cole wasn't watching the stage; his eyes were fixed on her. Was he thinking of proposing to her again? His behavior puzzled and disturbed her.

But now, as she turned her phaeton onto the Embarcadero, she caught her breath and her hands tightened on the reins; in an instant all thoughts of Cole were swept away.

Devlin.

Even from a distance she could never mistake him for any other man. That was his tall, wide-shouldered body, the self-assured set of his head, his long, easy stride. He had just come out of a warehouse and now was moving in her direction.

Torn by conflicting emotions, she forced herself to look away. She would drive past without giving him so much as a nod of recognition. But it took every ounce of resolution to keep her eyes fixed straight ahead.

"Briana!"

His powerful voice, which could reach his crew from the quarterdeck even at the height of a gale, now came to her above the uproar of the crowded waterfront. His resonant tone sent a swift current of heat coursing through her.

She jerked on the reins. The startled horse tossed its head, then reared up on its haunches so that she was flung back against the leather seat.

She cried out with fear as she fought to keep the horse under control. Then Devlin was beside the phaeton, his strong hands gripping the reins. He calmed the filly, speaking in soothing tones.

He looked up at Briana with a smile. "This is a handsome carriage. And a fine horse, if she's handled properly," he said. "But you need more practice at driving in this kind of traffic."

He spoke in an off-hand way, as if they had parted only a few hours earlier.

Then, before she could protest, he swung himself up on the seat beside her and took the reins from her hands. "Where are you headed?"

She should tell him it was no concern of his and order him to get down at once, but perhaps such behavior would reveal her feelings too plainly. She tried to speak as casually as he had. "I'm going aboard the *Star of Canton*. She docked this morning."

"Have you developed a sudden interest in the arrivals of the clippers on the China run?"

"Belle Cora told me—"

His dark brows rose and she realized that Belle's name was familiar to him. He didn't question her about how she had come to know the parlor-house madam. Instead he smiled down at her. "Surely the city's markets haven't sold out all their China tea."

"It's silks I need," she explained. "I've opened a dress shop—"

"On Sansome Street," he finished for her. "And from what Quinn heard you've been doing well for yourself."

Quinn had made inquiries about her; he had been more concerned about her welfare than Devlin. She pushed aside her chagrin and tried to sound brisk and impersonal. "I've been successful so far, but now I'm running short of dresses."

His silver-gray eyes glinted with amusement. "Don't tell me all those trunks you brought with you from Charleston are already empty."

"Not quite." She had been reluctant to discuss business with Cole, since he objected to her choice of customers, and it was a relief to talk about the shop with Devlin, who wasn't likely to criticize her for catering to women like Belle Cora. "I've hired a skilled seamstress," she went on. "So if I can get the silks I need—only the finest quality will do—I should be able to go on supplying my customers with all the latest Paris fashions."

She spoke quickly, a little breathlessly, telling him about the paper patterns she had ordered; about Abbie's skill as a seamstress. She did not dare lapse into silence, or he might sense the turbulent feelings stirring inside her. "I want to get the best of those silks before someone else buys them."

"Then you'd better let me come with you."

"I'm perfectly capable of conducting my own business."

"You haven't bargained for a ship's cargo before, have you? Even when he's dealing with a beautiful woman, Obadiah Tyler's a shrewd trader."

"You know him?"

"We've met from time to time. You'd be wise to allow me to handle this for you."

"There's really no need," she insisted.

"Don't be too sure." His eyes moved over her, lingering on the graceful curve of her throat, the enticing rounds of her breasts beneath her close-fitting bodice. "Tyler appreciates a beautiful woman as much as any man, but he's a rock-ribbed New Englander and he'll drive a hard bargain."

She hesitated. No doubt he could be of use to her. And yet a voice deep in her mind warned her to get away from him quickly.

"Why not let me get you the best merchandise at the lowest prices he'll settle for? I've been in the China trade myself, and I can judge the value of his cargo better than you."

"All right, then. Come along if you wish," she said. She told herself she was only being practical; if he could get the silks for less than they would cost her, it would be foolish to refuse. But as they came to the dock where the clipper was berthed, she looked away, fixing her eyes on the tall masts, the close-reefed sails.

Ever since he had seated himself beside her she had been stirred by the firm pressure of his wide shoulders, the well remembered scent of him—salt, brandy, and his own distinctive masculinity. Each time he turned his eyes on her she felt herself come alive, her whole being responding to his nearness.

How long would he stay ashore, before he left on his next river voyage? She didn't let herself think about that. He was here with her now.

* * *

They went aboard the *Star of Canton* and he introduced her to Captain Tyler, a tall man with a lean face and shrewd, pale blue eyes, then explained the purpose of their visit.

"I don't usually conduct business aboard my ship," Tyler told her. "I bring my cargo ashore to the warehouses and the customers bargain for it there. But seeing as how you're a friend of Rafferty's, I'll make an exception. And if it's silks you're looking for, I'm carrying some of the finest you're likely to set eyes on this side of the Pacific." He gave her a brief, canny look. "Such goods don't come cheap, mind you."

"Miss Cameron is an experienced judge of fine fabrics," Devlin said. "She'll look over your silks and decide whether they're up to her standards. If she's satisfied, then it'll be time to talk prices."

"Fair enough," Tyler agreed.

He ordered a couple of his crewmen to carry up the crates and pry off the tops; then he left Briana to make her selections while he and Devlin strode off down the deck. She caught only a part of their conversation.

"Running a skiff along these California rivers? That'll be a change for you, Rafferty—I remember that time we put into Java—the monsoon season, it was—"

She forced herself to concentrate her full attention on the merchandise. She saw that Captain Tyler had made no idle boast about the quality of his cargo. She smiled with satisfaction as she rubbed the silks between her fingers, and her eyes widened appreciatively at the myriad colors spread before her. So many rolls in subtle shades of pink, mauve, lilac, and azure; and others, in deeper tones—ruby, cerise, jade-green, and amethyst. Why, with silks like these, Abbie could set to work at once and create a fabulous collection of new gowns in all the latest styles.

When she had finished looking over the silks and the time came to bargain Devlin proved to be as good as his word. Tyler protested ruefully that he would be "giving the stuff away at such paltry prices," but at last he and Devlin struck a bargain.

"Now we'll have a look at some of the other goods," Devlin

said to the captain. "What've you brought back, by way of vases, screens, and such?"

She gave him a startled glance. "But I only came to buy silks," she protested.

Then, remembering that Belle Cora had explained the need to give her patrons a feeling of luxury and had paid well for Mama's china and crystal, Briana said no more. She stood by while Tyler ordered more crates carried up on deck.

Devlin studied their contents with a practiced eye. He gave most of them only a passing glance, but he told Tyler to set aside a fine hand-painted screen, a handsome dragon crafted in brass with a verdigris patina, a large porcelain bowl enameled with pinks and greens and highlighted with gilt, along with several other items. An ivory case for visiting cards, an inlaid trinket box lined with velvet, a fan that opened to reveal a detailed watercolor vista of an exotic harbor. "The Whampoa Reach anchorage near Canton," Devlin told her. "That's where these clippers take on their cargoes."

Even though he had proved his skill at bargaining, the final prices were still high enough to make her hesitate. She dared not go too far above the limit she had set for herself.

"Take them," he advised her with quiet assurance. After a moment's deliberation she agreed.

One of the crewmen escorted her to the gangplank, while Devlin lingered behind with Tyler, to go over the bills of lading and arrange for the prompt delivery of the goods. She could hear little of their conversation, but as they shook hands, she caught the words: "—a fine-looking woman you've got there—"

Was she Devlin's woman? She had given him all she had to give, but it hadn't been enough to change him; to subdue the hidden forces that drove him. That one night of shared loving hadn't stopped him from sailing off without her. He hadn't spoken of their future. He had made her no promises. He had left her to survive on her own, as best she could.

When they were back on the dock again he lifted her into the phaeton. "I'm most grateful to you for helping me deal with

Captain Tyler, but I mustn't take up any more of your time."
She tried to sound impersonal, but it was no use.

The next moment he was beside her on the seat again, his
eyes mocking her, telling her that he could see through her
pretense. Her voice faltered. "—There's really no need—I can
drive myself back to the shop."

With a swift movement, he shifted the reins to one hand and
let the other rest lightly on her arm. Even so casual a touch
awakened the familiar need in her. Why try to deceive herself?
She did not want him to leave her—not yet.

"You've done enough business for one day." He bent his head
and his gaze lingered on her face. "Beautiful as ever. But a little
pale. You need more color in your cheeks."

He turned the phaeton away from the dock, crowded with
heavily laden wagons driven by shouting, cursing teamsters;
with milling longshoremen, sailors and merchants. "Surely you
must have important business of your own," she protested.

"Quinn'll take care of it." His arm went around her shoulders
and she felt the hard strength of his muscles. She longed to lean
back, to surrender herself to the sensations that were racing
through her, but she held herself under tight control.

"How is Quinn?" she asked. "And Tommy?"

"They're both fine." His gray eyes danced with a hint of
amusement: He knew her far too well to be put off by her at-
tempts to hide her emotions. "Aren't you going to ask about
Jigger now?" He gave her a teasing grin.

"You took him along on the skiff?"

"We did. But he gave Quinn a bit of trouble along the way.
One of the miners in Gila Flats wanted to buy Jigger. Seems
the rats were overruning his tent and eating his supplies. He
offered fifty dollars for the cat."

"And Quinn refused, of course."

He nodded. "But the miner was persistent. He finally tried
to steal Jigger, just as we were casting off. Slipped the cat inside
his shirt and was heading back to his tent. But when Jigger
heard our skiff's bell he clawed his way free and came racing

down to the landing. He jumped aboard and climbed onto Quinn's shoulder. And off we went, up the Sacramento."

Briana smiled. "I wish I'd been there to see it." She broke off abruptly, then pressed her lips together. Never again would she give him the slightest reason to think she wanted to go out on the river with him.

They had met purely by chance today. Once she was back in the shop she would concentrate all her attention on business. She would tell Abbie about the silks to be delivered tomorrow and they would start planning the new winter clothes: smart promenade costumes, lavish ball dresses, along with seductive negligees and nightgowns.

If only she could take her gaze away from his. She had to break free, to conceal her urgent need to stay close to him. "I really must be getting back," she began. Then, as she forced herself to look away, she realized that she had lost all track of time. They were already approaching the outskirts of the city. The shacks and canvas tents were farther apart, and there were few other vehicles on the road.

"Turn around and drive me to the shop."

He brought the phaeton to a halt. Then he reached out and unfastened her bonnet, tossing it down beside her on the seat. His arms went around her. His mouth, urgent, demanding, claimed hers. She tried to hold herself aloof, but she couldn't. She made a wordless sound, deep in her throat, and let her head fall back against his arm. Her lips parted to receive his questing tongue. Through the layers of taffeta and silk that sheathed her body, her skin began to tingle. Her tongue curved around his. She was trembling. Shivers of desire were racing along every nerve of her body. . . .

No! She wouldn't—she mustn't give way.

She turned her mouth away from his. "Get down. I'll drive myself back."

He raised his head, but his silver-gray gaze silenced her. She couldn't hope to deceive him and she knew it. He released her from his embrace only to pick up the reins again and move on;

the phaeton went rolling along the shoreline, every turn of the wheels carrying them farther away from the city.

"Where are you taking me?"

"I don't suppose you've seen much of San Francisco since you've been shut up in that shop of yours."

"That's not true," she retorted. "I've been to the best restaurants, the finest theaters. Last week I went to the new opera house to hear Madame Anna Bishop in *Der Freischutz.*"

"You went with Cole Forrester."

"I didn't say that."

"You didn't have to. He has every right to enjoy your company in return for all he's done for you."

She turned on him, her amber eyes flaring. "If you're suggesting that he and I—"

"Spare me your indignation." His gaze held hers and she couldn't look away. "He got your trunks back for you, didn't he? And since you couldn't stay with Poppy that night he took you to his hotel."

"If you know that much, perhaps you also know that I stayed at the Tehama House only one night—in my own private suite."

"And Forrester is a gentleman. He didn't drop by for a midnight visit." His mouth curved at one corner in a mirthless smile. "He didn't buy that little shop on Sansome Street and set you up in business."

She fought back her impulse to tell him the truth: that she had never given herself to Cole. That, although he had put up the money to start her in business, she had paid him back every dollar.

Let Devlin think what he liked. She owed him no explanations.

She gave him a smile. "Perhaps you will drop by my shop, sometime before you sail again," she said. "Bring Quinn, if you like. And Tommy, too."

He didn't answer, but touched the whip to the filly's back, urging her to a brisk trot. His eyes had darkened and his jaw was set in a hard line, the skin pulled taut over his angular cheekbones.

She glanced at him uneasily. Had she pushed him too far? How could she have forgotten his volatile temper, his capacity for violence? She pressed her gloved hands together and tried to conceal her growing tension.

Now they were moving up a narrow, sloping path, and still he didn't speak or even look at her. She could no longer stand the charged silence between them. "Where are we going?"

"To the cliffs overlooking Seal Rocks." She gave an involuntary sigh of relief and felt herself relax at his even, casual tone. "You can see out over the city, and the sea," he said. "The view should be especially good today—San Francisco doesn't often have such clear, sunny weather."

His arm went around her again, but this time his touch was light and he made no attempt to draw her against him. It was better that way, she told herself. All she had to do was keep the conversation light. Once they had admired the view surely she could persuade him to drive her back to the shop.

"You know, when I first came here I could find nothing to like about the city," she began.

"And now?"

"It's not at all like Charleston. Or Paris. It's—young and untamed, with its own special kind of beauty. Sometimes, when the fog comes rolling in, thick and grayish-white, moving up the streets from the harbor, I can taste the salt on my tongue. Lately I'm starting to feel that I belong here. That it's my real home."

"I've never felt that way about any city."

"Not even back in—?"

She stopped herself abruptly, for she had remembered what Quinn had told her about Devlin's dismal childhood in that far-off land, of his parents' brief, tragic marriage and his grandfather's cruelty.

"In Australia?" He shook his head. "Except for Sydney, perhaps, there were no cities worthy of the name. Not when I was growing up there."

He slowed the horse to a walk. "The path gets steeper from

here on." His arm tightened around her shoulders. Was it only to steady her?

"Look up there."

She tilted her head back and caught sight of the oaks and pines, their branches swaying in the wind. "Over there, to the left." He pointed with the whip, and now she could make out a small square building; sunlight glowed softly on its weathered red-tile roof.

"That's the Gamborenas' inn," he told her. "Their food's excellent. We'll have *arroz con pollo,* black beans, tortillas, and a bottle of good wine."

They moved on, up the narrow, winding road, and now, as she peered over the side of the phaeton, she caught her first glimpse of the waves far below, dashing against the jagged rocks. Beyond lay the Golden Gate and the wide gray-green expanse of the ocean.

But when they reached the top of the cliff, he didn't drive on to the inn, as she had expected. Instead, he headed for a thick grove of pines; here, he brought the phaeton to a stop. She breathed deeply, savoring the spicy, resinous scent of the dark-green branches overhead.

He got out, reached up his arms to her, and swung her over the side of the phaeton. He didn't set her down at once, but held her close against him, so that her breasts pressed tightly against the hardness of his chest and her wide skirt was crushed against his thighs. The sea wind tugged at her hair, loosening the red-gold strands, whipping them across her cheeks.

Her heart quickened. When he released her and went to tie the reins securely to one of the towering pines she remained where he had placed her. She felt as if her legs were melting.

Now he stood a few feet away and held out his arms to her. The familiar need stirred inside her, deep and hot.

No! She wouldn't give in. Not this time.

She would stand here, unmoving. And if he was the first to yield to the current between them, if he were to come to her, even so, she knew how to turn him away.

Lie to him. Tell him you and Cole are lovers.

It was like a duel between them now; Devlin standing there, his gray eyes challenging her, and she, holding her distance, her body rigid, unwilling to give way.

Who took the first step forward? She didn't know. Didn't want to know. Now they were only inches apart and still he didn't touch her. And still she kept her hands clenched tightly, her head held high.

"Cole and I—"

His face was immobile, as if carved in granite.

"He's done so much for me. That night, when he came to my suite at the hotel—I couldn't refuse."

And still he did not speak.

"He's asked me to marry him. And I said—"

Then, with one swift movement he jerked her against him, his face looming over hers. "You said no."

"Damn you!" Damn him for knowing her as he did, for probing into the hidden depths of her mind, her very soul.

"He'll ask me again," she said.

"And you'll refuse."

"He can give me all I've ever wanted. All my mother wanted for me."

"You won't take any of it. Not from him."

She tried to deny his words, but she couldn't.

His voice was soft now, husky and deep. "You never made love with him."

"I—"

"Not you, Briana. Whatever you are, you're not a whore. You give yourself freely, as you choose. But you would never sell yourself to any man."

For a moment more she held herself unyielding, then slowly she gave way under the overpowering force of his words, his gaze. Her arms went around his neck, and she held on to him with all her strength. He lifted her against him and carried her deep into the shadows under the wind-tossed pines.

Fifteen

Devlin set her down, her back resting against the trunk of a tall pine. He bent his head and kissed her, a long, lingering kiss, then began to take the pins from her hair, one by one.

He tried to keep his hands steady, but his fingers trembled a little as he drew out the last of the pins. Her hair fell around her face and down over her shoulders in red-gold glory. He pressed his mouth against the silky waves and inhaled their delicate scent. With quick, automatic movements, he shrugged off his jacket, unbuttoned his shirt, and let them drop to the ground.

She reached out and stroked his chest, her fingers lingering in the dark whorls of hair.

He opened her close-fitting bodice, and his hands moved underneath to cup the fullness of her breasts. She rested against his arm as he removed her gown, her petticoats. How much longer must he wait to feel the touch of her satin skin, the curves of her body, molded against his?

Her fingers moved to one of her lace garters, but he gently pushed her hand away. The sight of her, clad only in her sheer silk stockings and slippers, stirred his senses.

"Not yet," he said, as he drew her down beside him on the thick, soft grass.

They lay side by side now, the look in his eyes sending hot flickers of desire moving through her. He slid off her slippers, and then her garters. His movements were slow, sensuous, as he drew the stockings down her long legs, pausing to caress the sensitive flesh of her thighs. His fingers drifted upward. He began stroking the soft triangle at the apex of her thighs, and caught the swift intake of her breath.

"Yes—Oh, yes—" Her voice was scarcely more than a whisper, yet it trembled with urgency as it mingled with the sighing of the sea wind in the pine boughs overhead.

Her legs parted so that he might explore the moist, hidden places of her. Gently, he slid a finger inside her. She pressed her hot mound against his hand. He felt her satin sheath tighten around his questing fingers.

Somehow he fought back his own driving need. Not yet . . . not yet . . . When he withdrew his hand he heard her give a small sound of protest. He bent his head and flicked his tongue up along the inside flesh of her thighs.

His mouth moved to the wet heat of her womanhood, his tongue probing, entering and withdrawing, thrusting. . . . She arched her hips in a silent plea for the release only he could give her. He raised his head and looked up into her face. Her lips were parted, her amber eyes smoky with desire.

He levered himself upward, resting his weight on his arms, and felt her hands stroking the skin at the base of his spine. Scalding waves went coursing through him.

Her fingers were pressing against his buttocks, drawing him closer. With a swift movement, he plunged his hardness inside her. She wrapped her legs around him, drawing him deeper . . . deeper. . . .

He felt the first soft throbbing of her sheath. He thrust harder, faster. He heard her rapturous outcry. A long shudder of fulfillment surged through his body as he released himself into her.

After they had dressed again, and she had pinned up her hair once more, they lingered beneath the trees. She knew that this sun-dappled grove would always hold a special place in her memories; when he had returned to the river she would relive their sweet, stolen hours here.

The delicious sense of fulfillment was touched with a faint sadness. He would be gone soon, and she would be alone once more. But she wouldn't let herself think about that, not yet. She must savor each moment of this golden afternoon.

He drew her to her feet and led her from the grove. They stood together at the edge of the cliffs, looking down at the glistening rocks, the foaming surf.

"The breeze is getting cooler," she said.

He lifted his eyes, as if gauging the angle of the sun's rays. "It's well past midday," he said, with seaman's certainty.

"I suppose we should be getting back to the city."

"Not yet, love. We'll go on to the inn."

He helped her into the buggy and got in beside her. "You must be hungry."

"Oh, yes. What is that dish you spoke of? *Arroz*— "

He smiled. *"Arroz con pollo.* That's chicken with rice, seasoned with saffron. And Señora Gamborena makes her black beans with her own special sauce full of all sorts of spices."

"It sounds delicious."

A teasing light danced in his gray eyes. "You've always had a lusty appetite."

She caught his double meaning, but she didn't blush, for she no longer felt the least trace of modesty. Not with him. Never with him. The loving they had shared back on the cliffs had been so right, so completely fulfilling.

Señora Gamborena greeted Devlin warmly, then served their meal on the small terrace behind the inn. They were the only guests this afternoon. The stout, black-haired woman smiled at Briana and gave a nod of approval.

The food was as good as Devlin had promised, but even as they shared the last of the bottle of wine she saw that the sky was growing misty; a few low-lying clouds were tinged with a rosy light, and the shadows were beginning to lengthen across the stone floor of the terrace.

She spoke with reluctance. "The fog will be coming in soon,

and the path down from the cliffs is narrow. Perhaps we'd better start back while there's still light enough to find our way."

His fingers closed around her hand. "Stay here with me tonight. And tomorrow we'll have Señora Gamborena pack a basket for us. We'll eat out on the cliffs, and then we'll climb down to the rocks. It's probably too late in the season to see the seals, but maybe there'll still be a few."

She longed to agree without a moment's hesitation, but although the wine had left her a bit light-headed, she wasn't too giddy to remember that, although they were up here in their private world, the city lay down below, crowded and bustling with activity.

"Abbie is expecting me. She'll be worried if I don't get back tonight."

"Send her a note and I'll have one of the Gamborenas' sons take it to the shop for you."

"Those silks are going to be delivered tomorrow afternoon."

"Tyler'll be in port for at least another week. He'll wait for payment."

But there was something more. She searched her mind, then remembered that she had promised to attend the theater with Cole that night.

But Devlin's eyes were fixed on hers, gray and fathomless as the sea beyond the cliffs. All thoughts of Cole, of Abbie, of the shop, were swept away. She wouldn't let herself ask him when he would board his skiff and go upriver again. She didn't want to know.

Love me tonight. Make me forget all the other nights to come. But she didn't speak the words aloud.

She only said, "I'll stay."

That night, with the silvery fog swirling outside the small windows of their upstairs room, she still couldn't bring herself to speak of the future. She could only lie naked in the wide bed, watching as he hung his jacket across a heavy carved oak chair. His fingers brushed against one of the pockets, and he smiled.

"Captain Tyler showed me this, while you were looking at the silks."

"I already have so much new stock," she protested in mock dismay. "I'll have to enlarge my shop."

"This isn't for the shop, Briana. It's for you." He drew out a small cedarwood box, came over to the side of the bed, and handed it to her. She opened the carved top of the box and gazed with pleasure at the delicate porcelain figurine.

"She's Kuan Yin," Devlin explained. "The goddess of good fortune." She looked at him in surprise, for she hadn't suspected that he would have the slightest interest in such fanciful notions.

He took off his shirt. "Kuan Yin will keep you safe for me," he said. "She'll—bring you luck."

The goddess would watch over her after he had left. Was that what he had been about to say? Quickly, he finished undressing.

She had never ceased to marvel at the masculine beauty of his body. Even now, when she longed to reach out to him, she paused, her eyes caressing his wide shoulders, his heavily muscled chest with its crisp black hair. She shivered with anticipation, her gaze following the straight dark line that arrowed down his lean, muscle-ridged abdomen—down to his manhood, already rock-hard with virile power.

She took his hand and he lowered himself beside her on the bed. His arms enfolded her. She pressed herself against him, molding her body to his.

They spent two nights together at the inn. Then, at dawn on the third day, he awoke before her. He raised himself on his arm, looking down at her as she slept beside him, her rose-tipped breasts rising and falling evenly, her lips slightly parted, her hair falling in tousled waves around her face. A light sheen of moisture still lay across her skin. Leaning closer, he caught the scent of her flesh, mingled with his own.

One flesh.

He had heard those words before, somewhere. . . . But where? At a wedding ceremony for one of his ship's officers; that was it.

His body went rigid, his muscles tightening as if to ward off a blow. What the hell was he thinking of? What had she done to him, to start him thinking this way?

She was beautiful beyond all his boyhood fantasies of women. Passionate and generous, giving herself to him freely, holding nothing back. But that didn't change anything. She could never be one with him.

He was alone; he always had been alone, always would be. It was better that way. Not only for him, but for her, too. If ever he asked her to join her future with his, what would he have to offer her?

Sorrow. Danger. Destruction.

He drew away from her and caught sight of the small porcelain figurine on the bedside table. He had told her that Kuan Yin would bring her good fortune; had started to say that the goddess would keep her safe. But he had caught himself in time. There could be no safety for her, not with him.

He got out of bed, moving carefully so as not to awaken her. He filled a basin with water, washed himself, then pulled on his clothes and went to the window. The early morning fog was thinning to a light, golden mist. The wind soughed in the branches of the pines and he caught the cry of the gulls as they wheeled and soared over the bay.

His hands gripped the broad window ledge, the whitewashed surface biting deep into his palms. Silently, he berated himself. How could he have lowered his guard, even for an instant?

He felt a sudden urge to escape from this small room with its white-plaster walls—to run away from her and not look back. He'd let her go on sleeping while he left the inn and returned to the city alone.

But he couldn't leave her, not that way. He would wait until she awoke. And while he waited he wouldn't allow himself to think of the past.

He had come ashore and spent a few nights with a lovely, passionate woman, as any other seaman would have done—given the chance. Now it was time to turn his thoughts to the future.

Think about the skiff, about Quinn and Tommy, already aboard and waiting for him. Think about the new cargo, and the profits it would bring. About anything except—

But it was no use; the memories of the past were too strong. They closed about him like the strands of an invisible, unbreakable net, enveloping him—drawing him back to that harsh, now-alien land far across the Pacific. . . .

He was a boy again. Ten years old. A boy crouching in the terrifying darkness of a small, hot cell, filled with a suffocating stench. Sweat poured down his skinny, naked body and over the burning cuts in his flesh.

"Bastard brat!—No better than your father!—your mother died—your fault!" His grandfather's voice and the searing stroke of the leather belt.

A beating no worse than any of those before it. But this time he had willed himself not to cry out. Pride had kept him silent, until he had bitten through his lower lip, to hold back his screams. He hadn't begged for mercy.

And so there would have to be something more—the punishment cell. The small, windowless box at the edge of the parade ground. It had been built for the most hardened convicts. A few had died of the heat, others for lack of food and water.

The boy knew this, and terror gripped his vitals. Alone in the blackness, he gave way at last. He sobbed, then started to scream for help. He pounded on the heavy metal door until his fists were bruised and swollen. And all the while he felt a growing certainty that his grandfather meant to let him die in here. He had killed his mother. His grandfather was going to kill him.

The walls started to move, to close in around him. Tighter and tighter. The ceiling was pressing down. Motes of light swam before his eyes. His heart stopped, then began to hammer in his chest.

He lay in the camp infirmary, on a narrow cot. The doctor, chosen from among the other convicts for his skill, leaned over the boy, bathing his face.

"Colonel Pendelton." He spoke the name like a curse. "The man's not human. Damn him to everlasting hell." The voice seemed to be coming from a faraway place. "To do this to his own grandson—"

The boy ran his tongue over his fever-cracked lips. "My father was a misbegotten rebel. . . . And I—killed my mother. . . ."

"That's a lie." The doctor was speaking quickly, as if he feared he would be interrupted before he could finish. "Lies, boy. All lies. Yes, the judge called your father a rebel, but those who followed him called him a patriot. Liam Rafferty was transported to this hellhole because he loved his land too much to see her people suffering under the rule of their English landlords."

The boy tried to take in the words, to grasp their meaning, but his head still swam with weakness and fear.

"You're no bastard, Devlin. Your father married your mother in secret before they ran away together. They were caught and brought back. He was hanged, and she died giving you birth."

The door of the infirmary creaked open, and the doctor stopped speaking. The boy dropped back into unconsciousness, the words lingering in the depths of his mind.

They lingered still, here in this cool, white-plastered room overlooking the sea. They would be branded into him, always. But he would never be sure if they had been a part of his delirium. He never saw the doctor again. If anyone in the settlement knew what happened to the man, they never spoke about it.

The boy hadn't been locked in the punishment cell a second time. The beatings had gone on, though, and his grandfather's brutal words were always the same. Those two strands of memory had blended together over the years, until now he couldn't be sure of the truth.

He didn't know. He only knew he dared not let down his guard, or get too close to anyone. If there was a chance he had come to love Briana, he had all the more reason to keep away from her. That way, she'd be safe.

Briana opened her eyes and reached out beside her, but he was gone. Raising her head from the pillow, she caught sight of him at the window. She called out his name, and he turned to her.

She saw that he had put on his clothes, his shirt-front clinging to his chest. A few strands of his thick, dark hair, damp with sweat, lay across his forehead.

Although he smiled down at her, there was a tightness around his mouth; his eyes were bleak.

What had happened to him since she had fallen asleep only a few hours ago, with his arm around her shoulders and his face resting against her breasts? His skin had been damp then, but only with the lingering warmth of their shared rapture. Now, even before he touched her, she could feel the change in him. When he bent and stroked her bare shoulder there was no trace of warmth in his touch.

"What is it, Devlin? What's wrong?"

He stroked her hair, his smile set and meaningless.

"Is it time to go back to the city?" she asked.

He didn't answer. With one swift, violent gesture, he jerked her to him. His kiss was hard and bruising on her mouth. Then he let her go so abruptly that she fell back against the pillows.

"I have to get back to the skiff. The cargo should be loaded by now."

"How soon before you leave port?"

"I'll be casting off tonight."

* * *

On the drive down from the cliffs, he told her about the mining camps; he spoke of cargoes and profits. "If I do well enough on this voyage, I have my eye on a paddle-wheel steamer. She'll carry three times the freight I can stow aboard the skiff."

His body had relaxed and his voice was casual. Now and then, she thought she heard a hint of the husky softness with which he had spoken to her during their loving, but it disappeared before she could be sure.

Her fingers rested on the cedarwood box in her lap. Kuan Yin: the goddess who would keep her safe until he came back to her.

In the weeks that followed Briana devoted herself to her work in the shop. Although she had had no word from Devlin since their parting that warm September afternoon, she couldn't put him out of her thoughts.

She threw herself into her work with all her energy, hoping to blot out the memory of those few brief nights of love. She pored over the new designs from New York and Paris; she served her customers with meticulous care and redecorated the shop to make it even more attractive, more enticing. And yet, no matter how hard she worked every day she still found herself lying awake at night, staring at the ceiling, tormented by thoughts of Devlin.

She tried to convince herself that there could be no future for them together. She should find another man, one who would make her a suitable husband—the sort of husband Mama had wanted for her. There were plenty of prosperous men here in San Francisco who would have courted her, if she had given them the slightest encouragement. But she couldn't.

Instead, she found herself wondering whether Devlin had found another woman somewhere along the river. Whether even now, as she lay awake in her bed, he might be making love with one of the women from the mining camps. Why not? He had made her no promises—she had no claim on him.

* * *

On a foggy evening late in November Briana sat with Abbie in the small workroom at the rear of the shop. The seamstress bent her head over the lamplit table, taking tiny stitches in a length of mauve silk. Although it was late, Abbie was a meticulous worker; the row of finished silk gowns on the rack behind her attested to her skill. "I wish I had a few yards of braid to trim the flounces," she said. "Purple, perhaps. Or do you think green would be more fashionable?"

"I think the purple's more suitable—" Briana broke off abruptly, silenced by the clanging of a fire bell.

Fires were all too common in San Francisco, where many of the structures were made of wood and canvas. The smaller blazes were quickly extinguished by the city's volunteer fire companies, but Briana had heard about the devastating fire some five years ago. Buildings had been dynamited for firebreaks; the flames had leapt across the spaces, driven by a fierce wind, and two thousand buildings had been burned to the ground.

Her heart speeded up as she ran to fling open the door. But she caught no smell of burning wood on the damp night breeze. With a sigh of relief she started to turn away when she caught sight of the crowd of shouting, jostling men rushing past her. She called to a heavyset man in a brown serge suit. "Please stop a minute!" His face was flushed and his eyes glittered with excitement.

"Where is the fire?" she asked.

"It's no fire, ma'am."

"That's a fire bell, isn't it?"

"Sure is—the Big Six Engine Company. But it ain't been rung that way since back in '51—last time they called out the Vigilantes."

"Vigilantes? But why—"

"Richardson's been shot, that's what! United States Marshal Richardson, ma'am. They've arrested Cora and put him in jail."

"Charles Cora?"

"That's right, ma'am. There's a new bunch of Vigilantes getting organized right now, and they're talkin' about a lynching."

"But Mr. Cora has the right to a trial," she protested.

"Lots of folks don't see it that way," the man told her. "Sam Brannan's making a speech in front of the Oriental Hotel right now. He's all for hanging Cora before the night's out."

The man moved impatiently. "I want to hear what Brannan's got to say—he's a real powerful talker." Then he gave her a look of concern. "But don't you even think about going over to the hotel tonight, ma'am. These mobs can get out of hand mighty fast. Go back inside. And stay away from the windows." He touched his hat and shouldered his way back into the rampaging crowd.

Briana shut the door, locked it, and turned to see Abbie standing close by. "I heard most of it," the seamstress said, her eyes filled with pity. "How dreadful for Miss—Mrs.—for Belle."

Briana's eyes narrowed with indignation. "How can they decide he's guilty without a trial? Just because he's a gambler, that doesn't mean he's capable of murder."

"A mob of drunken men won't wait to find out the truth." All at once, Abbie's her eyes glittered with unshed tears. "Sometimes I wish I had never come to San Francisco. It's still so lawless and violent." She turned her head away, and Briana suspected that she was thinking of her own husband, who had been killed by a savage drunk in a saloon brawl.

She put a comforting hand on Abbie's arm. "You'd better stay here with me tonight," she said.

"They sent in a troop of cavalry to break up the mob. And they arrested Sam Brannan for civil disobedience." The triumph in Belle Cora's voice quickly gave way to anger. "But the coroner's jury found Charles guilty of murder." Her gloved hand tightened on the handle of her parasol, as if she longed to use it as a weapon. "They were scared to vote any other way—the cowardly bastards."

"Who were they afraid of?"

"The Vigilantes," Belle told her.

There had been no customers in the shop all morning, and now, late on this bleak afternoon, Belle had arrived to tell them all that had happened.

Her green eyes burned with outrage. "It was self-defense. Richardson's a poor excuse for a marshal. He was drunk as a skunk when he drew on Charles. What choice did Charles have but to kill him—or let himself get shot down like a dog?"

"Belle, I'm so sorry," Briana said.

"I'm not here looking for sympathy," Belle told her. "What I need is a lawyer. The best in San Francisco. And I can pay whatever he asks. I'll spend every last dollar I've got before I let them hang my man." She paused to catch her breath, then went on. "Cole Forrester's one of the smartest lawyers in the city. And he's been chasing after you for months, hasn't he? You talk to him. Ask him to take the case."

Briana chose her words with care. "Mr. Forrester has a large practice. I doubt he'd be able to take the time to handle the case as you would wish."

"He'd do it for you."

"No, he wouldn't. He doesn't even want me to—" She felt her cheeks grow hot under Belle's keen, searching look.

"Your elegant gentleman friend doesn't want you to have anything to do with my kind of woman."

Briana nodded, too embarrassed to speak.

Belle's full rouged lips curved in a contemptuous smile. "He isn't too high-toned to come over to my place when he's hot for—Oh, lord! I never meant to say that."

"It's all right—I'm not in love with Cole Forrester."

"You must have a special man, though." Belle smiled. "It's that riverboat captain, isn't it? The one who took you aboard Tyler's clipper."

"Is there anything that happens here in the city that you don't know about?"

"Not much." Belle gave a small, rueful laugh. "You needn't worry about him. He's never been to my place—that's the truth."

"Then how did you find out?"

"Tyler's officers were talking about a Captain Rafferty, a big, good-looking man who came aboard the *Star of Canton* with a red-haired young lady to buy goods for her dress shop. So he's the one." She squeezed Briana's arm gently. "You care a lot about him, don't you?"

"Yes, Belle. I care—a lot."

"Every woman needs a man to love—even when the loving brings a whole heap of pain and trouble."

Remembering Belle's situation, Briana pushed aside her thoughts of Devlin and said, "I'm sure you'll find a good lawyer to defend Mr. Cora."

"You bet I will! My Charles isn't guilty of murder and no-body's going to hang him while I've got breath in my body."

She left the shop, her velvet skirts swirling about her. A coachman helped her into her shiny brougham and the hand-some vehicle was quickly swallowed up in the fog.

Briana sighed, and went back inside. She closed the shop and went upstairs to bed. But she lay awake, her thoughts with Devlin, out there on the river. How long would it be before he returned to her again? She turned her eyes to the figurine of Kuan Yin, on the table beside her bed. "Bring him back to me soon," she whispered.

Sixteen

Cole Forrester sat at the polished mahogany desk in his pri-vate office on Montgomery Street, his eyes fixed on the open folder before him. A breeze from the bay stirred the heavy red velvet drapes at the windows; pale spring sunlight glinted on the brass and ormolu clock and sent shafts of light across the thick Turkey carpet. Cole, however, was scarcely aware of his surroundings.

Lost in thought, he was also oblivious to the growing noise in the streets below: the measured tramp of booted feet, the tolling of the mourning bells that marked the passing of James Richardson.

He deliberately shut out all distractions, fixed his eyes on the papers in front of him, and carefully reread the latest information about Briana's background, which he had been gathering over the past year.

Cole's ability to concentrate unswervingly on one particular piece of business while ignoring all else had helped him to make a name for himself as one of the most successful lawyers in San Francisco. That same skill had aided him in his swift rise to power in civic affairs; although he didn't yet hold political office, he had proved himself a force to be reckoned with.

But during all these months, while he had been handling his legal cases with skill and efficiency and attending meetings of the Grand Tribunal, the leaders of San Francisco's Vigilance Committee, he had also gone on with his investigation into Briana's past.

Briana. He felt a hot stirring at the thought of her, an urgent need that made it difficult for him to remain calmly impersonal. Although he had seen little of her during these past months, he hadn't been able to get her out of his mind.

He would be escorting Eleanor Padgett about the city or sitting beside her at a dinner party in her father's house; strolling with her afterward in the moonlit garden, fragrant with the perfume of lavender, heliotrope, and lemon verbena, or waltzing with her at a ball in one of the mansions on Rincon Hill, listening politely to her flirtatious chatter. And then, all at once, a vision of Briana would arise to inflame his senses.

No other woman had ever stirred him as Briana had. It was useless to remind himself that she had refused his offer of marriage; that she had ignored his wishes and gone on running the shop her way, catering to madams, actresses, and other females of dubious character. He had decided to wait before proposing to her again, if he ever did. But he couldn't stop thinking of her.

Once he had begun his search into her past he had gone on methodically, refusing to abandon his quest. His carefully worded inquiries had gone out to certain friends back in Charleston, and after a long, tedious wait he had learned of the scandal that had forced her to leave the city.

No wonder she had invented that pathetic tale of her mother's death from malaria; the truth was far more sordid.

His lips tightened with distaste as he went over the details once more: the violent confrontation between her mother and the Marquis de Valmont in the lady's bedchamber; the struggle over a pistol; the accidental shooting of Lynette Cameron.

He resolved to drop any further investigation into Briana's past. He would find himself a more suitable wife.

He could go straight to Martin Padgett, declare his wish to marry Eleanor, and be accepted as his partner's son-in-law. And he would have done so, if not for his tantalizing memories of Briana.

Briana, with her burnished red-gold hair, and those bewitching amber eyes, shaded by long, dark lashes. Heat seared his loins as he remembered the enticing swell of her firm breasts, the curve of her slender waist. But it wasn't her beauty alone that had bewitched him. She possessed the poise and breeding, the sparkling wit, that would have made her the perfect wife for a man with his ambitions. If only she hadn't been touched by that deplorable scandal back in Charleston.

Without taking an inordinate amount of time from his business affairs, he had made use of his far-reaching legal connections to pursue his quest. It had led from Charleston to Paris and then to the startling discovery that Lynette Cameron hadn't been a respectable widow, living abroad in seclusion with her daughter.

After the death of her husband she had been pursued by the wealthiest men in France. At least, Cole mused with a faint,

sardonic smile, she had shown impeccable taste in choosing her
lovers; the Marquis de Valmont had been one of them.

He reread the most recent letter from the partner in a prominent French law firm, his eyes narrowing thoughtfully as he
weighed the intriguing possibilities. Briana bore the name of
Cameron, Lynette's late husband, who had been a respectable,
prosperous businessman. But if his informant was correct, Briana might lay claim to a far more impressive lineage; to one of
the largest fortunes in France.

He wasn't ready to come to any hasty conclusions, however.
Mere speculations were not enough; he must have absolute
proof. He dipped his pen into the brass and marble inkwell and
began another letter to the Parisian law firm.

An urgent knocking at the office door interrupted him. He
blotted the unfinished letter and slid it back into its folder, then
called to his clerk to enter.

"You're needed down at Fort Gunnybags right away, sir," the
clerk said. "Mr. Sam Brannan and the others in the Tribunal
are holding a meeting."

Cole opened the bottom drawer of his desk, placed the folder
inside, locked the drawer, and returned the key to his chain. The
tramp of marching feet was growing louder, and when he went
to the window he caught sight of a brass cannon glinting in the
pale sunlight; a troop of Vigilantes was dragging it in the direction of the jail. He reached for his tall hat, adjusted the pearl
stickpin in his satin cravat, and left the office.

The Sacramento River stretched out like a shimmering ribbon
of green silk, its banks shaded by oak, sycamore, and eucalyp-
tus. The river curved around the mining camp of Faro Flats,
with its canvas tents and lean-tos. The largest of the tents served
as a saloon and gambling house. Devlin heard the shouts of the
men inside, the click of dice, the rattle of the roulette ball. Guitar
music and the stamping of high heels on the wooden floor, and

the squeals and laughter of the Chilean girls in the fandango house nearby, added to the din.

But he had already turned his back on the camp and was heading for the *Barracuda*, his new paddle-wheel steamer. Quickly, he strode up the gangplank, with Quinn close behind him. The crew had been hastily summoned back to the ship and were already assembled on deck, looking to Devlin for orders.

"Cast off your stern line!" he shouted. "Cast off your spring line!"

"All clear!" Quinn called in return, then gave Devlin a puzzled frown. "We weren't set to leave until nightfall," he said. "We ain't even finished unloading the cargo."

Devlin didn't turn his head but made straight for the bridge, with the baffled Quinn still at his heels.

"We goin' on upriver?"

"We're going back to San Francisco," Devlin replied. "Give the order to turn her about."

When Quinn gaped at him in surprise his gray eyes went steely. "At once, if you please, Mr. Quinn." Such formality was rare between the two men, and Quinn hastened to obey.

"All hands!" he roared. "Stand by to come about!"

The sailors instantly sprang into action, their bare feet slapping against the planks of the deck.

"We'll be takin' nearly half the cargo back to the city," Quinn said.

Devlin's face was set in grim lines; a muscle twitched at the corner of his jaw. "You heard what that miner said back there—Casey's shot James King."

"There's shootings in the city all the time," Quinn observed with a shrug.

Devlin's eyes hardened. "This one's different. That firebrand King has been using his *Evening Bulletin* to crusade for what he calls 'law and order.' He published an editorial all about Casey's criminal record, his eighteen months in Sing Sing. And Casey shot him down. Now those Vigilantes have the excuse they've been looking for since last autumn."

"But King ain't dead yet," Quinn reminded him.

"He wasn't dead when that miner left the city. By now he may be. If he is, Casey'll hang. And Cora, too."

"Charles Cora! What's he got to do with it? He's still in jail, ain't he? Waiting for a second trial."

Devlin silenced Quinn with an impatient gesture. "Get those engines going. Full speed."

Quinn's powerful voice boomed across the deck. The ship's bell rang out; the engines started thudding and the paddle wheels began to turn, the water running off them in silvery sheets. The *Barracuda* churned into midchannel, swung about, and headed downriver.

Devlin's muscles went hard with tension; his hands locked on the wheel as if the force of his grasp could somehow move the ship faster. This time he wouldn't have to depend on the vagaries of the wind. The steamer's powerful engines would get him back to the city at top speed.

Back to Briana.

Each time he'd returned to the city during the past year he'd heard the angry talk in the saloons, the mounting demands for action to put a stop to the activities of the criminal element. San Francisco was changing from a sprawling, raucous port where gold-seekers came racing ashore, hot-eyed with the lust for gold, bought their supplies, then headed for the diggings.

It was becoming a thriving seaport metropolis, like Liverpool, Amsterdam, or New York, its waterfront lined with the offices of import firms; with warehouses and auction rooms crammed with valuable merchandise from the four corners of the world. Its newly completed custom house, an imposing structure with Corinthian columns, a granite portico, and mahogany furnishings, lent the city a look of solid respectability, as did the Merchant's Exchange, which. supplied information about ships and cargoes and served as a meeting place for successful businessmen.

Those same businessmen were growing ever more impatient with the officials of the city government; loudly they demanded greater protection from the lawless element. If Mayor Van Ness and his fellow elected officials couldn't be relied on to punish these criminals, then it was up to the Vigilantes to take affairs into their own hands.

The solid citizens had bristled with outrage when Charles Cora had managed to get off with a hung jury the first time, thanks largely to Belle's determined action and the skill of her high-priced lawyers.

Although he faced a second trial, there was talk that he would get off again, or that, even if the verdict went against him, his friends would break him out of jail before he could hang.

The shooting of King and the arrest of Casey had only provided the match to the fuse. The city was ready to explode into violence at any moment.

The miner who had arrived in Faro Flats only a few hours before had reminded his hearers that the Vigilantes now were well prepared, ready to march at the command of their leaders. "Cole Forrester—Sam Brannan—A word from them and all hell's goin' to break loose."

Devlin could well believe it. For months the Vigilantes had been meeting in a building that had quickly come to be known as Fort Gunnybags, because of the sandbags piled up around it. They had gathered an impressive supply of weapons and had drilled their troops: twenty-six hundred men, organized into companies of one hundred, armed with shotguns, knives, pistols, muskets, and cannon.

"Last I heard King was still alive," the miner had told his avid listeners, "but Casey shot him at point-blank range. Don't look like he'll make it."

The others had agreed. "If he dies, Casey's life won't be worth a plug nickle. Mark my words, he'll hang."

"And Cora, along with him."

Devlin, in the course of his wanderings, had seen the devastation wrought by other mobs in other cities. An icy hand clutched at his vitals as he thought of Briana, unprotected in her shop on Sansome Street.

"You'll be wantin' your coffee, Captain." Devlin turned and saw Tommy standing beside him. He took the steaming cup the boy held out to him, then set it down untasted.

"Don't you worry, Cap'n. No reason Miss Briana should be mixed up in this here riotin'," the boy said. "Long as she stays inside her shop she'll be all right, same as last year."

Devlin tried to tell himself Tommy was talking sense. The rioting last autumn, after Cora had killed Richardson, had been fierce but brief; the violence hadn't touched Briana.

"This time it'll be worse. The Vigilantes are a lot better organized now. They're out there, whipping up the mob." His eyes were hard. "No telling how far they'll go."

"Briana, no!" Abbie, usually soft-spoken and gentle, now stood blocking the door, bristling like a small, irate hen. "You're not going out in the streets today. I won't let you go."

Briana's arms tightened around the heavy cardboard box that was nearly as tall as she was. "I made Belle a promise and I intend to keep it."

"But she already considers herself Charles Cora's wife," Abbie reminded her. "And even if she wants a proper, legal ceremony before he's hanged—" Her voice shook, but she swallowed and forced herself to go on. "She has no need for a white wedding gown."

"You spent all last night working on that gown," Briana reminded her.

"How was I to know Fred wouldn't be here this morning to deliver it?"

Since Briana, with Devlin's help, had bought that first shipment of silks from Captain Tyler's clipper, she had not only kept her shop going, her trade had prospered beyond her expectations. While Abbie had turned out a new collection of silk gowns, other ships had come into port. Briana had bought satins and velvets, taffetas and brocades, Brussels and Valenciennes lace, and rolls of embroidered ribbon to add to her stock.

And she had hired a delivery boy, a skinny young man who hadn't been equal to the rugged life of the gold camps, but who had been unwilling to return, empty-handed, to Massachusetts to face the scorn of his family. Fred had proven himself industrious and reliable until now, but this morning there was no sign of him.

"I suppose he's on his way to Fort Gunnybags with the rest," she said uneasily. She glanced out the shop window. "It looks as if every man and boy in the city's out there."

"All the more reason you should stay inside," Abbie snapped at her.

Briana wavered, then remembered the anguish in Belle's face when she had come to the shop to order the gown. No amount of rice powder or lip rouge had been enough to hide her pallor completely.

"Maybe it's too late to save my Charles," she had said. "but when I stand up with him right in front of the preacher, I'm going to be wearing the finest wedding gown you can make me. White satin trimmed with your finest Brussels lace, over the widest crinoline you've got. A white veil with a wreath of orange blossoms. And a bouquet of roses and jasmine."

Belle Cora, parlor house madam, was possessed with a sudden determination to be married in white, complete with veil and bouquet. Under other circumstances Briana might have found the idea ludicrous. But not now. This was to be Belle's last gesture of devotion to Charles Cora, the man she had loved all these years.

Briana raised her chin and fixed an unwavering gaze on Abbie. "I'll take the phaeton," she said. "If I start right away, there'll be time enough to get to Belle's house and deliver the dress." Once, Briana would have flinched from the very idea of going to a parlor house, whatever the urgency of her errand. Now such proprieties seemed meaningless.

"Suppose the men at the livery stable have all gone to the fort?"

"Then I'll harness the horse myself."

Abbie, white-faced and trembling, clutched Briana's arm. "But you won't go anywhere near Fort Gunnybags. Promise me."

Briana repressed a shudder at the very thought of witnessing a hanging. "I'll give Belle the dress and come right back." Gently, she detached Abbie's clinging hand. "But if I'm going to get to her house in time, I've got to leave at once."

Last November, after Charles Cora had shot Marshal Richardson, the city had exploded into rioting. Now, as news of the death of James King spread through the streets, San Francisco had gone into solemn mourning; Briana found the silence far more ominous.

She drove her phaeton past stores draped in black bunting; past saloons and gambling halls shut down out of respect for the crusading newspaper editor. Bells were tolling the death knell, and she passed the procession leaving the church to take King's casket to its final resting place. Never had she seen the city in such a somber mood; even the warm spring sunlight did little to dispel the chill that had taken possession of her.

At last she caught sight of the tall, narrow wooden building, painted a vivid cerise and trimmed with intricate scrollwork. The shades were tightly drawn.

Briana got down and climbed the front steps, then shifted the long shiny box and raised the knocker. She had never visited Belle's establishment and only the exigency of the errand had brought her to such a place today. With the deathlike silence that lay across the city, broken by the tramping feet of the Vigilantes—with Charles Cora and James Casey already locked up in Fort Gunnybags—it seemed unimportant that she might be seen, standing on the doorstep of the most notorious parlor house in the city.

The sound of the heavy brass knocker was lost in the din from the adjacent streets: the tolling of the bells, the tramp of marching feet. At last the door swung open, and Briana found herself confronted by a plump maid in a black uniform, with a starched linen apron and cap.

"Belle ordered this gown from my shop. Please give it to her at once. And tell her—" But what possible words would serve to express her sympathy?

"Miss Belle ain't here, ma'am. She's gone off to the fort."

Briana's heart sank as she realized that, if she were to get the dress to Belle, she would have to go on to Fort Gunnybags herself. She remembered Abbie's warning and flinched at the prospect of making her way to the fort through a crowd of men bent on violence. Yet she was unwilling to return to the shop without keeping her promise.

"That there's a mighty big box," the maid observed.

And no wonder, Briana thought; it contained not only the dress, but also the wide crinoline underskirt, the satin corset lined with heavy whalebone, the long veil of fine Brussels lace, and the bridal bouquet. Briana had to hold it in both arms, but even so it was all she could do to keep a firm grip on it.

She couldn't bring herself to ask how soon the hanging might take place. She went weak with revulsion at the prospect. Instead, she asked, "How was Belle when she left?"

"Miss Belle's bearing up real well," the maid said.

Briana's throat tightened with sympathy. Belle would put a brave face on it, no matter what she was feeling inside.

"Perhaps she has a—male employee—who could deliver the dress to the fort," she ventured.

The maid shook her head. "We got a couple of big bruisers workin' here, keepin' the customers in line. But they both went off with Miss Belle. That's a mean crowd out there. She figured someone might try to stop her carriage." She sighed. "Miss Belle sure had her heart set on wearin' a fancy white dress."

Briana's thoughts went back to that day last autumn, when she had confided her feelings for Devlin to Belle, and she remembered what Belle had said.

Every woman needs a man to love—even when the loving brings a whole heap of pain and trouble.

Suppose it was Devlin who was locked up in the fort right now, awaiting death on the gallows. She dared not let herself think about it.

Instead, she forced her thoughts back to her errand. Belle had her heart set on being married in a proper wedding gown. All right, then—she'd see to it that Belle had at least that much to help her through her ordeal.

She turned and walked back to the phaeton, settled the big box on the ledge behind the seat, and grasped the reins in her gloved hands. She held herself erect and took a deep breath. She was a respectable businesswoman, delivering her merchandise. What reason would any man have to prevent her from carrying out her errand?

Devlin had never visited Briana's shop before. During the past year, whenever he had come ashore he had sent a note by Tommy, and she had come to meet him at the Gamborenas' inn up on the cliffs. Although Abbie didn't know him by sight, she quickly guessed who this tall, powerful man in his captain's uniform must be. "Captain Rafferty?"

"That's right," he said. She peered at him cautiously through the half-open door. She saw, on one side of him, a huge seaman with an orange tomcat perched on his shoulder; on the other side stood wiry, gangling boy with a shock of sandy hair.

Across the street, a gang of sailors stood waiting, their eyes fixed on their captain. They were a rough-looking lot, armed with pistols, rifles, clubs, and iron bars.

"Stand aside, ma'am." Devlin's tone was quiet but commanding, and Abbie moved out of his way. He came striding in with his two companions. "I've come for Briana. I'm going to take her aboard my ship."

"You're too late." The thin, wrenlike woman gave him a reproachful stare.

An icy tide moved through Devlin. "Where is she?"

"She went to take the dress to Belle's place. She promised

she'd come right back." A quaver crept into her voice. "She's been gone so long—and with that mob out there—I never should have let her go. Lord knows what's happened to her."

Devlin could deal with a mutinous crew or a raging storm at sea, but not with a hysterical female.

"You're Abbie Dawson, I believe." He gave her a reassuring smile and spoke with all the conviction he could muster. "Briana won't come to any harm. I'm here to see to that."

"But we don't even know where she is." Her fingers clutched at his sleeve. "I made her promise me she wouldn't go anywhere near Fort Gunnybags."

"Holy saints!" Quinn bellowed. "What would possess her to risk her neck goin' there at a time like this?"

"Belle's wedding gown. Briana promised to deliver it in time for the ceremony."

Quinn stared at Abbie as if he thought the woman was out of her senses. "That whorehouse madam's gettin' married?" Then he added, "Beggin' your pardon, ma'am."

"Tommy, you stay here with Mrs. Dawson.

The boy bridled at Devlin's command. "I ain't stayin' behind if Miss Briana's in trouble."

"Mrs. Dawson needs your protection," he said tersely. He turned to Quinn. "You and the crew'll come with me."

Quinn lifted Jigger from his shoulder and set him down on the floor. The cat gave his master a reproachful stare, then stalked off to settle himself on the plush seat of a small gilt chair.

Fort Gunnybags, a large, square building, was bounded by California, Sacramento, Front, and Davis streets. Along the front of the fort, the gunnysacks filled with sand were piled eight feet high; serving as a barricade with an imposing brass cannon at each end. Even as Briana's phaeton neared the building she caught sight of Cole, standing on a wooden platform behind the barricade, addressing the crowd.

He was a somewhat incongruous figure in his dark gray and

white striped trousers, cut fashionably narrow and strapped under his shoes; his satin cravat and embroidered waistcoat. But his audience, mindful of his importance as a leader of the Grand Tribunal, kept their eyes fastened on him in respectful silence.

"Ours is a solemn mission. We will have law and order in our city. We will have justice for honest citizens. These heinous crimes will not go unpunished."

She strained to hear the rest of his words; then her attention was drawn by a more ominous sound: the pounding of carpenters' hammers. They were working at top speed to finish the gallows.

"Hold it right there, lady." Briana choked back a cry as a Vigilante in a red flannel shirt and canvas jeans seized her horse's bridle. The phaeton lurched to one side, then came to a stop. His eyes quickly moved over her, taking in the neat black silk dress and bonnet and the pallor of her face.

Somehow, in spite of her rising fear, she managed to give him a cool stare. "Please let me pass."

"Sorry, ma'am, but this ain't no place for a decent female. You best turn round and go back home."

"Is Belle Cora inside the fort?"

He stared at her suspiciously. "What if she is?"

Briana twisted around and reached for the box on the ledge behind her. "I've got to go to her."

"What for?"

"I have to deliver her wedding dress." She rose from the seat and tried to get down, but the man barred her way.

"Not a chance," he told her. His tone, his look, were no longer respectful. "You a friend of Belle Cora's?"

She glared at him. "That's no concern of yours." He jerked at the reins and the horse whinnied in protest at such rough treatment. Briana cried out, her voice shrill with mounting fear. "Let go of my horse!"

The commotion drew the attention of the men who stood nearby. They moved closer, until their bodies pressed against the sides of the phaeton.

"Who is she?" one of them asked.

The man who held the bridle snorted with contempt. "Friend of Belle's," he said.

"What you got in that box, lady?" another demanded.

The mood of the crowd, which had been silent and somber until now, started to turn ugly. She felt the air around her crackle with tension.

"What're you up to?"

"Bet you're in on a scheme to help Belle get Cora free!"

Her horse tossed its head with fear, whinnied, then reared up. Briana was thrown against the side of the phaeton, and the box slipped from her hands and landed on the ground.

"Open that box, boys! Let's see what's inside."

"Don't you dare touch that!" she cried.

One of the men reached up and grasped her arm. "Cora's goin' to swing this time! Him *an'* Casey. An' if you're tryin' to help Belle get them out, you'll regret it."

"Likely she's one of Belle's girls!"

"She's a goodlookin' piece, an' no mistake."

An unkempt miner, his beard stained with tobacco juice, grinned up at her. "Maybe you're hidin' a pistol under that fancy outfit. Let's have a look."

He clambered up into the phaeton, seized her by the shoulder, and then shoved his hand inside her bodice, his rough fingers thrusting between her breasts, bruising her soft skin. Now other hands were reaching up under her skirts, tearing at her petticoats, clutching at her legs, tugging at the waistband of her pantelettes.

Revulsion surged through her. "Cole!" She called out his name, and her piercing cry echoed across the square.

Cole broke off in midsentence. She saw him turn his head. He was looking straight at her. A dark mist started to swirl before her eyes. Somehow she managed to hold onto consciousness long enough to cry out again.

"Cole—help me!"

Seventeen

Cole broke off his speech as he heard a voice calling his name, pleading for help. The cry came from the struggling woman in the phaeton across the square. He caught his breath in dismay as he recognized it.

Briana!

She was making a valiant but hopeless attempt to fight off the growing mob of men who surrounded her. One of them had already climbed into the phaeton, while another was scrambling up over the side. Narrowing his eyes, he caught a glimpse of her torn dress, her white skin bared to the avid stares of the men, the heavy waves of her burnished red hair disheveled and falling about her shoulders. What the devil was she doing here at the fort—today of all times?

"You men! Let the woman go!" he called out. "Get back from that carriage at once!"

His followers, members of the Vigilantes, had been well trained. They knew him as a respected member of the city's social structure, and also as a strong, demanding leader who would deal severely with any breech of discipline.

At any other time his command might have been enough to stop them. But now they were caught up in the growing tension, the lust for violence that had been stirred by the prospect of the lynching.

"You don't understand, Mr. Forrester," one of Briana's attackers shouted. "Belle's figurin' to get her man out before he swings! And this little slut's come here tryin' to help her!"

Cole stared at Briana and her tormenters in disbelief. Such a preposterous notion. He was about to speak out in her defense, but he stopped himself in time. Good Lord! Suppose the man was right? Suppose she had gotten herself involved in an attempt to free Cora. It was just possible. . . .

She'd always been impulsive, reckless; quick to flout conventions when it suited her. On the voyage to California she had agreed to share her cabin with Poppy Nolan, a common trollop. And she had disregarded his advice a second time, when she had gone on catering to the undesirable females who came to her shop.

Had Briana gone too far this time and gotten herself involved in really serious trouble? Had she agreed to take part in some dangerous scheme to help Belle spring Cora from the fort?

"Look at this here fancy box, Mr. Forrester!" an irate voice shouted out. The man raised the box high in the air. "It's big enough to hold a couple of rifles!"

"Four or five, more likely!"

"Bet she's got a couple of pistols stashed away under her skirts!"

"We'll find out soon enough!"

Briana cried out again, a wordless plea for help. Driven by instinct, Cole took a step toward the ladder leading down to the square. He had to get to Briana, to save her from the mob.

Then he hesitated, struggling to control his first impulse. This wasn't the time for rash action, he told himself. What happened here during the next few hours could play a decisive part in the success of his carefully laid plans.

He stood immobile, while the men were ripping open the box. A froth of white satin and lace spilled out on the grimy cobblestones.

"Look, boys! It's a wedding dress. And a veil, too."

A roar of cruel laughter rang out across the square. "A wedding dress for Belle. Ain't that somethin'?"

"Put them back!" Briana cried, momentarily distracted from her own desperate plight. "They'll be torn—ruined—"

"Now wouldn't that be a shame?" a rough voice mocked her.

Weak and dizzy as she was, she still found the strength to pull

herself upright, gripping the side of the phaeton. With her free
hand she managed to retrieve her whip and struck out blindly.

The man who was fumbling with her breasts gave a yell of
outrage. "Damn wildcat!" A thin red wheal sprang out on his
cheek. He growled deep in his throat, his florid face looming
over hers. She gagged at the rank stench of sweat. His thick
fingers closed like steel pincers on one of her nipples.

Fiery darts of pain shot from her nipple, radiating over her
breasts and out along every nerve of her body to the tips of her
fingers. The whip fell from her hand and she heard herself
moaning like a tortured animal.

A terrifying darkness, shot with tiny sparks of light, began
to swim before her eyes. The black cloud deepened until it
threatened to engulf her. But she mustn't faint. She mustn't . . .

A pistol shot rang out. "Let her go!"

Through the encroaching darkness, the familiar, powerful
voice, raised to quarterdeck pitch, came to her. It sent new
strength flowing through her.

She raised her head in time to see Devlin fire a second shot
straight up in the air. There was a murmur of anger from the
crowd, but those nearest the phaeton started to back off, stumbling into the men behind them.

Devlin, with Quinn at his side, was shouldering his way toward
her. Behind him came his bronzed, hard-eyed crew, all of them
heavily armed and spoiling for a fight. Other seamen from other
ships, recognizing Devlin and his crew, joined forces with them.

Briana gave a sob of relief as Devlin reached her. His gray
eyes narrowed with cold fury as he reached up and dragged one
of her tormentors over the side of the phaeton. He smashed his
fist into the fat, sweating face. The man's head snapped back
and he slumped to the ground. But Devlin hauled him up again,
threw him against the side of the phaeton, and struck him again.
And yet again.

Meanwhile, Quinn was taking on two of the others, swinging
his hamlike fists, knocking them down like bowling pins. One
of the mob, more daring than the rest, tried to lead a counter-

attack. "Law an' order!" he shouted the Vigilantes' rallying cry. But a blow on the head from a seaman's club sent him staggering backward.

Devlin climbed into the phaeton, threw his arm around Briana, holding her against him so tightly, she could scarcely breathe. He brought the whip down on the horse's back and the startled beast sprang forward, its flailing hooves scattering the nearest men in all directions.

The crew of the *Barracuda*, still seething with the lust for battle, went on fighting. They struck out with their rifle butts, clubs, and fists, clearing the way for the phaeton. As it sped down Sacramento Street, lurching and swaying, away from the fort, she let herself give way at last. Devlin was beside her; he would take care of her. Her head fell back against his arm, and she surrendered to the all-enveloping blackness.

Briana stirred, opened her eyes, and found herself lying in her own bed. Her body still ached, but someone had removed her clothes and dressed her in a silk nightdress. She gave a sigh of gratitude at the light touch of the delicate fabric; her breasts and thighs still ached from the manhandling of the mob.

She raised her head and forgot her pain as she saw Devlin beside her. He leaned over her, stroking her hair, his touch gentle. She reached up and pressed her fingers against his cheek. "It is you," she whispered, as if to reassure herself.

She stretched out her arms and clung to him.

"You came for me," she said shakily. "I needed you—and you were there."

How long had she been unconscious? Her eyes moved to the window and she caught sight of first wisps of gray mist, swirling up the slanting streets from the harbor to press against the windowpane. Twilight would soon be here. Then her gaze touched on the statue of Kuan Yin, the delicate figure gleaming softly, opalescent in the deepening shadows. "Perhaps the goddess brought you to me," she murmured.

He gave her a warm, tender smile. "I told you Kuan Yin would take care of you."

He dropped down on the side of the bed and she pressed her face against his chest, inhaling the scent of him: salt, brandy, and his own potent maleness. It felt so good, so reassuring, to be close to him like this; to hear the strong, steady beat of his heart. She burrowed even closer, as if trying to make herself a part of him. If only she could stay here, sheltered in his arms, forever.

But she couldn't hope to shut out the world for long. "The goddess had a little help, of course," he was saying. "One of the miners who came to Faro Flats brought news of the shooting of James King." He went on to explain how he had turned his ship around and come for her. His words forced her back to reality.

"What about all those miners waiting for your ship to bring their supplies?" she asked.

"They'll have to wait a little longer." His voice was low and husky. "Briana, if anything had happened to you—"

He bit back whatever else he might have been about to say. Maybe he was afraid to reveal his deepest feelings, she thought. But there was no need for words between them, not now.

For a timeless moment she went on clinging to him, trying once more to shut out everything else. But she caught the thudding of footsteps out in the streets. The bells had stopped tolling, and there was no shouting, no sounds of disorder. The men were silent, as if the lynching had left them drained of all violence.

She didn't want to think about Fort Gunnybags, or the pounding of the hammers. But she couldn't refrain from asking, "Cora and Casey—were they—"

"They were hanged," he said. His gray eyes were bleak, his voice detached. "I guess you could say Cora was the lucky one. His neck was broken right away."

"And Belle?"

"They let her marry Cora before he swung. She kept on denying that he was guilty of murder, right to the end. Still claimed the marshal's shooting had been self-defense. But she said that if Charles Cora was going to his death branded as a murderer, then she meant to go through the rest of her life bearing a murderer's name. They say she stood up strong and proud beside him, in her white dress and veil." He paused, then added, "They took him away, right after the ceremony."

He drew back and looked down at her. And she heard the swiftly rising anger in his voice. "That dress—Abbie told me all about it. What in hell possessed you to try to get it to her at the fort? Didn't you stop to think of the risk you were running?"

She wanted to say she'd been thinking, not only of her promise to Belle, but of him, too. Of her love for him. Of how she would have felt in Belle's place. But she stopped herself in time, knowing she could never make him understand.

"Hold me," she whispered. "Just hold me." He drew her close again, his mouth warm and seeking. His tongue traced the outline of her lips. She tightened her arms around him, and her lips parted to receive his kiss.

Her hands stroked the thick, dark hair that curled along the back of his neck. Then she moved her fingers inside his shirt, and felt the damp heat of his skin against her palms. Her fingertips pressed against his back, touching, caressing.

He raised his lips from hers. "Don't tempt me, sweetheart," he said softly, "or I'll get into that bed with you and take off that nightgown and . . ." He ran his hand over her shoulder and cupped her breast. She flinched slightly, for her breast still ached. He caught her response and drew his hand away. His mouth tightened. "I should have killed that rotten swine."

She shook her head. "There's been too much killing already."

"You've been through one hell of a day. What you need now is rest."

Slowly, reluctantly, he rose to his feet.

"Don't leave me," she murmured. "Not yet."

"I don't want to, but I've got to get down to the dock. I came straight to the fort without even stopping to fill out the papers and get clearance. If I don't get to the custom house fast, the authorities could impound the *Barracuda*."

She stifled all further protest. "I understand." He was possessed by his ships—clipper, skiff, paddle-wheel—it didn't matter. And drawn by the beckoning currents of the rivers and the seas. Always, they would take him from her.

Although she was exhausted, every muscle in her body aching, she longed for him to stay beside her, to hold her while she slept. But she warned herself that she mustn't ask for more than he could give. He took her hand, pressing it against his cheek, then brushed his lips across her palm.

"The city's starting to quiet down. Forrester has dismissed the Vigilantes. I don't expect there'll be any further trouble," he reassured her. "But I'll leave a cordon of my men to stand guard outside your shop, all the same."

"Mr. Forrester, you can't go up there. I've already told you Briana's resting." But Cole's footsteps were coming closer, up the stairs and along the hall. Although it was midmorning of the following day, Abbie had forbidden her to come down to the shop. The seamstress had brought her breakfast in bed and insisted that she stay in her room.

"I must speak with her, Mrs. Dawson. I won't tire her, I promise."

"It's all right, Abbie," Briana called out through the half-open door.

She had been brushing her hair, and now it fell over her shoulders in gleaming waves. She set down her brush and rose from the bench at her dressing table, reaching for an embroidered silk wrapper and slipping it on over her nightdress. A moment later Cole was there, standing in the doorway of her room. She motioned him inside and led the way to the chintz-covered sofa near the window.

He sat down beside her. Her amber eyes were cool and distant; for once he felt at a loss for words. He cleared his throat, but the carefully planned speech he'd been framing on his ride over to the shop now seemed hollow and unconvincing. Silently, he cursed Devlin Rafferty for having taken such daring action while he, himself, had been paralyzed by indecision.

"It's been awhile since you came calling," she said. "I certainly didn't expect to see you here today." Her voice was as remote as the look she gave him. "Surely you shouldn't be taking time from your many responsibilities as a leader of the Grand Tribunal to go about paying social calls."

"The Tribunal has completed its business for the time being," he said. "Justice has been served. Those two miscreants suffered the punishment they deserved."

"You're a most effective speaker," she interrupted. "But surely there's no need to waste your talent on an audience of one." She couldn't keep the irony out of her voice.

"Briana, I know how you must feel about what happened to you yesterday. That's why I came here. I want to explain—"

"There's no need," she said. "I've been told that Belle was able to wear her wedding gown. In spite of those vicious ruffians you call your troops."

"My men believe in their cause. They thought they were doing their duty in trying to prevent Cora and Casey from escaping punishment for their crimes. As for Belle, I warned you against becoming involved with a woman like that. No doubt you realize now that I was right."

Briana pressed her lips together to keep back an angry retort.

"But I haven't come here to talk about Belle," he went on.

She raised her eyes to his, her gaze direct, challenging him to continue. "Then perhaps you'll tell me why you have come."

He reached out and put his hands on her upper arms, then drew her toward him. His touch was light, tentative. She remained stiff and unyielding, but he wasn't put off.

Lord, but she was a sight to stir any man's hunger, with that burnished hair falling around the white oval of her face, fanning out across her shoulders. The embroidered robe she wore did little to conceal the firm roundness of her breasts, or the enticing lines of her long legs.

Even so, he warned himself to keep a tight rein on his emotions; to weigh the situation carefully before he committed himself.

He already had proof that she was the natural daughter of the Marquis de Valmont, his only living offspring. According to the documents from Paris, she had been born over a year after the death of James Cameron. And whatever her mother's reputation, the marquis must have believed he was her father. He had died naming her as his sole heir: his fortune, his estate in Brittany, his magnificent hôtel in Paris—except for a few bequests to loyal servants, she stood to inherit it all.

But even so, wouldn't it be wise to wait for confirmation that there were no other relatives, however distant, who might lay claim to the nobleman's estates and fortune? As a lawyer, he knew all too well that as soon as a man like the marquis passed away, individuals with the most tenuous claims often came forward to try to get hold of whatever they could.

Thank heaven she knew nothing of the great wealth she would inherit once the will was settled. She still believed herself to be the daughter of James Cameron. He had warned the lawyer in Paris not to start a search for Briana and had paid well for the man's compliance. But even so, if he waited too long, she might somehow discover the truth about her parentage on her own.

He spoke quickly, his voice soft and seductive. "Briana, my love, you injured me deeply when you refused my marriage proposal. But now surely you must realize how much you need a husband's care and guidance. You cannot go on alone."

"I wasn't alone yesterday," she reminded him. "Captain Rafferty was there to help me."

"A fortunate coincidence; nothing more. The man happened to be on hand, and he and his men were probably drunk—out looking for a fight, like all seamen when they come ashore." He dismissed Rafferty with a careless shrug.

"Had I been your husband, I would have seen to it that you were safe in your own home, as any decent woman ought to be. Instead you showed a lack of judgment, a shocking disregard for convention, when you came to the fort. It was your association with Belle that exposed you to such rough treatment by those men."

"I made her a promise. I did what I felt was right."

"But you were misguided." He caught the look of protest in her eyes, the stubborn set of her chin. He must choose his words carefully. "My feelings for you haven't changed," he said, his voice soft and caressing. "I still want you for my wife."

"Aren't you afraid that I would keep you from realizing your lofty ambitions? Perhaps you should find yourself a docile wife, one who could be relied on to restrain her impulses."

Her amber eyes were glittering dangerously. Had he gone too far in reproaching her conduct? He slid his arms around her. "You are the only woman I could ever think of marrying."

She freed herself from his embrace. "Indeed?" She didn't even try to hide the mockery in her voice. "And does Eleanor Padgett know that?"

Cole flinched at her words. "Miss Padgett is my partner's daughter. Naturally, we are often thrown together. She is a charming young lady, and I find her company agreeable. But I am not in love with her, and I've never led her to believe I was." He went on quickly, urgently. "Briana, you've got to believe me. It's you I love."

"Enough to take me exactly as I am?" Her lips curved in a smile. "I don't think so. You disapprove of my loyalty to Belle and the other women with whom I do business."

"Business! Good Lord, Briana, you've no need to give another thought to that paltry shop of yours. Why, once we are married there'll be no need——" He caught himself quickly. Once they were married he would tell her of her inheritance; he'd see to it that any possible legal obstacles were swept out of the way. Then, as her husband, he would have control of her fortune.

"Give up the shop," he urged. "Sell it, or turn it over to Mrs. Dawson. I'll devote the rest of my life to taking care of you."

"That's damned noble of you, Forrester."

Briana started, drawing in her breath sharply. She hadn't

heard Devlin coming up the stairs. Now he stood in the doorway, regarding Cole with a sardonic smile.

Cole got to his feet and approached him warily. "What's your business here, Captain Rafferty?"

"Briana needs a man to look out for her. You were saying so yourself." He grinned, his white teeth flashing against his deeply tanned skin. "So, here I am, ready and willing to take care of her, from now on."

She looked from one to the other and felt a hot tide of anger swelling inside her. She sprang up from the sofa, the skirt of her wrapper billowing out around her.

"That's enough!" she cried, her eyes snapping with sparks of golden fire. "How dare the two of you stand there, talking about me as if I were a—a piece of property?"

She glared at Devlin, and then at Cole. "Both of you, get out of my room. Out of my shop. Now!"

Devlin laughed softly, but Cole ignored him. He spoke soothingly to her. "My dear, you are beside yourself. If you will send this man away, we will talk like two rational people."

Her gaze darted about the room, then lighted on a porcelain vase. Her fingers closed around it and she picked it up. She drew back her arm. "Out!"

Cole stared at her in dismay. "You are obviously beside yourself. I'll come back when you've recovered from your ordeal."

He bowed and left the room. She heard his even tread as he went downstairs.

But Devlin remained where he was, lounging against the door frame, one corner of his mouth quirked in a smile. Unable to control herself another moment, she flung the vase at him with all her strength. He stepped aside with the swift, easy grace of a jungle cat.

The vase arced through the air and shattered against the wall. He kicked the shards aside and strode across the room to confront her. "I have to agree with Forrester," he said. "You do need looking after."

Before she could protest he pulled her against him. "I have

to go back upriver," he said, "but I won't be able to keep my mind on my ship. Not when I'm worrying over you. Next time there's trouble I might not get back in time to help you out of whatever predicament you get yourself into."

"I can take care of myself."

"You weren't doing a good job of it yesterday," he reminded her. She struggled to break free, but his hands gripped her shoulders with implacable force. "That's why I've decided to take you with me."

"You—you've decided!" She was too furious to choose her words with care. "Isn't there some woman in one of the gold camps to keep you satisfied between your visits back to San Francisco?"

All at once his eyes turned dark as the night sea; as his grip tightened, she realized that his hands were unsteady. "It's you I need." His voice shook. "I'll marry you, if that's what you want."

Two proposals in a single hour. She stifled a sudden urge to break into hysterical laughter. But she saw the tension in every plane and angle of his face. Why should he look like that at such a time? He wanted to marry her—he had just told her so. She searched his eyes, seeking the warmth, the tenderness, she might have expected to find there.

Instead she saw uneasiness. No, it was outright fear. Devlin was afraid. But of what? His look baffled and disturbed her.

"I said I'd marry you. Isn't that what you want?" he demanded.

"No, it isn't."

He stared at her, plainly taken aback by her refusal.

"I won't marry you, Devlin. But I will go upriver with you." Her lips curved in a faint smile. "How soon do we sail?"

Eighteen

"Sacramento's certainly changed since the first time I docked here," Devlin told Briana. They stood side by side at the rail of the *Barracuda* while the crew tossed out the mooring lines. "Every time I come into port I find there are more theaters, hotels, and shops."

"It *is* the state capital, after all," she reminded him, stopping herself from adding that, after the rugged, primitive conditions she'd seen in the gold camps along the river, the amenities of Sacramento would come as a welcome respite.

On each of their stops along the river, when she had accompanied him ashore, the men had treated Briana with the greatest respect. Few would have even thought of doing otherwise, with Devlin by her side. Nevertheless, she realized that by going away with him and living openly as his mistress, she had placed herself beyond the pale of respectable society once and for all.

Devlin had offered to marry her, she reminded herself. She was the one who had refused.

I'll marry you if that's what you want. It wasn't only his words, but the look on his face that had filled her with misgivings.

Plenty of men who were used to a roving life might hesitate to commit themselves to marriage. But with Devlin, the reluctance went deeper. Would she ever understand this man she loved? Maybe not, but so long as she was here with him, lying each night in his arms, giving herself up to the wonder of their loving, she would ask for no more.

She looked up at him and felt warmth flooding through her at the sight of his strong profile gilded by the sunlight off the water, his eyes smoky gray under his straight, heavy black brows. He put an arm around her shoulders and brushed his lips across her cheek.

"There's no need for you to wait here while I take care of ship's business." Then, seeing her disappointment, he added, "I'll meet you later, and we'll have a fine dinner at the Olympia Hotel."

A few minutes later she was descending the gangplank with Tommy at her side. Although the state capital might be getting more civilized, Devlin had still insisted that it was no place for a lady to walk about without a male escort.

"Tommy'll take good care of you," he said.

The boy beamed with pride, knowing that Devlin trusted him to look after her. He had scrubbed his face until it glowed, had brushed back his shock of sandy hair, and had changed into a pair of freshly ironed canvas trousers and a spotless white shirt.

Since she'd met Tommy on her first day out of Charleston, he had gone from a shy, skinny boy to the threshold of manhood. He had grown at least three inches taller, and his bony, gangling frame was beginning to fill out. These days he carried himself with a certain assurance. And no wonder, she thought, for any seaman who had rounded the Horn in the teeth of a blizzard need not fear lesser dangers.

Briana was grateful for Tommy's presence, his hand protectively under her elbow. As soon as they reached the levee, she noticed the speculative glances of the men who thronged the streets. Tommy glanced about, as if daring any one of them to approach her.

She had dressed simply during the stops at the gold camps; wearing thick-soled shoes to carry her through the mud around the tents and shacks, and gowns chosen for their practicality, although they were neat and becoming. But for this excursion in Sacramento she had given way to feminine vanity and decked herself out in one of Abbie's most elegant creations: her walking dress of honey-colored silk had been copied from one of the latest Parisian fashion plates; her imported Leghorn hat, with its tilted brim and dashing russet plumes, added a crowning touch of worldly elegance.

Tommy led her away from the levee toward the center of town. "Want me to hire a buggy?" he asked, but she shook her head. She welcomed the opportunity to walk about until it was time to meet Devlin at the hotel.

"This is K Street," Tommy told her. "There's lots of new shops here." Together, they strolled along, looking in the show windows. Then he paused before the window of a small shop that sold musical instruments and stared with interest at the display of harmonicas, accordians, and fiddles.

She glanced at the larger shop next door, and its neatly lettered sign caught her attention: JACOB PERLMAN—DRY-GOODS AND NOTIONS. The window gleamed in the summer sunlight, and the merchandise was arranged with care. She read the sign again and remembered the good-natured peddler who had found her wandering along fog-shrouded Pacific Street on the night she'd run away from her uncle's home. If not for his concern, heaven only knew what might have happened to her. But that Jacob Perlman had been a peddler traveling in a rickety wagon loaded with merchandise and drawn by a sway-backed horse.

She moved to the shop door, then glanced back at Tommy, who was still gazing wistfully at the musical instruments. "Wait for me here," she said. She caught the look of relief on his face; he would have been thoroughly bored by a visit to a dry goods store.

As soon as the proprietor came bustling forward, Briana felt a glow of satisfaction, for this was the same man who had brought her to Devlin's ship that night. But his suit wasn't shabby now; it was made of fine navy-blue broadcloth, carefully tailored for a perfect fit.

He smiled and bowed. "Good afternoon, ma'am. How may I serve you?"

She didn't see the slightest trace of recognition in his face, but that was scarcely surprising. She must look quite different from the frightened, disheveled waif in the torn dress who had stepped out of the fog and nearly gotten herself run down by his horse.

"You don't remember me, do you, Mr. Perlman?"

His dark, keen eyes moved over her; then he struck his hands together in surprise. "I'm afraid I—But wait! You're that girl from Pacific Street. The one who was looking for a clipper ship." He stopped to search his memory. "You're Miss— Cameron. That's the name, right?"

She nodded.

"That night on the Barbary Coast—so scared, you were, and trying hard not to show it. But you must forgive me for not recognizing you right away."

He studied her costume with professional interest. "This fine gown—the lines of the skirt. Right out of *Godey's Ladies Book,* it is. And your hat—the best quality Leghorn." His brow furrowed. "Miss Briana Cameron." Then he gave a wide smile. "You are the owner of that elegant dress shop on Sansome Street in San Francisco?"

"You've heard of my shop all the way up here?" She took pride in realizing that her shop was so well known.

Jacob showed Briana around his store, talking all the while. "That was a bad business you had in San Francisco back in May," he said. "I hope your shop wasn't damaged by the mob."

Briana assured him that the shop had escaped harm. He gave a deep sigh, his dark eyes holding a haunted look. "Such a world," he said sadly. "A man like me leaves the old country to build a better life. And even here, in this rich new land, again I hear about the mobs, the lynchings. Not a few drunken miners, a gang of ex-convicts, but a whole city, with a mayor, a government—and still the men turn into a pack of savages. All in the name of law and order."

She repressed a shudder at the memory, then decided not to tell him of how she, herself, had become involved in the ugly events at Fort Gunnybags. She only said, "My seamstress made Belle Cora's wedding gown. Belle was one of my best customers."

"You say she 'was.' The woman's left San Francisco, has she?"

"No, but she closed down her establishment right after the—after her husband's death. Since then she keeps herself shut away in the home he bought for her. She only leaves on Sundays to attend services at St. Francis Church."

Perlman sighed and shook his head slowly. "That Cora may have been a bad one, like they said. Even so, he was entitled to a fair trial." He gave a rueful shrug. "But with a man like Mr. Cole Forrester talking against him, stirring up the crowd—such a gift for speech-making, Forrester has. It's a pity he uses his talent to twist the law to serve his own purposes."

"Then you've heard Cole Forrester speak in San Francisco?"

"Not there, no. But he visits Sacramento often. He's going up and down the whole state, talking about how we need a strong leader to bring us law and order.

"He uses all the right words, but believe me, Miss Cameron, it's power he wants. That man's hungry for power. And he doesn't care how he gets it. *Ach!* I'm starting to think it's the same, the whole world over." Jacob smiled apologetically. "But this country has been good to me. I've worked hard, and I'm doing well. Soon I'll be able to send for my Rachel."

"You're married, Mr. Perlman?"

"Not yet. But we will be, God willing, as soon as she sets foot in California." He led her to the wide counter at the back of the store. "Come; I will show you some of my newest goods. You won't see any better in San Francisco, if I do say so myself."

She examined his merchandise with unfeigned interest and bought a pair of embroidery scissors in the shape of a stork for Abbie, along with an assortment of the best-quality trimmings: silk and cashmere fringes, buttons of jet and crystal; satin-covered garter elastics, and a brand-new innovation—an Imperial dress elevator.

"It's made with these weighted strings, you see? So a lady can raise or lower her skirt at will, and keep it from dragging in the mud," he explained. "I guess you still got plenty of unpaved streets back in San Francisco."

He made up the package, his hands deft. "I'll have them delivered to you," he said. "What hotel are you staying at?"

She hesitated a moment, then replied, "I'm staying aboard the *Barracuda*. She's a paddle-wheeler, anchored at the foot of J Street."

"I know the one. That's Captain Rafferty's ship." His eyes rested briefly on her face, and she caught the quick flicker of comprehension. Did he remember that the *Osprey* had also belonged to Devlin? "You'll have all your purchases by this afternoon," he assured her respectfully as he bowed her out of the shop.

She found Tommy still staring intently into the window of the shop next door, fascinated by the display of musical instruments.

"Do you know how to play any of these?" she asked with a touch of surprise.

"I can play a couple of tunes on a harmonica," he told her shyly.

"Come along," she said. She led the way inside and told Tommy to pick out the harmonica he liked best. But when she reached for her reticule, he protested. "Captain Rafferty pays me good wages."

"Please take this as a gift from one friend to another. I don't know how I would have managed without you, those first few days aboard the *Osprey*."

Outside the shop he fell into step beside her, running his fingers over his new treasure. "I had one of these once, when I was a kid back in New York. I nicked it off a stand in the Five Points."

"You stole it?"

"Sure did. But a bigger boy stole it from me. I'd have starved if I hadn't learned how to steal without gettin' caught," he explained. Briana gave him a troubled look. "But I ain't done nothin' like that for years," he assured her. "Because of Captain Rafferty—he got me straightened out."

They started down the crowded street again, and Tommy continued. "I belonged to a gang of river rats." Seeing her puzzled expression, he explained, "We used to row out to the ships anchored off South Street an' sneak aboard. We'd take whatever we could get ahold of. Telescopes, sextants, that kind of gear, 'cause there were plenty of fences that paid good money for them." He gave her a rueful grin. "Then, late one night, we went aboard the *Osprey*."

"And Devlin caught you?"

Tommy nodded. "The others got away, but he grabbed me and dragged me to his cabin. I hoped maybe I'd get off with no more'n a bad beatin'."

Her heart ached with pity; from the way he spoke, she knew he had learned to take such punishment as a part of his every day life. "I didn't care if he beat the livin' daylights out of me—long as he didn't take me to the police afterwards. 'Cause if he had, it would've been Blackwell's Island for me.

"He didn't hit me, though." Even now Tommy spoke with a touch of awe. "An' when I begged him not to have me locked up, he said that was somethin' he'd never do. He'd be damned— excuse me, Miss Briana—if he'd ever see any kid locked up in a cell." Tommy's brow furrowed. "He was lookin' kind of strange when he said that. Like he didn't really see me. Like he was lookin' a long ways off, at somethin' I couldn't see."

Briana nodded. "I know what you mean." She, too, had seen that remote look in Devlin's eyes.

"He asked me how I come to be mixed up with them river rats, an' where were my folks. I told him I didn't have none— that I lived in an alley in the Five Points.

"He asked me if I wanted to sign on aboard the *Osprey*, as cabin boy. I couldn't hardly believe my luck." He grinned. "He said if he ever caught me stealin' again, he'd wallop the tar out of me."

Tommy fell silent, and Briana considered what he had told her. She wasn't surprised that Devlin hadn't beaten a frightened, homeless child. But his reaction when Tommy had pleaded not to be sent to jail—what did it mean? Somewhere in the boy's story lay the key to the hidden side of Devlin's character.

She had seen his haunted look, even as he had asked her to be his wife. Asked her—no, hardly that.

I'll marry you, if that's what you want.

As if the words had been dragged out of him by force. But why? He had been gripped by some unfathomable emotion; she was sure of it. She loved him with all her being, yet she wondered if she would ever understand him completely.

"Miss Briana, look at that!"

Tommy stopped in front of a theater. He was pointing at the large black letters on the poster in front.

"Miss Poppy Nolan—that's what it says. An' there's her picture, too." He gaped at the brightly tinted likeness of Poppy, with her jet black hair and full red lips.

"She's performing here right now." Briana moved closer and studied the poster more carefully. "And there's to be a matinee today."

"Cap'n Rafferty never would let me go see her when she was dancin' at the Black Pearl," Tommy said. "But this here's a real theater, like the swells go to. Can we go in an' see her, Miss Briana?"

"We most certainly can."

She bought two tickets and a few minutes later they were seated in one of the velvet-curtained boxes. Tommy stared at the stage, wide-eyed; she guessed he had never attended a theatrical performance before. The matinee was already in progress and she had to restrain her impatience through the performance of a troop of muscular acrobats, a Chinese juggler, and a tenor who sang his soulful ballads about home and mother.

Poppy's act was the star spot; right before the one that closed the show. The men in the audience had been impatient for the main attraction and when Poppy appeared at last, in a gown of flame-colored velvet and elbow-length sequined gloves, the applause was deafening. She lifted her ruffled skirt and moved across the stage, whirling with lithe, sensuous grace, displaying her splendid legs in their black silk stockings, captivating her audience completely. They applauded and shouted for an encore.

Poppy obliged with another dance and a lively rendition of "The Miners Came in Forty-nine." When she had finished an usher came onstage to present her with a huge bouquet of scarlet poppies.

As soon as Poppy made her exit, Briana went off in search of her friend's dressing room, leaving Tommy to enjoy the rest of the entertainment.

Poppy was seated at her dressing table, taking off her makeup, when she caught sight of Briana's reflection in the mirror. She sprang up, ran across the room, and threw her arms around her friend. "Briana! It's been so long since I saw you last. What're you doing here in Sacramento? Did you see me dance?"

A little overwhelmed by her greeting, Briana said, "You were splendid!"

Poppy stood back and stared at her. "And you—you look like you used to before your uncle put you to work in his store. I bet you're not slaving away for that old miser and his shrew of a wife anymore."

"I left their house. I had to."

Poppy led her to a horsehair sofa and after they were seated Briana started to tell her all that had happened since the night she had run away. She told her friend about her visit to the Black Pearl and how she had gotten her start, selling her dresses to Hortense and the other girls. Quickly she filled in the rest.

"So you and Devlin Rafferty finally got together." Poppy gave Briana an affectionate hug and smiled with satisfaction. "I always hoped you would." She hesitated briefly. "But what about Cole Forrester? He was plenty hot for you, too."

Briana repressed a smile. Poppy still spoke without regard for propriety, and probably always would.

"I wouldn't have fit in with Cole's plans for the future," Briana said, without a trace of regret. "I believe he knows that now." Remembering her last meeting with Cole, she added, "He did ask me to marry him."

"But you turned him down to go off with Devlin." Poppy laughed knowingly. "I don't blame you a bit. Now Devlin Rafferty—he's the kind of man any real woman'd want in her bed. Those big shoulders of his. And that hard, tight butt. I always think that's a sure sign of a man who can give a girl all she needs in bed and leave her wanting more."

"Poppy!"

"Having a man who knows how to pleasure you—that's nothing to be ashamed of." She gave Briana a searching look. "But you used to have a lot of other notions. I remember you talking about getting married to a rich man, living in a fine house with a carriage and servants, and moving in the best society."

"I haven't forgotten." Briana fell silent, remembering the future her mother had wanted for her. The future she had thought would be waiting for her, once she got to California.

"I guess Rafferty ain't the marrying kind." Poppy gave her an encouraging smile. "But don't give up yet. You play your cards right and one of these days maybe you can get him to propose."

"He already has," Briana said quietly.

"Well, why didn't you say so?" Poppy's dark eyes sparkled with satisfaction. "When's the wedding goin' to be?"

"I told him I wouldn't marry him."

Poppy stared at her in complete bewilderment. "But you've been living with him all this time. And you love him." She shook her head. "I don't understand."

"I'm not sure I do, either. But for now, Devlin and I will go on as we are. It's better this way."

Unwilling to discuss her relationship with Devlin any further, Briana said, "From what I saw out there, I suppose you're besieged with admirers."

"They like my dancing. But I got one special gentleman friend now. And he's the one for me."

"Is he connected with the theater?"

Poppy shook her head. "Ross Warren's a reporter for the *Sacramento Dispatch*. He came here to the theater to talk to me one night, so he could write a piece about me for his newspaper, and—one thing led to another."

Then Poppy's dark eyes grew unexpectedly serious. "He's real smart. He comes from a high-class family back in New York. There's not much goes on here in Sacramento—or any-place else in California—that he don't know about." She put a hand on Briana's arm. "I'm glad you didn't marry Cole."

Briana gave her a puzzled frown.

"Ross has done a few pieces about Cole Forrester for the paper. He says he don't trust the man." She leaned forward. "That lynching back in San Francisco last year—Ross says that Cole was behind it."

"Because he helped organize the Vigilantes?"

Poppy shook her head. "That's not all. Ross told me it was Cole who started spreading the rumors about how Cora and Casey were going to try to escape from jail. He went out and hired a bunch of roughnecks to go around to the saloons and gambling houses. He got the mob all stirred up, to where they dragged the prisoners out of jail and over to Fort Gunnybags."

"But why would he do that?"

"Let me think how—how did Ross put it?" Her eyes narrowed with concentration. "To enhance his own reputation. Yes, that's what Ross said."

Briana listened with growing uneasiness. Ross Warren believed that Cole's plans extended far beyond his desire to be elected to political office. That he meant to lead a movement to get California to secede from the Union.

Back in San Francisco, and in the mining camps along the river, Briana had heard talk of the growing division between the men from the northern states and those who came from the South. But the issue of slavery was hardly a vital one, in a state where neither climate nor soil were conducive to growing cotton or sugarcane; where men willingly struggled to dig the gold from the earth or pan the rivers with their own two hands.

"We're so far from the east. California has interests of its own."

"Yes, but don't you see? That's exactly the argument Cole's been using to get the men here to back him up. He claims that

California isn't being treated fair. That she's kind of a stepchild, as far as those politicians in Washington are concerned.

"Cole keeps reminding the men who come to hear his speeches that California's been promised a railroad. But the leaders back east haven't kept their promises. He's been saying California would be better off on her own. Like she was before she became a state." Poppy smiled self-consciously. "I guess I never thought much about how the government worked before I met Ross. I still don't always understand all he says. But he's taught me a lot."

Poppy's smile deepened. "And not just about politics, either."

Even for Briana, who had dined in the finest restaurants in Paris, the large dining room of the Olympia Hotel was impressive, with its fluted columns, marble-topped tables, thick carpeting, and red plush banquettes. On one side of the room a string orchestra played softly.

A waiter hurried forward with the menus and Briana asked Devlin to choose for both of them. But though the first course, a rich oyster bisque flavored with sherry, was delicious, Briana found herself unable to relax and savor such unaccustomed luxury to the fullest. Her conversation with Poppy lingered in her mind, for it had left her deeply uneasy.

"What's wrong?" Devlin asked. "You haven't lost that hearty appetite, have you?"

She forced a smile, then realized that it would be no use trying to hide her feelings from him. "It's about Cole," she began. She told him first about her brief conversation with Jacob Perlman; then she repeated all that Poppy had told her about Cole's plans.

"You don't think Cole has enough power to lead a movement for California's secession, do you?"

"I wouldn't rule it out," Devlin said grimly. "And I never believed he cared a damn about law and order. Or about how soon Congress starts building a railroad to link this state with the rest of the country. He'll use any means he can find to gain more supporters."

Devlin spoke with growing conviction. "Cole Forrester could be dangerous. He's got to be shown up for what he is, Briana. He's got to be stopped before it's too late."

Briana stared at Devlin, shaken by the hard determination in his voice. "Why should you care if Cole does succeed? You said once that you didn't feel any special attachment to California. Or anyplace else on the face of the earth."

"I'm building a shipping line here," he reminded her. "Your friend Perlman is building a business. He's moved up from being a peddler to running his own store. But a man like Forrester builds nothing. A man like that can only destroy whatever stands in his way."

Devlin reached across the marble tabletop, his hand closing over hers. "That day at Fort Gunnybags, when he was making that fine speech, he wasn't thinking about Cora and Casey. He didn't care if they were innocent or guilty. He was using them as pawns in his own game. He sent two men to the gallows to satisfy his own ambitions."

A coldness began to spread through Briana as Devlin went on, his eyes darkening with anger.

"And what about you?" His fingers tightened around hers. "He said he loved you, but when it came to a choice between risking his hold over that mob or trying to save you, he acted out of his deepest instinct. His lust for power."

His voice shook with the intensity of his feelings. "Whenever I think of what might have happened to you I could break his neck with my own two hands."

"Then all this is about you and me," she reproached him. "Not about your loyalty to California—or to the United States."

"I care what happens to you, Briana—you know that." His eyes held hers and there was no mistaking the warmth, the tenderness, in their gray depths. "But there's more to this than my feelings for you, love." Devlin's face hardened. "I've been hearing plenty of talk about Forrester in the mining camps. How he

hired men to start the rumors that Cora and Casey were planning
to escape. If he worked out a cold-blooded scheme to have those
two men hanged, he'll stop at nothing to carry out his ambitions."

The words sent a wave of fear sweeping through her.

He gave her a hard, tight smile. "He's not running this state,
though. Not yet. There are still plenty of men who would band
together to stop him. If they understood his purpose. Those
same men who fought for California's statehood back in '50.
And a lot of others who've come here since then. They'd fight
him, and they'd win."

"But would such men be willing to fight on the strength of
rumors alone?"

Devlin shook his head. "I doubt it. They'd want absolute
proof of what he's done so far. And what he means to do if he's
given the chance."

"How can anyone give them such proof?"

"There's got to be a way," Devlin said, with calm certainty.
"And we'll find it."

Nineteen

In the weeks since they had returned to San Francisco, Devlin
had been spending endless hours in one of the boatyards on
South Beach, where he was supervising the construction of his
new steamer. Although he had made a substantial profit from
his trading voyages, the cost of this new vessel would take all
his savings. "But it'll be worth it, Briana. She'll be the fastest
paddle-wheel afloat on any river in the state," he told her.

She stood beside him in the boatyard office and saw a rare
boyish smile spread across his tanned face. Looking down at

the pile of diagrams spread across the desk, she tried to follow his description of the new vessel.

"She'll have a two-hundred-and-forty-five-foot hull. With a beam of forty and a depth of ten feet," he went on proudly. "She won't just carry cargo, either. I'm putting in cabins for passengers. And Mackenzie is one of the best in the business. He's designing a new kind of engine." He pointed to one of the sheets, covered with diagrams and figures. "See that? A single-cylindered model, a vertical beam with a bore of five feet."

"That's—remarkable," Briana said, trying to sound suitably impressed.

He laughed, put his arm around her shoulders and hugged her to him. "Briana, my love. You really don't have the slightest notion what I'm talking about, do you?"

"Certainly I do—most of it, anyway."

"All these diagrams make as little sense to you as your paper dress patterns do to me. When you and Abbie start going on about passementerie trimmings and pelerines, I don't understand a word of it."

"I do know how much the new ship means to you," she told him quietly, "and that's what really matters, isn't it?"

He turned from the table and his arms closed around her. He held her against him, his mouth covering hers. The familiar honey-sweet glow of anticipation welled up inside her as she brushed against the hardness of his chest. But she could hear the clang of hammers on metal, the creak of the horse-powered derricks, the voices of the yard hands outside; she realized that this wasn't the time or place for lovemaking—they could be interrupted at any moment. Reluctantly, she drew away.

He released her, his breathing ragged, unsteady; his eyes still smoky with desire. "You'd better drive back to the shop—while I'm still able to let you go. As soon as I'm finished here, I'll come to you."

"That's what you said last night. And the night before." But there was tenderness mingled with her reproach, for how could she blame him when she saw how hard he was working to make his dream of the new steamer a reality?

Every night, during these last few weeks, he had remained at the boatyard until after midnight, and when he finally came into her bedroom over the shop she was already sound asleep. But when he had stripped off his clothes and climbed into bed beside her, drawing her to him, she had awakened. His first touch was enough to bring a soft cry of anticipation from her. And when she felt his fingers stroking her shoulders, his mouth at her breast, she moved closer.

He entered her with slow, sensuous strokes, until she was fully aroused; until she locked her legs around him and arched upward, urging him to move faster, thrust harder . . . to take her to that dizzying peak of unbearable wanting. Together, they rose higher still, whirling to the ultimate reaches of ecstasy.

But these past two nights he hadn't come to her rooms at all; he had worked until dawn. Even when Mackenzie, the Scottish engineer, had left the boatyard, Devlin had gone on alone, stopping only to take a few hours' sleep on the lumpy sofa in the corner. Then he had set to work again. His enormous vitality, his immense powers of endurance, were fixed on the completion of the new ship.

Now, as she paused at the door, he gave her an apologetic smile. "Briana, about tonight—I want to be with you. But there are a few details in the design for the engine that need reworking."

She repressed a sigh. "Then perhaps I'll attend the theater with Abbie. She deserves an evening off."

"She's a hard worker," he agreed, a little absently.

"Or we could go to the charity musicale to raise money for the Ladies Missionary Society," she said. He nodded, but she saw that he was already immersed in his diagrams again; she slipped out of the office and left the boatyard.

Abbie could go to the musicale, but Briana had plans of her own. She hadn't forgotten her talk with Devlin, that night back in Sacramento. And she knew that, although he was possessed with his work on the new boat, he hadn't forgotten either. They had agreed that Cole had to be stopped. But how?

Only this morning she had read newspaper advertisements saying that Cole would be addressing a rally in the grand ballroom of the Oriental Hotel on Market Street. Although the audience would be largely masculine, she had no hesitation about attending; the Oriental Hotel, a handsome new building with ornate porticos and galleries, was patronized by the most prominent visitors to the city. Perhaps tonight she would be able to ferret out more information about Cole's plans.

Certainly it was worth a try.

The crowd leaned forward, their eyes fixed on Cole Forrester, drinking in every word he said. Briana was impressed by the skill with which he manipulated his audience. It took all her willpower to remain detached; to remember her own purpose in coming here tonight.

A month ago, at the Olympia Hotel in Sacramento, Devlin had spoken with passionate conviction of the need to stop Cole before he could gather so many loyal followers that he would be unstoppable. But how would he feel, she asked herself uneasily, if he knew that she was here tonight, instead of attending a charity musicale with Abbie?

She would tell him all about it later, and he would understand; right now she must concentrate not only on Cole's words, but also on all that lay behind them. This could be an opportunity to gather solid proof of his real intentions. But as he went on speaking, Briana realized that he was choosing his words with his usual care. He spoke in grandiose terms of "law and order" and "California's manifest destiny."

"How long are we to go on waiting for crumbs from the bountiful table of Washington's legislators?" he demanded of his listeners. "How long before we set ourselves free to follow our own path to a shining future?"

Briana stirred restlessly in her seat. Where was the solid proof

Devlin said they would need to prevent Cole from realizing his private ambitions? She would have to get him alone and persuade him to let down his guard. The thought of using her feminine wiles, even for so worthwhile a purpose, was repellent to her, but what other choice did she have?

When he had finished the audience applauded vigorously, raising their voices in support of Cole's speech.

"To hell with Congress!" one man shouted. Another jumped to his feet, his voice reverberating across the crowded ballroom. "Where's the railroad they been talkin' about—the one that'll join us up with the East?"

A well-dressed gentleman with an unmistakable Southern drawl called out for "States Rights"—a phrase Briana was beginning to hear on all sides. It appeared in the headlines of the newspapers that supported the interests of the South. Even a loyal Southerner like William McKendree Gwin, California's first senator, reluctantly admitted there was little need for slavery here, though he still insisted that his adopted state shouldn't be controlled by the government in Washington.

Would there come a time when Californians banded together to demand secession from the United States? For the last few years there had been no more than angry talk and uneasy compromises that satisfied neither side. But only a few months ago the San Francisco newspapers had carried lurid accounts of the sacking of Lawrence, Kansas, by the "Border Ruffians" and pro-slavery men. These reports were soon followed by others, about an abolitionist named John Brown and his followers, who had retaliated with a massacre at a place called Pottawatomie Creek.

It had all seemed so far off to Briana, until she had listened to Cole's speech tonight and heard the impassioned responses of his supporters.

After he acknowledged the applause Cole held out his hands for silence and came down from the platform. He was quickly surrounded by his friends. A brass band struck up a lively march. Unless she acted at once, he would be carried off in triumph to a saloon or some other all-male bastion where she couldn't follow him. She had to prevent that; to seize the opportunity to speak with him alone.

Only a few months earlier, he had asked her to marry him. But what were his feelings toward her now? Uncertainty stirred inside Briana, but she pushed it away. She had to revive his desire for her, to win him over long enough to get the information Devlin considered so necessary. She managed to get to his side, forcing her way through the crowd. "Mr. Forrester," she called out. He turned, his eyes widening in surprise.

"Your speech was splendid, sir," she said, with exactly the right mixture of maidenly propriety and open adulation. "If I might have a moment of your time . . ."

The men around him nudged one another and exchanged knowing smiles. Cole gave her a courtly bow. She placed her gloved hand lightly on his arm, gazing up at him wistfully, as if she was too shy to go on speaking in the midst of the crowd. "Your pardon, gentlemen," he said.

The men moved aside; Cole led her up the center aisle and out of the ballroom. They crossed the crowded lobby together, and once they were outside she moved even closer to him, drawing her fine cashmere shawl around her shoulders.

"My, it's getting chilly," she said. "I do believe there's already a touch of autumn in the air." She looked up at him from under the wide brim of her jade green bonnet. "Perhaps it was too bold of me, approaching you in public, but I couldn't leave without telling you how much I admired your speech."

"You are most kind." His words, his tone, were polite but distant. This was going to be more difficult than she had thought.

"Perhaps you wish to rejoin your friends," she said. "If you will escort me to my phaeton, I'll leave you to their company." But her hand remained on his arm, and she hoped he had caught the delicate yet enticing fragrance of her jasmine perfume.

"There's no need for you to go straight home yet, is there? Unless you're late for another engagement." He didn't mention Devlin by name. He didn't have to.

"There's no one waiting for me." She managed a wistful gaze.

This was the opportunity she had hoped for. If she could have
an intimate talk with him, convince him that she had broken
off with Devlin, she could find a way to win his confidence.

But where could they go to talk alone at this time of the
evening? She certainly wouldn't invite him to her living quarters
above the shop; he might take that as an open invitation to make
love to her.

"My carriage is over there." He was taking charge now. "I'll
send your driver away. Then we'll dine together at the Maison
Dorée."

The Maison Dorée had opened only a month ago and already
had established its reputation as one of the finest restaurants in
San Francisco. As soon as the proprietor, a portly, dignified man
in a gray frock coat, caught sight of Cole, he came forward and
bowed. "Mr. Forrester. It's an honor to serve you again, sir."

Cole drew him aside, while Briana paused to admire her surroundings. The Olympia, in Sacramento, certainly was a fine
restaurant, but it couldn't be compared with the splendors of
the Maison Dorée. Ladies in gowns of rich brocade and satin
were dining with their escorts beneath the huge chandeliers; the
light struck sparks from their jewels. The waiters moved quickly
between the tables, carrying trays laden with rare delicacies;
others opened bottles of wine. From a gilded balcony jutting
out over one end of the room came the strains of a waltz.

Cole returned and gave her an apologetic look. "I'm afraid
all the tables down here are occupied," he said. "But our host
tells me there's a private dining room upstairs."

She knew well enough that no respectable lady would take
supper with a gentleman in a private dining room. Yet she hesitated; it would be the perfect setting for the intimate talk she
had planned.

The proprietor led the way up a flight of heavily carpeted
stairs, then down a gaslit hallway papered in wine red cretonne
and decorated with gilt-framed paintings.

He opened a door at the end of the hallway and handed the key to Cole with a bow. "Your waiter will attend you at once," he said, withdrawing discreetly.

A small, round table, covered with a fine damask cloth, had been set with porcelain, crystal, and silver. Fresh flowers arranged in a silver epergne scented the air. Heavy red velvet drapes shut out the noise from the street. Briana shot a quick glance at a large couch, upholstered in brocade and piled with cushions. There was still time to make an excuse—any excuse—and get away. But a waiter was already opening the door. A swift flurry of uneasiness had taken the edge off her appetite, but she forced a smile to her lips as she allowed the waiter to seat her opposite Cole.

She tasted a little of each course—braised pheasant, veal Julienne, poached salmon—but she scarcely touched the wine; she must keep her wits about her every minute.

She praised Cole's speech again, then questioned him about the meaning of "manifest destiny." And what, exactly, had he meant when he'd spoken of the "path to the shining future"? But he seemed equally determined to steer the talk away from his speech. "You've no need to concern yourself with such details, my dear."

When they had finished dining Cole led her to the wide sofa. She seated herself a discreet distance from him, spreading her skirt around her as a barrier.

"Tell me, Briana, did you enjoy your trip to Sacramento?"

"You know about that?"

"Your voyage aboard the *Barracuda* caused considerable gossip." He refilled her glass and then his own. "But you haven't answered my question. Did you have a pleasant trip?"

Briana's mouth had gone dry and she swallowed the champagne more quickly than she had intended. All at once the room, with its tightly drawn drapes and flaring gas jets, was stifling.

"Those mining camps are dreadfully primitive," she said. "And the miners are a coarse lot. They work all day panning the gold from the streams, then squander their loot in the gambling tents and fandango houses. And the women . . ." She lowered her eyes and gave a slight shudder. "If I had known how it would be, I never would have gone."

"Devlin Rafferty knew," Cole reminded her. "Yet he saw nothing wrong with parading you about in such low company. Why should he? You went with him willingly, didn't you?"

"Cole, I—"

His blue eyes hardened. "You refused my honorable offer of marriage and went junketing off aboard his ship."

"I refused for your sake, not mine," she said. "And when I sat listening to your speech, when I saw how your audience was stirred by your words, I knew I'd been right. You have such a splendid future ahead, Cole. I've always believed that. I care for you too much to hold you back. If I'd married you, in time you would have come to resent me."

Was she going too far, flattering him so shamelessly? She paused and held out her empty glass; as he refilled it with champagne, her mind moved swiftly. She still hadn't learned anything that could be of use to her or Devlin. And she might never have another opportunity like this again.

"Your speech was so moving, so impressive." She lowered her eyes and looked up at him from under her lashes. "Of course, I didn't understand all you said—I know so little about politics."

"Nor should you. A lady as lovely as you need not trouble herself with such dull matters."

"But when you were speaking so fervently about the future of the state—I was so moved." Her amber eyes glowed over the rim of her glass. "Do you really think California would be better off as a separate nation?"

He gave her an indulgent smile. "We are already separated by geography, my dear. By all those miles of untamed wilderness that stretch between here and the East. With our vast, untapped wealth, we could become a powerful nation in our own right." She kept her eyes fixed on his face; under her adoring gaze, he let himself be carried away by his desire to impress her even more. "The people of California should never have agreed to statehood. That was a mistake. Once we're free we will shape our own destiny."

"But what about the *rancheros,* with their great holdings in the southern part of the state? Would they support your plans?"

"I've already made sure of that," he told her. "I've visited them, spoken with them in their homes. They are aristocrats—the blood of the Castilian nobility flows in their veins. They suffered a deep humiliation when they were defeated back in '48. Believe me, they only want an opportunity to avenge that defeat. They will join my forces when I give the word."

"But the peons who serve them—"

"They don't matter. They'll go on working the land as they always have. Except for those we send to the silver mines of the Sierra Madre. The mines will produce enormous wealth again, as they did during the days of the *conquistadores.*"

There was no need for her to feign astonishment now. She was shaken, frightened by his words. She had always known he was ambitious, but not until now had she grasped the full extent of his lust for power. "You and your followers would cross the border and try to conquer Mexico?"

He raised his head and spoke with assurance. "We will conquer. Does that seem so impossible to you? Perhaps it might be more difficult if we tried to do it on our own. But with support from the great powers of Europe—" He broke off abruptly and set down his glass.

She leaned forward, eager to keep him talking of his plans, but it was no use. "Enough of this, my dear. I didn't ask you to come here so that we might talk of such weighty matters," he said. His gaze caressed her. "If only I could have had you for my wife."

"Cole, please don't ask me again."

"I can't," he said, with a tinge of regret. "Not now. I want you as much as I ever did. But since you've flaunted your indifference to convention marriage between us is out of the question."

She pressed her lips together, forcing back the outraged words that rose inside her. She longed to tell him that even if he did propose again on bended knee, she would refuse him. Not only because of his grandiose dreams of conquest, his ruthless disregard for the rights of others, but because she loved Devlin and always would.

Somehow, she managed to hide her feelings. Now it was time to make a swift exit. "I've been foolish and headstrong; I see that now. I understand how you must feel about me."

"No—you don't understand at all. I want you. That hasn't changed. And I will have you." His arms went around her, and he was pushing her down into the deep, soft couch. She felt the heat of his breath against her cheek. He trailed kisses along the curve of her throat and the soft swell of her breasts, half bared by her low-cut basque. Although his words were muffled against her flesh, she stiffened with repulsion as she heard him say, "I'll set you up in the finest hotel in San Francisco. Or buy you a house of your own. Jewels, servants, a carriage—you've only to ask."

"Cole—no—" She struggled to free herself, but he kept her pinned down with his body.

"First I'll take you to Paris."

She looked up at him, startled by the driving determination in his voice. "Paris? Why Paris?"

He laughed softly. "You'll understand, at the proper time." The calculating look in his eyes filled her with uneasiness. He did nothing without planning carefully in advance. What had made him speak of Paris at such a time?

But now his fingers were moving swiftly, opening the top buttons of her basque; she felt his touch, hot and possessive, through the layers of taffeta and lace. She pushed his hands aside. "You're asking me to become your mistress." Her voice shook with indignation.

"Why not? You gave yourself to Rafferty—a common sea captain, an upstart without background or breeding. But I'm willing to forget that. Think, Briana—I can offer you so much more. The riches of an empire—my empire—"

She could restrain herself no longer. "You have nothing I want. Let me out of here, now."

"You came with me willingly enough."

Fear went racing through her. She had led him on shamelessly, had used all her wiles to arouse his hunger for her. She had no way to defend herself if he was bent on taking what she had offered. To pit her strength against his would be useless, and would only feed his lust for conquest. Her own quick wits, her understanding of the kind of man he was, were her only weapons. "A man like you—wouldn't take a woman against her will."

His hands dropped away. She saw his chest rise and fall, heard the harsh intake of his breath. "You're a gentleman—a man of honor—" He raised himself from her, then got to his feet; she saw his struggle between hot hunger and pride.

A shudder ran through the length of his body. "Get out," he said, his voice tight with anger. "Go back to the waterfront, where you belong."

She stood, willing her legs to support her; then she caught up her skirts and hurried to the door. She had been right about Cole—it had never occurred to him that she would refuse his lovemaking. But his pride, his breeding, had made it impossible for him to take her by force.

Her knees felt as if they had turned to water, but she kept going, through the doorway, along the gaslit hallway and down the carpeted stairs, past the crowded dining room. She didn't stop until she was outside.

She saw a cab approaching and signaled to the driver, who jerked his horse to a stop. She climbed inside, sinking down on the seat. "Sansome Street," she directed him.

She had gathered a great deal of information tonight, but she still lacked the hard proof Devlin said they would need to expose Cole's true intentions to his followers. She would leave that to Devlin. Once he'd completed his work on the new ship he would turn his full attention to this new challenge, with the fierce determination that was so much a part of him.

As she rested against the leather seat, she realized that she was still giddy from the champagne. Her thoughts moved from Cole's plans for conquest in Mexico to his offer to make her his mistress. She shook her head slightly, trying to sort out her racing thoughts.

Paris . . . He had spoken of taking her to Paris. That was natural enough, perhaps. With the Emperor Louis Napoleon and his frivolous Empress Eugenie setting a giddy pace, Paris was a city of worldly delights.

But when she had asked him, "Why Paris?" he had said nothing about the lavish entertainments they might enjoy there: the operas, the balls, the hunting parties, the endless round of festivities. Instead, he had given her a calculating smile and said she would find out his reasons at the proper time. Those words, that look, still troubled her.

She had been able to get away before he'd lost control completely and taken her by force. Should she tell Devlin about the private dining room, about Cole's attempt to make love to her?

Better not, she decided. Although she hated holding anything back from Devlin, she had glimpsed the streak of violence that lay beneath her lover's self-possessed facade. Now, when they were so close to exposing Cole for what he was, ruthless and power-hungry, driven by imperial ambitions, she mustn't give Devlin a personal reason to strike out before the time was right.

Twenty

Briana paused at the foot of the gangway and tilted back her head to look up at Devlin's new steamer; she caught sight of the name painted on the side in bold black letters: JESSICA RAFFERTY. She gave him an inquiring look.

"That was my mother's name," he said.

"You must have loved her very much."

"I never knew her. She died giving me birth."

Briana's throat contracted, but she knew better than to try to offer him sympathy. "It's a fine name for a fine ship."

In the soft gray light of the winter afternoon they strolled the deck, with its freshly painted white planks and gleaming brasswork. Devlin paused and opened the door of one of the new passenger cabins to show her the lavishly decorated interior, with its red plush chairs, plate-glass mirrors, marble-topped tables, and brass lamps.

"What do you think of it?"

"It's magnificent—as fine as the best suite in any San Francisco hotel," she said. "Have you started selling tickets for the maiden voyage yet?"

"Before we make the first passenger trip upriver we'll be taking her out for a test run. She'll not only be the fastest steamer on the river but the safest, too."

Briana was moved by the pride in his voice. Not since he had owned the *Osprey* had he spoken in such a tone about any ship. Her lips curved in a smile and her amber eyes sparkled. "The passenger cabins are splendid, but there's something more I'd like to see."

"If you think I'm going to take you to inspect the engines in that fine outfit, you're mistaken."

"I know nothing about engines." She laughed softly. "It's your cabin I had in mind."

He bent his head, and his mouth touched hers. "You are a shameless hussy."

"Only with you," she told him.

He grinned, then scooped her up in his arms and carried her to his quarters. He set her down on the bed and stripped off her clothes and his own; then he stretched out beside her. She thrilled to feel the length of his naked body against hers.

"I'd be neglecting my duties if I allowed you to go before I'd given you the complete tour."

"The complete tour?" she went warm all over at the implication.

His lips moved along the curve of her throat. "From here . . .

to here. . . ." She caught her breath as his tongue flicked at her nipple.

And now there was no more need for words. She gave herself up to his seeking mouth, his strong, caressing hands. The aching tenderness she had feared to express in words when they'd stood at the foot of the gangway she gave him now in full measure, blended with her rising passion, giving their lovemaking a new depth. And as they lay together in the afterglow of fulfillment, she drew his head to her breast.

"My love," she said softly, stroking his dark hair. "My dearest love . . ." He moved closer, pressing his face to the softness of her breast, his breath warm against her skin.

It was early evening when they went back on deck; the brisk wind ruffled her hair and tugged at her bell-shaped skirt. "Am I invited along as a passenger on your first trip upriver?" she asked.

"Certainly. If you can take time from the shop."

"Abbie can run the shop while I'm away. I've hired two more seamstresses to help her, and I'll be needing another delivery boy, too." She smiled with satisfaction. "Since I provided Eleanor Padgett—Eleanor Forrester, I should say—with her wedding gown, I've had more orders than I can handle."

"Cole Forrester's bride is one of your customers? You never told me."

"You were far too busy working on the ship to discuss such trivial matters," she reminded him.

"We'll make up for lost time," he promised.

Her laugh was soft, sensuous. "I'd say we've already begun." She was still warm with the memory of the hours they'd shared in his new cabin. But when she smiled up at him she saw that his brows were drawn together in a troubled frown.

"I should think Eleanor would have chosen another shop. One where she wouldn't risk brushing skirts with an actress. Or a sporting-house lady."

"Eleanor never set foot inside my shop," she said with a faint smile. "She sent for me, and I went to her father's house to work on her gown."

His eyes turned frosty. "You didn't need to wait on her at home. It's not your usual way of doing business, is it?" He gave her a searching look. "You already have plenty of customers who pay you handsomely."

"And not only sporting-house madams," she assured him. "These days, every actress who comes to perform here comes into the shop. And opera singers, too. Only last month Elisa Biscaccianti bought two promenade costumes, a satin dressing gown, half a dozen pairs of embroidered gloves, and—"

He interrupted her brusquely. "Then why should you go running to serve Eleanor Forrester when she snaps her fingers?"

"I want to build a reputation for providing the most fashionable wedding gowns in San Francisco. This isn't a city of adventurous bachelors anymore. Those men who struck it rich are building homes and settling down. If you read something besides the political news and shipping pages of the papers, you'd know all that."

"So you've been cashing in on these society weddings, have you? I guess that makes good business sense," he conceded.

"I'm getting more orders than I can handle from the ladies at South Park and Rincon Hill."

"But none of those ladies come into your shop, do they?"

"So long as they order their gowns from me, what does it matter?"

"It matters to me." His eyes darkened with anger. "You're as much a lady as any of them, and I won't have them treat you with the slightest disrespect." His arm tightened around her protectively.

She was moved by his concern for her. "It's not like that at all," she assured him. "After they've placed their orders they invite me to take tea with them in their parlors. Since I've let it be known that I grew up in Paris they can't stop plying me with questions."

"You needn't tell them. Your private life's none of their business."

"They don't ask about me—it's the court gossip they're after. They want to know if it's true that the Empress Eugenie once attended the opera in a gown cut so low that when she leaned forward in her box, the audience caught a glimpse of her royal nipples."

She was relieved to hear him laugh, and know she had succeeded in lifting his dark mood. "Eugenie's proud of her magnificent bosom," she went on. "That's why she started the demand for the extreme decolletage that's so fashionable now."

His gray eyes sparkled with amusement.

"And speaking of decolletage, I always tell the ladies about the visit of the Papal Nuncio from Rome. It seems His Eminence attended a ball at the Tuileries and found his path blocked by two ladies in enormous crinolines. The ladies apologized and moved aside."

She mimicked her mother's description of the ensuing conversation.

" 'Pardon, monseignor,' one of the French ladies said, 'but there is so much material in our skirts . . .'

" 'There is nothing left over to cover the top,' His Eminence replied with a bow."

She hadn't been present at the Tuileries on that occasion, and neither had Mama, but the tale had filtered down quickly from court society to the demimonde.

"Is that what respectable San Francisco matrons talk about over tea?"

"They're only too eager to hear about the foibles of Parisian society. The more lurid, the better."

"And does Cole's wife also clamor for such shocking gossip?"

"She's no different from the rest. She hasn't been abroad yet, but she's longing to go. I suppose Cole will take her to Paris, just as—"

She caught herself in time; Devlin mustn't know that Cole had offered to take her to Paris—as his mistress. "As soon as he can take a break in his busy schedule," she improvised quickly.

"In that case I don't think Mrs. Forrester'll be going abroad for awhile," he said. "Not until Cole's been elected governor. Or maybe he's got his mind set on a Senate seat in Washington."

"He set his mind far higher than that."

"How do you know?" he asked.

When would she learn to think before she spoke? She considered trying to evade his question completely, then decided against it. "I went to hear him at a rally in the grand ballroom at the Oriental Hotel," she admitted reluctantly. "His plans go far beyond the governor's mansion, or the U.S. Senate. He won't be satisfied until California leaves the Union."

"He really thinks he has that much influence over the people of this state?"

"Perhaps he will have, before long," she said slowly. "Sometimes he reminds me of Louis Napoleon."

Devlin's dark brows shot up in disbelief. "Isn't that a bit far-fetched?"

"Is it? Louis Napoleon returned to France and was elected President of the Second Republic, but he wasn't satisfied for long. He craved absolute power. He and his followers dissolved the National Assembly and declared martial law. Then Louis Napoleon seized the throne."

"But the French are used to imperial rule," he reminded her. "Louis Napoleon's the nephew of their lost emperor, Napoleon Bonaparte. We're living in a democracy here." He gave a short, scornful laugh. "Cole's family owns one of the biggest plantations in the Carolinas. But here in California that doesn't count for much."

"Maybe not. But Cole's possessed with limitless ambition." She spoke with rising urgency. "He means to win the support of the Spanish landowners, the aristocracy of California. With their backing, he'll move south to build a—a tropical empire. Right now he's playing on the loyalty of his Southern supporters, but he cares nothing for States Rights. For him, all that's only a means to an end."

Devlin's eyes narrowed with suspicion. "Are you trying to tell me that he stood up and said all that at the rally?"

"Of course not! But he told me afterward—" She broke off, too late.

"Afterward!" His powerful hands shot out, grasping her shoulders. His jaw hardened, and a shiver of apprehension moved through her. "And just where did you two exchange these intimate confidences?"

"Over dinner—at the Maison Dorée."

His fingers tightened, but she didn't try to free herself from his grip.

"You said we would need hard proof to stop him, remember?"

"I didn't tell you to go out looking for such proof on your own."

"We never had a chance to talk it over, not after we were in Sacramento," she reminded him. "You've been too busy working on your ship. I didn't think you cared about anything else."

"So you took matters into your own hands. You decided to go off to dinner with him. You used your charms on him, so he'd let down his guard. Tell me, just how far did you go to get him to confide in you?"

"Devlin, don't!" Hot tears stung her lids, but she blinked them back. "If you want to know whether I made love with Cole Forrester that night—or ever—then ask me outright!"

His hard grip eased, and she felt the violence go out of him. He drew a long breath, and when he spoke again she heard the contrition in his tone. "I don't have to ask. I know you, Briana."

"Then why were you so angry only a moment ago?"

"Because I know Forrester, too. He's been wanting you from the first moment he laid eyes on you."

"But he married Eleanor," she reminded him.

"Only after you refused him. When he couldn't get you he decided to marry a girl from a rich, influential family in order to further his ambitions. But it's still you he wants in his bed."

She pressed her face against his chest and her arms went around him. "He'll never have me."

"Damn right, he won't. From now on he'll keep away from you." Devlin said determinedly. "I'll see to that."

The wind from the bay drove the clouds across the winter sky. It tugged at the wooden signboards outside the shops along Sansome Street and shook the shutters on the windows of Briana's small parlor. But neither she nor Devlin noticed. He stood near the fireplace, his eyes fixed on the engraved card she had handed him a moment ago.

"When did this arrive?" he demanded.

"Eleanor gave it to me this afternoon. I went to her new house to help her decide on the gown she'll be wearing at her housewarming ball."

"And I suppose Cole found an excuse to come home from his office early."

"He doesn't have that office on Montgomery Street any longer. He conducts his business in his mansion on Rincon Hill. And he's not even in San Francisco."

"Where's he off to this time? Holding rallies up and down the state, I suppose."

"He's visiting a wealthy Spanish rancher, somewhere near the Mexican border. Eleanor said he wouldn't be back until the night of the housewarming."

Devlin still didn't look completely satisfied. "Why couldn't Abbie go to Rincon Hill without you? She's your head seamstress."

"Eleanor insists on having me there to show her the designs, and talk over every detail of the gown. This housewarming ball's an important occasion. Cole and Eleanor have invited the most prestigious people in the state. All the fine Southern gentlemen and their wives. Influential politicians and businessmen. Wealthy Spanish landowners."

"Isn't it odd she'd invite her dressmaker to such a great event?"

"I don't think she expects me to come."

"That makes no sense."

A slight smile curved her lips. "It does, to me. But I doubt a man would understand."

"Try me."

"Eleanor's jealous—she took a dislike to me the day Cole and I came ashore from the *Osprey*. She was waiting on the dock, eager to welcome him back, to show him how she'd missed him. I can still remember the look she gave me when he told her we'd made that long voyage together."

"That was nearly two years ago."

"But there was more. Cole set me up in my shop," she reminded him. "We went out together: the opera, restaurants, carriage rides. You were off on your skiff, remember—it was your first voyage upriver."

"All right; let's suppose she's still brooding over all that. Why would she give you this invitation?"

"To flaunt her victory over me. She adores Cole. She always has. She thinks he's God's gift to the female sex. I'm sure she believes I'm pining away because she snatched such a prize from me."

"And are you?"

"Devlin! I thought we'd settled that. I never loved Cole."

"But the rest of it? That mansion on Rincon Hill, the servants, the social standing. You might have had all of it."

She threw her arms around him and pressed herself against him. "I have what I want, all I'll ever want, right here."

He spoke her name, his voice deep, husky with passion, his breath burning against her cheek. His mouth claimed hers and her lips parted for his kiss. After he let her go he walked to the fireplace. "Let's get rid of this elegant invitation right now."

He stretched out his hand to toss the card into the leaping flames, then paused. "Maybe we can find a better use for it."

"What possible use—"

"I'm not sure yet. But this could be the chance I've been looking for." He scanned the card again, then tapped it against his palm, his eyes thoughtful. "You can't attend the ball without an escort."

"You want to go with me?"

"Maybe. Briana, somebody's got to make those influential guests understand what Cole's really up to. I'm not a practiced orator, but I'll make them listen to me."

"Will they believe what you say? You don't have any proof."

He fell silent, and she felt the tension in him as if it were a tangible force. She watched as he paced the parlor carpet, his gray eyes narrow with concentration, his mouth set. Then he stopped. "Papers," he said. "Written proof. That's what I need."

"But surely Cole's too shrewd to put his plans in writing," she interrupted.

"There's got to be something. Letters, maybe. Or a diary."

"But even if such proof exists, how would you go about getting your hands on it?"

"How much do you know about the layout of his house?"

"Eleanor showed me around the first time I went there. She even showed me the master bathroom. It has a tub encased in mahogany, with solid gold faucets. And a—convenience with one of those new overhead tanks."

"Cole wouldn't keep his personal papers in there."

Excitement raced through her as she began to understand. "The library. Or the office where he receives his clients. Both are in the west wing."

Devlin nodded slowly. "Now we're getting somewhere."

"I don't see how I can find an excuse to get away from Eleanor—not long enough to go searching through the house."

"I'd never let you take the risk." He grinned. "Besides, I don't think burglary's among your many skills."

"Then how—"

"Tommy'll know how to go about it. He had plenty of experience when he was growing up in New York."

"Devlin, no!" She clutched his arm. "Not Tommy. You had him promise never to steal again."

"He told you about that?" Before she could answer he went on with growing determination, "I'll deal with Tommy. All you have to do is find some excuse to bring him into the house on your next visit to Rincon Hill."

Eleanor Forrester, clad in her new ball gown, studied her reflection in the cheval mirror. The gaslight flickered over the soft luster of the blue Lyons brocade and picked out the details of the damask roses, crimson carnations, lilacs, and tulips embroidered on the wide overskirt.

"You've finally got it right," she conceded. She gave Briana a searching look. "You're sure you haven't sold any other lady a gown of this particular fabric?"

"I give you my word," Briana assured her. "This was embroidered to special order, as I told you. The pattern's the only one of its kind."

Unable to conceal her triumph any longer, Eleanor preened and smiled. "You've outdone yourself, Miss Cameron. This is the gown I wanted for my housewarming ball."

Under other circumstances, Briana would have been pleased by the compliment, but now her thoughts were with Tommy, who was moving about downstairs, following Devlin's instructions.

Eleanor had paid no attention to the "errand boy" who had carried in the shiny cardboard boxes, then disappeared.

"I'm not quite sure," Briana said slowly; she looked at the dress, as if studying every detail. "Would you mind turning around just once more?"

"Whatever for?" Eleanor demanded.

"I want this gown to be perfect in every detail." She forced herself to give Eleanor an ingratiating smile. "You see, Monsieur Worth insists on approving each of his gowns, before he allows it to leave his establishment in Paris. I don't mean to compare my talents to his—but I do wish to offer my customers the same quality of service."

Eleanor's impatience gave way to interest, and she listened, wide-eyed.

"Monsieur Worth always wishes to see how the lady will look when she stands at the head of a grand staircase. And I assure you, Mrs. Forrester, even in the homes of the nobility no staircase, no ballroom, is more impressive than yours." She lowered her eyes and managed a small, wistful sigh.

"No doubt I'll visit the House of Worth when Mr. Forrester and I go to Paris," said Eleanor.

Briana nodded, then went on. "Monsieur Worth used to say the ultimate test of a truly great ballgown was the way it moved with the wearer. This gown must pass the test before I can consider it completely satisfactory.

"When you descend the stairs and later, when you dance the first waltz with Mr. Forrester, all eyes will be fixed on you. I can't let you have the gown until I'm sure it will be suitable for such an auspicious occasion."

Eleanor gave her a patronizing smile. "Your attention to detail is most commendable, Miss Cameron."

Briana's eyes met Abbie's; the seamstress inclined her head slightly. Between them, they would see to it that Eleanor didn't stir from her bedroom for at least another hour.

"There're two locked drawers in the office desk. I could've forced them open, but I only looked them over, like you told me to." Tommy grinned at Devlin with pride.

Briana sat listening in silence, rain pelting against her parlor windows. "I'll get the right kind of keys down on Pacific Street. It might take a couple of days, though. Back in Five Points I'd know where to go right off."

"You're not back in Five Points," Devlin reminded him sternly. "And if it wasn't necessary, I wouldn't allow you to go back to your old trade, even for an hour."

"It ain't my trade no more." Tommy gave him a reproachful look. "I'm an able seaman now. Actin' under orders from my captain."

Devlin clapped the boy on the shoulder. "Then off you go. And be careful."

"Pacific Street's no worse than the Five Points," Tommy assured him. "I can look out for myself." He touched his cap and hurried out of the parlor, bound for the Barbary Coast.

When he was gone Briana looked up at Devlin anxiously. "Will he be safe down there on his own?"

"Quinn'll be keeping an eye on him. I've ordered him to follow the lad at a distance. He'll be staggering around stinking of whiskey, like any drunken sailor on shore leave. But he won't let Tommy out of his sight if he can help it."

"Does Tommy know?"

"Of course not. It would be a blow to his pride if I told him." She put a hand on Devlin's arm and smiled up at him. "That boy would risk his life for you. And I can understand it. What other captain would have caught him looting the ship and then given him another chance, as you did?"

A shadow crossed his face. "Don't give me more credit than I deserve. I helped the boy for reasons of my own."

"If not for you, he'd have gone to jail," she insisted. "A child like that, in a prison cell. I can't bear to think of it."

"Then don't."

Why should Devlin sound so annoyed when she praised him for helping Tommy? Was he embarrassed that she had learned of his generosity, or fearful that she would think him weak for having been moved by the boy's plight?

No, that wasn't likely. Devlin was far too self-assured to be troubled by such misgivings. Why, then, was he reluctant to discuss the incident?

"What if Tommy's caught when he goes back to Cole's house? You won't be able to help him then."

"The boy'll never see the inside of a jail cell," Devlin told her.

She changed the subject hastily. "We don't know if he'll find any papers that we can use to convince Cole's followers."

"It's a big chance, but maybe the best one we'll ever get," he reminded her. "You have your part straight, haven't you?"

"Certainly. I've already told you—"

"Tell me again."

"Tommy comes along to Rincon Hill again. He unlocks the drawers and takes all the papers inside. He gives them to me once we're out of the house. You and I look them over together. We keep whatever we'll need, and Tommy puts back the rest of them." Fear stirred inside her. "If only Cole doesn't change his plans and come back before the night of the housewarming. If he were to find those papers missing—"

"We've got to risk it." Devlin pressed her hand, and she drew reassurance from his touch. "You've told Eleanor you'll be going to her ball?"

"Not yet. But the invitation will get me in."

"Get *us* in," he amended. "She may be taken aback when she sees me as your escort, but she won't make a scene."

"Not in front of all her important guests." Briana smiled at him. "Besides, you're a respectable member of the community now, Captain Rafferty. The owner of a shipping line."

"I've never given a tinker's damn for respectability. Not for myself." He gave her a troubled look. "But it's different for a woman, isn't it?"

She stiffened, half hoping, half fearing he might be about to repeat his offer of marriage. "If I'm going to get that gown to Eleanor, I'd best get back to the shop." She spoke hastily. "And your engineer's waiting aboard the ship to show you the adjustments on the engine, remember?"

But after he had gone she didn't return to the shop at once. She stood at the parlor window until she saw him pause outside the shop; he pulled up his collar against the driving rain, then strode off into the darkness.

He hadn't asked her to marry him again, but one day he might. And if he did, what would her answer be? He was the owner of a prosperous shipping line now; whether he cared or not, he was respected by San Francisco's business community. His new steamer would enhance his reputation. In a few years he might even be able to build her a mansion as fine as Cole's.

Her mother had wanted her to marry well, to enjoy a life of respectability as the wife of a wealthy man. Indeed, it had become an obsession for Mama.

And now there might be an even more urgent reason for her to marry. A few weeks before she had noticed a change in her female cycle. She had always been quite regular, but now she was delayed. She couldn't be sure yet, but it was possible she was carrying Devlin's child.

There was no reason to share her suspicion with him. She wanted to wait until she was sure. And even if time proved she was with child, she knew she would still hesitate to tell him. She didn't want him to offer to marry her out of a sense of obligation; a need to shield her from scandal. She stiffened and pushed away the thought of his going through a meaningless ceremony only because he felt he owed her that much.

She longed to bear him a child—but not yet; a shadow lay between them. She sensed there was a dark side of Devlin's life, a part of himself he still concealed from her. Only when he was ready to share it with her would she agree to be his wife.

Twenty-one

"Did you find them papers you wanted, Miss Briana?"

She looked up from the pile of folders spread on the table and shook her head. "Not yet, Tommy But there has to be something here we can use."

Devlin's plan had been carefully thought out and Tommy had

done his part with expertise. Last night he'd slipped into the Forrester mansion on Rincon Hill, used the key he'd bought on the Barbary Coast to unlock the two drawers in Cole's desk, and gotten away with the papers. Early this morning he had brought them to her apartment over the shop.

But so far she had found nothing that could be used to expose Cole's plans to his followers. Her lips tightened as she went on taking out each folder, studying its contents, then laying it aside.

Only two more weeks to New Year's Eve—the night of the housewarming hall. She had accepted Eleanor's invitation, but what good would it do to attend the ball with Devlin unless they could confront the guests with absolute proof of Cole's scheme?

Had Tommy made his dangerous foray to Rincon Hill for nothing? Doggedly, she went on scanning the papers before her. Gray winter light filtered through the parlor windows. Although it was already midmorning, she had kept the gas lamps turned up.

"You've done a good night's work," she assured Tommy. "Devlin will be proud of you." But as she examined each document, then set it aside, her spirits sank.

Tommy stood near the fireplace, shifting from one foot to the other, watching her. Reluctantly, she closed the last of the folders.

"Ain't they the right ones?" He gave her a crestfallen look.

"I'm afraid not—but don't blame yourself. No one else could have done as well. You carried out your orders to the last detail."

But her reassurance did not seem to cheer him. With an abrupt movement he picked up the heavy woolen jacket he had left near the door and brought it to her. When he set it down on the oval walnut table she heard a muffled thud and realized that the jacket concealed some heavy object. Before she could question him, he pulled the cloth aside and she stared in dismay at a polished teakwood box with an inlaid design: figures of mandarins, of bridges, willow trees, and flying cranes. The polished brass hasp was fastened with a small padlock.

"What's this?"

He shuffled his feet. "A tea chest."

"Where did you get it?'

"From Forrester's house."

She shot up from her chair and confronted him, her voice shaking with indignation. "How could you? Devlin gave you strict orders—I heard him. You were to open those two drawers in Mr. Forrester's desk and take whatever was inside. But nothing else."

"I remember, Miss Briana. But—when I saw this chest I just couldn't leave it behind."

Devlin was still working in the engine room of the *Jessica Rafferty,* going over every detail before he took the steamer out for the test run. But she'd' sent him a message an hour ago, and he would be here soon. When he found out Tommy had disobeyed him, he would be furious.

She, too, should be angry with the boy, but her disapproval was tempered with understanding. Was it his fault that during his early years back in the Five Points, he could only hope to survive by stealing? Now Devlin had ordered him to use his skills as a thief again; how could she blame him for reverting to his old ways and taking the first object of value that had caught his eye? But she couldn't condone what he had done.

"Tommy, you know you shouldn't have taken this. Devlin trusted you." She tried to sound angrier than she felt. "I'll have to tell him when he gets here."

But if she gave him a stern lecture right now, if she got him to admit he'd done wrong, she could speak out in his defense when Devlin confronted him. But even so, she was afraid for Tommy. She didn't think Devlin would beat Tommy for his disobedience, but he might send him away, and that would hurt him much more.

"Devlin would never have sent you to get the papers, except that he thought they might be the only weapons we could use to keep Cole Forrester from—" How could she explain the scope of Cole's plans to the boy?

"But I never meant to keep the chest for myself, Miss Briana." He gave her a reproachful look. "I was goin' to get it back to Forrester's house tonight, along with the papers."

"Why did you take it, then?"

"Because I figured there might be something important inside. Look at this." He pointed to the small padlock. "Them ordinary tea chests ain't locked.

"This is what them Chinese merchants call a presentation box. They only put their best teas inside—the fancy kinds. An' then they give it to the captain of a tea clipper for a special present. One of these boxes is worth a heap of cash in any port in the world."

"That's still no excuse for your taking it." She put a hand on his arm. "Devlin trusts you, and so do I."

His lean young face flushed as his eyes met hers. "I ain't no thief, Miss Briana. Not anymore. That day back in New York, when the captain offered me a chance to sign on the *Osprey,* I gave him my word I'd never steal again. I never broke my promise."

She was moved by his straightforward look and the ringing sincerity in his voice. "Go on."

"Last night, when I found the chest, I started wonderin' why Mr. Forrester kept it hidden out of sight. It was shoved all the way under his desk, an' I couldn't figure out what it was doin' there."

Tommy's words made sense. Knowing Cole as she did, she was sure he was proud of his mansion and its expensive furnishings. Why wouldn't he have kept this beautifully inlaid box out in the open, to impress his visitors?

"I would've told Captain Rafferty about the chest, but he said to come straight over here. He'd been busy all night, him an' that Scottish engineer. They've been workin' down in the boiler room."

She gave him a searching look. "Maybe you were afraid to tell him you'd disobeyed his orders."

"A little, I guess. But I couldn't have asked his permission before I took this chest. I only found it by accident, while I was workin' on them desk drawers."

Her heart was racing. It was a slim chance, but maybe . . . "Will that key of yours open it?"

He looked doubtful, but he tried to fit the key into the tiny opening of the padlock. "The key wasn't made for nothin' as small as this. I guess I could go back and find the right kind down on Pacific Street."

A rising excitement swept through Briana. She had to examine the contents of the chest right away. Yet she hesitated. Cole must have no suspicion that his office had been searched and looted. "Can you break the lock without damaging the wood?"

Tommy glanced around the room, then hurried to the fireplace and seized the brass poker. He pulled out a heavy bandanna, wadded it up, then shoved it between the padlock and the box. With skill and precision, he struck the lock once, twice. Then he grinned at her in triumph. "There you are! An' not a scratch on the wood!"

She opened the lid; although the box was still fragrant with the scent of fine tea, it now held a stack of neatly arranged folders. With an upsurge of hope, she bent over the box and pulled out the first folder. She began poring over the papers inside.

She studied the maps of lower California and Mexico marked with symbols that meant nothing to her. Maybe Devlin could make sense of them. She looked at the contents of another folder, shook her head, then set it aside. But when she opened a third her lips parted with a sharp intake of breath. The paper she held bore a coat of arms she had seen before, in Paris. She turned it over; it was signed *Auguste Jean Hyacinthe, Duc de Morny*

The Duc de Morny, illegitimate son of Hortense Beauharnais, who was the daughter of the Empress Josephine. Half-brother to Louis Napoleon. A nobleman with the instincts of a gambler, de Morny had helped plan the coup d'etat that had placed Louis Napoleon on the throne.

She stared at the letter in bewilderment. Why had Cole been corresponding with de Morny, who, as president of the *corps legislatif,* wielded enormous power in the French government?

As she scanned the lines, her legs grew shaky and she sank back into the chair.

Tommy looked at her anxiously. "Miss Briana? You all right?"

She nodded. "I think I've found what I was looking for." But she needed time to study the papers carefully.

"You must be hungry," she said. "There's a pot of coffee and bread and butter in the kitchen. Help yourself."

Tommy headed for the kitchen, and Briana began reading the extensive correspondence between Cole and de Morny. That night at the Maison Dorée, when Cole had told her his plans, he had already started to put them into effect; the dates on these letters proved it.

First he would persuade his followers to support him in the movement for the secession of California; then he would extend his power southward into Mexico. The letters described the boundless wealth of the Mexican silver mines. Cole promised that, in exchange for French mercenaries to support his own forces, he would share the spoils of conquest with Louis Napoleon.

She was stunned by the sheer audacity of the scheme. Was it possible that his dream of conquest, so daring, so fantastic in its scope, could possibly succeed?

She heard Devlin's footsteps on the stairs. The door swung open. She pushed back her chair and hurried to his side. "I've found what we need! Come and see."

She clasped his hand and led Devlin to the table. Tommy came out of the kitchen, and Devlin nodded at him approvingly. "Good work," he said.

Then he caught sight of the chest, and his dark brows drew together in a frown. "Where'd that come from?"

She spoke quickly. "It was under Cole's desk. Tommy noticed it was padlocked—hidden out of sight." She stepped between Devlin and the boy. "You won't punish him—you mustn't. He brought us what we were looking for." She pointed to the top of one of the letters. "The crest of the Duc de Morny. Cole's hoping to get the duke to use his influence with Louis Napoleon."

Devlin seized the paper, then seated himself at the desk. She leaned over his shoulder. "French mercenaries in exchange for Mexican silver," she said. "And maps, too."

He spread the maps so they covered most of the table and started to examine them, then looked up at her, his gray eyes shining with triumph.

"We've got him!" He glanced at the chest. "Anything else in there we can use?"

She carried the chest to the sofa, where she began scanning the remaining folders. One held documents involving land deals up and down the state; another dealt with the structure and activities of the Committee of Vigilance.

She set these aside and reached for the next folder, then stifled a cry of surprise. She had caught sight of her own name on the topmost paper. And here was her mother's name, too: Lynette Cameron. Cole had been making inquiries into her past. Some of the letters were to friends in Charleston. Others were written in French. He had been corresponding with a lawyer in Paris, seeking information about her and Mama. How dare he pry into her past! Her jaw tensed with indignation.

She glanced at Devlin, who was still engrossed in the maps. Her hands trembled, but she kept silent as she went on reading. The names seemed to leap out at her: Lynette Cameron. James Cameron. Briana . . .

The words swam before her eyes. *Briana . . . bears the surname of Lynette's deceased husband, James Cameron . . . citizen of Charleston, South Carolina. . . .*

. . . bears the surname . . .

She bit back a cry of outrage. Of course she went by her father's name! Yet even now a curious anxiety stirred inside her. She set aside the letter and caught sight of a legal document—a will. She skimmed the first page. Her fingers tightened spasmodically around the heavy paper.

This wasn't true. It couldn't be true.

All at once her surroundings—the small parlor with its plush furniture, the flames crackling on the hearth—Devlin, bending over the maps—everything was blurring before her eyes.

Once more she was standing on the threshold of Mama's bedroom, in their house on the Battery in Charleston. And Mama was lying on the carpet, her robe, her nightdress, crimson with blood. A man was running down the stairs. She heard again the slamming of the front door, carriage wheels moving down the drive. . . .

"This will be more than enough to convince Cole's followers he's been deceiving them!"

Devlin's voice brought her back to the present with a jolt. She slid the will, the letters from Charleston, and those from Paris, back into their folder. She would need time to read them carefully, to try to make sense of them.

Her world was rocking around her, but somehow she managed to hold on to some vestige of her self-control, to slide the folder under one of the sofa cushions. Then she brought Devlin the chest, and the papers about the land deals and the Committee of Vigilance. "Did you find anything else we can use?" he asked.

"Maybe—I'm not sure—" She had to force the words past the tightness in her throat. He pushed back his chair, took the chest from her, and set it down, then caught her in his arms. "What's wrong?" He looked at her anxiously.

She couldn't speak; she could only hold on to him, to try to draw strength from the heat of his powerful body.

"Easy, love." He cupped her face in his hand. "Cole isn't going to carry out his plans; we'll see to that. We've got enough right here to stop him." His lips were warm on her forehead.

If she looked pale—and she probably did—if he felt her trembling, let him go on thinking she was still shaken by the discovery of Cole's outrageous schemes.

Later that night Briana sat alone in the parlor. Although she'd drawn the heavy drapes, she could hear the winter rain beating against the panes. Thank heaven Devlin had returned to the steamer, to work with his engineer until dawn. Although she missed the comfort of his presence, she needed this time to herself.

Somehow, she had to get over the shock she'd felt after she'd finished reading the will. Her father's will. The Marquis de Valmont was her father. She had to sort out her contradictory feelings at this revelation; to find her way through the maze of deception Mama had created for her; the protective lies that had shaped her own sense of identity. Whatever Mama had done—whatever mistakes she had made—she had acted only out of love.

She must hold on to that one truth, for it was all she had to cling to now, with the rest of her world shifting around her. Mama had allowed her to believe she was James Cameron's daughter, but surely that had been an attempt to save her from the stigma of bastardy.

What had passed between Valmont and Mama on the night of the shooting? Perhaps Mama had been trying to frighten the marquis into leaving Charleston. Or perhaps she had tried to force him to give her a financial settlement for Briana's dowry. She would never know the answers to the questions that had tormented her since her discovery of the will.

She leaned closer to the fire, but the heat from the leaping flames did little to dispel the knot of coldness inside her. She pressed her fingers against her temples and shut her eyes. And saw Mama's face, drained of color, her tangled black hair, the spreading crimson stain on the front of her robe and nightdress.

She blinked rapidly and tried to calm her whirling thoughts. Valmont had fled the house, a dark shape brushing past her in the hall. Later, she'd heard that he'd left Charleston on the first ship bound for France.

Mama had been shot accidentally in the struggle over the pistol; Odette had kept assuring her of that. And she had believed the maid. She still did. Mama never could have deliberately killed anyone, and certainly not the man who had once been her lover.

According to the letters from the French lawyer, the marquis had lived only a few years after the accident; secluded in his chateau in Brittany. Perhaps he had become convinced that he was her father during those years. Another question never to be answered. But he must have been tormented by guilt; possessed with a sense of obligation, for he had willed her his vast fortune, along with the chateau, another estate in Auvergne, and his magnificent house on the boulevard de Strasbourg in Paris.

She glanced again at the will, then riffled through the correspondence between Cole and his friends in Charleston and the lawyer in Paris. Once more, a wave of resentment surged through her. How dare he go prying into her most intimate affairs?

She forced herself to control her emotions as she looked at the dates on the letters. He must have begun his investigation shortly after he had proposed to her for the first time. No doubt he'd felt he had acted too impulsively in asking her to marry him. He'd wanted to check out her account of her early life and the circumstances surrounding her mother's death. Before he proposed again, he had to be sure she would make a suitable wife.

But now her brows drew together in a puzzled frown. According to the dates on the letters he had already known of her mother's dubious past, her own illegitimacy, the day he'd come here and asked her to marry him again.

It wasn't easy to follow the workings of Cole's devious mind, but she had to try. He had desired her, had wanted her in his bed—she was sure of that. But for a man like Cole physical desire was not enough to cause him to flout public opinion. Then why . . . Perhaps, after he had learned the truth about her, he'd been willing to overlook her past, in order to make use of her fortune.

Even after his marriage to Eleanor, he had still wanted her. When they'd met at the Maison Dorée he'd asked her to be his mistress. And he had said he would take her to Paris. Of course! Because once there, he could have taken the necessary measures to help her claim her fortune. Even if there were other claimants to Valmont's property, Cole would use his impressive legal skills to see she got all that the marquis had wanted her to have.

Although he wouldn't have had a husband's right to her fortune, he'd been sure he could easily gain control over her by sheer force of will. Her lips curved in a faint smile. Cole was clever and thoroughly amoral, but this time his boundless arrogance, his monstrous conceit, had led him astray. He had never understood her and never would.

She loved Devlin; there could be no other man for her. She pressed her hand against her stomach in a protective gesture. With every passing day she was more convinced that she was pregnant.

She could keep the secret of her parentage, her inheritance, from him forever. She need never try to claim her fortune. But this other, more intimate secret—she couldn't conceal it much longer. In a few months he would know that she was carrying his child.

"You asked Briana Cameron to our housewarming without consulting me?" Cole, his blue eyes frosty, confronted Eleanor in her bedroom.

After the first few weeks of their marriage, when she had submitted to him out of a sense of duty but without a trace of warmth, she had insisted upon having her own bedroom, now lavishly decorated with pink satin curtains, marquetry cabinets, and gilt and velvet chairs.

"I've a right to invite anyone I choose. Besides, you've been away all these weeks—you only got back this morning." Her voice took on the petulant whine he'd come to know and dislike so thoroughly during the months of their marriage. "I asked her on impulse—I felt sorry for her, still unmarried, poor creature. Working so hard in her shop. But I doubt she'll come to the ball."

"You just told me she's accepted your invitation," he reminded her. He pushed his hands into the pockets of his dressing gown, trying not to show his rising irritation.

"By now she'll have changed her mind. She must have real-

ized she'd be out of place among our other guests. She'll probably lose her nerve at the last moment and stay away."

If his wife thought that, she knew nothing of Briana's fierce
pride, her strong will. Poor creature, indeed! The young woman
who had stood up to Devlin Rafferty on the Charleston dock
and had embarked alone on a dangerous voyage around the
Horn; who had refused to agree to an arranged marriage and
had gone on to build one of the most successful businesses in
San Francisco; who had forced her way through the mob at Fort
Gunnybags—such a woman wouldn't withdraw before the challenge of attending a ball on Rincon Hill.

"Even if she *is* foolish enough to come," Eleanor was saying,
"the ladies will snub her and she'll go slinking off like a scared
cat."

He was finding it increasingly difficult to hide his contempt
for his wife's judgment. The ladies might snub Briana, but every
man in the ballroom would be stirred by her warm, sensuous
beauty.

"I'll admit she has excellent taste in clothes," Eleanor said
as she smoothed the folds of her billowing brocade skirt. "All
those years of living in Paris, I suppose. She assured me that
this gown was the height of Parisian fashion this season."

"You bought your gown from her?"

"I didn't go down to Sansome Street, if that's what you
mean," Eleanor said with a prim little smile. "One doesn't know
what sort of female one might meet in her shop. I sent for her
to come here, of course."

She went on, but he could scarcely keep his mind on her
chatter. He was remembering that night at the Maison Dorée.
Briana beside him on the sofa in the private supper room. The
scent of her perfume. The glow of her red-gold hair. The satin
skin of her shoulders, the swell of her high, firm breasts. A
wave of scalding heat flooded his body; he was seized by an
almost painful tightening in his loins.

Suppose Briana had agreed to become his mistress that night?
A series of vivid erotic images rose to torment him. Briana's

breasts bared to his touch, the rosy peaks of her nipples beneath his fingers; her thighs parting to receive his first thrust of possession.

He could have taken her by force that night, but such an act would have been an offense to his pride. He had wanted her to come to him willingly, with a hunger that matched his own.

"Cole, really! I don't believe you've been listening to me. I just asked if you would take me to Paris."

"Certainly I will, my dear." The response was automatic, but she didn't notice that.

"I'll adore visiting the House of Worth . . . a whole new wardrobe . . . do you think I might be presented at court?"

He turned away from her, restraining his impulse to tell her that it was Briana he'd wanted to take to Paris.

He started for the bedroom door.

"Where are you going?" That whining tone again. It set his teeth on edge.

"You must excuse me, Eleanor. It's getting late and I've not yet dressed," he said. "Our guests will be arriving soon."

Twenty-two

Briana stared at Devlin, blinked, then stared again, taken by surprise at seeing him for the first time in formal evening attire: the dress shirt with starched white ruffles, the pearl gray silk cravat, the embroidered silk waistcoat, and the black evening trousers. A black cape lined with pearl gray silk swung jauntily from his wide shoulders.

He swept off his tall silk hat, bowed, then helped her into the phaeton. "Better get a good look now. By the time this evening's over this outfit will probably be the worse for wear."

She put a hand on his arm and looked up at him anxiously. "You're expecting a fight?"

"Cole's not about to give up his dreams of glory easily. And there'll be plenty of followers who'll back him up, no matter what proof of his treachery I have to show them."

"But he wouldn't start a brawl in front of so many important guests—Senator Gwin and Sam Brannan and—"

"Don't be too sure. He's been getting more unpredictable all the time. With his back to the wall, there's no telling what he may do." His gaze locked with hers. "If a fight starts, get out fast." He spoke in his commanding, quarterdeck tone, and she didn't question him. "Tommy says there's a big garden behind the house," he went on. "At the first sign of trouble go there and wait for me."

But when they arrived at the Forresters' imposing mansion, and Devlin maneuvered the phaeton into the line of waiting vehicles, she tried to tell herself that he might be mistaken. It was hard to imagine a pitched battle in such elegant surroundings.

Candles glowed in the tall windows, and each time the butler opened the massive oak door the enticing strains of an Offenbach waltz floated out to greet the guests. Bejeweled ladies in billowing crinolines descended from their carriages; Briana smiled as she recognized some of those gowns, for they had come from her own shop.

In creating Briana's gown of cinnamon-colored silk, Abbie had outdone herself: the bodice with its daring decolletage, the wide, bell-shaped skirt trimmed with gold lace flounces, reflecting the latest Parisian mode. Her black velvet cloak was lined with honey silk, to accentuate her warm amber eyes. Her hair was drawn back from her face, arranged in a cascade of red-gold ringlets. The light from the half-open doorway struck sparks from her topaz-and-diamond necklace and earrings.

When Devlin had presented them to her earlier that evening she had caught her breath in delight. "They're beautiful—I'll treasure them always. But you've spent so much on the steamer. You shouldn't have—"

"You're right," he agreed with a careless laugh. "I'm just about tapped out now." He fastened the clasp of the necklace, and her senses stirred at the touch of his fingers against her skin. "But I'll make it all back, and more, as soon as the *Jessica Rafferty* takes to the river. The tickets for her maiden voyage are sold out already. And I have a full cargo waiting in the warehouse." She heard the ringing pride in his voice; the ship meant nearly as much to him as she did.

He helped her down from the phaeton, and they walked up the curving pathway, lit by torches on either side. Again, she was impressed by the magnificence of Cole's mansion, its turrets and pinnacles, its parapets and carved brick chimneys dark against the sky. It reminded her of the ornate castles of Europe, and why not? No doubt Cole already saw himself as the ruler of his own empire here in California.

Now they were inside the wide, high-ceilinged foyer, with its floor of black and white marble squares; she was enveloped by the heady fragrance of pine boughs and hothouse roses, mingling with the ladies' perfumes. A liveried footman took her cloak and Devlin's tall hat and cape.

In the upper hallway Eleanor and Cole stood side by side, receiving their guests. Briana caught the flicker of surprise in her hostess's eyes. She'd been right, then; Eleanor hadn't expected her to come here tonight, and certainly not with Devlin as her escort.

"I'm so pleased with my new gown, Miss Cameron," Eleanor said with a forced smile; she raised her voice slightly, so that the ladies nearby could hear. "Your little shop has lived up to its excellent reputation."

Cole bowed over Briana's hand, then greeted Devlin in his usual polished manner; he gave no sign that Devlin was an uninvited guest. "All San Francisco's talking about that new steamer of yours, Captain Rafferty. A floating palace, so they say. Maybe you'll find me on your passenger list once again." He permitted himself a faintly patronizing smile.

"You'll be most welcome—you and your charming wife."

Briana caught the brief glint of mockery in Devlin's eyes. Was he reminding Cole that he'd been there to witness the man's proposal to her, and her firm refusal?

Later, as she and Devlin waltzed together in the magnificent ballroom, in the light of the glittering crystal chandeliers, she let herself forget all about Cole and Eleanor as she gave herself up to the sheer delight of whirling and swaying in perfect rhythm with him; to the sensual pleasure of his hand, warm and strong at her waist. Where had he learned to waltz with such skill? Surely not in New South Wales.

But all at once another sensation made Briana catch her breath. Under the folds of cinnamon silk and lace and the wide crinoline petticoats, deep within her body, she felt a flutter of movement. It filled her with awe and wonder. The baby had stirred for the first time. Devlin's baby. Her steps faltered for an instant, but she recovered herself and caught the beat of the waltz again. She longed to share her secret with him—but not now—not yet.

Abbie already knew about her condition. During the first fitting for her ball gown those sharp eyes had studied her closely. "Briana?"

"Yes." No use trying to deceive her friend.

"We'd best move the waistline a bit higher," said Abbie, reaching for her pincushion. "No one will guess—the Empress Eugenie's already set the fashion for high-waisted gowns."

Briana had felt her face grow hot, but she had tried to sound self-possessed. "By next week our customers will all be clamoring for the same style. Now about the petticoat; I want you to—"

But Abbie hadn't been put off so easily. "Have you told him?"

"No, I haven't. And don't you dare say a word."

"He has a right to know." Abbie had placed a reassuring hand on her arm. "He loves you, Briana."

"He's never said so."

"He doesn't have to. I've seen how he looks at you. Once you tell him, he'll marry you."

"He's not ready for marriage; not yet."

"But you are," Abbie had said with a meaningful look at her waistline. "Good heavens, Briana, the man's not blind. How long do you suppose you can go on keeping your secret?"

She hadn't answered; she'd pushed the question to the back of her mind and gone on with her detailed instructions about the petticoat.

"A pocket?" Abbie asked in surprise. Briana nodded, unwilling to admit to the superstitious side of her nature.

But now, as she and Devlin danced together, she took comfort in remembering that the pocket hidden in the lace and cambric ruffles of her petticoat held the small, intricately carved figurine of the goddess Kuan Yin.

Deep within her womb, the baby stirred again, then kicked. She took in her breath sharply.

"Briana, are you all right?"

She looked up at him with a dazzling smile. "Certainly I am."

But he wasn't satisfied. "For a minute there you looked—distracted." His hand pressed firmly against her waist, and he gave her a reassuring smile. "If you're worried about what may happen later tonight, don't be. I've got the crew of the *Jessica Rafferty* positioned all around the house, just waiting for my orders."

"I didn't see any of them as we came in."

"You weren't intended to. But if I need them, they're ready to go into action, the same as they did that day at Fort Gunnybags."

Briana glanced uneasily at the elegantly dressed gentlemen circling the ballroom with their partners, or grouped around the silver punchbowls set on the long, damask-draped tables. Some of them were Southerners like Cole.

Others were *rancheros,* men of regal bearing who took pride in their Castilian ancestry; the owners of the great tracts of land in southern California or across the border in Sonora. Their short, tightly fitted black jackets and trousers and crimson sashes made them stand out from the other male guests.

After the first waltz Cole introduced Devlin and Briana to one of them: don Alfredo Montoya, who had spent the holidays as a houseguest. He was in his early fifties, tall, lean, and straight as a ramrod, with an aquiline nose and black hair touched with silver. He bowed and asked Briana for the next dance. As they moved across the polished floor, she was impressed by his courtly manners and his quiet dignity. After that she was besieged by partners; her dance card, a tiny white square suspended from her wrist by a satin cord, was quickly filled.

At midnight the bells rang out, echoing across the city, from the narrow, twisting streets and alleys of the waterfront to the highest hills, to mark the start of the new year. The guests cheered, kissed, and embraced. Devlin held her close to him, his lips warm and seeking. If only they could slip away now, she thought longingly. But she reminded herself of their reason for being here, and when he released her she took his arm. Slowly they moved into the dining room along with the others.

The guests strolled to the tables, to find platters bearing turkeys, glazed hams, suckling pigs, and venison. The damask tablecloths were decorated with thick loops of evergreen fastened with silver ribbons. Servants in livery hurried forward to fill glasses with champagne.

Cole stepped forward, welcoming the guests to his new home, then lifted his glass and proposed a toast.

"To the shining future of California," he began. "A free and independent California. Once we have shaken off the chains that bind us to the United States, a glorious—a limitless vista lies ahead for us." He cast his gaze about the room. "For my compatriots from our own beloved South, the opportunity to return to our traditions—unhampered by those fanatics who would impose their radical views upon us." Not a word about slavery, but his meaning was plain enough. Her hand tightened on Devlin's arm.

"To our friends, the *rancheros*, in whose veins flows the blood of the Castilian nobility, I pledge myself to the restoration of all that was taken from them in an unjust war."

He went on, and Briana, glancing about the room, saw the rapt, upturned faces of the guests, who were caught in the spell of his practiced oratory. Without offering any specific promises, he was convincing them that, under his leadership, they could achieve whatever they most wanted.

Beneath her gloved hand, she felt Devlin's muscles go rock hard. She caught the icy glint in his gray eyes, the set of his jaw. Her heart speeded up and, in spite of the perfumed warmth of the room, she felt a growing chill.

Soon, she thought. Whatever he meant to do, he would take action soon.

"We who are here tonight seek only what is ours. The right to govern ourselves as we see fit. Free from the domination of outsiders—"

"And you think Louis Napoleon will agree to that?" Devlin's powerful voice rang out, silencing Cole, reaching the farthest corners of the huge dining room. She felt a thrill of pride. Although he was no trained orator, his words, his bearing, had never failed to control a rebellious crew or a mob of angry passengers. She drew a measure of reassurance from the memory of the way he'd handled the near riot on her first night aboard the *Osprey*. But he wasn't in command of one of his own ships now. Cole's guests looked startled at this unforeseen interruption.

"I scarcely see what the French emperor has to do with our plans." Cole's voice was a soft drawl.

"I think you do, Forrester." Devlin reached inside his jacket, drew out a folded paper, and held it high. "You wrote this to the Duc de Morny—the emperor's half brother and a most influential member of the imperial government. You took it upon yourself to promise that, in return for the help of French troops in Mexico, you would offer an enormous payment in silver from the mines of Sonora."

The *rancheros,* many of whom had interests in those mines, fixed their eyes on Devlin. He had captured their complete attention now.

"As for you Southern gentlemen who favor States Rights and secession," he went on, "I'm here to tell you that you've been deceived. Cole Forrester is using your loyalty to the South to gain support for his own purposes."

"Just a moment, Captain." Martin Padgett, a tall, distinguished-looking man, spoke out; his soft drawl didn't conceal his rising anger. "Cole Forrester's my son-in-law and my law partner. No man here is more devoted to the honor of the South. He favors secession, as we all do."

"That's true enough, sir," Devlin said. "He wants secession. But not so that you'll gain the right to hold slaves in California, to run your affairs without interference from the federal government. He's determined to establish his own empire here in the west. To make himself absolute ruler. After that he'll extend his sphere of influence right down into Mexico." He paused, his gaze sweeping over the room. "But to do that he'll need the help of the French government. The services of French troops."

Cole's face had gone white, except for the red splotches that burned on his cheeks. He set down his glass and advanced on Devlin with a measured tread. "If you think these men will accept this fantastic story on the strength of your word alone, Captain, you're mistaken."

"Not my word, Forrester."

The crowd parted as Devlin strode forward to meet Cole, flourishing the folded paper. "Your word. This is only one of your letters to the Duc de Morny; I have plenty more. Along with his letters to you." Devlin turned to look about the room again; he was speaking to the others now. "A most informative correspondence, gentlemen."

"It's a damn forgery!" someone shouted. "Forrester wouldn't sell us out—"

"Judge for yourselves. The letters are under guard at the custom house, in the possession of the United States Collector of Customs. You're all welcome to come down and read them as soon as you wish."

The men stared at Cole, then eyed one another in confusion and dismay. Before Briana knew quite how it had happened, Cole was surrounded by a phalanx of loyal supporters, while others advanced on Devlin. But he didn't give way; he stood, arms folded across his chest, feet set apart, as self-assured as if he commanded his own quarterdeck.

"This is an outrage. You will leave my house at once, Captain Rafferty," Cole said.

"Not a chance," Devlin told him with a tight smile. "Shall I pass around this letter? Or would you care to read it aloud to your guests?"

A big, bull-necked man whose well-tailored evening coat covered a pair of massive shoulders made a grab for the paper. In that instant Tommy stepped out of the shadows.

Briana gave a low cry of surprise. Where had the boy been hiding until now? Quick as a cat, he snatched the letter from Devlin. The burly man reached for Tommy, but he grinned, dodging away easily, and darted through the crowd and headed for one of the windows.

"Now, lad!"

At Devlin's command, Tommy picked up a gilt and velvet chair and swung it with all his wiry strength. The glass panes shattered, the glittering fragments showering down on the carpet. The damp night breeze came streaming into the room; the heavy satin drapes billowed and swayed.

Eleanor gave a shrill scream; another lady swooned against her escort. Devlin turned to Briana, who had already flattened herself against the nearest wall. And now she heard it, too—the pounding of heavy footsteps in the hall below, the raucous shouts of men primed and eager for battle. Servants cried out ineffectual protests. Devlin's crew came surging up the stairs.

"Stop them!" Cole shouted to his followers, but his voice was swallowed up in the growing din. The crew of the steamer, led by Quinn, exploded into the room, brandishing clubs, belaying pins, and boarding pikes. A wide grin split Quinn's face and he swung his huge fist, knocking down the nearest defender and sending the man lurching backward against the table.

Another man came at Quinn with a knife, but Tommy tripped him up. When he grabbed at one of the pine swags to regain

his balance he only succeeded in dragging down the whole tablecloth. Before the dazed man could make a second attempt
to get to his feet Tommy picked up a potted plant and brought
it down on his head. "Good work, lad!" Quinn shouted, and
went on swinging.

Women squealed in fright and clung to their escorts, who
tried to get them out of the melee, but other men braced themselves to fight back the intruders. A silver punch bowl went
crashing to the polished floor. Wine splattered across the white
tablecloth and down onto the carpet.

For an instant Briana remained frozen, her eyes fixed on
Devlin. "Get out of here!" he called to her, even as he drew
back his arm and swung on the bull-necked man. Lifting her
skirts, she edged toward the doorway, still keeping her back to
the wall. She moved carefully, possessed by her instinctive need
to protect the precious life within her.

After one last, anxious glance at Devlin she managed to get
out into the long hall. Lifting her skirts, she raced down the
corridor's length, thankful that she knew the layout of the house
well enough to head directly for the rear stairs.

No time now to stop for her cloak. With the screams of the
frightened women, the shouts of the men, the crash of china
and glass still ringing in her ears, she got downstairs and
wrenched open the back door. Then she sped across the flag-
stone terrace and down the steps to the garden.

The branches of the trees creaked and swayed in the night
breeze. She filled her lungs with the damp, salty air, and it
steadied her. Although she was anxious for Devlin, she knew
he was well able to defend himself.

She started down one of the winding gravel paths, between
two rows of tall, flowering shrubs, then sank down on a marble
bench, her eyes fixed on the rear windows. It looked as though
the fighting had spilled out from the dining room and into the
rest of the house; she saw two struggling figures at the window
on the lower floor, and then a long ray of light pierced the
darkness of the garden. One of the fighters must have clutched

at the heavy drapes and torn them down. Moments later a window shattered, and a marble statue came hurtling out onto the terrace. The impact smashed the marble to pieces.

Briana felt a pang of sympathy for Eleanor, who had taken such pride in her splendid new home; who had expected this New Year's Eve to be a night of social triumph.

But her thoughts quickly returned to Devlin. He'd been right to order her outside, yet she longed to be with him, to see for herself that he was still holding his own in the fight.

Cole, caught off guard, his towering ambitions threatened, was capable of anything. Even after Devlin had denounced him he still had commanded the unshaken loyalty of a hard core of supporters. There were plenty of Southerners, as well as those hot-tempered *rancheros,* who weren't convinced that he meant to betray them. They'd fallen under the spell of his oratory, been convinced by his promises. They would go on fighting for him—they'd kill for him.

A shudder went racing through her. She rose from the bench, took a few steps in the direction of the house, and then stopped, remembering Devlin's orders. And there was the child she carried; even if she was willing to risk injury to herself, she realized that from now on she must always consider the life inside her.

Her muscles began to ache with tension. Her gloved hands were balled into tight fists. She flexed them, and saw that her dance card still dangled from her wrist. She snapped the satin ribbon and the card went fluttering off, to be caught in a nearby shrub.

She started, then gave a sigh of relief as she heard footsteps on the graveled path. Devlin had come for her.

But the welcoming smile on her lips froze when she saw Cole, rounding the stand of bushes. She shrank back, hoping to conceal herself, but it was too late.

His hand shot out and closed around her wrist. "Briana." She saw his blue eyes narrow slightly. That quick, shrewd mind was at work, seeking to turn this unforeseen meeting to his advantage.

He drew her against him. "I knew you'd be waiting for me, my dear."

"Miss Cameron?" She recognized Señor Montoya's deep voice. She wasn't surprised to see him here. He had pledged his loyalty to Cole and meant to keep his word.

"Let go of me!" She tried to break Cole's grasp, but he was too strong for her.

He laughed softly, lifted her in his arms, and carried her along the path, followed by Montoya.

She bucked and writhed against his chest, then realized it was useless to waste her strength in an unequal struggle. She forced herself to remain still, her head lying back against his shoulder. Overhead, the clouds went scudding off; in the moonlight she caught sight of a long, low brick building ahead, and recognized the smell of hay and horses.

"You, there! Frazer!" A stablehand roused himself and hurried to answer Cole's summons.

"Hitch up the barouche. And be quick about it!"

The startled man rubbed his eyes, then called into the darkness of the stalls, "Seth, get up and bring out them grays." Another man shambled forward, and together they hitched a pair of powerful geldings to a large, ornate carriage. "Want me to wake up one of the coachmen, sir?" Frazer asked.

Cole shook his head. "You'll do the driving tonight."

Frazer mounted the high seat, while Seth stood watching, openmouthed. Briana began to struggle frantically, striking out at Cole's face, his shoulders. She fought for breath, cursing her confining whalebone corset.

She hadn't counted on this turn of events—but she should have. She should have known that Cole, although convinced of his ultimate success, would have made plans for a possible temporary retreat. "Put me down—Devlin knows where I am— he'll come looking for me—"

But he ignored her cries as he ignored her flailing fists.

"A moment, Señor Forrester, *por favor*," Montoya protested. "You said nothing about taking this lady with us."

Cole's soft laugh chilled her to the bone. "She's an unpredictable creature—it's one of her charms. She promised to wait for me, but I couldn't be sure."

"That's a lie! I was waiting for Devlin!" She aimed a blow at the point of his jaw, but he shifted so that the blow struck his shoulder. "Señor Montoya—please believe me! Make him let me go!"

"I do not fight against women, señor. You will release her."

"You mustn't be misled by her little charade," Cole said. "Believe me, the lady is willing. She traveled from Charleston to San Francisco in my cabin. A most delightful voyage. We have—an understanding."

Now he motioned impatiently to Montoya. "After you, señor." But the man didn't move. "You have already offered me the hospitality of your estate in Sonora," Cole reminded him. "Surely you're not backing down now."

The man raised his head, his lean body taut with outraged pride at the suggestion. "A Montoya does not break his word."

"Come, then."

"The two of us could make greater speed on horseback," Montoya pointed out. "Your fine carriage will prove unwieldy on the narrower roads."

"We'll use the carriage only as far as Point Lobo, then hire a boat to take us the rest of the way."

Yes, Cole had thought it all out, down to the last detail. Now he was lifting her, forcing her through the open door and into the carriage. She tried to clutch at the door frame but lost her grip and went bouncing onto the soft leather seat. She started to rise, hampered by her wide crinoline.

"Let me down, damn you!"

"Enough, Briana! No need to keep up your performance any longer. It grows tiresome." He turned to his companion. "Come, señor. We've no time to waste."

Montoya hesitated, then climbed inside. He seated himself opposite Cole and Briana. Cole closed the door, then called out to the driver, who cracked his whip; the barouche moved forward, away from the stables, down a wide, tree-lined path.

She cried out Devlin's name, but she knew he would never hear her. They were too far from the house, where the battle still raged. The barouche wasn't moving quickly, not yet. She thought of lunging for the door and throwing herself out. But she couldn't risk the baby's safety. She sank back against the seat and stared out at Rincon Hill already receding behind them, a dark shape against the moonlit sky.

"I looked all over the garden, like you said—but Miss Briana ain't there."

Devlin gripped Tommy's shoulder. "I told her to wait."

Quinn appeared, his shirt torn, the side of his face swollen. He stepped over the shards of a smashed vase and rested his bruised hand on the railing of the upstairs hall. "Maybe she went home by herself. Wouldn't blame her, with all that ruckus goin' on."

The house was a shambles, but the fighting was over; those of Cole's vanquished followers who could still walk had helped their battered friends to get away. The noisy, triumphant crew of the *Jessica Rafferty* had staggered off to the Barbary Coast, to drink to their victory.

The last of the guests—those who had been unable to escape and had been forced to take refuge in whatever empty rooms they could find—now came out cautiously.

All around them, the signs of battle remained. The gray light of dawn, pale at the windows, revealed the torn swags of greenery and flowers trampled underfoot. A priceless painting had been ripped from the wall, its gilt frame smashed, the canvas marred by muddy footprints. A lighted silver candelabrum had been knocked over; someone had stamped out the flames, leaving a blackened place on the thick carpet and the acrid smell of scorched wool overpowered the scents of pine needles and roses.

Eleanor stood, white-faced and rigid, her father beside her.

Devlin approached her, indifferent to his disheveled appearance: the blood that streamed from a cut above his eye and stained his ruffled shirtfront; the livid purple bruise on one side of his jaw. He forced himself to speak quietly, for he sensed that she was on the edge of hysterics. "Where's your husband?"

The corner of her mouth jerked spasmodically; her fingers plucked at an ostrich feather in her fan. "Gone," she said, her voice expressionless. "He's gone."

"You will leave this house," Martin Padgett intervened. "At once, sir."

But Devlin ignored him and spoke to Eleanor. "Where did he go, Mrs. Forrester?"

"He left with Señor Montoya—I don't know where he's—" Her voice broke.

Devlin stiffened with apprehension. It wasn't like Cole to run away in the face of violence; whatever else the man might be, he was no coward.

"I've already told you to leave," Padgett cut in. He put a protective arm around his daughter. "Must I have the servants throw you out?"

Quinn gave a harsh bark of laughter. "Not likely. Them jackanapes in their pretty uniforms are probably hiding in the kitchen—"

Devlin silenced him with a gesture. "I've no wish to upset Mrs. Forrester any further, sir. It's her husband I'm looking for."

With a sudden, violent movement, Eleanor jerked away from her father and confronted Devlin. She was breathing quickly, unsteadily, and her eyes burned with malice. "He's gone! Señor Montoya went with him! I don't know where!"

"He didn't give you any idea where he might be going?"

Her gloved hand closed around the handle of her fan, and he heard the ivory sticks give way with a small, snapping sound.

"Why would he tell me? Go ask your trollop—ask your precious Miss Cameron. If you can find her!"

Devlin ignored his anger at the insult to Briana. As Eleanor's meaning sank in, he turned away from her and gestured to Quinn and Tommy. "Come on!"

He strode down the hall and out the back door, with the other two close behind him. The hot excitement of battle, the triumph of victory, drained out of him. He had sent her to the garden; he'd placed her in harm's way.

Outside in the misty garden he called her name, but there was no answer. He stood staring into the swirling fog, and from the depths of his memory the familiar guilt arose to torment him once more. He hadn't married her, but he had joined his life, his destiny with hers. He'd gone against his long-held resolve never to become too close to any other human being.

Had he, like his father before him, sent the woman he loved to destruction?

Twenty-three

In the light of the lantern suspended from the overhead beam, Devlin confronted a startled Seth. "How long since Forrester left?" Devlin demanded. The stable hand eyed him warily, retreating a step.

"A couple of hours, maybe. He took the big carriage—the barouche. Frazer, he had me help hitch up the horses. He was drivin' Forrester and that Señor Montoya—"

Devlin grabbed the man by the shirtfront, his powerful hand twisting the collar. "Was there a woman with them?"

The man hesitated for a second. Devlin's grip tightened. "Yes—a lady—real good-lookin'—"

"Where were they heading?"

"I don't know. But they were sure in a hell of a hurry—they didn't even stop to change out of them fancy duds they were wearin'." He glanced at Devlin pleadingly. "I couldn't have stopped them, mister."

"Why would you want to?" Devlin demanded.

"Well, the lady—seemed like she didn't want to go along. Mr. Forrester said she was only puttin' on a—a charade. But he finally had to pick her up and toss her into the barouche, and even then she kept makin' a fuss— Hey—stop that, mister! I'm tryin' to tell you—you don't have to—choke it outta me."

Devlin slackened his grip slightly. "Where were they heading?"

The stable hand drew a ragged breath. "I don't know." Devlin's jaw muscle clamped down hard and Seth's eyes went wide with fright.

"Where? Talk, damn you!"

"Mr. Forrester didn't say—I swear he didn't. Why would he tell me?" He cringed, struggled to break free, then abandoned the hopeless effort. "I guess he was tryin' to get as far as he could from the riotin' in the house. I heard the racket all the way down here—woke me out of a sound sleep, it did—"

Quinn took a step forward; his shadow loomed menacingly against the stable wall. "You want me to help him remember, Captain?" His hands closed into fists.

Devlin shook his head. With an effort, he controlled his fear for Briana and spoke more softly. "Try to remember everything you heard."

"Well, that Señor Montoya, he wasn't happy about takin' the lady along. But then Mr. Forrester asked him, was he goin' back on his word. An' he said a Montoya wouldn't do that, an'—"

Devlin's insides knotted tighter. "Did you hear Forrester give directions to the coachman?"

"He didn't even wait to call the coachman—he said for Frazer to drive. Like I told you, he was in a big hurry, an' I don't blame him, what with them yellin' savages tearing up the house an smashin' the windows."

"Savages, is it?" Quinn began, but an ominous look from Devlin silenced him.

Through the open doors of the stable came a pale ray of sunlight; the early morning fog was starting to thin away. With a tremendous effort, Devlin kept control of his temper. "Where's Montoya's ranch? In Baja California? Or across the border?"

"He didn't say! I told you, mister—Captain—"

"Why didn't they go by horseback?" Tommy interrupted. "They could've made more speed that way."

"That's what Montoya said. An' he was right—you take a big barouche along one of them narrow coast roads in the fog, an' at top speed—you could have a bad accident. An' Frazer ain't a proper coachman—only a stable hand like me."

For one terrifying moment Devlin could visualize the barouche, careening down a fog-shrouded road, out of control. Briana crying out with fear. Or limp and still, lying on the rocks at the foot of a cliff, her slender body shattered, her amber eyes wide but unseeing, fixed on the sky.

He forced himself to shut out the terrifying vision; to concentrate on the stable hand's stammered words. "—an' Mr. Forrester said they'd only be takin' the barouche as far as—" Devlin saw the man's brow furrow in his desperate effort to remember. "Point Lobo! He said they'd leave the barouche an' take a boat the rest of the way from there."

Devlin let out his breath with a rasping sound. "Point Lobo? You're sure that's what he said?"

"I'm sure!"

Devlin released him, and Seth scurried off into the darkness of the stalls.

"There's plenty of little skiffs they can hire at the Point," Quinn said. "With a good wind they can get to Mexico fast and put in at any one of a hundred coves you won't even find on a map."

"They won't get that far." Devlin's voice was dangerously quiet.

"I ain't had much practice ridin' a horse," Quinn said, "but we can get that fella to saddle three of Forresters' best an' try to catch up."

"We don't know what road they've taken, only that they're

heading south. We could ride over half the state and never catch sight of them."

"Then how do you figure on—"

"The steamer'll get us straight to Point Lobo."

"The river's too narrow, once you get past Big Oak Bar."

"We're not going by river," Devlin said. "We're taking the steamer out to sea."

"She ain't even been out for a trial run," Tommy protested.

"She'll have her trial run, just as fast as we can raise anchor."

Tommy and Quinn exchanged doubtful glances. "It'll take more'n us three to handle her," said Quinn. "The rest of the crew's scattered around in the gin mills on the coast, an' them that ain't layin' under a table are rollin' with a whore in a feather bed."

"You and Tommy will round them up. Bring me at least half a dozen; more if you can. I'll head straight for the *Jessica Rafferty* and start the furnace. We have plenty of coal in the bunkers, and Mackenzie'll lend me a hand."

Quinn and Tommy headed for the door, but even as he followed them, his hot fury against Cole Forrester slowly ebbed away. Now a fierce guilt was clawing at his vitals. If Briana should come to harm, he, not Forrester, would be to blame. Because he had allowed his feelings for her to grow, to deepen, to penetrate that hidden place inside him; the place he had kept guarded until now. He had let down his defenses. She had become a part of him. He hadn't wanted it that way; it had just happened, so gradually he'd scarcely realized it.

He'd hunt down Forrester and drag him back to San Francisco. He'd make the letters public, all of them. Forrester's dream of conquest would be destroyed.

He'd bring her back, too. He pushed aside the icy fear that threatened to engulf him. She had to be alive, unharmed.

But once she was safe in the city again, he would distance himself from her. She'd be hurt and bewildered, but he couldn't help that. He would turn back to his ship, to the world of wind and tide. The only world where he belonged. Although parting from her would leave fresh scars on that dark place inside, he would learn to live with them.

The fog had already burned away and a pale sun lit the winter sky as the crew gathered on the deck of the new steamer. Although Devlin had changed from his ruined evening clothes to his uniform, his face still bore traces of blood, now mixed with coal dust. Mackenzie's light blue eyes peered from a blackened mask. "I designed these engines, Captain, and I'm telling you, you can't push them up to top speed."

"Go ashore then." Devlin spoke hoarsely. His eyes moved over the milling men, who'd been dragged from saloon floors or sporting houses and herded aboard. "Mackenzie's right," he told them. "It'll be dangerous taking her to sea at full speed. I'm not ordering any man here to come with me." It took an effort to go on; he wasn't used to asking for help.

"That bastard Forrester's got the captain's lady. He took her off against her will." Tommy's voice, only recently deepened, now cracked under the stress of the moment. "I'm goin' along to help get her back."

The rest of the crew looked at the boy, then at one another. There was a moment of taut silence. Then one of them shouted, "We'll get 'er back for ye, Captain."

"That we will."

"An' we'll beat the bejesus out of Forrester."

Devlin was moved by the loyalty of his crew. Experienced seamen, all of them, they knew the risk they'd be taking. He turned to the engineer. "We're ready to cast off. You'd best get ashore now, Mackenzie."

"And leave one of these ham-handed sailors to wreck my engines?" He gave Devlin an outraged glare. "Not a chance, Captain." Before Devlin had time to thank him the Scotsman turned and headed below.

* * *

The sun was overhead now, slanting through the branches of the towering trees. The barouche went jolting along a road that was little better than a rough wagon track. Briana clung to the seat and tried to keep from falling against Cole; his closeness repelled and frightened her. She was grateful for the presence of Señor Montoya.

Since they'd left the estate behind and driven out of the city Montoya had maintained a tight-lipped silence. She wondered if he was still troubled by Cole's insistence on taking her along. Perhaps he hadn't fully accepted Cole's facile explanation of their relationship after all.

Even now, in spite of her growing anxiety, she felt a deep sense of outrage. Cole had said she'd made the voyage to California in his cabin, but he had neglected to mention that he hadn't shared the cabin with her. He'd implied that she had been his mistress, that she still was.

At the first opportunity she would find a way to get Montoya alone and try to convince him of the truth. But would he believe her? He was one of Cole's devoted supporters, after all. And perhaps Eleanor had dropped certain hints about the reputation of Briana Cameron, even while she had been whirling about the ballroom last night in the arms of one partner after another.

Briana Cameron, owner of a fashionable dress shop; a young lady who wasn't above dealing with the madams of the most notorious parlor houses in the city; who had befriended Belle Cora. Who had cast aside the last claim to decency and gone sailing off with Captain Devlin Rafferty.

She shut her eyes tightly. It hadn't been like that at all. She loved Devlin—had loved him from the beginning, although it had taken time for her to realize it. She had refused his proposal only because she'd sensed it wasn't what he really wanted. Even now she could see the look of torment in his eyes when he'd said he'd marry her. *If that's what you want*

Had he already discovered she'd gone off with ole? For a moment hope flared within her. He'd know she hadn't left willingly. And he'd come after her. But then hope ebbed away. How could he ever find her before Cole had her hidden at Montoya's hacienda across the border?

"Miss Cameron—you are feeling ill, perhaps?" Her lids flew open and she saw that Montoya was looking at her with concern. She wanted to speak, but Cole's hand closed on her arm. His touch warned her to remain silent.

"I'm sorry this stretch of road's so bad, my dear," he said to her with feigned concern. He put his arm around her shoulders as if to steady her. "As soon as we embark at Point Lobo, we'll have a smooth passage. A fair breeze, a calm sea. And you'll find the accommodations at Señor Montoya's home as luxurious as you could wish. I'll make sure you're comfortable." His breath was hot against her cheek. She stiffened but didn't try to pull away.

He wanted her as badly as ever; she saw it in his face, sensed it in his touch. But he might restrain his hunger, at least for the length of the journey—unless she lashed out at him and told him what she thought of him in front of Montoya. If she humiliated him that way, she couldn't be sure what he might do to punish her.

The fierce ambition that had driven him so long had grown steadily. As he had gathered supporters and exchanged letters with the Duc de Morny in an attempt to gain the support of Emperor Louis Napoleon, his dreams of glory had soared to fantastic heights.

He'd left Eleanor behind last night without a backward glance; he hadn't even considered how his wife would deal with the destruction of her home, the scandal that would inevitably follow when Devlin exposed him before his guests.

She threw him a quick glance and saw the cold intensity in his eyes. She had to get away from him somehow. "I'm not ill, only exhausted," she told Montoya. "Perhaps we might stop for awhile."

"Not yet," Cole interrupted. "We're close to Point Lobo, my dear. We'll keep going until we get there." His implacable tone silenced her. She started to draw away from him, slowly, carefully. The next moment she cried out as the barouche gave a sudden lurch that jolted every bone in her body. She heard a shout from above, where Frazer was struggling to control the frantic horses. Then came the screech of metal, the cracking of wood. Her side of the barouche slammed into the nearest tree and she was flung against the door. Her arms closed instinctively across her belly before she went spinning down into darkness.

"You heard what I said, Captain." Under stress, Mackenzie's Scottish burr grew more pronounced. "We're already making fourteen knots. We can't get a pound more steam pressure out of her than we are. Not unless you want to blow her to hell, and us along with her."

Devlin respected the engineer's judgment, but he couldn't bring himself to take back his order to increase their speed. Possessed by his driving urgency, he clamped his lips together, turned, and went up on deck. He looked at the twin stacks overhead, and the dark streams of smoke trailing across the pale winter sky.

Quinn came hurrying to his side. "Better hold to this speed, Captain." He glanced down at the deck. "Feel that?"

Only now Devlin noticed the searing heat of the deck through his heavy-soled boots. He led the way up onto the bridge that stretched between the paddle boxes.

The sailors down below were glancing at him anxiously even as they went about their duties. But he knew they'd keep the steamer on course until he gave other orders.

Briana looked about a small clearing, on a cliff high above the ocean. A few wind-twisted cypresses stretched their branches over the edge, grotesque shapes in the misty afternoon light. Cole had wrapped his satin-lined cape around her shoulders and propped her against one of the rocks. She shook her head to clear her dazed senses, then tried to rise.

"Careful, señorita," Montoya cautioned. "You don't seem to be badly hurt, but one never knows."

She glanced around the clearing but saw no sign of Frazer. "The driver—where is he?"

"He's gone down to the village to hire a boat," said Cole. "The barouche was wrecked and the horses went galloping off as soon as they were unhitched."

"You struck your head on the side of the carriage," Montoya put in. She put up her hand and felt the bruise beneath her loosened hair. Only now was she aware of the dull ache, but that didn't concern her. As full consciousness returned, she feared for the child she carried. Had it been harmed? She concentrated on the sensations inside her but felt no movement. Maybe that was natural; she knew little of such matters.

"You should have a sip of brandy to restore you." Montoya sighed. "It's a pity the flask in the carriage was smashed."

Cole patted his lean waist. "I had the presence of mind to retrieve this, at least." Briana caught sight of the pistol butt protruding from the waistband of his trousers, looking incongruous with his evening attire. But it was only common sense to carry a weapon when traveling in this untamed land. Bandits, lawless miners, prowling cougars, could be lurking close by.

"Try to rest, señorita," Montoya said. "As soon as Señor Forrester's servant returns, we'll take you down to the boat and make you as comfortable as possible."

Montoya's concern was genuine. "You are most kind, señor," she began. Then she stopped short. "What's that?"

She leaned forward and caught the sound of a steady throbbing, far off. A steamer's engines. Her heart stopped, then started again, lurching erratically. Could it be the engines of the *Jessica Rafferty?*

She reminded herself that there were many steamers plying the coast of California. She dared not let herself hope, and yet . . .

With one swift movement she was on her feet. She was vaguely aware of the pain from the bruises on her body, but that didn't matter, not now. She started toward the edge of the cliff. A moment later Montoya was at her side. "Señorita, what is wrong?" She felt his arm supporting her.

"That ship down there." The throbbing of the engines grew steadily louder. She broke free from Montoya's restraining arm and moved closer to the edge, then gasped as she felt herself slipping on the damp grass; Montoya caught her in time.

"You must be more careful," he reproached her. He stretched out his other arm. "Look down there."

She stared in the direction to which he was pointing. She caught her breath as she saw the sheer drop. Far below lay the dark, jagged rocks, the foam-edged waves. But her gaze moved swiftly from the rocks to the sea beyond. To the twin plumes of black smoke against the sky.

She narrowed her eyes, trying to get a better look at the lines of the approaching steamer. But it was still too far away . . . she couldn't be sure. One thing she did know: It was moving with unusual speed.

She'd spent enough time on the river to have heard yarns about the steamboat races. One captain would challenge another, each determined to prove his ship the fastest. But she could see no other ship close by.

She forced herself to turn away with feigned unconcern. She ran her tongue over her lips, swallowed, then cast Cole a pleading glance. "I'm terribly thirsty," she complained. "Perhaps there's a stream nearby."

"Nice try, Briana." He gave her a cold, derisive smile. "You're hoping that's Rafferty's ship down there—your gallant captain racing to the rescue."

"Devlin's steamer isn't nearly ready yet. He said something about making a trial run soon after New Year's Day."

But Cole ignored her and went on. "I suppose you'd enjoy watching the two of us fighting over you."

He turned to Montoya. "These ladies are a fickle lot. I think they take a positive pleasure in arousing our jealousy, playing one man against the other. It flatters their vanity.

"And this charming lady's skilled at the game. It's hardly surprising, when one considers that she learned such wiles from her mother. She couldn't have had a better teacher. Lynette Cameron was well known in Paris. Or perhaps I should say notorious."

"Enough, señor!" Montoya shot him a scornful look, but Cole didn't seemed to notice. If he had recognized the steamer, if he felt even a trace of uneasiness at Devlin's approach, he certainly didn't show it.

Unable to restrain herself a moment longer, Briana turned on Cole, her cheeks hot, her body taut with anger. "You've managed to convince yourself and your followers that you will build an empire. That nothing, no one can stop you. Even now you think you're invincible."

"I am."

Cole's words, his unwavering stare, confirmed her growing suspicion that, under his calm facade, the man was gradually losing touch with reality. If he could turn so many others into loyal, unquestioning followers, believers in his great destiny, how could one woman resist him? He wanted her—not only her body, but all of her. He wanted her to worship him, to give herself to him freely.

She'd hoped to wait for a private moment to try to gain Montoya's help, but she dared not delay any longer. The words came in an uncontrollable torrent. "Señor Montoya, listen to me—I beg you. I didn't come with Cole willingly. And I never shared his cabin on the *Osprey*—I'm not his mistress!"

"Careful, Briana," Cole warned. But it was too late.

"Devlin Rafferty, the man who spoke to all of you last night—" She spoke without a trace of shame. "He's my lover. The father of the child I carry."

Cole stared at her, as if willing her to take back the words she'd just spoken. And when she stood still, her steady gaze fixed on his face, her head high, she saw a terrifying change in his expression. Disbelief gave way to cold fury. He took a step toward her, but Montoya moved between them.

"I believe you," he said. "And I give you my word, Señorita

Cameron—I will not permit this man to do you further harm. I, myself, will return you safely to your home. I—*Madre de Díos!"*

Briana cried out, and even Cole started violently at the deafening explosion from the sea below. The sky went black, then crimson, as tongues of flame shot up from the shattered steamer.

Twenty-four

With the coming of twilight a gray mist settled over the clearing. A chill wind blew in from the ocean, whipping Briana's hair in loose strands across her cheek, but she didn't put up her hand to push it back. She stood motionless, her eyes fixed on the vessel below. She told herself it could be the wreckage of any ship, burning red on the gray water, but she had to set her jaw to keep it from trembling. A terrible coldness began to spread through her.

She turned as she caught the sound of footsteps on the path leading up to the left of the clearing. She caught sight of Frazer, breathing hard after the steep climb; his face and hands were blackened, his jacket scorched.

But Cole did not give him even a moment's rest. "How soon do we sail?" he demanded.

The man stared at him incredulously, then shook his head. "Not until morning. I couldn't find us a skiff, Mr. Forrester. That was a long climb down to the village. I came close to breakin' my neck more than once."

Cole advanced, his face merciless with anger. "You had your orders, you fool!"

"Yes, sir. But you gave me them orders before the accident. Right now them folks down there are all tryin' to save their fishin' boats. I never got to the village until just a few minutes before the *Jessica Rafferty* exploded. Lord, what a sight! All them pieces of burnin' wood came flyin' through the air, and what with this wind, the sails of the other boats caught fire. . . . I pitched in and helped. I've been carryin' buckets of water."

Frazer went on speaking earnestly, but his words came to Briana through a dull roaring in her head.

The *Jessica Rafferty*. Devlin's steamer.

Until now she had tried to convince herself that it wasn't possible. But Frazer had robbed her of the last vestige of hope. A terrible numbness began to spread through her.

Montoya stared into her face, then quickly took her arm and led her back to the outcropping of rocks. Her legs were unsteady; her knees gave way and she sank down. The rising wind tugged at her torn silk skirt. With a mechanical gesture she pulled Cole's cape closer around her.

From somewhere a long way off she could still hear Cole berating the stable hand. "If you hadn't dawdled you could have reached the village and gotten us a boat hours ago. We'd have been on our way south by now. You lazy, good-for-nothing fool!" He drew back his arm.

Frazer didn't retreat. "Just you hold it right there, Mr. Forrester. You pay my wages, but that don't give you the right to lay hands on me. I ain't one of them slaves on your plantation back East."

His unexpected defiance only drove Cole's fury to a higher pitch. "You wretched imbecile! First you smash the barouche with your clumsy handling. Then you fail to carry out a simple order. And now you dare to make excuses, to try to justify your stupidity."

"I ain't stupid, and I ain't to blame for the barouche gettin' smashed up, neither. That fancy rig was built for a drive on Rincon Hill on a Sunday afternoon. You never should've taken it on these rough roads. Señor Montoya tried to warn you, but you wouldn't listen. You wouldn't even wait for one of the regular coachmen. We all could've been killed." Frazer jerked his head in Briana's direction. "The lady, too. An' she never wanted to come along. You kidnapped her; that's what you done."

He ignored Cole's infuriated stare and went on. "I know you got your notions about secession—you and your high-toned friends. But California's still part of the United States. A free state. And there's plenty of ordinary folks who want to keep it that way." He gave Cole a hard look. "If you still got a hankering for life on your plantation, maybe you should haul ass out of here and go back home."

To Briana, crouching on the damp rocks, it was like a play being performed on a distant stage. For her, the only reality was the smoky crimson light over the wind-ruffled surface of the sea; the smoke, black against the gray sky. Glowing sparks and shards of burning wood were still blowing in the direction of the small village.

Her nails cut deep into her palms, but she felt no pain. Her throat contracted, as if it were encircled in an ever-tightening iron band; an unbearable ache gripped her chest. For just an instant she wished she had been aboard with Devlin when the steamer had exploded. That she had died there on the deck, locked in his arms.

Then she reminded herself of the new life inside her. Somehow she would have to fight back this tide of despair that threatened to engulf her. She would have to keep her emotions under control; to try to survive for the sake of Devlin's child. The child who was all she'd ever have of him now . . . the only tangible proof of her love.

She looked up to see Cole push past Frazer and walk quickly across the clearing; he was heading for the path leading down to the village. "I'll get a boat for us," he said grimly, his hand on the butt of his pistol.

But Montoya hurried to his side and placed a restraining hand on his arm. "You will have to be patient. Those people down there are still fighting to save their boats. Perhaps their houses, too. Your threats will be useless." Cole stopped and eyed him coldly.

"Wait until the fire's out, at least." Montoya looked him up and down with a hint of contempt. "Then, if you still wish to go to Mexico, you may be able to find some fisherman to take you there."

"To take us there," Cole amended, his voice steely, his blue eyes hard. "You gave me your word you'd go along, remember. The word of a Montoya." He didn't bother trying to keep the cold sarcasm out of his voice.

"I made that promise before I discovered how you had deceived me, señor." He gestured in Briana's direction. "Look at the lady. It's plain enough she was speaking the truth from the first. She cares nothing for you—I doubt she ever did."

Cole stiffened at this unexpected opposition from one of his staunchest supporters. This couldn't be happening, not to him. First, that lout, Frazer, had dared to defy him. Now Montoya was saying that he was abandoning the cause.

For a moment the ground seemed to shift beneath his feet, but he quickly regained control. All great leaders had faced such reversals and had triumphed over them. He would, too.

At least Devlin Rafferty was no longer a threat; the man was dead—he had to be. And it served him right. Rafferty had dared to confront him in his own home, to show his guests that incriminating letter. And there were others in the Custom House under guard, or so Rafferty had said.

How the hell had he managed to get hold of them? Had Briana helped her lover? She must have been in and out of the house several times to oversee the creation of Eleanor's lavish ballgown. But the chest had been carefully hidden under his desk.

He pushed aside the unanswered questions. He must look to the future. He would get hold of a boat and go down the coast to Mexico. Not to Montoya's ranch, as he had planned; that refuge was closed to him. But he had made other acquaintances in Mexico; owners of great estates, of silver mines. He would find another wealthy Mexican who would give him shelter. He'd devise a new plan. Then, when the time was right, he would return to San Francisco. He'd win back the loyalty of his followers.

But what about Eleanor, and her father? Did they already know he had taken Briana with him? That could cause a problem when he returned. He needed Martin Padgett's support.

Why had he brought Briana along? He glanced over at her, huddled beside the small fire. Even now, with her face drained of color, her amber eyes bleak, and her red-gold hair falling in a tangle about her shoulders, he felt the familiar stirring in his loins, the overpowering need to possess her.

She would grieve over Rafferty for a while, but once they were in Mexico together he would make her forget her foolish infatuation. Sooner or later she would turn to him for consolation—what other choice would she have? She'd be friendless in an unfamiliar country. And she was pregnant, too.

The memory of her disclosure stabbed at him, but he managed to thrust his resentment aside. It would be another obstacle to be overcome; he'd find a way. As soon as the baby was born, he would take it from her and turn it over to some peasant family. He'd tell her the child had died at birth. He'd give her time to recover from her loss. He would treat her with gentleness and understanding. Then, if she still resisted his advances, he would take her by force. Surely he had waited long enough—too long. For all her carefully cultivated airs and graces she was no better than her mother. She'd been trained in the ways of the demimonde. Not a suitable wife, but a most desirable mistress.

And there was her fortune to be considered, too. If Martin Padgett turned against him, her inheritance would certainly prove useful.

He glanced across the clearing, to where Montoya was standing at her side; now he put a sinewy, comforting hand on her shoulder. "Forgive me for my mistake, señorita, *por favor,*" he said. "I can do nothing to ease the pain of your loss. But I can get you safely back to San Francisco, and I will."

He ignored Cole deliberately and spoke to Frazer. "It's getting colder," he said. "Gather enough wood for a fire." When Cole's servant hesitated he added, "For the sake of Señorita Cameron. She must not take a chill."

Frazer nodded, then began gathering dried branches from the heavy tangle of underbrush around the edge of the clearing. He heaped them up near the rocks where Briana still sat motionless and lit a small fire. It took time for him to get the fire going because the damp mist was growing heavier now. But even after the wood started crackling the heat couldn't touch the frozen place inside her.

She stared at the ocean beyond the cliff. Was the hulk of the steamer burning less fiercely now? She couldn't be sure. But even from up here she caught the smell of ashes on the wind. Her heart contracted with pain. Devlin had been so proud of the *Jessica Rafferty;* he'd spent so many hours watching it take shape. He'd given the project infinite care and patience; he'd wanted it to be perfect in every detail.

She looked away and tried to fix her attention on the steady, rhythmic beating of the waves against the rocks; the creaking of a cypress branch, the shrill cry of a night bird from the woods beyond the clearing.

She turned her gaze on Señor Montoya. She was sure he would keep his promise; he would take her back to San Francisco, back to the apartment above the shop on Sansome Street. And what would her life be like then? How could she get through the rest of the winter, the first days of spring? Each of those small rooms would be filled with memories of Devlin.

Devlin, sitting in the lamplight, going over Cole's papers, seeking proof of the man's traitorous schemes. Devlin, pacing the carpet with his restless, long-legged stride. And, in the other room, Devlin asleep in the wide bed where he'd held her close against him. Even now she was overwhelmed by the memory of their embraces. Of her arms locked about him, her legs closed around his lean hips, the heat of his flesh on hers; the friction of his hair-roughened chest moving against her nipples, teasing them into hard peaks. Her whole body throbbing with the urgency of her need to be possessed by him. Devlin, his breathing harsh and jagged as he buried himself deep inside her, filling her, pouring his seed into her.

It would be unbearable torment for her to return to those rooms, yet where else was she to go? Abbie would be there to comfort her, to help her get through the months that lay ahead. She would immerse herself in the details of running the shop. Perhaps the work would keep her thoughts occupied—during the days, at least.

And then, with the return of summer, she would have Devlin's child to care for, to love. The child he would never see. A fresh wave of agony gripped her. Her fingers closed on the torn skirt of her ruined ballgown. And touched something small and hard.

Her hand had brushed the tiny porcelain figurine in the pocket of her petticoat. Kuan Yin. How could she have been foolish enough to believe that a bit of porcelain, shaped into the likeness of a heathen goddess, could have the power to protect her and Devlin? She felt the tears burning her lids and turned her face away.

And drew in her breath at the sight of a pair of round, yellow eyes, peering out from the thick underbrush. Was it one of the cougars that roamed here? Even as she tensed with fear, she saw the tomcat come stalking out, his wet orange fur plastered to his lithe body. Jigger. There was no mistaking those jagged notches in his ears, the scar on one side of his head—souvenirs of his many battles. A pulse began to hammer at her throat and she bit back a cry.

The cat was heading toward the warmth of the fire, tail switching, belly low against the ground. Cole caught sight of him and picked up a small stone, flinging it in his direction. The cat gave him a baleful stare, then retreated to the edge of the clearing.

"He must've come up from the village," Frazer said.

But Briana knew better. She kept her face carefully expressionless, even as she was seized by a swift upsurge of hope. Was it possible that only the cat had escaped from the inferno down below? Or had any of the crew survived?

Had Devlin?

She caught her lower lip in her teeth and leaned forward as she strained to catch the sound of men's footsteps, of voices from below. But there was only the rhythm of the waves, the wind in the trees.

Cole came stalking over to her, seizing her arm and pulling her to her feet. "We're going to start for the village right now," he said. "I'll find a boat and a crew to take us to Mexico."

"Don't bother. I've already hired a couple of boats."

That voice, deep and resonant, came from the darkness of the path. "But you're not heading for Mexico, Forrester. You're coming back to San Francisco with me and my crew."

Briana went weak with relief as she caught sight of Devlin. He stepped out of the shadows and stood at the opening to the clearing. His torn, blackened shirt was soaking wet; it clung to the heavy muscles of his chest. His dark hair was plastered against his forehead. She had to get to him, to touch him, to be sure that he was real.

She tried to wrench free from Cole's grasp, to run to Devlin. But now Cole's arm was around her waist. He drew his pistol and pressed the hard muzzle against her side, shoving her in front of him.

"Devlin!" she called out to him, but he stayed where he was. She caught sight of Quinn close behind him; heard the rumble of angry voices. Devlin gestured to his men to be silent.

"Let her go."

But Cole's arm tightened until she could scarcely breathe. "You are in no position to give orders here, Captain. You and your men—step out where I can see you. All of you. And throw down your weapons."

Again she heard a low roar of hostile voices from the shadows of the path. Devlin moved into the firelight, followed by Quinn, Tommy, and the rest.

"Do as he says." She caught the barely restrained fury in Devlin's voice as he gave the order. He dropped his Colt to the ground. Quinn swore as he threw down his gun. One by one, the others obeyed their captain's command.

She kept her gaze fixed on Devlin. Then, from the corner of her eye, she caught the flash of a knife blade in the firelight.

"No!" Devlin called to Montoya. "Don't try it."

For a moment the blade was frozen in Montoya's hand. Then he let it fall.

"You and your men will walk over there," Cole said to Devlin. "You two go with them," he added to Montoya and Frazer. Slowly, reluctantly, they obeyed.

Devlin fought against his instinctive urge to rush Cole, to tear Briana from his grasp. A slow, corrosive bitterness stirred inside him. He'd survived the explosion of the steamer, and most of his men along with him. But Cole had Briana. He'd kill her if he had to; Devlin was sure of it.

"I'm taking her down to the village with me."

"Wait for morning," Devlin said. Somehow he managed to keep his voice steady. "You won't make it in the dark."

"I'll find my way."

Invincible, Devlin thought; he really believes he's invincible.

"Then go alone," Devlin told him. "Go to Mexico. Or to hell."

Cole shook his head. "She goes with me. And you won't try to follow." He gave a bark of mirthless laughter. "You don't want me to kill your woman—or your bastard brat?"

Devlin felt as if the ground had shifted under his feet. His gaze locked with Briana's, and he knew that Cole was speaking the truth. She was carrying his child. Why hadn't she told him? *Bastard brat.* The words pounded inside his head like hammer blows. Every muscle in his body ached with the need to rush Cole here and now, to free her and carry her to safety. But he didn't dare, not as long as the pistol was pressed against her side. He could only call up every ounce of willpower to force himself to stand immobile.

Briana, unable to bear the agony in Devlin's agate eyes, let her own gaze fall away. She caught a stirring in the grass close by. A snake, perhaps, or a weasel. Then she glimpsed the wet orange fur plastered against the long, lean body, the twitching tail. It was Jigger, his ears flattened against his head, cautiously making his way toward the warmth of the fire again.

Cole nudged her with the pistol. "Come along," he ordered. "We're starting down now."

"No—we can't! It'll be pitch dark before we're halfway to the village." She lunged against his encircling arm, but he tightened his grip on her waist. She twisted, trying to kick his legs.

Ignoring her futile efforts to escape, he took a step backward, then another, moving in the direction of the path. He felt something crunch beneath his foot. A shrill, unearthly yowl split the night air. The cat turned and sank his strong teeth and sharp claws deep into the flesh of Cole's calf. Cole swore and tried to kick the cat away, but the infuriated beast held on.

Briana felt Cole's grip loosen for an instant and seized her chance; she twisted with all her strength and she was free. She threw herself facedown on the wet grass, rolled over, and saw Devlin racing across the space between them. He was moving fast, running straight for Cole.

She cried out at the crack of the pistol. Jigger let go of Cole's leg and streaked away.

Devlin stopped short, stumbled backward. She saw the red splotch soaking through his shirt. No! She couldn't lose him, not now. She started to get up, bracing her weight on her arms. She had to get to him.

"Stay down!" he shouted.

Even as she obeyed he was moving forward again. He lunged with the speed of a jungle beast. Cole raised the pistol again, but Devlin brought the side of his hand down on Cole's wrist. The pistol fell to the ground.

Devlin lost his footing on slick, wet grass. He went down, and Cole was on top of him. Cole's hands closed around his throat.

Devlin fought for breath, then broke the hold, and now he was on his feet again. They were close to the edge of the cliff. He felt the sea wind raw and chill against his body and a burning pain seared his left shoulder.

Cole swung at him. Devlin dodged, feinted, then drove his fist into Cole's belly.

Cole doubled up, swayed, but remained on his feet. His blue eyes were glazed, his face a chalk-white blur in the firelit night. He was moving in again. Devlin's back was to the cliff. He tried to shift away, but Cole lashed out, slamming a blow into the wounded shoulder. Dizzying pain seared through Devlin's body. Cole swung his fist to strike again, with all his weight behind the blow.

Devlin heard Briana's shrill cry and leaped to one side. Cole, caught off balance, tried to grab for the twisted limb of the nearest cypress.

His fingers slid away. He went stumbling back to the edge of the cliff. Devlin reached out, grabbed at his shirt. The cloth ripped and Cole went over the edge, out of sight.

Briana got to her feet and ran to Devlin's side. She clutched at his arm, and saw Cole's body plunging down into the darkness.

In the rosy light of early morning the skiff moved swiftly past the shards of floating timbers, the fragments of gilded furniture—all that was left of the *Jessica Rafferty.* Briana sat in the stern, with Devlin's arm around her. His shirt lay across his shoulders, and a bandage gleamed white against his tanned chest.

One of the wide ruffles from Briana's petticoat, folded into a thick pad, had staunched the flow of blood; another had served to keep the pad in place and support his left arm.

"It was a clean shot," Quinn had said as he fastened the bandage in place. "The bullet tore the flesh and went right on through. You'll be fit to steer a ship again in no time at all."

Now, in the growing light, she could see Quinn standing at the helm of the rented skiff, guiding the vessel north. Back to San Francisco. Tommy stood beside him, while Jigger lay stretched on the wide rail, sound asleep.

Another skiff followed close behind, bearing the rest of the crew, along with Señor Montoya and Frazer.

"Mackenzie didn't make it," Devlin was saying, his voice rough-edged with pain. "He called out a warning to the rest of us, right before she blew. But he stayed with his engines. He was trying to get the pressure under control. It was too late."

"And the others?" she asked.

"A couple of them are badly burned. We'll get help for them as soon as we dock at the Embarcadero."

He fell silent, and Briana felt the tension in his body. His eyes were fixed on the sea and the distant horizon; the skin was tightly drawn over the angular bones of his face.

When he spoke at last she sensed how difficult it was for him to say what had to be said. "How long have you known about the child?"

She hesitated, then forced herself to meet his gaze. "A couple of months. Then, at the ball, when we were dancing together—I felt life for the first time. A kind of flutter."

"And you still said nothing to me. Why? I had a right to know."

She tried to look away, but he cupped her chin in his hand and turned her face to his.

"We'll be married as soon as we get back."

"Devlin, I'm not sure—"

"I am. You'll do as I say."

"Is that an order?" She tried to force a teasing note into her voice, but she couldn't quite manage it.

There was no tenderness in his face, his voice. His gray eyes were remote. "Bastard brat." His voice was jagged with resentment. "That's what Cole called him." He drew a long breath. He was already retreating into that hidden place, but this time she wouldn't allow him to withdraw from her.

"Why should you care what Cole said?"

His gaze was as fathomless as the depths of the sea around them. "Bastard brat. That's what my grandfather used to call me."

She put a hand on his arm. "But your parents were married; Quinn told me so."

"It was a secret marriage, and my grandfather refused to recognize it. That's not how it'll be for us. For our son. We'll get married properly. In a church, with you in a fine white gown and veil."

She gave him a long, searching look. "Why should that be so important to you?"

"You can ask me that, even now?"

"I've got to know. It's only because of the baby, isn't it? To protect him—her—Or maybe to pay back your grandfather for the hurt you've carried around inside you all these years."

He was close beside her, so that she could feel the warmth radiating from his body, but a part of him was far away. Her fingers tightened on his hand. "I didn't tell you about the baby right away because I thought you'd ask me to marry you—for all the wrong reasons."

"I asked you once before, remember?"

"How can I forget? You said you'd marry me—if that was what I wanted."

"Did you want me to make a fancy speech with a lot of flowery words?"

She shook her head, her amber gaze unwavering. "I wanted much more than that. I still do."

Gently, carefully, he lifted her hand from his arm and drew away. He got to his feet and stood looking down at her. With a sudden movement he drove his fist into his palm. Pain shot up his arm, helping to distract him from that other, deeper pain that had lain inside him so long.

Then he turned on his heel and started for the other end of the boat to join Quinn and Tommy.

Twenty-five

"Ain't you had enough?" Quinn asked Devlin.

They were seated at one of the small tables downstairs in the Black Pearl. Although it was too early for the first performance to begin, the low-ceilinged room was starting to fill up with customers. A few seamen had stopped briefly to commiserate with Devlin on the loss of his ship, but he'd only nodded brusquely, and something in his cold, gray stare had discouraged them from further comment.

Now he gave Quinn that same hard-eyed look. He ignored his friend's question and poured himself a shot of whiskey from the bottle that stood between them. He stared at the glass moodily, then drank down its contents in one swallow. But it had little effect; he realized that he was still cold sober.

Probably that was just as well, considering his plans for the evening. He had waited long enough. Tonight he'd have to confront Briana and set a definite date for their marriage.

It had been nearly a week since he had brought her back to the city. As soon as the skiff had docked at the Embarcadero, he had hired a buggy, driven her back to Sansome Street, then lifted her in his arms and carried her into the shop.

Abbie had left her customers and run to the door.

"Briana! I've been out of my mind with worry. When you didn't get back from the Forresters' ball I couldn't imagine what had become of you. I went down to the shipyard, but all the watchmen could tell me was that Captain Rafferty had taken the steamer out to sea. . . ."

Her lips quivered and she touched Briana's arm, as if to reassure herself that this apparition in the torn, muddy gown, with her hair tangled around her face, was the same elegant, fashionably dressed young woman who'd gone off with the captain on New Year's Eve.

The customers left the counters and crowded around Devlin and Briana. One excited lady forgot that she was wearing only her petticoat and chemise; she popped out of the curtained dressing room, caught a glimpse of the big, dark-haired man who was holding Miss Cameron against his bandaged chest, then retreated hastily, pulling the velvet curtain closed behind her.

Although Abbie had been shocked and frightened by Briana's disheveled appearance, she had quickly recovered her self-possession.

"You carry her straight upstairs," the thin little seamstress ordered Devlin in a brisk, no-nonsense tone. He mounted the steep flight of steps at the rear of the shop and Abbie followed them up into the bedroom and pulled back the blankets. Devlin carefully placed Briana on the bed.

"I'll take care of her now," Abbie said. She looked him up and down, her gaze resting on the bandage across his chest. "Are you badly hurt?"

He shook his head impatiently. "Briana's the one who needs a doctor," he said, his voice taut with concern. "There was an accident—the carriage overturned in the woods near Point Lobo."

Abbie didn't waste a moment asking whose carriage it had been, or where Briana had been bound for. "The baby—" Her voice shook slightly. "Briana, what about the baby?"

"It's safe," she said. "I was afraid at first, but then, on the trip back to the city, I felt it move again. I'm quite sure no harm's been done."

"Good Lord!" He turned an angry stare on Briana. Why had she waited so long to tell him? Abbie had known about the baby. And how many others?

But this wasn't the time for a confrontation. Although Briana spoke confidently, she looked exhausted, her face drained of color. He bent over the bed, brushed his lips across her forehead, then went stalking down the steps and out of the shop. She would be safe enough with Abbie to care for her.

He had other pressing responsibilities. Two of his men had been taken to the nearest doctor's office, to be treated for the burns they'd suffered when the boilers had exploded. He'd have to look in on them, see that they were getting the best possible care.

And there was Mackenzie's spinster sister, the engineer's only close relation, back in Scotland, to be notified. He didn't look forward to writing the letter informing her of her brother's death. He'd send her Mackenzie's pay, and however much more he could scrape together.

He and Quinn had been living aboard the steamer these past weeks. Now they would have to find themselves a room in one of the less-expensive lodging houses on the waterfront. He clamped his lips together as he tried to fight back the wrenching ache that rose inside him. First he'd had to give up the *Osprey;* now the *Jessica Rafferty* was gone as well. Was he forever doomed to bring misfortune not only to those whose lives were linked with his but even to the ships he had cared about so deeply?

In the days that followed he'd kept moving, and if he suspected that he was deliberately keeping busy to avoid seeing Briana, he ignored the suspicion. He had reported Cole's death to the proper authorities; both Montoya and Frazer, along with his crew, had confirmed his sworn statement about the circumstances that had led to the confrontation at Point Lobo.

Devlin had found an unexpected ally in Montoya; the Mexican aristocrat, disillusioned when he had learned how Cole had deceived him, had informed the other *criollo* ranch owners who had come to San Francisco to join Cole's cause. He had even offered to call on Eleanor and inform her of Cole's death and how it had come about. "It will, no doubt, be difficult for you to face the unfortunate lady, Captain Rafferty. To make her understand what happened out there on the cliffs."

Devlin had refused Montoya's offer. "It's generous of you, señor. But I have to do this myself."

Montoya had given him a look of respect. "As you wish, señor."

But he hadn't been faced with the painful necessity of confronting Eleanor after all. Although she had remained in her ruined house on Rincon Hill, a solemn-faced maid had informed him that her mistress was confined to her room.

The maid led him to the library, where Martin Padgett motioned him to a seat. It seemed to him that Eleanor's father had aged in the brief time since he'd seen him last; there were new lines in his face, but he held himself erect in the high-backed leather chair as he listened intently to Devlin's account of Cole's death.

"I misjudged the man; I won't deny it," Padgett said. "He deceived me, as he did all those others. But even before you exposed his plans for conquest, his secret dealings with the French, I'd began to suspect that his ambitions went far beyond those he had confided to me."

"Yet you said nothing about it?"

"Eleanor worshipped him." He sighed and shook his head. "My daughter is in a state of shock, Captain Rafferty. She already knows that Cole's dead. Perhaps she might have been better able to bear up under her loss if she hadn't also heard that he had taken another woman away with him."

Devlin stared at him in surprise. "She knows about that?"

"From the day you returned to San Francisco with Miss Cameron the gossip's been spreading. A few of her so-called friends came to call on her as quickly as they could." His eyes were bleak and troubled. "Eleanor has kept to her room ever since. She's scarcely eaten or slept—I've heard her pacing the floor at night. I tried to persuade her to return to my home, but she insisted on staying here."

Devlin felt an unexpected stirring of pity for Padgett and his daughter. "I didn't mean for Cole to die." He gave the older man an unwavering look. "I wanted to bring him back to San Francisco to make a full confession, and to face whatever charges the federal government might have directed against him. But out there on the cliffs he tried to use Briana as a shield to make his escape. He was prepared to risk her life, as well as his own. I tried to stop him, but he wouldn't listen to reason."

Padgett nodded slowly. "You did what you had to do," he said. "I can see that you had no choice. Not after Cole threatened the life of your—" He paused, obviously seeking the most tactful choice of words.

"Miss Cameron and I will be married," Devlin told him.

Now, sitting here with Quinn in the Black Pearl, he knew there was no point in putting off the encounter any longer. Briana had said she didn't want to marry him, but he'd get her to change her mind.

He pushed away his glass and got up from the table. A few of the dancers, their faces white with rice powder, their lips and cheeks bright with rouge, had already come downstairs. The Black Pearl was beginning to fill up with its usual raucous crowd.

"Want me to walk you over to the shop?" Quinn asked.

Devlin gave him a tight smile. "I think this is one matter I'll have to handle by myself."

"Holy saints! You look like a man on his way to his own wake. She'll say yes to you. She's in love with you. She has been since she ran away from her kin and came aboard the *Osprey.*" When Devlin didn't answer he added, "And now that she's—what I mean is, things bein' how they are—"

"Now she's pregnant she should be anxious to accept. I suppose most women would be, but she's different."

"Don't be so sure."

"I asked her on the way back from Point Lobo. She said no."

Quinn's thick brows shot up. "Did she, now? But she was still shook up bad. Likely she didn't know what she was sayin'."

Devlin gave him a long, level gaze. "She knew. And she had her reasons for refusing."

She had wanted more from him than he was prepared to offer her, or any other woman. All the same, tonight he would force her to agree to the marriage, one way or another.

"There *is* something you can do for me." His voice was tight.

"If you want me to stand up with you in church, I'd be honored," said Quinn.

"Thanks. But first I want you to start asking around, in here and down on the waterfront. Find out which of the big owners are looking for a master for a China clipper. I'll sign on the first one I can find."

Quinn stared as if he couldn't believe he'd heard right.

"You're gettin' married. What's more, your bride's already expectin'. And here you are, making plans to go halfway 'round the world." Quinn shrugged his massive shoulders. "I suppose she and the baby can go with you—plenty of captains take a wife and child along. Although, if you ask me, it ain't the ideal way to start married life."

"What the hell would you know about married life?" Devlin demanded.

"Nothin'. And with any luck, I mean to keep it that way. All the same, don't you think Briana'll be having something to say about your plans? I guess she's got enough put aside from the shop to keep her and the youngster in comfort. And there'll be your pay—captain's share—to add to that."

"I'll provide for them."

Quinn looked embarrassed. He wasn't used to discussing such intimate matters, even with Devlin. "But ain't it never crossed your mind she might expect somethin' more? Maybe she'll want you there with her, when her time comes."

Devlin started to speak, then thought better of it. He wasn't prepared to discuss his reasons for wanting to distance himself from Briana as soon as possible. Quinn, tough and unimaginative, wouldn't begin to understand his feelings. The mate would think he was losing his wits. But he was convinced that, in leaving Briana, he was doing what had to be done to protect her.

He was unlucky for her. Cursed, like his father before him. He'd put everything he had into the *Jessica Rafferty,* and now she lay, a rotting hulk, beneath the waters of the Pacific. And his love for Briana had brought her into danger; it had almost destroyed her. She might have been killed when the barouche had overturned. Even now he could see her back on the cliff, Cole's arm locked about her waist, the pistol pressing into her ribs.

He had to leave her before he brought her even greater disaster. All at once a dark, icy tide of foreboding moved through him. Suppose he did marry her, to give her and the child the protection of his name; to be certain no one would ever call his son a bastard. But what would happen when the baby came? If he got command of a China clipper within the month, he'd be half a world away in early summer. Briana would be left to face the dangers of childbirth alone. Most women survived the bearing of children—sometimes a dozen of them. But it hadn't been like that for his own mother. She'd died giving him life.

He winced as the Black Pearl's small band, a melodeon and a few shrill fiddles, started tuning up for the first show. He glanced in the direction of the door.

"Will you be comin' back here tonight?" Quinn asked.

Devlin shrugged, turned on his heel, and went out the door into the darkness. It had started raining, a steady downpour that would likely last through the night.

"Why are you still working at this hour?" Devlin demanded. It wasn't the way he had meant to greet Briana after not having come to see her since the night of their return to the city. But when he found her in the shop with Abbie, unpacking boxes and arranging a new shipment of merchandise, he couldn't suppress his irritation.

She wore a blue challis gown, simple enough for work yet fashionably cut. Her hair was parted in the center and coiled in a neat chignon at the nape of her neck. "Please stack that pile of patterns at the end of the counter, Abbie."

Then, looking up at him, she said calmly, "It's only a little after eight. And I want to have the shop in order when we open tomorrow. I think we'll have a good many customers, all eager to see the latest patterns from New York. And to order their spring wardrobes."

Her lips curved in a faint smile. "And to get a look at me, I suppose," she added.

"What for?" he demanded.

"I've been the subject of local gossip ever since you carried me in here in that shocking condition. By now I'm sure everyone in the city has heard how Cole—" She hesitated, but only for an instant. "How he forced me to go off with him on New Year's Eve. No doubt those ladies who were guests at his home have spread the story, and embellished it."

Abbie sighed. "I'm afraid so," she agreed, shaking her head.

Briana forced a smile. "Don't look so downcast," she told the seamstress. "That sort of gossip can be good for business."

She kept her voice light as she went on arranging the new selection of feathers and silk flowers from France, but deep inside she felt a surge of anxiety. She could guess why Devlin had come here tonight, but she was still uncertain how to answer him when he asked—no, commanded—her to marry him again.

If she had only herself to consider, she knew what the answer would be. But there was the child to think about. A warm current of tenderness moved through her at the thought of her baby. What did she owe the child she was carrying? Her lips tightened. Society could be cruel to a child born out of wedlock.

Mama had done what she could to protect her by giving her the name of Cameron. Mama had died fighting to keep up the illusion of respectability, at least long enough for her daughter to make a suitable marriage and take her place in Charleston society.

She repressed a sigh. How long ago all that seemed now.

"Come upstairs," Devlin said. "Abbie can finish up here."

"Since when have you taken over the running of my business?" She tried to keep her voice light and teasing, but Devlin's bleak stare made her uneasy.

He took her arm in a firm grasp and led her to the rear of the shop and up the stairs to her apartment. It had been raining off and on for the past few days and a damp chill permeated the rooms. He shot an impatient look at her. "Don't you have sense enough to look after yourself properly, now of all times?"

Before she could answer he was bending over the small fireplace, scooping coal from the brass scuttle and starting a fire. He thrust at the coals with a poker, and the flames shot up.

"Really, Devlin," she said, touched yet irritated by his concern. "A woman doesn't have to be treated like an invalid just because she happens to be pregnant."

She knew it wasn't proper to speak so directly, even in the privacy of her parlor. A real lady would have said she was "in an interesting condition," or "in the family way."

His face tightened. "You didn't just happen to get pregnant," he said, with a directness that matched her own. His eyes were dark with self-reproach. "Maybe you didn't know how to take care of yourself. But I can't make excuses for myself. I'm the one who's to blame."

She took a step away from him, and her heart sank at his words. Was that all the baby meant to him? Did he see her pregnancy only as an unfortunate accident?

"There's no need to blame yourself," she said. "I could have asked any one of a dozen customers for advice. Not those fine ladies from Rincon Hill, but the others—I'm sure a woman like Belle Cora knows all about how to prevent a pregnancy—or to get rid of an unwanted—"

His powerful hands were gripping her arms with such force that she couldn't go on. "Don't!" His tone grated harshly. "Don't even think about trying anything like that!"

His arms went around her and he held her against him, as if he were protecting her from some impending danger. Although she was baffled by his swift change of mood, she was comforted by his concern. She let her head rest against his chest, then moved closer, molding herself against him.

If only it were possible to stay like this, enfolded in his arms, close and warm and safe. But even now he was moving away from her.

He stood looking down at her, but his eyes didn't quite meet hers. "I'd have come to see you sooner," he said. She heard the uneasiness in his voice. "But I had a lot to see to. Papers to be filed. The steamer was insured, but under the circumstances there's little chance of my collecting."

Bewildered by his sudden shift to such practical matters, she didn't know how to reply. "I suppose you've got some money of your own from the shop," he went on, his tone crisp and matter-of-fact. "And you'll have more." He paused, drew a long breath, then went on quickly. "I'm going to find myself a master's berth on a clipper. Quinn's already started asking around. The captain of a China clipper's allowed to carry a cargo of his own. I can make a good profit that way."

"Devlin! You aren't planning to go back to sea as captain of another man's ship?"

He shrugged. "I don't see that I've got much choice," he told her. "We'll be married, as soon as it can be arranged. Then I'll sail."

"And you'll leave me behind?" Was he only anxious to do what he considered his duty and then get himself as far from her as possible? The words came from her, unbidden. "You can't! I won't let you!"

"Briana, be reasonable. You're in no condition to go along on a voyage to China. Even if I wanted to—"

"Even if you wanted to take me with you? That is what you were going to say?"

"Why can't you try to understand?"

"I understand," she said, surprised at the icy calm in her voice. Could he sense the tumult inside her? "This has nothing to do with me, or the baby. You want to marry me because you can't forget what it was like for you as a child, with your grandfather calling you a bastard. Punishing you for something that wasn't even true!"

He turned away from her and strode quickly to the window. His hand shot out, and he jerked aside the drape and stared at the silvery streaks of rain streaming down the window; at the blurred ovals of the gas lamps below.

But now he wasn't seeing the dark, wet streets of San Francisco. He was looking backward into the past.

He saw the hard sunlight blazing down over the barren ground of the convict settlement in New South Wales. He was back in his grandfather's study, listening to that cold, inexorable voice again. "Convict's spawn. He called me that, too. He said

I was to blame for my mother's death. Said he'd beat my father's bad blood out of me."

He scarcely realized he had been speaking aloud until he caught the sharp intake of her breath and felt her hand, small and firm on his arm. "Devlin! Look at me."

He turned and saw her amber eyes, glistening with tears, filled with understanding and tenderness. She reached up and rested her palm against his cheek. "Why couldn't you have talked to me this way before? Why didn't you tell me—"

"About my grandfather? And that hellhole in New South Wales? What's that got to do with you?"

"With us," she said. "You've kept me at a distance from the first. Even when you were making love with me you never let me get too close. I wasn't sure why, until now."

"I don't know what you're talking about."

But she wouldn't let him keep her at a distance any longer. "I think you do." Her arms went around him and she clung to him with all her strength. He didn't push her away, but remained stiff and unyielding in her embrace. "You're afraid of me, Devlin. I think you always have been."

"That's enough," he interrupted. "When we were coming back to the city I asked you to marry me."

"You didn't ask me. You told me, in no uncertain terms. I'd have to marry you because of the baby. But it's not that simple. Not for me."

He went on as if he hadn't heard her. "We'll set the date for the wedding tonight. Quinn will stand up with me. Abbie can make your dress. This won't be any secret ceremony. There'll be no question that you're my wife."

"And afterward?"

He drew a jagged breath. "I'm going to find myself a clipper."

"Why not a riverboat? In time you'll build up your own line again."

"No riverboat." His voice, his look, silenced her. "A clipper bound for China."

She felt a sinking sensation. He was willing, even anxious, to give her and the child the protection of his name, but he didn't want to stay with her. He was determined to go back to sea.

"If you sail aboard a clipper, I'll go with you."

"That's impossible now."

"Then wait until the baby's born."

"No!" His chest rose and fell with his harsh breathing. "Don't make me say it, Briana. When the time comes just let me go."

But she didn't flinch before his hard stare, or the tight, set thrust of his jaw. Until now she had always thought of him as the stronger. Tough, self-assured, a man who could give her his strength and protection.

She had yielded herself to him, not only her body but all of her; she had tried to tell herself she was content to take only what he was willing to give in return. Even after she had discovered that dark, secret place inside him, she had sensed that he wouldn't allow her to intrude there.

But now all that had changed. She was no longer a frightened young girl, fleeing from Charleston to escape the taint of scandal, bent on reaching San Francisco to make a good marriage to a man of wealth and social position. That had been Mama's dream, not her own.

Since she had come here she had grown, changed, proved that she could make a place for herself. When she had walked out of her uncle's home she had taken the first step toward independence. Then later, as her shop had grown and flourished, she had gained new assurance.

Now she would have to make use of her hard-won confidence. She glanced at Devlin's set face, but she didn't waver. Not only her own future, but that of their child, depended on her.

"I do understand," she told him. "You don't want to leave me to face the shame of bearing your bastard. You want to spare the child from suffering as you did. That's why you're so determined to marry me."

For a moment she thought he might strike her. But she stood her ground, her eyes fixed on his in a searching stare.

"But there's more." She felt a new strength coursing through her. "Tell me, now—I want to hear all of it."

He looked away. "I can't take you with me. And I can't stay here with you. I'd only bring you grief. In the end I'd destroy you. As my father destroyed my mother."

"Devlin, you're not making sense. Quinn said your father was a brave man, a patriot, fighting for his country. He knew the risk he was taking."

"And my mother? What about her?"

"He gave her his love. I think it was the only love she ever knew."

"Maybe so. But for how long? They shared a few wretched months of running, hiding, like hunted animals—and that was all."

"That's what you believe, because that's what your grandfather taught you to believe. But how can you be sure? You speak of weeks, months. Love's not something you measure that way. I think those few months may have seemed as rich and fulfilling to her—to both of them—as if they'd shared a lifetime of loving."

"That's enough, dammit!"

She saw a shudder run through the length of his powerful body, and she reached out to grip his arms, to steady him with her own inner strength. "Listen to me, Devlin. I won't die in childbirth. I'm going to give you a son, and I'll live to bring him up to be a fine, strong man."

She put all her conviction into her words, her look. For a moment he remained rigid, unmoving. Then slowly, gradually, she felt the tension begin to go out of him. He drew her into his arms and she lay her face against his chest and heard the steady beating of his heart, felt his familiar warmth surrounding her, filling her.

"I want to believe you," he said slowly. But there was still a lingering doubt in his voice.

"It will take time," she told him. "And meanwhile . . ." She raised her eyes to his, then took his hand and led him away from the window, into the bedroom. She reached up and began to unbutton his shirt.

"Briana, should we—can you?"

For a moment she stared at him. Then she understood. She laughed softly. "You won't hurt me."

Even as she spoke she started unfastening her gown, letting it drop down around her feet. She smiled at him as she opened the small, beribboned pocket in her petticoat.

"What's that?"

She held out the tiny, delicate figurine. It glowed white in the lamplight. "Kuan Yin." She set it down on the bedside table. "I took her along with me on New Year's Eve," she told him. "The goddess protected me then." Her lips curved in a smile. "Or maybe it was our love that saved me from harm."

They lay side by side in the wide bed. He drew her soft, yielding body against his, but she could still feel a certain hesitation. "Lie back," she said. He gave her a quizzical look but obeyed. She moved so that she was above him, the heavy, red-gold masses of her hair brushing his chest, trailing across his throat.

"You're sure it will be all right?"

He wasn't yet completely free of his fears for her. But he wanted her. Her eyes slid downward and she saw his arousal, hard and demanding; his body had a will of its own.

Her eyes held his as she straddled him, kneeling above him with one leg on either side of his lean hips. She bent closer and one of her nipples touched his mouth. Slowly, deliberately, she ran the nipple over his lips.

She heard the swift intake of his breath, felt the muscles of his thighs go rock hard under her buttocks. His lips parted and he drew the nipple into his mouth. He nipped at her lightly, then began to suckle. Waves of liquid fire coursed through her.

She reached down, her fingers curving around his hardness, stroking him lightly. Then she moved so that his arousal was pressed against the hot, hard bud of her womanhood. Still looking down into his eyes, now smoky-gray with mounting desire, she rubbed the rounded tip of him against her.

Then she took him into her, filling herself with his hardness. She began to move her hips, drawing him deep inside, then sliding back. Her body moved in a slow, sensuous dance, as old as time. His breath grew hoarse, his chest rising and falling, his eyes narrow and burning with the force of his need.

And now he reached out and grasped her buttocks, his fingers gripping the satin rounds. He pulled her close, and closer still. She felt the first tentative throbbing. It grew more intense with every movement of her hips, every thrust of his hardness inside her.

She gripped his shoulders and threw back her head. With a wordless cry, she gave herself up to the glorious tide that swept them both to fulfillment.

The rain still beat with a steady rhythm against the bedroom windows . . . a soothing sound, lulling her into drowsy contentment. But she didn't want to sleep, not yet.

Devlin had drawn the comforter over both of them. He held her against him, his body curved protectively around hers. He stroked her hair, his hand light and caressing.

When he spoke the words came slowly at first. He didn't sound at all like the self-assured man she'd always known. It would take time for him to put aside the long-held fears that had been a part of him since boyhood.

"I love you, Briana," he said softly. "I think I've loved you since that first day I saw you, on the dock in Charleston. I guess maybe I was afraid to tell you." He drew her closer. "But now everything's changed. Now you're a part of me. I can't sail for China. I can't leave you." He hesitated, then went on. "If I stay here, I can build another steamboat line. But it'll take time. Years, maybe. I won't be able to give you all I want to. Not right away."

"There's no need for you to worry about that," she began.

She felt his muscles go hard beneath her fingers. "If you think I'm going to live off my wife's earnings, you're mistaken. But I did have almost everything tied up in the *Jessica Rafferty.*

And since I took her out to sea without a trial run, pushed her engines to the limit and beyond—the insurers aren't likely to make good on the loss."

She put her hand across his lips. "We can start with another small trading skiff, if we have to," she said. "A cargo of pans and shovels, flour and whiskey."

"You love me that much?" he asked.

"That much and more," she told him. Then a smile tugged at the corner of her mouth. There would be no need to start from such humble beginnings again.

Later, much later, she would show him the will and tell him of the fortune left her by the Marquis de Valmont; it was waiting for her in France, whenever she chose to claim it. There would be more than enough to build a whole fleet of riverboats. When the time was right she would explain how she had come to discover the truth about her parentage.

Right now she was content to lie in his arms, to listen to the steady rhythm of the rain beating against the window; to look ahead to the years of loving, of sharing, of building a future together.

JANELLE TAYLOR

ZEBRA'S BEST-SELLING AUTHOR

DON'T MISS ANY OF HER
EXCEPTIONAL, EXHILARATING, EXCITING

ECSTASY SERIES

SAVAGE ECSTASY   (0-8217-5453-X, $5.99/$6.99)

DEFIANT ECSTASY   (0-8217-5447-5, $5.99/$6.99)

FORBIDDEN ECSTASY   (0-8217-5278-2, $5.99/$6.99)

BRAZEN ECSTASY   (0-8217-5446-7, $5.99/$6.99)

TENDER ECSTASY   (0-8217-5242-1, $5.99/$6.99)

STOLEN ECSTASY   (0-8217-5455-6, $5.99/$6.99)

FOREVER ECSTASY   (0-8217-5241-3, $5.99/$6.99)

Available wherever paperbacks are sold, or order direct from the Publisher. Send cover price plus 50¢ per copy for mailing and handling to Penguin USA, P.O. Box 999, c/o Dept. 17109, Bergenfield, NJ 07621. Residents of New York and Tennessee must include sales tax. DO NOT SEND CASH.